To John
Thank
Oliver
July 2012.

Acts of Defiance

First published 2012

Cover design – Jules T. Smith
Cover illustration – Oliver Bayldon

Text prepared for digital printing by John Didlock
Set in Times New Roman

ACTS OF DEFIANCE

A MARRIAGE. A THEATRE.
A TOWN

2004 is Chekhov's Centenary Year
Garrick Jones is full of great plans.
The women in his life expect rather more.

by

Oliver Bayldon

For my wife Britta, Colin Cant and John Didlock.
Without them this novel would not have seen the light of day.

CONTENTS

Biographical Note

Writer and designer, Oliver was brought up in small villages in Rutland. He worked briefly as a theatre designer in Northampton before moving to London where he is better known as TV and film production designer, winning a Royal TV Society Award for "Never Come Back", and a Bafta Design Award for Jack Clayton's TV film "Memento Mori". Also gained nominations for such successful BBC series as "The Onedin Line", "Fight Against Slavery" and "Poldark". He has frequently filmed in Lancashire and Yorkshire.

He has held design exhibitions at the Royal Society of Arts, the British Film & TV Academy and Northampton Art Gallery. He is a Life Fellow of Royal Society of Arts and a Fellow of Chartered Society of Designers.

His short stories were broadcast for several years on BBC Radio 4 and the World Service, read by such luminaries as Alfred Molina, and he has had poetry broadcast on BBC Radios 3 and 4. His short poem "Morning" was published as a pamphlet edition. His English version of "The Papermaker's Art" was published by John Mason's "12 x 8 Press", illustrated by Rigby Graham, and is a now a collector's item, as is "Towards Handmade Paper" for the same press. Other poems and articles have been published in magazines and the national press over the years.

This is his first novel. Another is under way.

INTRODUCTION

Garrick Jones is a man with problems. One is his dubious past as a Media Magnate spiced with exaggerations and lies. Having hyped himself up he is finding it hard to back down.

Family life has been under pressure since his wife developed an independent career. Then his American mother-in-law started to visit. Now London feels very exposed. Soon family history begins to intrude because 2004 is the Centenary Year of the death of Anton Chekhov, the great Russian playwright. Verity and her mother demand that Garrick makes amends by producing a series of Chekhov plays to honour their family connections. This they say is his chance of a lifetime, the chance to redeem himself

On their insistence he leaves a comfortable house-husband rôle with two small children, for a minor Lancashire town which has great hopes of expansion. Bluffing his way through an interview and surprisingly getting the job at Norston's one theatre, he stumbles into local politics. Temptations and corruption abound. It is then he begins to realise why he was selected and what the nature of Norston's controversies are.

As property values boom, personalities and relationships clash in this sometimes satirical look at the nature of sexual passion and fear. The whole town is embroiled in fierce competition, exposing people's intimate lives. As the women of Norston rage at the state of their world, they confront the forces of change, leaving their secrets and dreams unfulfilled. The theatre becomes their only escape but other people have other ideas.

When Verity comes up to Norston to visit, Garrick's marriage is put under intolerable stress. The atmosphere is palpable: rivalries intensify. The result is disturbing as events quickly build to a climax. The denouement comes as a shock.

This is a vivid and troubling account of a society on the cusp of great change.

CHAPTER ONE

NEW BEGINNINGS

How had he got in this mess? He kept asking himself the same question. How? There must be an easy way out. Surely?

Garrick had hoped his arrival in Norston would make some small difference if only by marginally tipping the scales. Say, by a single gram? A smidgen of a smidgen perhaps? A tad? Okay, one molecule then? A single solitary atom? But if his brain wouldn't function, the answer was to concentrate harder, except that didn't work. The more he read the less he retained.

It wasn't true he was out of his depth or starting to dread the whole project. No, not at all. As his wife said, it was merely a question of digesting facts and celebrating great lives. As simple as that.

So he took another deep breath, "Anton Pavlovich Chekhov (1860 -1904)," He cleared his throat, then reread the opening passage aloud to himself, "Anton. Pavlovich. Chekhov . . . Russian dramatist and writer of short stories. Born on January 29th, 1860. Died July 14th, 1904 in the German heath resort of Badenweiler."

Garrick knew he was no academic, but he did like to think he absorbed details, even if studying textbooks meant banging one's head against Kultur complete with a capital K. As for being dyslexic or autistic, just adjectives! Words! He forced his finger to follow the print:

". . . Born the son of shopkeeper Rostoff Yegorovitch Chekhov and Evegeniya Morozova (one of the later Morozoff clan) in the port of Taganrog on the Azov Sea . . . Studied medicine at the University of Moscow Medical Faculty from 1879 and . . . and . . . and . . .

In this, Chekhov's Centenary Year, this anniversary mattered. It was his job. He tried to read on, but something moved on the edge of his vision. He tried to shut it out.

". . . And married the actress Olga Knipper on May 6th 1901. Wrote 'The Seagull' (1898), 'Uncle Vanya' and 'The Three Sisters' (1901), and 'The Cherry Orchard' (1904) but . . . Damn!"

His brain would not co-operate; it chose to react at more primitive levels. His eyes kept being drawn to that window, so who were they? Those miniature figures down there, scrabbling around like clowns in the mud?

Garrick first glimpsed them through drizzle; identikit figures with striped poles and clipboards. Their bright yellow helmets caught his attention: men in grey suits, white shirts, and ties, with fluorescent anoraks. At first he'd found them amusing, like deviant bumblebee larvae performing some surrealist pageant . . . Or something from Grimm's Tales? Even Edgar Allan Poe? Now they'd seriously begun to intrude.

He sheltered his wandering eyes with one hand. He was meant to annotate scripts. This was why he was here. Directing classics could not be some slapdash affair. As he understood it, great art required dedication, absolute, total, intensive and . . . Jesus! . . . He slammed the book shut, pressing his forehead onto the window, squinting down through the haze. There was something cartoonish about them, these tiny Day-Glo figures bumbling around in their miniature landscape. He must have been watching some time, repeatedly wiping his breath from the glass.

Norston can be depressing. In winter its twilight seems endless. From sunrise to sundown a haze envelops the landscape till everything blurs and fragments. Eventually cherry trees would blossom pink outside the Town Hall and daffodils bloom in their big concrete urns, but winter asserts itself first. Here in this monochrome greyness anything luminous jars.

First they'd stand here; then they'd stand there, posture, pose, squint at each other and signal. Now they were walking backwards and forwards, pacing out geometrical patterns like some Freemasonry rite, but that was the way of surveyors. Next they'd be enforcing everyone's morals, then taking total control of their souls.

His own father had ended up distributing propaganda for God, but Edwin had been a late convert, an atheist aiming at Saint. Religion to him was the blind acceptance of words, always quoting Proverbs and Psalms. Nowadays who cared about Faith? There were too many distractions. Garrick wasn't helped by The Majestic's resident staff, obsessed with their wage-rates and pensions. He was an artist not Human Resources Consultant. He was solely here to fulfil an obsession exactly one hundred years to the day. But as he pressed close to the window his best intentions condensed on the glass.

It was time to test Vee's reactions. After all, she was why he was here. There'd been times when she had sympathised, but since the births of their children she'd spent most of her time phoning back home as if Massachusetts were just down the road. Verity was so self-contained and her lecturing life so straightforward . . . Then on the day he'd moved up here, all that changed.

"To me, family matters," she'd announced, "You always respect the love of your parents." Then she'd invited her mother to stay.

Usually such visits were short. Roseanne flew in, Roseanne flew out, like an annual migration. As Verity said, it all came down to genetic components. People were ingredients too. A pinch of this, a pinch of that. Life came down to Michelin Stars. Verity was Acacia Honey with a sharp dash of cayenne. That's why he loved her. The complications were other people.

"Gary," she'd told him, "Blend in. Make friends. Make a name. Earn cash. They'll judge you by that. Momma says the provinces aren't bad. Miami, Chicago, Las Vegas, The Bronx. That's where local colour counts. It's cheerleaders versus drum majorettes. It's living. It's live. There's pizzazz!"

Up here in his turret above a crumbling theatre facade, he overlooked 360 degrees. Nothing could creep up unseen. The building with its twin towers felt like some sectarian church dominating the centre of town while down below in the shadows, officials in helmets slithered like yellow-capped snails. He only needed giant-sized boots and he could easily stamp them all out. That was the great hidden danger of Chekhov. "Guest Director" could go to your head.

He spat out his nicotine gum then stubbed it under the desk. He needed a meal. From Day One of their meeting Vee had invaded his diet. Fish-cakes and chips gave way to Pan-American, then to Haute Cuisine. He'd followed her cosmopolitan route; peppers and aubergines, tortillas, flapjacks, herb salads, and clams. Hispanic meets Cape Cod. Organic, low calorie, fat-reduced, flavourful concoctions. Add to that the Rostoff palate. It proved the power of the Rostov cuisine. Include Paté de fois gras and fine truffles. Then from deep maternal roots she'd introduced him to Dostoyevsky, Tchaikovsky, Shostakovitch, Tolstoy and Chekhov, all filtered through New York and flavoured with New England accents. But Lesson One; involvement means you risk hurt, and Lesson Two; he had got bloody hurt "You don't escape, you re-locate," Verity said when he'd once left, then come back. He'd never left her again.

Below him surveyors were spreading out plans, typing details into a laptop. Soon there'd be multi-storeys and car parks galore. Demolition moved like a plague, but one thing for sure, 'The Majestic Theatre' would be here long after those buggers were gone. He leaned forward and wiped the glass clear with one hand. It looked like the mating of insects combined with pagan fertility rites, comic and oddly compelling. At that moment one of them looked up and pointed. As Garrick ducked out of sight, his telephone rang. He must have automatically answered, because slowly he became aware of a voice:

"Hello? Hello? . . . Did you hear what I said?" a woman's voice was asking, "Well? . . . What do you think?" . . . and she waited. "Hello? . . . Hello? . . . Hello!" he registered Lancashire vowels, "Will you be available then?"

"Available?"

"Like I just said, for the Theatregoers Club Meeting?"

"Sorry? . . . It's an atrocious connection." But the voice had not stopped, so he rustled papers close to the mic. "Say that again?"

"Mrs Roberts," it repeated, "Louise Roberts."

A faint whiff of oestrogen blew on the wind. Beside him the photo of Verity frowned.

Wet hair has a satisfying feel. *Schleef*! *Schliver*! It slides through fingers, aqueous and live as wild eels. Jilly Craske was rinsing Highlighted Bronze, watching water stream down the basin and gurgle away in an energy spiral. Her client laid back, head cupped in the bowl, humming away to herself. That's the joy of a sculptural Coiffeuse. All that pain just washing away.

"You see, it's pollution what does it, Louise. Free radicals and acid rain. It damages the roots, you see. It's scientifically proved. That's why we use conditioners. Everything herbal, everything pure. we'll soon have you back to your glamorous self."

When it came to Louise Roberts there wasn't much else she could say because 'Crowning Glory' had one vital function, dispensing peace of mind. This was its paradox too; compensating for others. She who could have been somebody else, was busily dispensing salvation; she whose own body clock ticked; whose cellulite nudged at her brain; whose aging symptoms she tried to ignore.

"Jilly, did you see him? In the local paper, love?" Louise's voice rose distorted from down in the basin. "Did you?"

Louise Roberts always came dressed to the nines. In Norston social niceties mattered. It emphasised 'the difference'. Jilly in green nylon smock with 'Crowning Glory' stitched to its breast pocket epitomised Crowning Glory, and Crowning Glory was her. Whereas Mrs Roberts was just a married name, despite financial assets, expensive pretensions, and friends on the council . . . But everything about her was dated. Her clothes, her bangles, her earrings, her taste. Her husband ran a small cafe. Proprietor and sole chef. Now Louise planned to open a night club herself and in her own name, as if in direct competition. It did not seem appropriate somehow.

Jilly sighed, "Who?"

Working beside the front windows, she had views of the street through her wall-to-wall mirrors. Reflections reflecting reflections. Back-to-front repeated front-to-back. In a couple of weeks, street decorations would clutter things up before you were quite in the mood. Christmas was anticlimax, but she only had to close her eyes and think summer. One sniff of Rose Water Essence from her new electronic dispenser provided an instant escape.

"It's all very well, but it's our theatre!" Louise's voice continued muffled, face-down over the basin, "All their fancy talk! . . . Chekhov! . . . Who? . . . They don't understand community needs. Not our spiritual needs. Who watches TV, or video games, or gets varicose veins in the movies? There's locals crying out for live entertainment . . . And what's more . . . what's more . . ."

Jilly was thinking how clients were probably at this very moment booking Christmas cruises, or buying presents they could not afford. Luckily theirs was a credit card culture. Forget dole queues and unemployed marchers; recessions were a thing of the past. With everyone booking for ski slopes or Caribbean beaches, she took comfort from Hollywood stars leering down from her walls.

But Louise kept gabbling away, ". . . an' it'll take more than some . . . some toff from down London, no matter how lah-de-dah. And as for that stuff about Chekhov? . . . Why Russians? They're all Communists. What's wrong with ourselves? . . . Chekhov? . . . People want Noel Coward . . . I mean, did you read that in the paper? . . . Hello? Did you?"

But something caught Jilly's eye. Two staring faces. Splattened faces, noses against her front windows. Hands and foreheads flattened on glass. She gave a start. Water cascaded over her feet. A tall skinny lad and short scruffy friend were cupping their heads to her windows, staring straight in.

Louise talked on about Mary Sloe and Lucy Katchel and their interminable problems; proof no man could be trusted and emptiness never be filled because marriage was always disaster.

"Jones, did you say? " Jilly sounded weary, "Garrick Jones?"

By leaning sideways, still running the hairspray, she managed to keep both youths in her eye-line, making mental notes, convinced they'd be captured on CCTV

"Hey!" Louise spluttered and jolted, "Hey! Bloody mind!"

Water was pooling out on the floor, pale and diluted as urine. Dabbing round the client's feet, Jilly's humiliation was total. Explanations would make it all worse.

Louise's wedding-ring hand rose up in front of Jilly's face. "Listen. Every woman knows about risk." Jilly was coiling warm towels round Louise's head. "That's why I'm opening my club." Louise felt the comforting warmth of soft cotton and relaxed. "Yes, cultural style with more class. 'Self-improvement with coffee'. That's my new 'Club Arabica'."

"And how's your daughter?"

Louise jerked, "What? She wants to 'express' herself. Express herself! At fifteen going on sixteen? She's soap opera, her. No certificates. No boyfriends neither, thank God . . . no, my love, just remember the name Garrick Jones. Garrick Jones! He's to blame."

Jilly repeated the name under her breath. Then she caught sight of her overweight self in her mirrors. Her shadow seemed to expand and inflate, adding the caption 'obese' and cutting her off from her friends. Self-loathing thrived on distortion. That was why women married their biggest mistakes, then compensated the rest of their lives. That's why her salon was so hectic at Christmas, that season of divine retribution, bleaches, dyes, backcombing, and historical perms. Who cared about the birth of Our Lord? Few women could relax in their skins because most were atoning for failure, emerging like new Barbie dolls, renewed and perfected.

Everything was sexual, that was a fact, with customers overindulging their organs then giving her gruesome details. This confirmed her mixed feelings for men. Jilly recalled those two flattened male faces and shuddered; their threat was implicit. A perm or new shoes helped, but for women, violence was prowling the streets, fleshing out those urban myths. Her function was Mother Confessor. She offered superficial compassion as clients poured out their incomplete lives. Hair-styling was symptomatic. Her role was to simply agree.

As Jilly continued to snip at loose ends she recalled Louise's carotty daughter. She'd not seen the girl for some time. Abigail must be growing up fast.

She felt Louise's head jerk in her hands, "According to The Mercury," Louise was saying, "Norston's due to be 'New global city. The Internet centre of Europe'. New transport, trams, pedestrian walkways." Louise's hair squirmed to escape, "Yes, and shopping arcades, multiplex cinemas . . . Cycle tracks, pass-overs, crossovers and . . ."

Jilly grimaced as internal spasms clenched bladder and bowels. Curse was an appropriate word. She knew her own body. Monthly eviscerations grew worse. Certain things had begun to go wrong. It wasn't cystitis. Things you didn't discuss. Tensions combining with menstrual failure. Functions you never referred to. Failure was the keyword; an all too-familiar concept. She'd always dreaded the doctor. With all these rushes of hormones another diet had failed.

"Yes, act, says Abigail, act!" Louise put on her mock poshest voice, "'I want to join Chekhov Players!' she says. Fat bloody chance!"

Jilly's film stars gazed down from the walls as Jilly's eyes fixed on a fine shaft of sunlight. She watched its pencil-beam sneak through dark clouds. Its draughtsmanship dissected the street like a laser. Outside was her personal Road to Damascus. The Lord could move in mysterious ways.

Across the road a traffic warden leant over somebody's car, punching details into a handset. As Jilly removed the protective cape, fluffing out Louise's hair and holding a hand-mirror up for approval, Louise was onto her feet.

"So don't forget," Louise was insisting, "Café Arabica. Another name to remember, 'Cafe Arabica', cultural Mecca of the North. Come to my opening night. I'll send a complimentary ticket."

Jilly watched her striding away through the traffic. On reaching her shiny new black BMW, Louise stopped before ripping the fine from her windscreen as Jilly backed into the shadows.

Garrick was reflecting, how had he ended up here? Memories fade or get overwritten. That very first interview seemed a lifetime ago. He wished he had carried a pocket recorder, but details began to come flickering back like reels of old nitrate film.

His first appointment had been made at short notice. Vee had dialled an advertised number and booked his interview for him, reserving a train seat for Norston via Manchester Piccadilly. Euston had been crowded. Beside him a bearded Sikh ploughed through the whole Financial Times. Businessmen communed with laptops. Others texted. Most were on cellphones or plugged into music, sealed into airtight cocoons. As stations came and went, they passed between hills, across plains, over bridges, through tunnels and cuttings with shifting landscapes. He barely recalled changing platforms let alone changing trains, but not long after Manchester you sense those cold moors around Norston. You feel its approach in your bones, but the railway slices straight through, carving whole graveyards in half. Repetitive suburbs are followed by 1950's estates spiked with high-rise blocks. Slatted spokes of old terraces radiate from Victorian mills. Factory sheds abut railway marshalling yards. Now you plunge under soot-blackened bridges, over dark swathes of canal, then storm through a short tunnel, emerging beneath an opaque glass roof beside the North Union Canal.

Fading posters announce "Norston Central". "Bollocks!" retort the graffiti, exactly as the committee had warned. As they said, their town was unique. Mosques, chapels and multiplicities of temples all jostle. Here Christians pray for common approval and hopefully a cathedral, because Norston is a town without status or Charter. It celebrates obscurity. The world may be booming elsewhere, but just such boom had once caused its near-terminal slump. Now self-denial was seen as a virtue. 'Pride Before Fall' was its motto. Mediocrity prospers; its public monuments commemorate this. Norston stays true to its past.

Inhaling fumes of stale urine, Garrick emerged into that forecourt where visitors are confronted by a vast architectural model. "Norston Station Development Scheme," it says "Buy a share in the future. Apply Manwess Development Co." Here even Chekhov would have feared for his values, but Garrick was forced to confront that unresolved Southern concept 'The North', with Vee's newspaper cutting still folded up inside 'LIFE OF CHEKHOV' (unread). The terms of that advert were clear, so perhaps he had been in some state of denial.

Arthur Ruddock was waiting. It was like being met by a bank; formal, pompous and brief. Their single-car motorcade shuddered off with Arthur in 'populist' mode like a presidential campaign. Despite driving back and forth across time zones, no trace of any theatre appeared although once Arthur waved to a hair-styling boutique where a large woman waved frantically back. When they finally drew up at an open-air market, Arthur ushered Garrick ahead before lunging between fluttering stalls, gesturing Garrick to follow. Then vanished.

A marketplace was in full sail. Fleets of storm-tossed canvas bulged. Scaffolding yardarms flew saris, all yellows, saffrons, oranges, hennas and reds. Armadas of tarpaulin tacked among blizzards of polythene bags. No hypermarkets. No branches of multiple stores. Signs in every known language. He could have given up then but Garrick's luck had already run out, or was it the albatross curse? Instead he plunged blindly on after Ruddock, knowing Vee would never forgive him.

He didn't see the van till it missed him. All he recalled was its logo, two Trumpeting Angels over a Paradise Shopfitters' Scroll, memorable and outrageous. As Garrick broke into a run, two schoolgirls got in his way, giving him two-fingered gestures knowing for certain they'd never see him again. Ahead a narrow alleyway cut through the brickwork like a geological fault. Down this shrinking canyon Arthur was a diminishing shape, but before Garrick could reach him, he'd turned and walked through a three-storey wall. Over its doorway a rusting sign announced 'STAGE DOOR' like the entrance to a lost era.

By coming to Norston that day, Garrick accepted his fate. His mission encompassed his wife and her mother, together with generations of Morozoffs back throughout all mitochondrial time. Russian blood in Morozov veins was a specific mutation with family trees to prove it. From there the Caucasus spoke with the accents of Moscow, and Georgia seemingly flourished wherever émigrés prospered. Easterly winds blew all the way from the Ukraine. Their hero was a doctor and playwright. A man from the Sea of Azarov. You couldn't be more Russian than that. Even if Vee and her mother made certain assumptions, Garrick learnt never to argue. Confessions weren't in his tradition, so from the start he had acted his role. That's why they both later felt so betrayed.

Watching his Aspro dissolve, he tried to pinpoint the moment when things first began to go wrong. It began with those big dinner parties at home. Verity loved entertaining. Her recipes soon multiplied and ingredients overflowed until slowly, imperceptibly, her hobby became a profession. Then when her career began to take off, students were calling all times of the day. Her schedule fitted no pattern; lecturing at ungodly hours in ungodly places. To compensate for this disruption she invented elaborate routines. Everyone was forced to adapt, even down to that craze for 'Baked Clams with Garlic à la Cape Cod' each time a child was expected. During such emergencies she'd first started phoning her mom. Around about then Vee first began to asking those difficult questions. Then when Roseanne in person arrived she brought all the dirt she'd unearthed.

Garrick stirred up the water, his plastic pen clinking the glass, churning the mixture into suspension. He swallowed it down in one gulp.

Praed Street was just a few streets from their home. In a hastily converted warehouse alongside Paddington Station, North London Catering College couldn't be easily missed. Extractor fans blasted concoctions of herbs. Her students hung around local bars, and NLCC became the big trend. Soon her 'Cuisine' extended to pastoral care of all students, as if that were an end in itself. Soon journalists interviewed her.

When their inquiries extended to him, Garrick rewrote his career. He blanked his name from professional handbooks and destroyed any press cuttings. So no more Gerelda, Wild Boys, Divinas, contortionists, nudes or exotic dancers. Omissions and evasions worked, so he rewrote his entire CV. When the future lies in the past, respectability counted. Being invited to functions as Verity's escort meant further adjusting his facts, so showbiz was turned into "Culture" and clubs became "Opera Houses". It worked. He found himself on the establishment lists. Vee and Roseanne were impressed, together with college investors, well-wishers, donors and high-minded wealthy subscribers.

London is a hotchpotch of villages crowded together but kept well apart. Scratch any resident and you'll find a commuter. So he avoided former hangouts, changed his phone numbers, took himself off registers, cautiously reinventing his life. Soon he began to believe it himself. In those early days when she'd not thought to ask questions, he'd begun to feel almost self-righteous. Paternity redefines a man's status, so his kids became welcome distractions, and he was secure in the fatherhood role as long as no-one asked questions. Deep down in his temporal lobes he felt fully reinstated. His reinvention had worked. Everyone accepted him. At least till that day when Chekhov paid them a visit.

'The Biography' by Arnold G. Steiner, subtitled 'Acts of Defiance', arrived by airmail direct from Boston, Massachusetts. The accompanying letter came like as a bolt from the blue, 'BIG DISCOVERY' it said in bold capitals, with records of recent research underlined. It confirmed this scholar's researches, including letters, photos and revised family trees proving what Roseanne suspected. She was descended from the great Russian playwright and author, Anton Pavlovich Chekhov. Therefore her daughter was too.

When Garrick considered the full implications, an inconsistency struck him. He pointed out that if Morozova was Chekhov's mother, then how come the Morozovs descended from Chekhov? (Let alone Stanislavsky). Morozov was Chekhov's maternal grandfather's name. They were only tangential. They did not have that Chekhov DNA; therefore the Morozoffs could not be descendants of Chekhov. Done. Q.E.D. It was pure common-sense and no more complicated than that. But whatever followed from pointing this out, Garrick would trace back to that day.

In his first few days in Norston he'd travelled no more than the route from lodgings to theatre. Okay, you take easy options. You quickly get into routines, it was that kind of town; its early expansion had led to a sudden contraction. When cotton mills died it retreated back on itself in some kind of auto-sclerosis. So different from Manchester, Burnley, Sheffield or Leeds, but unlike many small towns it still retained its old theatre. For Garrick its remoteness had an attraction. He was free from unrealistic expectations. Here he could safely make his mistakes.

As he set out today he felt adventurous, careless and unrestrained. He kicked at loose pebbles, watching them clatter over stone sets. He turned down an overgrown alley to take a shortcut along the canal. On rounding the corner, a demolition crane blocked his way like a faded red monster, sci-fi and rusting, bearing the logo "Craig Demolition" in flaking white paint. As Garrick looked up, its gantry moved overhead.

Perhaps he did hear the siren, but before he could move, a rusting steel ball swung barely metres above him. It seemed to move in slow motion following an invisible arc, dragging gravity with it. Like plasticised Lego, walls burst in a spatter of bricks, followed at once by the echoes, before swinging back on its chain as if it had all eternity left. At that moment Garrick's mind flashed to his children. One day they would understand, but again the ball swung. Walls caved. Boards splintered to firewood. Signboards blazed CRAIG DEMOLITION as if contradicting some claim. Garrick shielded his eyes and seemed to smell rotting corpses mingled with charcoal and faeces, the burial pit and the funeral pyre. Soon bonfires would reduce the whole district to ash.

As Garrick ducked he saw someone approach; a stocky man in a trench coat, oily grey hair coiling from under his helmet and straggling down his bull-neck. As Eddie passed, billowing dust-clouds enveloped the theatre beyond, like St Paul's Cathedral swathed in the smoke of the Blitz.

Eddie Craig did not see Garrick. He'd bigger things on his mind. His was the maths of the circle: a given mass in an inevitable arc striking a preordained target, an instant testosterone high. Its maleness tingled the groin; addictive, compulsive, dangerous too. He was ringmaster. Impresario. King-of-the-castle, Eddie was self-contained and ambitious. Showmanship guaranteed contracts. This was his Art. 'Creative Destruction' summed up the mood of the time, the ultimate self-expression. He shouted for workmen, and when Eddie shouted, everyone jumped. Helmeted labourers jumped out of nowhere and ran. Eddie assembled his foremen, then up the lane came Arthur Ruddock, strutting past the barriers and brushing caution aside, a clumsy greatcoat flapping like wings. He was followed by young George de Vries at his heels, as gawky as a three-legged foal. Seconds later a sudden gust blasted the alley, funnelling ashes and smoke, thick with the powdered remains of old Norston laced with asbestosis, and impregnated with plague. The wind continued to blow as Arthur was introducing young George to Eddie Craig, pointing and gesturing as if signing decrees to the deaf.

Behind them trailed assorted officials. The two stood centre-circle: Arthur v. Eddie! The clash of industrial Titans! A cameraman was filming away. A council official held out a wallet of pamphlets, but Eddie Craig swept them casually aside. He and Arthur burst into laughter and shook hands. As if on cue, generators roared into life, pneumatic drills drummed, and workmen started to hammer away. This was a sledgehammer moment. Everything would be recycled. That was a political promise. Every reclaimable brick and every reusable beam. Here charitable status would join with divisible profits, so everyone present shook hands. Behind all of this, The Majestic rose like Mount Olympus above acres of rubble, frozen in that moment of time.

Garrick had other things on his mind. They took it for granted he was a seasoned director, but at any stage he could have cried 'stop'. It was always the same. You tell them what they want to hear. By completely reinventing his past he had colluded. Forget all those showgirls, chorus girls, models, usherettes, dancers, who'd previously peopled his life. Everyone fucked, but they'd all been firmly consigned to a past where he hoped they'd stay. He owed his survival to Vee. Her innocence and the birth of their kids outbalanced the death of his father, so when her virtues overcame his, they felt innately his own. It felt like a moral progression. He'd never been so secure in his life. Then Vee's mother intervened. That was when Lola, Rachael, Suki and others came back to haunt him.

But why Suki? That was a big misunderstanding. Body language is ambiguous. It's open to misinterpretation. The girl had been hired on four weeks approval, officially labelled "Trainee Intern", meaning she wouldn't be paid, so when told to make cuts, Garrick had listed the staff and their jobs, scratched it all out, then started again. It wasn't about economics. The theatre committee was Arthur Ruddock. He'd simply rehired Rex Schulman's old team without consultation. There'd been no consideration of Chekhov. The list of employees seemed endless. Phyllis Corbel, Bert Battley, Reg Diamond, Danny Utama and others, with Suki Warrington on a Work Experience Course.

Phyllis was the only exception. She was the eyes and ears of the theatre and evidently trusted by Arthur. Apart from her, a cautious pruning was needed, and Suki was the obvious choice. She was forgetful, disorganised and always complaining. Of course he admired the bulge of her buttocks, the turn of her calves, the voluptuously prearranged cleavage, and those glossy pink quivering lips with their fatal addiction to smoking. But wearing high-heeled impractical sandals with ultra-short miniskirts was distracting. Worse she was incompetent.

Aware of his doubtful responses, Garrick wavered. Couldn't Suki see she disturbed him? She must be autistic. Or was it some hormonal effect? Anyway, when he finally gave her that Letter of Notice, she looked uncomprehending. He'd felt almost ashamed, but his decision was made. She continued to stare without moving. He spread out his hands, shrugged sympathetically, and gave that famous rueful smile.

"You!" She gave a raised finger, "You bigoted shit!"

"Hang on! I'm sorry Suki, I know how you feel, but if I'm forced to be frank . . ."

"So fuck off Frank!"

As she stormed out slamming multiple doors, he knew this would echo and echo.

Phyllis glared over her glasses. "I know you're on the phone! But I've just spoken to Suki. Poor child, it doesn't make sense!"

She loomed across Garrick's desk. He tried clamping a hand over the mouthpiece. In desperation he held up his phone and pointed.

"All right." She made a concession sound like an order. "Finish your call then I'll talk to you later."

She spun round on low sensible heels, slamming the door behind her. Exactly like Suki, that sense of communal outrage, identical flurries of gestures.

"Jesus, Gary! What was that?" Verity's voice came indistinct from his phone. "I was telling you about little Markie's addiction to skateboards. Then like . . . It's crazy! . . . How come?"

"The wind caught the door. It slammed, that's all."

But he knew she was smarter than that. She'd have to reassure her mom that Chekhov was well on his way. This was their great family epic, a personal Morozov quest: that Chekhov's apotheosis was on schedule. His 'Three Sisters' would be followed by a new 'Uncle Vanya' heading a Festival of Great Classic Drama to be transferred to London's West End. Then perhaps Broadway, major world tours, followed by the film of the show? He could hear a child's yells in the background and Vee was shouting asides. Seconds later the line disconnected. He decided against ringing back.

When Garrick reached Phyllis's office she continued to rattle away at the keyboard.

"Ah! Yes!By the way . . ." Without looking up, she selected a folder, ". . . Here. Mr Ruddock wants a detailed breakdown of costs." She continued flipping pages "And by tonight."

Garrick blinked. A lifetime's inexperience showed.

"And so," Now Phyllis was sounding almost indulgent, "Bearing that in mind, I'll complete an estimate for you, based on Rex's last season. All right?"

Still without looking up, she pointed to a framed photograph showing a middle-aged man with swept-back grey hair, lantern jaw, and prominent teeth smirking. "Dee..ear, darling Rex. Those lovely old professionals."

Her printer started whirring out lists: past pantomimes churned, reduced to statistics. This, thought Garrick, is how it would be; everything judged by seats sold, never by classic performance because this was the Internet era. Secrets were no longer private. His mother-in-law had tuned into that. She'd poked around Garrick's roots like a naughty child prying. She'd muddied the Internet waters by trawling, then pushing detritus on him.

Before Roseanne's interference their marriage was happily coasting along. Not any longer.

"Truth is always sacrosanct and everything's there to be found," Roseanne announced.

Already his marriage had suffered. At first Vee had a lecturing post while he dipped and dived by freelancing. The educational establishment suited her. Verity thrived. She devised new culinary styles. Recipes were perfected. Famines came and went. Starvation and malnutrition joined forces. Charities responded and Michelin awarded more stars. Garrick bathed and fed babies, did shopping and chores. As their paths began to diverge, Vee began seeking Professorship status, aiming at Head of Department. She got the College Principal job and a place on the board. Okay he could adapt. They were in love. From potty training to chaos at bath-time he'd coped, and somehow it worked. It was U.S. paramedics that failed.

Verity's father collapsed one afternoon in L.A. Morton's second stroke came as a shock, but once Roseanne was widowed, she rediscovered herself. After the funeral and love-in with lawyers she'd sat on the phone to U.K. or dabbled at family trees. Only then did the Morozov connection emerge; the Unique Unsurpassed Morozov Line. Roseanne bought software wholesale, obsessively searching Morozov, Morozoff, Morozzo, Morozova, Morozavitch . . . She'd turn over stones where there weren't any stones.

"Family history brings obligations, I guess," she'd said, "Russia has deep pre-historical roots from way back before even the days of the Czars. I'm planning on checking out every link, or whatever."

That's when it happened. Evegeniya Morozova surfaced. Evegeniya Dolzhenka, the long-suffering mother of the great Anton Pavlovich Chekhov, that Morozov link with the Chekhovs. Verity had been so excited.

Later out of the blue, Roseanne sent Garrick obscure links extolling 'temperance', 'abstinence' and 'cures for desire', commenting how easy it was to check anyone's past. She referred to morality, truth and orthodox values, plus how much, much else she was longing to ask him, adding (hint, hint) how lonely she felt, missing her dear darling daughter in London. She needed quality time with her grandchildren. All the Morozovs had so much in common.

Garrick threatened to return to work if Roseanne moved into town. In which case he warned they'd have to hire an au pair and child-minder. To his surprise Vee took it all very calmly. She actively encouraged him. A career for him would revive their marriage, she said, because one never knew where it might lead: their routines needed spicing up, which had come as a bit of a shock.

12

Looking back, it was Vee who'd originally produced that newspaper clipping referring to Norston. It was Vee who'd composed his first application and printed out his CV. But Norston? He'd barely heard of the place, but by then it was too late to back down. What he hadn't realised was this would be his Mecca, his own sectarian Hajj. Mission and Odyssey weren't in his lexicon either and self-sacrifice looked like a suicide pact. He was here for Anton Chekhov, not Evegeniya the mother. Why call them 'The Morozov Players'? He'd registered 'Chekhov Players' instead.

Whenever Garrick questioned his personal motives he'd hear his late father declaiming the King James Bible. Edwin stood in for a conscience. He'd recite the Book of Isaiah between smoking those black cigarillos of his and hiding the brandy away. On any whim he'd spout Plato and quote St Augustine, oblivious to his own failings. When tragic combined with the comic it turned into terminal farce, so Garrick knew what was expected. What mattered was Chekhov himself not Phyllis's schedules. 'Mission creep' must be contained. He would not be sidetracked from Verity's aims.

Phyllis's spectacles glinted, their intricate hinges catching the light. "Contracts are normally handled by our Mr. Ruddock," she said, "But I'm sure you'll do what needs to be done." Her pale eyes imperceptibly hardened behind blue-tinted lenses, "So I'll leave the detailed selection to you. Along with preparing the costings and schedule." Shutters slammed down as Phyllis washed her hands of the subject.

On the day they'd first met, Vee made it plain to Garrick she wanted a family. Fine. So no ambiguities there. He'd accepted that children and home would come first. Garrick's dad encouraged them: in fact he'd been so confident Garrick himself never foresaw any problems. He'd felt free to tell Vee whatever she wanted to hear. She maybe even embroidered his tales. When babies were born, Garrick adapted his stories still further, amending and improving on details, gradually raising his status and extending his fabulous cultural contacts. He turned himself into producer/director, Shakespearean scholar and reticent establishment star. His list of famous acquaintances grew. He erased former contacts, destroyed press cuttings, removing his name from professional handbooks. He avoided regular hangouts and completely reinvented himself. He'd even thought about knocking some years off his age. In retrospect he'd gone too far. A woman as smart as Roseanne would spot such inconsistencies the moment her luggage dropped on their doorstep. Or sooner. And sooner came first.

At least Phyllis was no Roseanne. Her office was the antithesis. Nothing precise or rational here. Cabinets crammed with decades. Shelves bent under files. Posters papering available space. Paperweights. Fans. Figurines. Plants like living mementoes cluttered any available surface. On the crowded mantelpiece a large plaster toad commanded eclectic assortments of frogs. Except Phyllis knew where everything was. As Chekhov understood so well, it wasn't earthquakes or wars that disturbed us. It was the jammed carton, missed phone call, broken button, or misplaced pen; the symptoms of everyday lives.

Garrick knew he had to speak out, "Phyllis, I do appreciate how you must feel. After all those years of dedication, I'm aware . . . very aware . . . you aren't happy with change, but I'm afraid my schedule will be extremely demanding."

She glanced up from her screen, eyebrows raised in a question, watching him intently. He explained the absolute rigours of Chekhov and demands of serious drama. It wouldn't be like the old days of Rex Schulman, all Rattigan and Noel Coward. It would require total and absolute change.

". . . And I'll need a personal assistant of course," he said, "Someone wholly committed."

From her fixed position she watched him pacing about. Mediocrity ages men, but she could see he wasn't much younger than she. She liked the level playing-field image. What this latest contender lacked was Arthur's gravity or Rex Schulman's charm. She knew the local set-up back to front and Garrick was just one more in a line. So she prepared to take notes until eventually he sat at her desk.

"Now, Phyllis, I'm sure we'd pay cash in lieu of notice. Change doesn't have to be feared. We understand how you feel." He gave an indulgent smile "To be honest, I don't blame you at all."

He could hear a road drill grinding away. A distant aircraft toiled overhead as Phyllis gazed around. For one fleeting moment he doubted his judgement. He would not spell the obvious out, but he'd leave her to reach her conclusions. Redundancy had its attractions and would help them all start from square one.

Her lips stretched into a welcoming smile, "Of course Garrick. Don't worry. That's settled."

He almost gasped. He'd underestimated her. In his eyes she'd visibly bloomed. No questions; no threats to go to appeal. She'd read his mind and not made him spell everything out. He almost wanted to kiss her. She knew she'd get a generous redundancy package, so she wouldn't lose out.

He tried to envisage her office renewed. Busts of Chekhov and Stanislavsky appeared, followed by maybe an Oscar, a Bafta or two. He pictured white walls, black leather and chrome. He was mentally refurbishing the block, creating the commercial hub of an entertainment empire. Theatre, film, television and maybe even Internet too.

"Garrick, I see just what you're saying." She examined him thoughtfully, "Yes, we think alike, you and I. You don't need to say any more. I'll organise Suki's replacement. But before that . . ." She dialled, sniffed and wrinkled her nose. "There it is again , and I've warned Arthur too. But oh no! He's no sense of smell, Surely that's gas we can smell? I'm calling Manwess contractors at once. Before we're all asphyxiated. After that we'll get down to planning our season and casting."

As Garrick tried to take it in, a cloud the size of a man's hand seemed to float in from outside.

14

CHAPTER TWO

LOCATION, LOCATION

Garrick stared down in a reflex reaction. From the north turret his office surmounted the world. If you twisted then craned, you could see down for almost 360°. Sometimes it caught him off-balance, spinning in all directions. Away to the right lay the main shopping centre, as concrete as a siege emplacement. Far to the left stretched industrial terraces surrounded by rings of Victorian suburbs, organic as annular growth. Beyond this urban sprawl straggling estates dissolved into haphazard farmland, which petered out into moorland and fells.

He took a mental photograph. Behind the theatre ran a nineteenth century canal like a bleak, overgrown moat. Alongside this, the old industrial town jutted with iron-tipped pinnacles and long-redundant chimneystacks looking like trunks of fossilised trees, monuments to penile dysfunction. But all those great industries died. Dyeing, weaving and printing perished. Cotton had long gone as had car parts, freezers and knitwear. Instead supermarket chains and financial services ruled from bleak wedges of glass. Throughout all this, call-centres spread like a virus. In prime position here, The Majestic rose like a twin-towered Cathedral, brandishing two fingers at life. It gave a new sense of perspective. Most of all it gave him hope.

By standing on tiptoe and facing South (while bearing just a touch left) Garrick could zero straight in on London. Forget the curve of the Earth. Forget about geometry. By focusing exceptionally hard he could think himself directly into St George's Mews. That was the power of the mind. However whenever he'd tried calling home, the connections were always engaged.

Phyllis was sorting out forms, "Here. These are top priority." She pushed a random assortment towards him. "All correspondence has to be read, then acknowledged. Just initials'll do. The Council relies on questionnaires. We subscribe to consultation exercises, focus groups, efficiency tables and all the suchlike. I'll lay these out in order, right?" She scattered additional forms. "Arts Council Grants . . . Heritage Subsidies . . . Private Subventions . . . Scholarships for Creative Expression . . . Industrial Initiatives . . . And of course your own detailed budgetary plans." She indicated dotted lines "And if you can raise extra finances yourself?" She smiled a one-sided smile, " Then all the better! Right?" She patted the bundle, thrusting it into his hands.

Garrick needed a nicotine fix. Like other ageing hippies and roadies he'd become more and more like his father, always compensating for something; a father who mistrusted his son. Garrick tried shutting his mind. Hadn't Chekhov trained as a doctor and failed to cure his own illness? Who could diagnose themselves when the hemispheres of the brain were at odds, undermining each other? Result? A split personality crisis, facing both backwards and forwards. Which is how he had ended up here. And again the old contradictions. As much as he needed tobacco and sex, Norston needed its theatre. Yet Manchester, Preston and Liverpool thrived while Norston went into decline. Without live theatre no town could be itself. Did Urban Regeneration have to mean cheap compromise? Across the skyline, rows of lopped-off sycamores ached; beyond them, shorn hedges straggled between dismembered shrubs and barbed wire. A greyness hung on the air, intensified by the season. Escape might be his only way out.

As he tried to slip downstairs, Phyllis waved from her office. It was too late. As unlighted stairs and dark passages went into peristaltic contractions, disgorging him onto the pavement, he could still hear her calling his name. In front of the theatre stood a skip and generator emblazoned with 'Manwess Gas' logos. Flashing lights and orange cones marked out a wedge-shaped plot in the road, like the lid of an oversized coffin. Blue workmen assembled a chrome yellow drill. Discordant colours fused with aromas, uproar and din like acute synesthesia.

He found walking helped. He trudged round the block twice, past hairstylists, fashion stores, dry cleaners, cake shops, charity shops, more charity shops, coffee bars, takeaway curries, Halal and Kosher, second-hand fridges, multi-screen cinemas, computer/video traders, cut-price home entertainment. All emerged from a mist as if someone had lifted a filter. Forget voters' lists. This was real life. This is where his audience lived. When she'd talked about 'cultural deprivation' maybe Louise was right? Maybe they hungered and thirsted for Chekhov? In a state of deep concentration he stepped out from the kerb as a waiting car slid away. As traffic lights changed a Black Ford Mondeo raced a Manwess van.

Garrick instinctively dived as streaks of slow-motion blurred, frame after frame. As if on a fader, screeching brakes, hootings, dissolved into silence. Out of this darkness Vee appeared like a ghost, hand-in-hand with his kids at the kerb, mournfully shaking their heads.

A tall bronzed man in navy-blue suit and long whiskers was bent over Garrick, his uniform topped by a navy-blue turban emblazoned with the Manwess Gas badge. His hands pressed together in greeting.

"Praises be, you're alive. I saw what just happened, you see. Call me old reactionary, but it's a jolly sight safer with handcarts and bullocks! No thought for eternal existence. No social conscience, you see."

He padded off, shaking his head.

Garrick's interview for the job came back again in even more minuscule detail.

He clearly remembered walking into that room confronted by a long table arranged like Leonardo's Last Supper. There at the centre the Chairwoman smiled through silver-rimmed lenses, her tiny manicured hands immaculate against grey silk. Lady Peggy de Vrie's delicate neck rose from an Aquascutum silk blouse. She must have been a beauty once. Barely in her sixties, soft powder clung to fine hair on her cheeks. Pearlised lipstick marked the faint course of a smile. Pale tinting heightened neatly trimmed hair. She had leaned so far forward he'd glimpsed dry cleavage beneath strings of wild pearls. Only a membrane of chintzy silk lay between them.

"Tell me," she'd asked, "How do you see your future in Norston?"

Before Garrick had time to reply, Arthur Ruddock had intervened, implying the theatre was minting big money. Audiences queued round the block. Everything was booming, he'd said. No hint of financial restrictions. Looking back, the wilder Garrick's proposals became, the more that committee seemed to approve. He'd been encouraged by their reactions. He'd flailed around for wilder and wilder ideas.

"Yes, and Chekhov aids neurological responses," he'd found himself claiming, "Chekhov has anti-viral effects!" Sensing everyone's thrill of excitement as rhetoric fed on itself, "Chekhov's the answer to anyone's programme."

He felt an adrenaline rush. A crumpled note in his pocket spelled out "Go for it dad" in Rachel's smudged crayon. Apparently cost was no object. If he'd suggested 'Odysseus on Ice' with a cast of thousands, plus two complete orchestras, they'd probably have cheered. In retrospect it did seem odd, but at the time they'd loved it. He'd recommended Chekhov plus Ibsen and Strindberg. A major cultural breakthrough, he'd claimed. He's talked of 'Creative Renaissance', borne on a verbal tsunami. There'd been a stunned silence before their applause.

"Hear hear!" they'd all chorused, "Hear hear!" They'd thumped their palms on the table as he'd bounced their own slogans back, confirming every prejudice. They'd applauded again and again. Or that's how he remembered it, seemingly scripted and planned.

Next moment he'd been outside in the corridor on a wooden bench, awaiting a formal rejection. He'd seemed to hear deep subliminal grindings as if the whole building vibrated. A numbness seeped from his brain to his bowels. He was trying to shut it all out when a workman in overalls appeared, sweatshirt stamped Manwess Gas. Behind him a cascade of mortar and rubble was followed by more broken bricks, then in the silence, the faintest aroma of gas.

By the time he was invited back into the room, Garrick knew it was over. No congratulations. No speeches. A closely typed document lay on the table. Ruddock slapped him on the back:

"Not hard to sign your name, is it? You'll not need a legal consultant. First find the dotted line, then mark it with your personal cross! You're not signing for Manchester United, okay," and everyone laughed . . . but memory plays its own tricks.

When he returned to start work two weeks later everything had changed. No one was waiting to greet him as promised. As he crossed the station forecourt, rumbling his suitcase behind him, a gleaming black car had brushed him aside before accelerating away. He'd tasted burnt oil in its wake. Feeling the first specks of rain, he decided to find his own way to the lodgings.

'Baker's Row. Desirable town-centre first-floor apartment,' evoked a cosy alleyway scented with freshly baked bread. The letting agents implied a five minute stroll from the station, but by the time he'd tramped down Sammihall Street, Cavanham Street, Fox Lane, and Bullocks Way, through Weavers Street and Market Place, Verity's warnings seemed right, "Get a taxi," she'd said as if reading his mind, his cellphone had started to bleep. Vee's extrasensory perception had worked.

"Hi!" He'd tried to sound positive, "Hi darling! I'm nearly there."

A silence. "You what? . . . It's Rocko! Your agent, remember? . . . An' don' give us no more shit! Jus' think 'Crazy Bull', that snooty striptease joint, awright?" Garrick held the phone from his ear. "Smarty-farty clientele, footballers, models. Off Gresham Street? Wi' live music? It's cultural bigtime! Starting next Friday. Okay?"

The drizzle was turning to serious rain. Garrick switched off his phone, and sheltered under a bookstall. Here the local press ruled, no national dailies. No paedophiles. No pregnant beauty queens. No serial adulterers. No drunken drivers. No terrorists. No drug-trafficking thieves. Even a shortage of muggings. A seven day total absence of murder. With so little news Garrick's younger self stared out the page surrounded by 'Unrepeatable Offers, Amazing Discounts, Sales of the Decade, Clearance Bargains and Astounding Cut Price Deals'. Alongside, a column headed 'New Faces' was by-lined 'Elizabeth Scott', accusing Garrick of being 'Pillar of the London establishment'.

She warned that Chekhov and Strindberg were "not icons of popular culture, but totems of white middle-aged, middle-class values". It questioned his allegiances. The North was being patronised, she said, but theatregoers would always remember the great glory days of Rex Schulman. "Come the Day of Judgment, Lancashire will supersede London, and Norston will attend Garrick's demise and celebrate entertainment again."

As raindrops plopped onto newsprint, he unsprung his fold-up umbrella.

Phyllis could not know his thoughts. She'd quickly started to prey on his diary, adding appointments, writing illegible comments, repeatedly asking if he took sugar in tea and rearranging his desk. Garrick began to feel over-observed. Budgets and schedules were more like Sodoku. Add algebra to chronometry and you get just another equation. His calculator tried to join in but what everyone wanted was schedules.

After cutting up several calendars, creating date-charts and cut-and-pasting schedules, he began to feel less of a fraud. Any activity helped. Lancaster Gate seemed planets away, but his expectations grew until single cherry trees grew into great flowering orchards. Then someone cut the orchards down. So he knelt on the floor to reorganise rosters and casting, spreading loose pages around him.

Allowing, say, one day for read-through, followed by at least three weeks rehearsal, the time was damned tight. Maybe dress rehearsal on Sunday? Followed by a run of five weeks, once-nightly Monday to Wednesday, then twice-daily Thursdays, Fridays and Saturdays. He'd open with Sheridan's 'The Rivals', then Chekhov's 'Cherry Orchard', or maybe 'Three Sisters' or even 'The Seagull'? And then Ibsen's 'Rosmersholm' or maybe 'Hedda Gabler', and naturally a Strindberg or two? Or maybe start with 'Cherry Orchard' and . . . he stood up and returned to his desk. Reality was an Arts Subsidy world. You needed bait for government grants? Throw in deals for the disabled, disadvantaged, pensioners and children, ticking possibilities off. Next, get your Stage Management, Cast, Choreographer, Designers, Musical Director. He underlined 'The Three Sisters', then circled it and starred it in red, before crossing it out and starting again. When the phone rang his pen skipped the page.

Phyllis was in switchboard persona, "A Mrs. Roberts for you! Says it's very personal?"

Verity was in a mood she hardly recognised; her sense of enormous relief was boosted by new confidence; new achievements added new undisclosed hormones. She no longer felt the need for excuses; apologies were due from elsewhere. She'd just got home from campus, spent half an hour with the kids, then fed Scooby the insatiable cat before unwinding in her usual way. She took a deep breath and felt almost reckless, pressing the phone to her mouth. Fresh lipstick and mentholated toothpaste were tinged with at hint of Sauternes. With confidence comes relaxation, and her lips and tongue re-established control.

"Hi honey," she said, "So how's it all going?"

For Garrick another day had gone down the pan, but her voice sounded liquid and teasing. She squelched him a watery kiss while signalling the kids to keep quiet, then muffled a giggle impeded by tongue, teeth, and brain.

"Like, how's things, like, working out?" she began, then felt herself involuntarily tensing. "My secretary said you talked 'kinda curt'? And hey, why call me at work?"

Something was not being said. Anyway, why should Professors of Cooking be protected by answering systems? That 'Professor Jones always unavailable' stuff, "But can we take a message?" So what was he meant to do? As he heard consonants blurr from the phone, Phyllis peered round his door frame, signalling 'T' with both hands. He signalled frantically 'No'.

"But Vee! I've tried you several times a day . . ." he repeated.

Vee motioned both squabbling kids from the room, mouthing out silent instructions:

"Gary, I can't call you from lectures, for chrissakes! Here I am, midways through creating a range of vegetarian menus featuring Flavocol soya, Flavocol pulses and hydrolysed Flavocol products. and that's between interviewing staff and giving lectures! None of that's funny." She sipped from the glass and then waited.

Garrick tried to fill in the pause. "So how's the domestic? No, forget Roseanne. Just joking." In the background he heard Rachel shrieking, "And how's the kids? Did you get it, their special bubble shampoo? The two hundred milligram pack? The one with the green dragon logo?"

"The what? Trouble is, Gary, I always know what you're thinking. It's not worthy of you. Get real, they're fine! Their shampoo's fine! We're all of us fine. So what's with you? You will do 'Cherry Orchard' first? And who've you cast to play Masha? Who's playing Vershinin? Anyone we've heard of?"

The roots of the American Rostoffs ran via mother and daughter right through to his children, entirely bypassing himself. He blamed Evgeniya Morozova, but paradoxes remained. How could the Chekhov line run in the Morozov blood? Even if the Chekhovian Tree flowered in the US of A? Garrick pictured Phyllis and Arthur surrounded by the Majestic's board, examining his draft proposals and striking red lines through them all. His attention strayed to the window, caught by a polythene bag blown on the thermals, swooping and floating over the town. In a wave of self-pity he knew how that paper bag felt.

But Vee was still talking away, "Oh never mind honey!" She mouthed him a kiss, "Just give my love to Norston. Bye."

As Abigail braced herself on the footbridge, she committed her mind to the slow-moving water. The canal was her private escape. From great fundamentals right down to every bite'n'scratch and each kiss'n'tell, everything was a problem. Everyone hid behind rules. "Do this" or "Do that." No rhyme or reason. None of it made any sense. Everybody wore masks. Only Stacey understood, because they were alike, she and her friend, as matching as semi-identical twins, their birthdays only a few days apart. Utterly unreliable Stacey! The rest were all strangers. In such a world everyone was alone. Utterly alone and adrift, everyone unrelated, because families were no more than words. With "Mrs. Louise Elsa Roberts", even her signatures were scrawled to impress. It was all a façade. The maternal hug. The sympathetic smile. All for effect. Even Louise's greying hair was restyled in the latest old-fashioned perms then plasticised beneath layers of gilt. As for the hairdressers' guild? Crowning Glory? That was her club; more like confessional, according to Stacey. Yet Louise's latest project was opening a nightclub! A niteclub in down-and-out Norston? It gave social glamour by adding a frisson to culture: apparently that set her apart. "Like mother, like daughter," they'd say.

Would Abigail would end up like her? She felt hot at the thought. A living cadaver? Mangled to fit through a mincing machine? The name-tag Abigail Cynthia Roberts tied to the corpse in a mortuary drawer? As for her gingerous hair, her loathsome white skin, its unsurpassed baby-doll smoothness peppered with transparent freckles, these were the labels of being an outcast. Pain was the only distraction: she relished its silent forensic incisions, the pinkness of scars, and the rush of contentment. The forearm uniquely engraved. Then came the healing and hiding. It secretly set her apart.

She spat down at her startled reflection. The canal tried to drift it away. From the cast-iron rail of the footbridge the water looked dark and deep, yet oddly inviting. She felt she could hang from the stanchions and stroke its sensitised skin, trespassing between living and dead. She dared the floods to rise up and engulf her. But as she looked down, skies above darkened. Imperceptibly everything changed. The oil-scummed surface seemed to blur. Sulphurous wastes churned up the spectrum. From crumbling banks, fractured pipes pissed entire lifetimes away. Flecks of steam skimmed oily ripples over its mirrors. This was the bottomless chasm that channelled millions of litres direct into Norston, cutting the town into sectors, and endlessly draining its soul.

In one convulsive gesture Abigail spread out her palms, exposing bare wrists to the wind. A challenge. A dare. Skin was irresistible; the largest organ by far, and this fading freckled complexion was hers. It tightened and stretched around body and soul, a surface on which she could draw. A filigree of fresh scars was already fading, sketching pale outlines of something she could not describe. Something potent, disturbing and abstract. That was the greatest temptation. Contours needed emphasis; their shapes required filling out. Rusty blades cutting at flesh? Or take the ultimate plunge and just jump? It was almost alluring. She'd not be the first nor the last. Without hope there was no future, only flawed dreams like her mum's. But Abigail's dreams would not end if she drowned. She knew this for certain. She knew she would rise from the water transformed. But not even that cured the anguish. Then, as she tensed and leaned out, she heard running. The footsteps slowed. They stopped right behind her. A gust of wind wrinkled the moving reflections; Abigail's features shimmered; dispersed. But as she leaned further out, a second face appeared beside hers, Abigail spat and the image dissolved into intermeshed circles.

Abby turned, "You're bloody late!"

But Stacey was doing a twirl, her coat and hair spinning out. "Well shitface?" Stacey balanced on tiptoe, twirling a leatherette satchel. Laughing, "Look. Got sick of brunette! Men lust for silvery blondes." She awaited reactions, "Don't bloody look like that. It cost us me savings. And styled at Crowning Glory too!" She fluffed her hair through thin fingers. "Next I'm planning on studs. Gold ears, nose, lips, bellybutton, tongue and gold nipples. The lot." She laughed. "An' maybe a tiny red rosebud tattoo. On each boob! And another gold ring in the crotch!" She performed another slow twirl, swinging her school-things around her, performing a walking investment. "An' I've got a paid job!"

When Abigail failed to respond, Stacey seemed to explode.

"Then fuck you too!" All her frustrations combined into one. "It's thanks to my office cleaning I'm working full-time. From today I'm somebody new." False fingernails trailed through her freshly bleached tresses. "And I want it to show." She peered over the handrail and frowned at the water."'Cept you can't see a thing in that piddle!" She looked back at Abigail. "Hope you're prepared?"

Abigail nodded, "An' you?"

"Like I break promises? That what you mean?" She braced herself, hands on hips, head to one side, posed in anticipation.

Against a cyclorama of clouds Stacey looked electrically charged, her silhouette rimmed with pure daylight, her ample flesh squeezed into tight pants. As Abigail screwed up her eyes, extended silence took fright. Leaking pipes continued to plop into echoes. Waterfowl took to the air. Above droning traffic she could make out the barking of dogs.

Stacey flaunted her newly found halo, "Well, thanks a lot, cowface!" Bulging cheeks tightened on tightly clenched teeth. "Does Miss Disneyworld want to be an actress. That it? When she looks like the fucking Witch of the West!" Stacey stalked to the handrail, calmly unzipping her schoolbag. "All right. Now!" She pointed at Abigail's bag, "I keep my word. School uniform binned. Plus all sports gear burnt, an' you?" She taunted the lack of a response, "Or will lovey stay on till the end of the year? Conform? That it? Too bloody frit? Student of the Century, eh?"

Faint shafts of light blew with the slow-moving clouds. Time went into reverse. Years of spats drowned out everything else, leaving Abby with nothing to say. Existence had only evolved into uncontrollable symptoms, physical bulgings, and internal changes, resulting in blood then more blood, all of it involuntary; everything pre-programmed. She was no longer herself.

At times she had secretly thought she had cancer, even convinced she was dying. Adapting to this and surviving meant you forgot who you were. But Stacey? She was so cool, so kinky; undaunted. Now Stacey was unfastening her coat, button by button performed like a stripper, savouring Abby's discomfort. Defiance gave added conviction. A short knitted top patterned with Lurex left her broad midriff exposed. She stood semi-naked in wind-factor 6, swinging her schoolbag of books and forcing her lips to a pout:

"Unless you're planning like heading back to the womb?" Stacey's pose was defiant. Abigail's posture accepted defeat.

Stacey shimmered her golden-bleached tresses. "We both promised. Remember? Swore on an oath." She ran a long finger over her coffee-cream throat, "Cross your heart and hope to die."

This turning point, once crossed, could never be revisited. Like crossing a threshold. No turning back. Each put a hand to their heart, slapped palms, and began to count down. Together they leaned over the rail. Ten, nine, eight, matching each others' movements. Six, five, four. Like initiation, Abigail thought; final and unavoidable. Stacey was resting her bag on the rim. Together they took a deep breath.

Stacey leaned forward, "Today we begin the rest of our lives! Now!" Then let go.

They spun their bags at the sky, watching them loop and then dive. Textbooks like broken-necked birds plummeted into the water. Mathematics, Media, Social Studies, Community Relationships, as satchels upended and burst. Book followed book, flapping, fluttering, gurgling, sinking. Some bobbed to the surface; waterlogged pages, broken spines, indices trailing loose. Computer Techniques, Media Studies, all drifting away with their pasts, to sink without trace. As if in response, a sharp gust of wind scoured their faces, stippling eyelids and cheeks. In that same moment a trillion circles wove chain-mail across water, turning polished expanses to matt.

It was done. The first rites. Anticlimax was laced with the briefest regret. Now for stage two.

"It's like what the law says. Sixteen. Right? Well, now it's official." Stacey produced cigarettes and a lighter. "More kills and thrills in one giant pack! Eh? An' cheaper than hash."

Her nostrils seemed to expand. She lit and inhaled, sucking warmth into her lungs, feeling the gases expand. As Abigail started to cough, Stacey breathed out blue smoke.

She nudged Abigail's ribs, "Still planning on doing a runner?" She ruffled her newly uncontrolled hair. "Well I'm way ahead, babe." She unzipped her collar, rolling the knitted top down, observing Abigail's cautious confusion. "You want to be an actress, right?"

Dramatically Stacey thrust out a bare breast. As the sky caught it, a hardening nipple tightened the bulge of goose-pimpled flesh. Stacey blinked and pouted in girly-mag pose, lips like red anemones. She fluttered her tongue like some pink, tremulous undersea creature exploring the edge of its world. Stacey was grinning, back in command. As Abigail faltered, Stacey inclined slowly forward, suddenly kissing her full on the lips.

"This is what actresses do! So if you want to be . . ."

Abigail staggered, shocked at the imprint of teeth. She turned and ran, spitting, coughing, choking, back to the footbridge through curtains of rain haunted by Stacey's loud laughter. As she reached the main span, she stopped in her tracks. Midway a figure knelt by the handrail, peering down. Below, in a belching of bubbles, pages were floating back to the surface. Soggy books bobbed like dead sheep. A skinny young man in loose top and jeans, his long face hinting at stubble, flipped back his hood. Abby stood half-blinded with rain. The frozen seconds persisted.

Josh pointed down at the mulch in the water. "Hope no-one's fell in." With a clatter of footsteps Roddy suddenly emerged down the alley. His pace never faltered.

"Come on!" he yelled as he dragged Roddy off, "Let's get fuckin' drinkin'!"

Memory loves playing tricks. Sometimes it muddles intentions, sometimes befuddles the facts, but Garrick's seemed crystal clear. On his very first visit to Norston he clearly recalled telling that committee to stuff their damn contract, then storming out. By sheer repetition its details were fixed. He remembered his principled stand, "Forget terms and conditions," he'd said, "I'm off'. It sustained his hagiography. His promise to Vee surpassed everything else because she had underwritten his mission (countersigned of course by Roseanne). He had kept the train ticket as absolute proof. As he recalled, everything was so detailed and vivid. He replayed it again and again, first being chauffeured around before being dumped in a market. When Arthur Ruddock had walked on ahead and disappeared down that alley, Garrick could, or should, have turned back. Everything would have ended right there.

Instead Garrick stumbled on down the tunnel. Then in a deep-set recess he'd spotted a low, blistered door scaling like psoriasis. Garrick pushed. It had swung open. A dim bulb in a rusting wire cage glimmered inside a windowless cube, its shadowy surfaces peeling with scrofulous posters, layer on layer like eczema. But no sign of Arthur. As he ventured further in. Bang! The door slammed behind him. Sudden pressure popped his ears. Garrick fumbled in half-light for exits. Everywhere there were warnings. "No loitering" "No Smoking" A steel door marked "Fire Door. Keep Shut" was sealed. As his eyes adjusted to the dim light he noticed calling cards and fading messages sprouting round a notice board. "Rudolf is a reindeer," read a felt-pen graffiti, "It's the only damn part he could get!" A printed notice stated, 'Stagehands always required', to which someone had scribbled 'Unpaid !'

"Hello?" he had hollered, "Anyone there?"

He'd tried forcing a heavy steel door before noticing its lever. One tentative tug and it suddenly gave. He edged through to a tiny cramped landing. A zigzag of treads plunged down a deep shaft; an expressionist maze packed with ambiguities where vertical halflight plummeted into perspective like a Marc Escher ladder, defying all logic, vanishing down a Black Hole. He could hear distant footsteps, descending and ever-descending, their echoes filling a surrealist void.

"Jones?" A disembodied voice came spiralling up. "Where the hell are you?"

Gorky and Chekhov had plumbed human depths: Tolstoy and Pushkin put their own lives on the line. Garrick took his own first step, trudging down, till treads hit the floor behind tall canvas flats. Beyond this opened a basin of darkness. No sensation of scale. Huge shadows circled a pool of grey light enticing him on. He was half-expecting applause. Then an explosion of light! Spotlights smashed with a physical force, pinning him to the spot.

"Not bad, eh?" Arthur's voice emerged from the dazzle. "State of the art digital switchboard. Parabolic circuitry. Remote control. Super-halogen centralised beams." A bulky figure was spreading both arms, its overcoat flapping like Batman. "And this, as you already know, is our good friend, Lady de Vries."

Garrick saw eyes in a mirror aimed directly at him. The hand mirror snapped shut. A figure emerged from the shadows and into the spotlight. All sight lines converged upon her. Neatly trimmed silvery hair surmounted a fragile complexion. A navy-blue suit was heightened with strings of pebble-sized pearls. A diamond brooch glittered.

"You like Norston, Mr. Jones?" adding, "Good!" without waiting, "Because we're all of us striving towards the same aims. Literature is civilisation. Drama is the song of the soul. Culture means self improvement." She faced the auditorium. "And this is our small miracle."

Garrick screwed up his eyes. Between dazzling star-bursts he could just make out rows of tip-up seats. There other half watched the living perform. With a faint click, white blinding spotlights shrank to red dots, stamping green haloes onto his brain. "Majestic" suggested imperial splendour and Edwardian values. Garrick had pictured baroque cornices, gilded cartouches and sweeping balcony curves with crimson plush, gold cord and tassels. Instead, tubular railings and stepped industrial ramps linked salvaged cinema seats. Panelling was chipped and worn. Even the structure

24

looked shaky. But as Arthur explained, a corn exchange was built on the site of a foundry constructed before the canal, converted to a cotton store, then opera house, then music hall, and latterly a cinema before the council stepped in.

"Therefore we welcome you." Lady Peggy de Vries unconsciously mimicked the Queen. "This place is very dear to us. Majestic by name. Majestic by nature. Our past master, Rex Schulman, left us great aspirations. Which includes my forthcoming 'Christmas Theatre Soirée' to which you'll be an 'Honoured Guest'"

"Hear hear!" came Arthur's voice from the shadows, his clapping scattering echoes.

Strangely since his interview, no-one had once mentioned Chekhov. Yet that was why he was here. Garrick's plan was to announce his own prospectus directly to Arthur as a fait accompli, but bypassing Phyllis was tricky. She guarded Arthur like Securicor. You couldn't even tiptoe past. Uneven stair risers, irregular handrails, worn edgings, and distinctive creaks of each tread revealed each intimate detail. She recognised every shadow and creak. When Garrick eventually cornered the Chairman, Arthur was still in a hurry.

"Sorry. Can't stop. It's the Gas Executive visit. Soon they'll be ripping out piping then drilling bloody great underground shafts, condemning every pipe and stopcock then replacing the whole bloody lot. That's Health & Safety for you. Just give Phyllis your schedules and budget. Goodbye."

As Garrick trudged round the block, redialling, redialling, his hand went into repetitive strain. Mobile phones were useless here. The signal kept breaking up. He cursed Norston's strange micro-climate where clouds drifted so tantalisingly low they scuffed at roofs and aerials, coiling round towers and spires and blotting out radio links. These very same clouds could have blown here directly from London, passing straight over Lancaster Gate.

At tenth time of dialling Verity answered, "Call back later," she snapped, leaving him out of sight out of mind.

He found Phyllis deep in a phonecall too. She glanced up as he entered then thrust her phone in his hand. A multifaceted diamond on her third finger concentrated available light. This he hadn't noticed before.

"I've a very special lady here," she announced, "It's our Mrs. Roberts," and smiled.

His doppelgänger took over, "Ah, Mrs. Roberts. Sadly I'm in a big meeting." Phyllis raised both eyebrows, "Our whole committee is here. We're just about to vote." He turned to go.

"Then it's lucky I caught you. I've popped your invitation in the post. And while we're on publicity, we saw that latest advert of yours. We'll all be signing up."

"Sorry?"

Phyllis slid the Mercury classifieds over, extending a thin bony finger clamped to an advert announcing a new drama course run by the theatre.

"Yes. That's you," she whispered, "It's good for public relations We run one every year." She handed him a leaflet, "All the details are here."

As he slumped with his head in both hands, Garrick knew he was filling Rex Schulman's shoes. He'd never intended to teach, but everything was compromise. He ploughed alphabetically on through the theatre's disparate library. Here was the whole gamut of drama. With Roseanne and Verity poised at his shoulder and history looming behind, he knew he hadn't a choice.

Eventually he selected Sheridan's classic 'The Rivals', for Christmas, then 'The Cherry Orchard', followed by 'The Seagull', after that 'Uncle Vanya' building up to Chekhov's great masterpiece, 'The Three Sisters. This meant Vee and Roseanne would be fully appeased, thus keeping his marriage on hold. All the same, he was taking a risk. That bastard Arthur had offloaded teaching on him; he who'd never taught in his life. He wasn't a natural teacher but once you'd faked absolute truth you were fine. He was an expert at fooling himself.

A wind started to rattle the eaves. The weather was changing; another scudding skyscape was blasting from the Azores through to Bergen, its cold fronts sweeping the charts. Today he was usually scheduled to 'take kids swimming'. Cue Rachel and Mark. Full slide-show. First expressions. First steps. First milk tooth. First new teeth. First day at playgroup. First day at school, learning to read from alphabet soup, adding up pasta numbers without ever reaching conclusions.

This time Phyllis knocked before walking in, "Here you are. Your new handbill for door-to-door distribution." Two thousand more were neatly packed in her cupboards.

The Majestic Theatre

by public demand

Reopens under its new Director of Productions

GARRICK M. JONES

presenting the Chekhov Players in best-seller award-winning classics
A brand new era in the history of social services
Something for all social groups
****

Support your own community theatre.
Backstage staff required
Director's Assistant Required.

List of part-time posts available on application
– Apply for interviews now –
Auditions to be announced
See local media for opening schedules and dates

Garrick's rooms were advertised as 'fully furnished'. The creaking metal-framed bed was teamed with rickety table, unmatched chairs and a peeling PVC chest of drawers, all perched above a tobacconists next to a Laundromat seemingly miles from the theatre. Grey dust infiltrated windows and pollution yellowed the curtains. Garrick slumped onto the cobble-filled mattress. He heard neighbours coughing. If poverty were a fungal condition he could almost taste its spores. What would Roseanne or Verity think? The terrace bundled takeaways and newsagents with Adult Bookshops, Halal Butchers, Pinpoint Tatooists, and Kosher Retails. Shadowy drug-dealers loitered in doorways.

Chekhov had trained as a doctor, analysing character while dissecting livers and brains. The human condition ran from his 'Three Sisters' and 'Uncle Vanya' right through to 'The Seagull', but sometimes that seagull mutated. Any dying albatross could scatter the best of laid plans. Garrick stared up at the bulge in his ceiling and groaned. Edwin could be merciless from his grave. "You've made your bed, son. Lie on it," was all he'd got to say, but Garrick's dependence on Vee and the children was total.

He popped one lager and opened another, 'The Cherry Orchard' could save him? Prunus cerasus could be chopped into acceptable twigs? The more he drank, the more Louise's suggestion appealed. He could base the teaching course on his rehearsals? Unless he'd a better idea. He unpacked his travelling files and read till his vision was blurred, but as he flipped the last pages, an unmarked folder slithered out, scattering shiny black-and-white stills.

Tight close-ups of sequinned G-strings and naked breasts gleamed in the light. In disbelief he examined the shots. Glossy buttocks compounded bulging vaginal smiles. Pubescence postured in plumes and stilettos, doing the splits, or squatting in impossible poses. Pouting folds of thick vulvas and dark nipples squeezed into the photographer's lens. He sat up in shock. Two enlarged prints of extreme penetration were heavily scribbled 'obscene'. He thought they'd been destroyed years ago. As he tore them all up, a sliver of negatives slid away under the bed.

Bleep! Bleep! Bleep! But his alarm clock refused to switch off. Bleep! Bleep! Bleep! Bleary-eyed he reached instead for his phone, frantically fingering keys. Bleep! Bleep! Bleep! So where the hell was he? Not St George's Mews. No, not even Lancaster Gate. Darkness came flooding back as he pressed the phone tight to his ear.

"Mmm? Hello?" he croaked, desperately controlling his bladder, "Hello?"

Verity sounded suspicious, "Gary? That Phyllis woman said you'd meetings all day." Her voice rose a pitch or two, "I've not heard a thing. Your cellphone was off so I guess nothing's come in the mail? Nothing, like . . . special?"

"No why?" More likely she'd been forwarding bills.

"Okay, but Momma's here! Really. She's sitting right ahead like she's commuted for years. I mean, wow, you got to admire her whole generation. She says it's the immigrant's DNA. The Rostova Spirit. The soul of Evgeniya Morozova Chekhov. And that's pure Stanislavsky I guess. By helping our kiddies, she says, she'll help you reactivate British drama. So how about that for ambition?" She took his silence amiss. "Look, I thought you'd be pleased. We'll all come down for opening night. Okay? Forget Harvard and Yale. The Chekhovs and Morozovs will be resurrected as one. That's the family destiny. I mean, she's sixty-nine . . . and still relates. Both kids adore her. She's bought Markie a new Zappo game. He zapped two hundred victims first go!"

"Was that what you rang up to tell me?" She'd sounded too upbeat and the cold was numbing his feet.

"Jesus Gary! It's tough with momma and kids. That's why I'd gotten to thinking . . . I mean, just think how many years . . . you and me . . . Hello?"

He'd positioned himself in front of the loo. Floor tiles were icy and chipped.

"You listening Gary? It's momma's suggestion. Communicate, she says. Reach out. Touch base. So I call you for emotional feedback, and then." She paused, "Is someone with you? Is that what you're telling me?"

"Jesus, no!"

If humans were 70% H_2O, he knew where every molecule was. Either his prostate or bladder would burst. He let his sphincter muscles relax.

"Does marriage mean nothing? No love? No commitment? Aw, shit!" The phone went dead.

Back in bed, he projected his family onto the ceiling, as comforting as a home movie. No problem. He'd phone home first thing in the morning. But as always his brain intervened, subverting his vision, piling image on image with composite heavens and hells. The questions kept asking themselves. Why ring him at two in the morning? There was something in her manner. Something contradictory. In desperation his brain switched to auto, and there it was: the cast list for The Cherry Orchard rolling in ghostly white credits,

Madame Luba Ranevsky. (As yet uncast) ?

Gayev (Leon)– (As yet uncast) ?

Boris(Simeonov-Pischik)– (As yet uncast) ?

Alexander Lopakhin– (As yet uncast) ?

Anya– (As yet uncast) ?

Varya– (As yet uncast) ?

Charlotte– (As yet uncast) ?

Epi--------------------"

A sudden crash! He awoke. No time had passed. Hammering at his door was followed by a loud bang like a gunshot. He rolled over cop-style hitting the lino, upending the standard lamp whose parchment shade rolled in eccentric circles . . . followed by silence.

He tiptoed up to the peephole expecting a drugs squad in bullet-proof vests. He pressed an eye to its miniature lens. A wide-angle showed empty landing. He pressed an ear to the door. BANG!! The crash jarred his eardrum and brain. He snatched the door open.

"Package for you, man." The voice came from skirting board level.

Garrick adjusted his eye line. A grey-stubbled man was jack-knifed into some high-voltage frame. The bloodshot eyes swivelled upwards.

"Come midday. This 'ere" His breathing was hoarse. "T'old bag upstairs dropped it in. Signed for it too. Looks after stuff, I does, like. Else things gets stole, see." He thrust a package at Garrick's crutch. "Came ornerry post. No charge this time, but next . . ."

The hybrid from Forbidden Zone coughed then scuttled back over the landing. Rattling chains were followed by slamming of bolts. Norston returned with a long-sustained roar.

Crowning Glory Salon was freezing. Jilly Craske waited, hands in pockets, overcoat buttoned up to the neck as 'Classics of Cissie Miami' twanged in the background. Life was all about image, yet here she was, relentlessly putting on weight. Whenever she internalised problems, physical symptoms emerged. No diet worked. Her feet were swollen; her body felt clumsy and bloated; her veins seemed swell and congeal. Where was the justice in that? Cellulite compounded a sense of despair with always that residual ache. There was no avoiding reflections when everything was watching. It was the world in reverse seen through a silver-backed glass. Bloodshot eyes blinked back. Their tear-ducts started to brim. Carefully she rolled down her collar revealing those usual dark swellings. Purplish patches shadowed her neck like photographic exposures. She ran her fingers over the skin . . . and flinched

Mirrors could be merciless. Smiling was a welcome distraction. Her clientele expected as much. They claimed her attitude helped, but despite all her greetings two had recently suffered from cancer. So much for all her outpourings. They'd both looked so well; once even seemed to gain weight. Next moment they'd shrivelled and died. Such lessons could not be ignored. Goodwill had limitations. She tried to impose a broad grin on the glass.

The morning was unusually dark. Mist hung the valley. A crystalline frost coated cars, encrusting both windscreens and steel. Tom as usual had dumped her then driven off with that screech of burnt rubber. Then her Salon door had jammed. Today her gallery of Shakespearean kings looked self-absorbed and dejected, the back boiler was coughing, and her poly-cotton smock was frayed. She couldn't resist an ironic laugh.

She loathed early morning appointments, but Louise had insisted of course. These days competition was fierce. People expected 24/7 on standby. Like that Josie West with her ludicrous braiding. Or Doreen Cranmer whose wisps were dyed indigo blue. But the most frustrating was always Louise. Louise Roberts, her so-called very best friend. Shopping was all they had in common. It barely stopped them floating apart. As if times weren't tough enough, she could not even trust cleaning contractors, mostly part-timers after hard cash. Last night they had done such a really poor job, their attitudes hung on the air, and deodorants lingered as viscose as asthma. As for her cleaner girl's name? All skimpy skirts and see-thru blouses? Stacey Someone-Or-Other? She'd arrived, made-up to the nines to sweep mountains of hair. It didn't make sense. With so many rivals moving into the district, Cavanham Street should be renamed Hairdressers Row. Their flashy facades made her own frontage look dated. She regretted postponing modernisation. Warming herself with a hairdryer she also regretted no breakfast. Her ribs were sore. Her body ached. And as always her eyes returned to the clock. To pass time she began reading those pamphlets which plopped through her doors overnight. Indian takeaways. Romanian Pizzas. Polish Builders. Charities of every description. Cut-price hairdressers too.

One leaflet caught her attention. 'The Majestic Theatre, by public demand . . .' It announced in an oddly dated style, black on vermilion red. Like her, they were looking for staff. She'd make a good actress herself. She'd had enough practice. Once she'd won a talent show. Sadly you don't get to live your life twice. But she'd slipped the leaflet into a pocket.

Louise Roberts was over twenty minutes late. She breezed in unrepentantly with a swish of her brass-buckled Italian boots. Even before she was over the threshold she was rubbing her hands. Refusing to remove any layers she kept to her purple alpaca Sylvestre Camus and new orange Romani shawl. Everything she was wearing was new. Her message was clear.

"As for that traffic warden last time!" Louise was always pursued by injustice, "Do they pick on Eddie Craig's trucks? No! Nor bloody Manwess Gas, digging its mine-shafts all over. There's dumper trucks everywhere. But no! They bloody fine me when you're doing my hair!"

Jilly worked to calm her down. There was something narcotic in massaging scalps, feeling each curve of the skull, sharing that therapeutic effect. Jilly brushed tangled hair, uncoiling its fine errant spirals. With each swish of bobbed bristles, Louise sank deeper into a trance. Not until Jilly mentioned the theatre did Louise react.

"Them! Call themselves Majestic! Bringing in outsiders!" She faced Jilly directly. "I call that provocation. My daughter's as good as them lot."

Jilly didn't need to read between lines. This was one woman's plea to another, as if mother-daughter relationships were Louise's confidence crisis. Jilly remembered unguarded remarks made as if to a confessor. Little hints. Clues. Symptoms. Admissions of rage and frustration. It didn't need deep diagnosis. Abigail was at that age and Louise was at odds with her daughter. Jilly had heard it all before but miracles could be achieved simply by trimming the fringes and streaking the hair. Physical was mental and vice versa. Hairdressing was a religion. Lost faith could be restored simply by bleaching and tinting. It was like doctor with patient or priest with the flock. No matter how much Louise was frustrating, her failings kept the salon in business.

Louise closed her eyes. "It's my responsibility, see. I'm a mother. It's got to be done."

Jilly had heard this one too: mothers threatened by daughters. She'd not seen Abigail lately, but when parents start to feel old, the generation gap widens. No. What Louise needed was urgent restyling. Her regular tint looked too harsh. Her silhouette needed judicious trimming. A total makeover was needed. So Jilly leaned confidingly forward.

"A drastic solution, you mean. Just leave it to me."

"I knew you'd understand. You always do. It's like you're reading my mind." Louise gave a deep, satisfied sigh.

Jilly felt the neck loosen and head slump under her hands. "Yes Louise. We all feel the same. It's taking first step's that's the worst. It's not like hysterectomy. It's much more basic than that!" She felt Louise twitch, "No, no. I mean it. Some folk aren't self-critical."

30

Jilly gazed round at her framed acting heroes from Richard Burton to Peter O'Toole, Tony Curtis and Larry Olivier, all in theatrical crowns. "We're all of us celebrities. Leave us to take years off you!" they choroused.

Louise seemed to suddenly tense. In this sudden silence a darkness passed as if in a sudden eclipse. Gone was the sun. Then another Eddie Craig truck rumbled past, vibrating plate-glass till shrunken putty dislodged and the ill-fitting doors shook on worn hinges.

Louise twisted angrily round. "Not me, Jilly! Abigail! . . . My impossible daughter."

Eddie Craig thought of himself as a practical man, easy with judgements and quick to demand explanations. He liked to reconnoitre first. He parked his car, tried to look anonymous, then walked the last few hundred metres calculating the odds. It wasn't as simple as editing sums on computers. Reality had bigger perspectives. It meant global warming, religious conflict, racial tensions, political fashions, continental drift, "known and unknown unknowns". The problem was, big issues had no demarcations whereas trivia could be measured in lives. Like every damned cigarette he'd smoked. Every bottle of whisky. Every breath of asbestos. Every minute genetic mutation. Every cholesterol trace. Every virus. Every scar. That theatre too was becoming an issue, and his image was starting to matter.

Eddie played safe in public. He wore leather-soled shoes and insisted on wearing silk ties. He'd comb his hair back, keep his vegetarianism secret, avoiding all mention of class. From his first dealings with Norston he'd learned to be wary. Political bosses talked socio-economics and orthodox diversities. No bugger thought profit and loss. None of this lot took any risks.

It hadn't been till his very first meeting with Arthur that Eddie first heard the term 'metamorphosis', it sounded good and meant nothing, which gave it immediate appeal. It rolled well on the lips. It summed up his business where locals dreaded any mention of 'Change', yet without the Great Fire of London there'd have been no Sir Christopher Wren . . . and without the 'rural clearances' (like Henry de Vries demolishing villages to create fancy vistas by Capability Brown) there'd be no Temple Storford, nor landscapes leading up to those moors. The result was this dump which clung to a Dinosaur era, expecting to be subsidised. This included the art school, the gallery, the local museum, the libraries and parks and similar sites of which the prime site was here right in the centre of town. So where would Arthur be without Eddie? Great Projects were started by bombers, arsonists, or dictators. All modernisation depended on warlords and rogues. Here they needed a practical man.

Crossing the road at the lights, he smiled to himself, indulging the blessings of civilisation while totting balance sheets up. But halfway across . . . an edge-of-vision flash. A black Ford Mondeo like retinal blur. Its tailwind tugged at his clothes. Eddie ducked instinctively. He glimpsed a Manwess Gas logo wedged in its windscreen. The car slewed on its brakes then was blocked out of view. Eddie barely noticed the sudden dull pain in his ribs or that transitory ache down the left arm. Metamorphosis; that's what was needed. More metamorphosis. Redundant factories into glass towers. Valleys into landfills. Landfills into multiple car parks. See 'New Improved Norston,

Revision 26A', locked away in the 1950's Town Hall extension (available to view on demand, provided you knew the right codes). Soon they'd redraw the whole map of this town.

Eddie stood at the kerb and looked up. The theatre didn't match function with form. Anachronistic, he reckoned (That was another good word; plenty of sharp consonants) Their advertising changed nothing. Their annual rebranding emphasised obsolescence. The Majestic's new hoarding was headed 'Reopening Soon'. He should have brought a camera. There was something epic and tragic about it. Such moments needed recording. Trying to decipher the small print he could just make out the name, but strolling back to his car, Garrick Jones still meant nothing. That's why as he drove off past the theatre Eddie leaned forward to read the whole poster.

A juggernaut cut him up. As he overshot the turn he swerved down a slip road, his tyres drummed over loose rubble. Barely yards from the towpath he juddered to a halt and knew at once where he was. Every millimetre was marked on his maps. This was unmistakably his, marked luminous red on the chart. He switched off his engine, turned off the lights and sat back. Canal mists condensed on his windscreen. He wound the driver's side down and breathed in the vapours. His ample nose tingled. Blood vessels clotted his cheeks. Half closing his eyes, he inhaled the sweet'n'sour tang of decay. From here he could sense the town's modest landmarks.

Such targets could not be missed. Resting an arm on the cill, clenching his fist like a pistol, he took careful aim. "Pow! Pow! Pow!" The old chapel. The Depository. The auction house. Picking off each, one by one. Finally, reloading his fingers, he fired at the theatre itself.

Verity had begun to feel guilty. London never slowed down. One hectic meeting followed another as conference followed more presentations. She leaned forward and massaged the folds of her neck. Her mouth remained stubbornly dry. She ought to be feeling exultant but dabbing both cheeks with a tissue only smeared her carefully matched blusher.

All day she'd been bombarded with Garrick's texts. As a dietary expert she'd needed peace to plan the latest recipes, let alone time to eat for herself. She dreaded more Chokski Bar samples, feeling an onrush of kilos, but dietary gum only hastened a migraine causing more rows with her mother. Or was it the other way round? Everyone demanded their slice. First Rachel, then Mark, now Roseanne.

She switched off her laptop, carefully closed, then locked, her door. She sat for a moment, head in both hands, before tapping out Garrick's code.

Eddie still sat in his car by the bridge. Seen through a foreground of mists, Norston resembled a three-dimensional Lowry peopled with living cartoons. As for Norston's future renaissance as 'European City of Culture', it didn't fit global perspectives. Whatever anyone planned, continents still drifted, volcanoes erupted, and land was being forever recycled. Whatever remained was the oceans and seas. Soon ice would trim this leaky canal where he and Arthur once played. Here in long-ago summers they'd dog-paddled planks while barges drifted alongside. They'd scrumped apples and collected frogspawn together. As kids they'd challenged both God and the Devil and in a way still did. Soon these stagnant wastelands would become a new gleaming marina. Monaco of the North. A future glowing with promise. That's what resurrection meant.

He needed to stretch, but as he clambered out, a chill wind snatched at his dreams. His innards contracted. His prostate rebelled. He felt an inconvenient urge as his bladder shrank like a leaky balloon. He edged through rusting nettles right up to the arch of the bridge. As he steadied himself, his practised eye automatically analysed structures. His instinct was to look closer. The brickwork was traditional. Flettons faced with Staffordshire blues and bonded with lime mortar in Flemish-bond stretchers and headers, no doubt enclosing tons of loose rubble. Such quality brickwork deserved to survive, unlike the Majestic with its mismatched appliqué and spreading Victorian cracks. But whatever was built would one day be demolished.

Eddie had unzipped his flies and was taking a breath . . . "Well now!" A rasping voice floated from nowhere , "Marking out your territory, eh?"

Eddie looked up and spattered his trousers. A head was perched like a coconut shy. A disembodied Arthur grinned over the parapet.

"You fuckin' voyeur!" Eddie yelled.

"Desecrating council-owned structures! You deserve to be bloody well fined"

Then Arthur was gone, his cackles still ringing, but Eddie's trousers were soaked.

He edged beneath the arch of the bridge as vehicles drummed overhead. Lime mortar plopped into echoes. He knew that beneath these very same vaults, hundreds of navvies had died. According to folklore, Irish corpses still lined the cut, haunted by drunkards, hookers, illegals, and addicts. Even now Eddie could hear drunken mumbling. Someone was coming.

He backed out of sight, clumsily re-zipping damp trousers. Reaching his car, he reversed with a grind of transmission. Hard tyres swung him round on the handbrake before heading him back to his site-manager's shack, stirring up rubble and grit.

Garrick had been reduced to a mumble. The towpath was greasy, reception was poor, and there were too many distractions. Feral cats scampered from mountains of tyres, mallard and moorhen flew off, but Vee was sounding impatient. His keyword was Chekhov, repeated again and again, but either she could not hear or was unimpressed. She kept changing the subject. As he picked his way down the rut, high-stepping from outcrop to outcrop, the bridge repeatedly broke up his signal, catching loose words in invisible mesh.

"Sorry? What?" He slithered past muddy brown pools; her speech came and went, "Hello? Hello? I can't hear." But she wasn't listening to him.

It seemed she had sent him a package. She'd put in the ordinary post. She'd only sent it two days ago. His explanation was simple. He'd left before the post arrived. He explained how neighbours collected the post and brought it direct to everyone's doors. Nothing was simpler or safer, so where was her sense of proportion? He raised his voice as hers faded, pressing the instrument tight to his ear

"Sorry? Eh? . . . What was it? . . . Hello? Hello?" as its circuitry faded.

As usual his battery needed recharging. He did try re-dialling, but somehow by balancing sideways, avoiding puddles and holding his neck at an angle, he managed to keep a faint signal.

Then, frictionless, fast as an ambush, paving stones slipped like greased glass.

Zhunk! Space-time turned turtle, toppling, frame-by-frame in slow motion. As he pitched headlong his knees cracked on granite; his elbow clipped a loose brick, and Garrick found himself sprawled on the coping, his legs hanging over the brink. As he lay winded, shingle plip-plopped into water. His phone was lying close enough to relay his drowning live.

He guessed Vee must still be on about great Russian plains and tales of Roseanne's Morozov dacha. Around him luminous spectra mingled with chemical mists, their carbon monoxides tinting both sunsets and dawns. He felt like an island about to submerge. Suddenly a swan hit the water, surfing on its crash-landing gear before gliding sedately away.

No pleasure came without pain. Chekhov would have endorsed that. As if in a coma Garrick continued to think about saunas, and oxen and peasants. Of wild deer and wolves. Of forests of birches, echoing harness, and jingling sleighs.

The cold began to seep into his bones.

CHAPTER THREE

DIALOGUES

Garrick twisted and turned. An ear-splitting whine was detaching itself from his dreams, leaving a three-masted ship drifting through icebergs beset by flesh-eating gannets.

He fumbled blindly trying to regain his bearings. No warm sleeping body beside him. The side-lamp blasting his eyes. This wasn't Lancaster Gate. 'Fully furnished Apartment' had been a complete misrepresentation. As for 'location, location, location', this was a back-street miles from the theatre.

The alarm clock had drilled through his head. Now Garrick was freezing. He padded barefoot over cracked lino through a curtain of PVC ribbons and into a hardboard-framed alcove. The toilet bowl defied Feng Shui. The washbasin hung on loose brackets. An encrusted shower-head dripped behind plastic curtains like folds of loose ageing skin. He nearly slipped. Something had stuck to his heel. Holding it up to the light he saw a dim transparency through which he perceived naked figures coiled in a drug-fuelled embrace.

It burned to a bubbling crisp on his hot-plate, its acrid fumes stinging his nostrils. While all-night traffic rattled his windows and paper-thin walls, he obliterated his early career. At the time he'd been young. Once it had seemed very daring. It paid. But now it was coming to haunt him. Unable to get back to sleep he unwrapped Verity's parcel of scripts and flipped through Russian History before blanking out. Agreeing to teach had been a mistake.

At five in the morning the whole block came to life. At half-hourly intervals stampede followed stampede as another shift headed downstairs. Garrick decided to show some communal spirit. Neighbourliness was a virtue and ought to be encouraged. Especially here. To survive he would need to fit in, therefore that almost Ancient Mariner figure 'grey-stubbled with glittering eye' from over the landing who'd rescued his package, needed rewarding if only to salvage Garrick's own conscience. So, when the last footsteps faded, Garrick sneaked out and slid a banknote under the door before setting off to work.

In early morning darkness Baker's Row was coming to life. Gopal's the newsagents. Gerry's discount store. A Chinese girl in oilskins tugging her hair through a glitter-edged comb. A figure pitched up in a doorway. A chain-smoking Sudanese setting up stall. Shuffling figures straggling around the Social Security Centre . . . were these potential audience? . . . He doubted they'd celebrate Chekhov. Culture would not exactly be top of their list. Their first need was survival.

He decided to take different routes every day and gradually acclimatise.

Abigail woke with a start. As she tried to open her eyes, lashes and eyelids stayed firmly gelled. She wrestled with Dippy Duck duvet as Emeline fell off the bed. Somehow she got out of bed to an alien world where suddenly nothing made sense. It was weird, as if overnight something occurred; something immense and momentous. She waded through abandoned clothes, kicking stray shoes, discarded books, scattering knickers and makeup. Everything was ordinary but nothing was fully convincing. A soundless cartoon had been on replay all night. Lilac walls were plastered with pinups, pink ponies, pastel boys, and white kittens with blue saucer eyes. It was like an old self she'd discarded. Every step was uncertain.

Half-obscured among beads and brass chains she caught sight of herself in the mirror. That puffy unrecognisable face with its freckles and pouches! It belonged to a stranger; its ravelled hair glared unacceptably orange. About some things Stacey was right. Families were embarrassing and Louise was a figure of fun because everyone knew who she was. Club Arabica was dragging her family down. It wasn't fair, but as always it was Stacey who thrived, always kept blooming, taking raunchiness to extremes and succeeding. Stacey could revel in buttocks and breasts. It was Stacey in step with the world but keeping that one step ahead.

It was all right for Stace but first you had to feel secure. Next you had to conform. Overnight the world had changed. Hips reconfigured. Body-line expanded. Worst of all was the blood, the unwelcome surges of blood. Each morning Abigail hated herself. Starving and cutting were comforts. She carefully renewed her disguise. Even if the internal process went on, its polished surface was scarred.

In Human Biology classes, fertilised embryos transformed into adults like eggs into tadpoles, nuclei to foetuses, diagram by diagram in clever animation. Initial fascination was merged with disgust, but Stacey was totally hooked. She loved all that. Whole lifetimes were stretching ahead but ageing and death were for failures. Everything else was for sale. That was the difference. That's what had changed. Getting out of school was escape. Like breaking old chains. That moment her textbooks had floated away she'd felt an unbearable freedom. Day One of the rest of her life!

With fingernail precision she began unpeeling adhesives from cupboards and doors, stripping the posters away. Turning onto her mirror she unlooped strings of badges and beads, coming face-to-face with a stranger. Behind stark glass lurked alien features with tight gingerous hair, as gawky as Stacey was smooth. This was what ugliness meant. Now she was ripping at walls, trampling the shreds into carpets, then scooping up every mascot and doll and jamming them all in the bin.

"Abigail?" Louise was downstairs yelling up, "Are you deaf?" Then a moment's silence. "Right, my girl! One last final last chance . . . I'm starting to count . . . I'll count up to ten . . . One . . . two . . . three . . ."

As Garrick headed through waves of early commuters, preparing to confront his first day at the theatre, he pictured his children in parallel time heading up Westbourne Grove towards school. He tried to visualise details such as were they with Vee or Roseanne? Were they chattering? Giggling? Counting bikes? Miserable? Chasing pigeons? What? He was tempted to phone straightaway. It was all about synchronisation, but some invisible timer was flicking the seconds away; at that very moment millions would be heading for work thinking similar thoughts. It was more than simple concurrence, he thought, it defined everyone's lives because living creatures needed routines.

Cutting through Wilberforce Row he arrived in Cavanham Street from the North. At the pedestrian crossing he was mentally holding his children's hands, but would they give him a thought? Soon they'd take his absence for granted. An ageing black saloon swerved lane to lane without signals. As buses braked and revved, the old jostled new in a strangely familiar landscape whose geometry had already started to crumble. It struck him that everywhere High Streets mimicked each other, chain stores crowding out local shops. Amongst fading facades only hairdressing salons rejoiced in a smell of fresh paint. Some were flashily new but "Crowning Glory Hairstyling Salon" looked suitably aged. A bourgeois shabbiness set it apart, its interior like a Hollywood set. Waves of nostalgia were picked out in neon, hung with film stars as kings in ancient black-and-white portraits featuring Sir Laurence Oliver as Richard III (his wig looking like Edith Piaf), Richard Burton (teeth gritted) as Henry the Fifth. An illuminated sign in the window spelt out the signature *'Jilly Craske, Stylist'*. A young woman tried to hand him a leaflet but Garrick pressed on, thinking then quickly forgetting.

A car kept to the inner lane, slicing through gaps. Its front wheels clipped the kerb barely centimetres away and narrowly missing Manwess gas excavations, before disappearing beyond The Majestic as if it dicing with death were quite normal.

Garrick began to believe he was getting a sense of the place. He desperately wanted to merge, to belong, to conform. He wanted to capture the spirit of Norston, but more than this he wanted acceptance. His future might yet be bound up with this town where people were greeting each other while breakfasting on the run, everyone snacking'n'slinging. Soon a whole stratum of styrene would be laced with cholesterol mulch.

Jilly's concern was survival. She'd make daily journeys with eyes tightly shut trying to switch off her brain. The salon had to be open on time but Cavanham Street always delayed them. The problem was Thomas replaying old Hollywood stunts, broadsiding into No Parking bays, overtaking at lights. There was something autistic about it. He talked Capacities, G-forces, Octanes and Aerodynamics as though nothing else mattered. If meter inspectors lacked satisfaction and status, his heroes were Mafia gunmen, not Shakespearean kings. His cars were Viagra. Testosterone ran in their fuel. She knew exactly where it would lead as facts and fantasy merged into one. Thomas stepped on the gas forcing a cyclist to swerve.

Garrick was half up the hill when their car passed. Neither noticed each other. A microsecond either way they'd have been accidents-waiting-to-happen, but lifetimes are crammed with predictable flukes. Jilly was too preoccupied. She scrambled out the moment they stopped. Maybe the district was edging upmarket but winters still depended on Christmas. Survival meant fulfilling appointments, then paying off debts. The annual restyling business was booming but festivals should be for children. She quickly shut the thought away.

Her one consolation was theatre. It offered a fleeting escape. Thomas did not agree. She'd read about a new London director whose promise of Chekhov raised hopes for people whose every day was a trial. Jilly could identify. In a way her own life was like being an actor stepping onstage, with each client requiring a private performance. All the time hair styles and techniques kept changing as multiple clients ratcheted tension, "Coiffeuse by appointment. Trichologist to the masses!" She felt more like a prostitute grooming everyone's ego.

Looking round her salon walls she wondered about her Shakespearean kings; Laurence Olivier, Mark Elwes, Peter O'Toole. As for their Queens? And mistresses? Sadly the Garrick Jones of this world always turned up a decade too late. The story of her life.

As the car drove away she turned her keys in the locks. The shop was unheated and dark. She'd barely entered when someone outside banged on the window. She opened the door on a chain. Some nearby leaseholders were gathered.

Scott the Jeweller brandished a clipboard, stubbing his finger onto the page. "Threatening us with penalties! Bastards! Sending round bloody assessors! Orderin' us to tart our premises up!" The jeweller thrust papers at her. "Fight the fucking landlords. Sign our petition."

When they'd gone she locked the door. Her overnight contractors had ticked the job "finished", but such was the nature of hair. Like emotions it strangles and chokes. Wisps, clottings, snippings, knottings and strands clogged extractor fans and grilles.

"Ooh Stacey!" she groaned, "Lazy damn cow!

She ran her fingers around. A mesh of invisible tensions throttled fixtures and fittings because hair was as subversive as sex. That was its universal law. It took its revenge. You either compromised or fought. Soon it would be opening time and with it the ritual laying out towels. "Overture and beginners!" But first she'd spend private time communing with her collection of Kings. Shared contemplation helped. Aches and pains disappeared, dizziness vanished and with it old fears. Meanwhile the street came to life like a time-sequence film.

Something else was disturbing. Today her clothes felt unexpectedly tight. Everything seemed to have shrunk. Waistlines tightened the flesh and her body bulged over her bra. She unbuttoned her salon topcoat, gained a moment's relief, then slumped in a shampooist's chair with aching feet on the basin. She read the circular from The Majestic. Mind you, there weren't any crowned heads in Chekhov. She knew that, but at least there'd be compensations. She turned to Norston Mercury. Parochialism gave everyone purpose, and she deserved her own moment of fame.

There was another sharp rap at the windows; a pallid man in overcoat, his frameless spectacles catching the light. His narrow eyes glittered. She peered round the door. A balding head reflected the halogen lights.

He produced an ID. "Brinkhold Estates, that's us. Yes? The Brinkhouse Brinkside Group." He seemed to expect to walk in, "We like to be out bright and early. Just like yourselves." He produced a crisp white business card, his manner brusque and efficient. "You must have read our documents, yes? Under the terms of our lease, Mrs Craske, renovations are due, completion by the end of the month. We haven't heard from you yet. Our architects can recommend contractors." He held out his pen. "I'll leave it for you to sign."

From behind the newspaper headlines she watched the surveyor continue his rounds. 'Norston Venice of the North' the centre pages announced. As she spread out the paper she spotted an advert for "Backstage staff at the Majestic Theatre" below an item headed "Hairdressers urgently required". It was time to face up to events. She would no longer be victim, but it wouldn't be easy to change. Opening a new box of chocolates she noticed a short stubby man in large flapping coat looking up at the roofs, but Eddie Craig barely registered humans while mentally flattening whole streets.

Jilly returned to the Freeholder's leaflet, intending to throw it away. She remembered a local shopfitter's van. It often came past. Its graphics were very distinctive; so distinctive she even remembered the name. Those two intertwined angels had struck sensitive nerves. The ludicrous logo was indelibly pressed on her mind.

She checked name and number, then phoned them before her shampooist arrived.

Louise understood community values. Hadn't the Roberts survived generations, outlasting enclosures and industrialisation? Today she saw a puritanical town, proud of Nonconformist roots, clinging onto its past. To open her nightclub might contradict this, but speculators had to surf waves. Expansion, inflation, boom and then bust? When property prices were rising and banks were prepared to invest, this was her God-given chance. She sorted through her jewellery. With her hair newly styled she chose the very best earrings, holding one to an ear while smiling into the mirror.

Never mind theatre, her new club would be an irresistible magnet. Its prime situation near St Giles's Close guaranteed attention, and though barely a hundred metres from the church she'd won planning permission by promising aid for the parish. Provincialism held anywhere back, so her First

Annual Arts Festival would be the big Pre-Christmas event to which Norston's cultural elite was invited (with husband Carlos providing the food). Understatement was out. Club Arabica was bound to succeed. Everything was perfect. They'd announce to the world how Norston was new and expanding. Casinos with floorshows were next. Inevitably taxes and incomes would grow as turnover reached Las Vegas volumes. The bandwagon would gather pace as soon as foreign investors piled in. Civilisation would flower like the glories of Paris or Rome. 'Venice of the North' would guarantee 'City' status for Norston.

She chose a necklace of emeralds set in sliver links with real diamond clips. Expensive not vulgar. Not bright plastic baubles such as her daughter might wear. The official opening would be a 'Great International Event'. The watchword had to be Taste.

When Louise's invitation dropped on her doormat, Jilly Craske was disconcerted. For a moment she'd dithered, but having once yearned for Rex Schulman she jumped at a chance to meet Garrick himself, even if that meant taking risks. Whatever the danger you had to seize chances, and Abigail was bound to be there. So that morning Jilly surreptitiously put on her best clothes beneath her longest overcoat and let her man take her to work. She watched as his car pulled away. She would have to trust her shampooist to cover. Besides it was time Veronica learned to be responsible. A full-time assistant had to grow up, and when it came to dealing with clients, experience mattered, because Thomas mustn't know she was out. For just those few hours it only needed some basic discretion: fingers on lips, plus a bit of avoidance. Anyone could manage that.

By the time Jilly arrived at the nightclub, late guests pressed like iron-filings to magnets: writers, artists, teachers, businessmen, lawyers, golfers, divorcees and council officials all huddled, eying each other. Jilly knew she was being observed. Some regular clients even avoided her eyes, as if having hair treatment was shameful. Or were they afraid of their husbands? Or worried about what they'd confessed at the basins? Or did she look so ungainly? Didn't they know her function was vital because everyone sometime has hair? All those tiny follicles? Growing by the billion whether you wanted or not? Even death couldn't restrain them. She'd heard newly shaved corpses were known to sprout stubble urgently needing a trim. Unless it was her accent? Or Class? Was she seen as a servant? Was being obese a stigma, just as she'd feared? All these ambiguities hurt, and sipping pomagne in a corner, she felt extra heavy and hot. No sign yet of Garrick Jones. No sign of Louise.

The trumpet fanfare caught her off guard. Dinner-suited heavyweights strutted in like Nigerian boxers, heads shaven, bulbous ears studded with gold. The martial group parted to reveal Louise like a games show hostess. No reticence here. Just a coup de theatre. "Bling-bling!" it announced, "Newly imported from London!" Everyone burst into applause. Here was Louise as no-one had seen her, in multi-beaded gown and tiara, extending freshly nailed, glittering fingers. Two uniformed attendants stretched out a red ribbon before her. Headlines were guaranteed, plus coverage on local TV.

"Welcome to Club Arabica." Louise sounded tired but triumphant. "The trendiest spot in the trendiest town!" Brandishing a pair of gold shears, her voice boomed over loudspeakers. "No more talk. I now declare my club open." As slices of ribbon floated apart, Louise became Wonder Woman made flesh.

As everyone cheered Jilly looked furtively round, but no sign of her theatrical guests or Louise's mythical daughter. Abigail was an enigma these days. To think, over shampooist's basins Louise once talked of little else. She'd talked so much Abigail felt like Jilly's own surrogate child. It was like adopting a stranger, until when Louise stopped bringing photos, she watched this foster child drift away. It was like a bereavement. She needed some resurrection. She wanted to tie up loose ends while everybody was here. She recognised Eddie Craig with the mayor, together with solicitors and other local businessmen. In a far corner she noticed Arthur Ruddock and cronies chatting away to her freeholder's agent. Wine merchants jostled with estate agents. Bookmakers entertained dentists. The circumstances were perfect. However, no sign of Garrick Jones.

A sudden hand gripped Jilly's shoulder. "Gillian! Darling! Not sloping off?" Louise was noticeably flushed. "You've not seen her? That daughter of mine? 'Cause I've bloody not!" Then one of her cackling laughs. "You're right of course. Kids! It's live-for-the-moment, expecting everything free. Next it'll be contraceptives and . . . Whoops!" She put a hand to her mouth. "Before you can say Increased Income Tax, it'll be abortions for kids! They don't share our hopes. Nor our dreams. So I'm trying to save my own child from herself. But . . . but . . ." She dabbed at her eyes. "That's why I've got to talk about . . ." A bearded man in a shiny grey suit dragged Louise away in mid-sentence.

At that moment Jilly knew she would never meet Garrick. The omens were wrong. She was too bulging. Too old. Too demeaned. Nor would Thomas approve. He despised bohemian types, just as he'd loathe Club Arabica and everything it stood for. He abominated bright colours and hated nude paintings as if any culture posed awful, unmentionable threats. If everything filled her with guilt, why had she come? Maybe she panicked. Electrodes fired as chemicals imploded, bloating her body and catching her unawares. She took a large swig of Pomagne to fight off the retching. But next came the cramps. That was the trouble with art. Its psychosomatic effects.

"Sorreeee!" Louise caught Jilly's wrist. "Never get married to men! Now our kid's mardy as well!" She shepherded Jilly aside. "You know how it is. She's got this special interview. Tomorrow that is." Helplessly she spread her hands. "So it doesn't give us that long. Remember us saying? My makeover plan? And . . ."

At that moment Jilly's eyes swivelled . . . and zoomed. In a moment of recognition she'd almost missed it. One of life's seminal moments. Yes. It was him! Garrick! It must be. Her eyes widened. Her mouth slipped open. Those crinkly eyes? Those lopsided features? That shadow of stubble? Exactly as on the front pages.

When a Jilly got back to the salon, Veronica was in a 'missed-ciggy' state. She'd found coping a strain, and the fault-lines between them both widened. Now the girl needed calming down. As if there weren't enough complications. The business would only tick over so long as women believed they could alter their lives simply by changing their hair. Survival of the prettiest hairdo? Or absolution through shampoo and trims? Freeholder pressures could tip them all over the edge. If styling couldn't change anyone's future, then maybe brain transplants were needed. Was it all in the mind? Every day Jilly was putting on weight, and it didn't make sense? Even her salon blouson seemed tighter. It got to the stage she was having to eat to calm down. She'd tried low carbohydrates, high proteins, reduced sugars, salts and fats . . . but no diets helped.

She bit into a Chocolate Praline. This influx of new hairdressing franchisees was not only slicing her margins but forcing her on the defensive. That pre-Christmas rush had not materialised yet because Crowning Glory looked dated, outmoded, and even passé. They had to revamp and rename. A refit could be an advantage.

Veronica suddenly jumped up and yelped. "Oh shit!" She shuffled wildly through papers. "Sorry love, I forgot It was them Paradise lot. Some shopfitting outfit? Yeah? What's already spoken to you? Like, you'd left them a message? And like, asked them to send someone round? Yeah?" She presented what looked like a crudely drawn crossword, scribbled and revised several times. "This 'ere's the details. Can you ring back and confirm?"

Garrick considered his duty was done. As the anonymous Celebrity Guest he'd made his split-second appearance at Club Arabica as promised. Not that anyone noticed. As an invisible presence, he'd observed them. They only talked to themselves, wincing at mentions of Shakespeare or Chekhov, while back in metropolitan London, Vee and Roseanne were deluded. Roseanne insisted culture improved the further it got from smart trends, but here they spelled 'theatre' P.A.N.T.O And at Club Arabica they rated touring musicals tops. The five-star classic was still Noel Coward!

Phyllis gave him a questioning glance as he returned to the theatre, but what Garrick needed most was tobacco. It haunted him still; its flavours were ingrained in his clothes. Back at his desk, chin in hands, he could hear Phyllis humming away to herself. That summed everything up. She was downstairs. He was up here. Theirs was a clear-cut a division. It was staff in their dens versus him up here in his turret like a squatter preparing fake cures. What made it worse was the former Rex Schulman. Rex had branded everything with a possessive obsession. You couldn't get away from the shit.

Garrick's instincts kicked in, so as usual he tried phoning Vee. They blamed urgent staff meetings and overrunning seminars and offered to take a message. In a fit of energy he dumped anything labelled 'Rex Schulman' into bin-bags and felt his first sense of achievement. All that bloody clutter was gone. But maybe something else too? Seeing the now-empty shelves, perhaps he'd dismembered the past. Like a black hole it sucked everything out, leaving him wholly exposed. Now only internal politics ruled. The solution was clear. He needed an interface with the world.

He began writing captions on postcards and spreading them over the floor. 'Timekeeping' 'Reliability,' 'Literacy,' 'Communication,' 'Filing skills,' and so forth, expecting some new revelation. He tried triangles, rectangles, squares in different layouts, but nothing seemed to add up. Then suddenly, there was the answer. Those splayed turret walls! That's why he couldn't think straight! There were no right-angle reference points. Octagonal wasn't a practical shape. There had to be another solution. He lay on his belly, adjusting each sheet with a fully extended forefinger and thumb, considering subtle perspectives . . .

A loud cough at his shoulder! As Garrick jumped up, he cracked his skull on the underside of a desk. The whole room tottered and swayed. Bright planets spun among billions of stars. Somehow Garrick managed to focus. A deputation crowded his doorway. Albert, Danny, and Reg took a unionised stance trying look like the masses. Albert jiggled heavy plastic-framed glasses up and down before clearing his throat.

"We're a deputation." he growled as the other two nodded, "Us need specifications. We got no calendar sorted, and fundamentally, time's running' out. Basically, this panto takes all us human resources . . . what with gas men and the whatnot . . . an' dozens of special effects. An' beggin' your pardon, we're right short-staffed."

Supporting himself on the desk, Garrick tried to respond. The room was beginning to stabilise round him.

"We'll be doing the complete Chekhov canon. Starting with either The Cherry Orchard or The Three Sisters. I've advertised for trainee staff and . . ."

"No! No!" Danny Utara, the sparks, intervened. "An' what about de pantomime? An' de new lightin' switchboard? 'Cos everytin' computerised now. An' what we needs is investment. On de technological basis." He produced a crumpled leaflet. "The new GRC594K multi-functional memory keyboard with SP6 Polychrome halogen output is capital write off agin' income. Know what I'm saying?"

Albert was clearing his throat. "An' speaking from experience, no pantomime's owt but explosions, flashes, trapdoors, ghosts, acrobatics on wires, transformations an' suchlike. We're leaving them decisions to you." He checked his watch. "Official warning timed at four-forty-seven P.M." And with that the whole delegation turned on its heel and departed, the door left swinging behind them.

Pre-Christmas business rarely lived up to expectations because Jilly's regulars became insecure, reverting to colour-tint perms instead of essential restyling. She'd be glad when her new drama classes began. She urgently needed distracting.

She carried on snipping loose ends, chatting through the mirror as usual. "Mmm. Hair's just fantastic". She ran the woman's soft hair through her fingers. "No nerves, no blood, nothing. Amazing. Like cuticles or toenails. Organic extrusions like silk." She glanced at the wall clock, knowing Thomas would arrive on the dot. "A secondary sexual characteristic," she added, "Nothing but dead scaly tissue."

When the last customer left she turned down the lights. Auto-technology shut off the heating, steaming up rickety windows as chlorine mingled with Bouquet Garni, corroding both decor and flesh. It wasn't until she flipped 'OPEN' to 'CLOSED' she realised it had been dark for some time. At least 'Trend!' magazine was packed with actors, celebrities, stars. This was a substitute life, but skimming its frictionless pages, something else caught her eye. In a full-page colour-spread, an overdressed woman was subtitled 'Famous cuisinière, Verity Jones Teaching the Pure Kama Sutra of Food'. Beside her hovered a man reminiscent of Garrick, but on closer inspection it looked too young to be him. As temperatures dived and condensation hung on the air, she reverted to watching the street like a movie. This was the pits of the year. Bad light and delays provoked Thomas's fury.

Maybe her first marriage failed, but little Sophie Anne was perfect; everything in miniature; the tiniest most exquisite creature, with minuscule fingers and toes, all in faultless proportion. They diagnosed 'cot death', citing 'allergic responses'. That was ten years ago. Ten years! But the very day after, Darren fucked off without leaving a forwarding address. Never even sending a wreath.

One man was much like another, their testicles directly linked to their brains filled with androgen-alcohol mousse. Now Thomas was claiming illness had left him infertile, which is why he . . .

A loud bang at the door. Through gathering gloom she caught sight of two faces squashed on plate glass. Lips and noses shapeless as slugs, grotesque as masks. On their trade card, two trumpeting angels surmounted 'Paradise Shopfitting Co'.

"'Scuse us, missus!" One brushed spiky hair from his eyes. "Like you never rang back, so we took a chance. We're shop fitters right. Josh and Roddy." He looked around disapprovingly. "Floor to ceiling replacement, right?" He pointed at his twin angel logo. "That's us. We give you a quote by next day. Soonest measured, soonest repaired."

The window frames were noticeably warped. Keyring graffiti scoured the plate glass. Safety panels were bulging. The signboard was flaking.

"We jus' done Club Arabica. They loved it."

Roddy unfurled a measuring tape, stood back and grinned. They were Laurel and Hardy, Abbot and Costello, Morecambe and Wise, Ant and Dec. A tall lanky lad and short dumpy partner. As she watched them measuring, the skinny one did all the work. The other talked and talked till everything gleamed with added expense. Planning permissions. Ventilation. Insulation. Utilities and so forth. She wanted them to leave her alone, but Josh was suggesting an upgrading deal plus more discounts.

"Ignore my colleague, madam. We're offering. Hollow chrome frames. Extra-tough laminate glass to EU double-star thermal standard. Including integral euro-alarms. Plus solid-state air vents and electronic extractors. We've taken all the measurements. We need to check the fascia trim and measure up for the sign." He kicked Roddy's ankle. "But someone's not bloody packed our steps!"

From sheer desperation she let them borrow two best leather chairs, covered with towels for protection. Then at the back of her mind she glimpsed wee Sophie Anne curled up in her cot, and felt that familiar pain. Then a loud thud! A muffled crump! A black silhouette filled the window! It clawed without friction, hung in mid-air, before sliding down like some mock crucifixion. Even as their van drove away, this after-image remained. A desperate spread-eagled figure.

Thomas would soon thunder back in his ZXS Special, carbon black from fender to hood and so understated it barely showed on CCTV. Even a smudge on its multiwaxed surface troubled its aerodynamics. Its customised wire wheels and window glass polished like charcoal, all announced phallic and danger. She closed her eyes tightly to shut out the world. Then something brushed against her.

As she screamed in the darkness a louder scream merged with her own. "It's me!" The voice was faint but determined. "It's Abigail . . . Abby."

Garrick was feeling more settled. He accepted solidity was only perception; just atoms, molecules, and electrons held together by theories. Nothing is airtight, nothing is fixed; he realised that. Between stage and auditorium the Pass Door looked solid enough in its reinforced steel, painted bright red, but it only maintained an illusion. A cultural airlock, thought Garrick, dividing them from us. Fire regulations were only a pretext. The old order kept itself safe by locking and guarding that door. Not until it slammed tightly behind him Garrick he feel free to relax, knowing he'd finally, utterly, exorcised Rex.

Bert began quoting union agreements in infinitesimal detail. The stage crew demanded concessions. They could not accept their deals were with Arthur, not him. Soon it was "Rex Schulman this . . ." and "Rex Schulman that . . ." It rang on in his ears as Manwess contractors continued dismantling pipework and smashing conventions. He needed help. No ghost could ever be laid.

In her Consulting Senior Lecturer role, Vee would no doubt recommend asking Phyllis. She'd know what to do. Okay. He'd have to see Phyllis alone. First he'd confront her, then tackle Ruddock himself, but as he approached the main foyer, a stocky figure swaggered downstairs, its navy-blue overcoat flapping. Arthur Ruddock glanced at his watch then exited before Garrick had time to react. Once through the main doors he'd vanished behind Manwess trucks.

Her office door was open. Phyllis was facing away, ambiguously rocking. She was opening her handbag, taking out tissues and dabbing her eyes. The silence teemed with unspoken words. Surely she must have heard him come in? He coughed aloud. She jumped and spun round in one movement, cannoning into her desk.

"Hello, I was just . . ." Phyllis blew her nose noisily. "Sorry, it might be a cold. Yes, or an allergy maybe." She sniffled through pink paper tissues. "My nostrils, you see."

"I, er . . . I happened to be passing."

With scarcely a glance, she gathered her handbag and coat, and left. All he could hear were those classic court shoes clipping the rim of each tread.

Garrick knew his own limitations. He urgently needed a chat with his kids, but back in his office the line was engaged. He hurled a paperball at the bin. As always it sheered away under the table. But of course! That was the answer. The octagon syndrome! Rooms should always be square. Maybe his old man had seen other truths? Like Culture having no moral function? It didn't cure diseases and it wasn't holding his marriage together. Chekhov recognised paradox too. He knew life itself was cheap drama which got the ironic laughs it deserved. Ambivalence ran like a thread through his work.

Garrick kicked the wicker bin under the desk and heard it bounce off the wall.

Jilly combed at wild hair as Abigail leaned over, face down, deliberately masking her features. Call it red, sandy, ginger or Titian, this mane of hers was uncompromisingly wild. As alive as wet snakes through your fingers. In one single strand you could read whole generations, like 'Blackpool' through peppermint rock.

"Anyway, I always say, hair styling's an advanced state of Karma," Jilly persisted, "It's like carving a sculpture while dancing and playing guitar." Static crackled over the teeth of the comb like bolts of miniature lightning. "Don't you reckon? No?"

Conversation continued one-sided as Jilly circled her sitter, her model, her subject, inviting divine inspiration, but Abigail did not respond. Most times she couldn't stop clients talking. She'd codify them by their intimate details. It was hard to think this was Louise's daughter, that happy child that once danced around singing, now stiff as cold pudding and as skeletal as a corpse. Those high cheekbones, thin fingers, sharp angles, began to make Jilly feel gross: so much so her fingers grew podgy, seemingly detached from her brain. Her hands even started to tremble.

She applied weak peroxide to metal-foil strips like rites of anointment; almost baptismal acts. Hers was both cutting-edge science and art. She felt like a priestess preparing some sacrificial princess. Only once did Abigail open her eyes, big bluey eyes, before snapping them shut. The supplicant's head was so fully adorned it shimmered with metallic wafers. It was like anointing the dead, but Louise wanted miracles. So was she meant to make the blind see? The dumb speak? Thomas must be already on his way. She had to be ready on time.

Abby's voice emerged as a whisper. "That's why I answered that advert, you see. I'll not get an interview else. You know . . . for that theatre. You know."

A Transit van turned off Cavanham Street, taking third exit towards Oldcross Square, and accelerating away with Josh and Roddy at odds.

"You know what an 'airdressers is?" Roddy kept shouting, "It's a great place to dye! 'Air today, gone tomorrow. 'Air we go, 'air we go, 'air we go! An' you know what they call a transsexual giant's coiffure?" But engine revs drowned the rest out.

Josh was feeling fulfilled. He was the one who'd clinched the deal despite strict company rules. It was he who'd devised their campaign. This was their chance to go "freelance", earning some cash on the side. But Roddy continued aping around, always bloody joking, wallowing in negative values. He always had to satirise. Life to him was repetitive puns, but ceativity mattered. You had to fulfil your potential and question what life was about. At school they had both been a unit; best mates, a combo, a team. Whoever had changed it wasn't himself.

46

Partnerships had real obligations because there were rules about sharing. For instance, if you compared their two contributions, who was the one with the best motivation? Yes, always Josh. Always himself. He kept their scores because he never stopped clocking up points. In gaming arcades he won 'Star Trek by Numbers' each time. His target was a million in cash in five years, so when they'd first heard of that hairdresser's query it was Josh who'd jumped first. By offering seasonal discount, he knew their bait would be taken. Her old-fashioned windows were quickly worsened by neatly-placed screwdriver jabs, proving free enterprise worked! It was artistic licence. He had the vision, but when they'd reached that critical mass he'd take his profits and quit like that Hollywood movie. First he needed a few tubes of lager, but traffic was slowing them down.

Roddy kept nudging his shoulder. "Yeah an' you know what tragedy is? It's getting caught short at the movies." He ignored Josh's groan. "But comedy? It's when some other poor bugger falls off a cliff!"

In front a dusty ten-tonner swerved. Josh stamped on the brakes. Flashed all his lights. Repeatedly thumped on the horn. The truck braked again sharply, blocking their path. Beneath layers of mud Josh deciphered the words "CRAIG DEMOLITION". Its reek of testosterone blew on the wind. Two occupants, shaven skulls gleaming, leaped out, claw-hammers glinting in holsters.

"Oh shit. I forgot!" Josh banged on the wheel with both hands. "We bloody forgot."

Roddy stared at the oncoming fitters. "Eh? Forgot what?"

Josh was manoeuvring, braking and swearing. With a force of 10g, they spun round and accelerated away. Somewhere in the distance a police siren started to wail.

Jilly had kept calmly combing and snipping, softening a curve, straightening a line, counting the seconds away, knowing Thomas would be on his way, so risks would have to be taken. She'd ended up fully committed. Now Abigail had to succeed. It was vital. It was more like the plot of a play. Abigail would be her personal proxy, uniquely designed for seduction. Abigail was messenger. Garrick Jones the target. It cheered her up. It made her smile. It was classic, this feelgood factor made good!

She spun the adjustable chair on its axis and examined her subject more closely. Youth bloomed and then faded. It was unavoidable. You aged. As Jilly kept snip-snipping away, clipping a single hair at a time, she seemed to plunge into a bottomless pool, deeper and deeper until both hands were lead weights and bodymass was dragging her down. She was ugly, obese and dyspeptic. Her own substance had begun to engulf her. Silence accented those snip-snipping scissors. Jilly looked up at Sir Larry and at Ribero da Ponte. Both gave their reluctant assent. Everyone must get involved.

"Anything prepared?" Jilly leaned expectantly forward. "For your interview? Learnt any speeches?"

But Abigail's eyes remained closed. No vital spark. No curiosity. If this were Jilly's surrogate, she'd fail, and Jilly was too far committed for that. Her understudy would have to rehearse.

"But this man . . . Garrick Jones? I mean, he'll have big expectations."
She let the thought sink in. "Never heard of women's lib? Suffragettes?" She
guided the head into position. "Women have to stick for themselves, or else."
She gripped Abby's tight skinny shoulders. "For Christ's sake, woman,
bloody wake up!"

Abigail's eyes snapped open-wide. An image began to form in plate
glass. It wasn't the someone she knew. It mimicked her every manoeuvre. It
imitated her features. They'd chopped back her hair. They'd cut away her
disguise! They'd compromised and exposed her, leaving her nowhere to hide.
Then as she looked she began to relax. She liked what she saw, and her
reflection seemed to agree.

"Now lass," Jilly was saying, "It's time to practise cosmetics."

Taking corners on two wheels, the lads headed back into town.
Gridlock piled upon gridlock, diversion upon diversion, as Manwess Gas
extended its hold and One Way systems made everything worse. Then the
clouds opened up, each droplet exploding like mortars as if individually aimed
at their windscreen. By doubling round back streets, repeatedly crossing
canals, they found themselves in East suburbs heading back into town.

Cavanham Street looked different from here. Amputated chimney
stumps vied with twisted convulsions of steel marking Manwess's former
headquarters. Everywhere looked under siege. Earth-movers rumbled with
headlights full-on. Pile-drivers lurked heavily armed in reserve. This was
undeclared war and battles were still being fought. As flattened landscapes
emerged from the gloom, Roddy started to run out of gags. They saw
Manwess Gas had fenced everything off with strings of flapping red pennants.
A pantechnicon was parked in the gap. A man in scruffy anorak dragged away
crates and hampers. This was the mood of a siege. The Majestic in floodlit
defiance, was going down with all guns firing and every flag flying.

At this moment, rods of hail shattered on windows, miniature bursts of
refraction then magical liquefaction of crystals. Here was classic Cavanham
Street poised on a time-switch, wholly committed to Christmas. That
hairdresser must wonder where they had gone. The project might even be
threatened.

As Jilly Craske worked away, her motto was dedication. And didn't all
artists have that in common? Botticelli, Titian, Rembrandt? Even Chekhov?
Sublimation was the essence of art. Bodies were her medium and Abigail the
canvas. Same with her walls full of stars: life itself was their palette: each
single pore, each flake of skin, sebaceous gland and every strand of fake hair.

Despite her tendons starting to knot, a growing excitement sustained
her. Pinks, golds, browns, beiges, lilacs, blues. Refreshing, plucking and
trimming, tinting and painting, but with Abigail's lips, no more innuendo was
needed. The sexuality was already there and Jilly knew what she was doing. It
was exciting. She was creating a subject, perhaps a dependant, conditioning
subtlest responses, using every technique she knew. Cosmeticians could
reduce human beings to icons by raiding their subject's subconscious, then
subtly implanting themselves. Why not? Why not? It was like psychic radar.
No. More like a portrait. A Jilly Craske self-portrait. And as Abigail was

48

younger and slimmer, she could be made more attractive to Garrick. The idea was very appealing.

Abigail started to watch herself change and have doubts. Was she being demeaned or improved? A daughter's response was to blame her own mother. She began to feel over-promoted. If her mouth didn't feel like her own, what would that do to her words? And what about Stacey's reaction? One minute she'd flatter, promising love and affection. Next she was scathing, because Stacey's one motive was men. She knew every sexual aid and position. Wine by the litre had no effect. She never got drunk. That was part of the game.

Jilly was standing back, head to one side. This latest creation expressed Jilly Craske . A living work of art! She'd projected herself in the principal role, but the understudy would get the applause. She felt almost jealous . . . then slowly it dawned. While Thomas thrived on his vengeance she would be deceiving him, conveying her uncontrolled passions by proxy.

As Jilly tidied Abigail up, their eyes met in a sudden convergence of mirrors. For that split-second, ten thousand volts fired, repeating ad infinitum. In that exchange of looks both women recognised something; something that left them complicit.

Jilly leaned forward. "Remember what I'm doing for you. So you keep your half of the bargain. Agreed?" She stretched out her hand. "You publicise me at the theatre. You also keep me informed. If we help each other we'll . . ."

A movement caught Jilly's eye. Dim silhouettes were holding up shapes as heavy rain beaded around them. Two madmen were pounding the door. Over their heads were her very best Italian chairs! As Jilly unlocked the door, bedraggled figures brought in her rain-sodden seats and dark rivulets spread on her floor. Josh started to apologise, looking wildly around. His clothes were soaked and his hair turned to mush. When Abigail started to laugh he spun round. Perhaps in that instant, images froze like stopping the disk and fixing the course of events.

With all neurones still firing Josh stumbled out, and nothing would be quite the same.

Garrick needed constructive help. He knew that. He needed support while he still felt positive. The nitty-gritty still had to be faced. His season was coming. The weather chart had gained a new format as daylight trimmed and Earth redeployed on its axis.

He'd texted greetings to Vee but got no response. He tried sending texts to his kids with no luck. There was too much to do. He ploughed through questionnaires and letters from agents. A full-time assistant was urgent. Despite a disappointing response he was due to see some applicants, like taking a shot in the dark. His advantage was limited vision: he only saw what he saw. He unpacked copy-typed scripts, stacked them onto shelves and requested translations of Chekhov, Ibsen and Strindberg. He'd started on some dialogue. Page One, Act One, Scene One, 'The Cherry Orchard'. 'World Drama Season'. Poor Charlotte, Varya and Anya. Poor Dumyasha. Poor poor bloody everyone.

This time Bert cornered Garrick to complain about 'non-practical boilers'. He said he'd monitored temperatures and amassed statistics. Now they had statutory rights to walk off the job. The 'Brrrr Brrrr' of a road-drill echoed up from the street as the building adopted the mood of its staff and refused to respond. Like some ancient mariner, Garrick was left prowling the decks of a vessel already adrift. He couldn't help thinking 'Titanic'. To make it worse his hand-written 'plan of campaign' for the Board of Trustees had been cross-checked by Phyllis and returned with queries, exclamations and cross-outs.

He walked in dead men's shoes, and everyone knew it. His schools initiatives had not worked. He'd ended committed to teaching. He'd signed up to giving night classes in town.

He finally traced Verity back to her office.

"Gary, I'm fine." She sounded wary. "Just fine. But kind of busy. And you?"– He could make out the clatter of office machines.

"Me?" He must have sounded piqued. "I'm busy casting, commissioning, and suchlike, and . . ." His positive thinking ran out. "Vee, darling, I miss you. I mean that. I do."

"I do appreciate that . . ." A slight irritation had entered her voice. "But you don't need to say it. I take that as said." Office acoustics grew in the background.

"But you need a break," he insisted, "You're missing out on new restaurants here." This would gain her attention. "It's no way provincial. Nothing as narrow as 'ethnic'. I mean this is Norston. It's got finest Bengalis, Goans, Jamaicans, Cantonese, Turkish, Iranian, Irish . . . whatever. You name it. We're Europe's next City of Culture!" He had offered the titbit.

"Oh yes? You're having it tough."

"Come on. I'm interviewing assistants. Next I'll be casting. It's like spinning dice."

"Poor Gary." She sounded unsympathetic.

"No listen. I'm starting with 'The Three Sisters', the definitive production. I won't bore you with details, except to say . . ."

"Back in London we only get pantos. 'The English Art Form' we're told, but Momma calls them crude burlesque. They're quite the dumbest thing around. An' for kids? All Goldilocks and Aladdinses . . . Perverts and four-letter expletives? So tacky! Jeez! You've luckily cornered the culture in Norston. Kultur with a capital K. It's my opinion, you . . ." Garrick heard muttered asides.

"Sorry Vee, I can tell you're busy. Give my love to Rachel and Mark, and tell them daddy keeps trying to call but they never seem to be in. And I've found this new war game for Markie. He's just the right age. And I'm looking for something with furry animals for Rachel . . . Hello? Hello?"

But the line had gone dead in just the same way love vaporised into ether. He unwrapped a rye sandwich and bit into 'tuna'n'cheese'. He was getting nowhere. One thing he could see from his windows. It was really the Sun that revolved round the Earth. People were quick to assert human values, like putting a human face on the moon. If Garrick really strained hard enough he could catch glimpses of the canal, like links in some opal-grey necklace. The rest of the Universe appeared to implode.

Suddenly his intercom buzzed. He dumped his ciabatta and went straight onto the offensive.

50

"Phyllis! How's my interviewees? I trust you've everything all under control? All names and dates confirmed?"

Verity's voice sounded loud. "And who the hell's Phyllis?"

He must have pressed redial again. "Sorry darling, it's intercom problems. She's our receptionist. Phyllis."

"Is this what you called back to tell me?"

"No darling." He took a deep breath. "I've had this wild and crazy idea." "Go for it," he thought. "Listen. Why don't you come down this weekend? And bring the kids. I'll book a hotel and show you round town. We'll have a spectacular time. We can do the whole Lancashire bit . . . visit some heritage sites . . . restaurants too if you like." He waited in anticipation. "What do you say?"

"Thank you for ringing back." Formality anglicised her vowels. "Can I postpone our decision?" Sounding more like a call centre now.

Even her acoustics had changed. Smaller space. No background noise. Presumably in her office and sounding very official, but that's what the establishment does. It sets targets, creates bureaucratic regimes conforming with tests and exams. It produces millions of students. Too many cooks literally spoiled all the broth. Everyone's pressures on Vee were enormous. They owed her the principal's job. This was the title she craved.

"Vee? What's going on?"

"Thank you. Of course. We need to agree contracts. Thanks." She gave a quiet embarrassed laugh, adding in a low voice. "It's kinda tricky right now. Give me a moment." He heard a deep breath, followed by changing acoustics. "Listen Gary, I'm in the Ladies. Now don't take this wrong." He foresaw news about Roseanne's latest outburst, or Rachel's growing pains. "You see," she continued, then paused. "They've just made me this offer. Promotion. I mean . . . a new job!"

He was momentarily taken aback. "Congratulations! Lavinia Miller's retiring?"

"No, not exactly." She sounded almost piqued and those East Coast vowels were becoming pronounced. "Except, wow, it's sure not as simple as that."

"Then Deputy Principal job?"

"No. Much better. I've gotten this offer. Straight up. Pre-selected. Personally. To do this video. Yeah, and there's a TV series to follow! Naturally it's all about cooking . . . and . . . and . . . anyway . . ." She took a breath and changed gear. "Come on Gary, they're pretty damn serious. They've approached the college direct. It's high-octane stuff. We're discussing formats. They've come up with dates."

His eyes drifted over the fast-moving clouds. "What are you saying?"

"Saying?" She gave a short laugh. "Guess they couldn't find anyone else in a hurry. It's Channel Twelve Digital. Their first choice went sick so I'm striking the feminist blow! Oh, and I start from exactly ten minutes ago . . . as red-hot as oven-baked cookies!" She giggled, "And you're first to know!"

The clouds seemed to go out of focus. "Vee. Look, I don't want to sound off-putting but . . . but, are you sure it's all on the level? I mean, the way you talk, I know this business. There's bastards out there. You need something in writing. You need proper advice. You can't just put your job on the line."

"How come I always know what you'll say? You give off such negative vibes. Even momma sees that. Don't you see, Gary? I'm flipping the Ace. Same as you when you got to do Chekhov. That's your dream. You want to resurrect Chekhov. Now, this producer calls our college and he's in some panic. Some celebrity chef drops out. Food poisoning or stuff. He needs someone to front his cookery chat-show. Anchor it, right? Would you believe it? Another show about food? Well, it so happens this is my dream. And they're off on location next week. It's everything from barbecue sauces to casseroles and Chinese woks. It transmits in two months!" She waited for Garrick's response. "If that isn't that luck, then what the hell is? "

Verity still hadn't referred to the news cutting he'd sent about him from last week's Norston & County. Somehow during their phone conversation Vee's photograph's eye lines had changed, neatly averting its gaze.

"What've you told them?"

"Told them? Like what?" She didn't wait for his answer. "Gary, it's me asking you. I'm asking my husband's opinion. I value your judgement. Come on. You say."

Low clouds heading east scuffed across tower blocks. The air felt warmer and muggy. Way down below, tectonic plates were swapping whole continents round. It felt like the earth on the move was leaving him out on a limb. When Vee referred to obsessions with Chekhov, this Odyssey wasn't his choosing. Or was it now his private Hajj? His pilgrimage? His penitence? What? A husband must back his wife.

Instead he heard himself asking, "But is this what you really want?" because he was the one with professional standing and years of experience. "What about our kids?"

"What about them? Come on Gary, this pays more for one episode than I'd earn in three whole semesters. That's got to be good for us all."

Dizzying pigeons zoomed past his window. One landed on his windowsill, parading its chest, bobbing and cooing to taunt him. Phyllis would be collating queries from actors' agents. He hoped they'd be desperate for prestigious Chekhovs. They might value class between better-paid jobs.

Garrick felt dry in the throat. "Look, what if I give it some thought? Maybe . . . maybe we'll offer them a good old provisional 'maybe' . . . *perhaps*. But don't sign. Not yet. I'll get my agent checking it out. Rocko could manage. Okay?"

In the long extended pause, he noticed how lumbering clouds exuded gold shafts like painted backcloths rumbling over traditional rollers. Their cumulo-nimbus had frothed up en route from the States. Now they were threatening storms.

"Garrick!" Verity's voice had noticeably hardened. "I've gotten my own agent, thanks. Lucy's drawn up my contract. I signed the option this morning." She took his short gasp as acceptance. "There. See, it wasn't so bad! I knew you'd be thrilled. And Roseanne's delighted, our kids overjoyed." She blew kisses. "Right now I've visitors waiting. We knew you'd be tickled to death!"

As he slammed his phone down the pigeon took off with a flutter. His children still grinned from their frames. 'Rachel and Mark on the swings', 'Family with dog in the park'.

Then came the buzzer again! "Ah, hello Garrick," Phyllis simpered. "It's our Mister Arthur Ruddock. We have him here in person. He's in the building. And he's seen your proposals for Chekhov and Strindberg. He's telling me you're due for a meeting."

"No Phyllis. I'm not."

"I'm sorry but you are. And he'll see you downstairs in one minute."

As Phyllis followed Garrick down, Garrick sensed she was purring. Arthur was in the main auditorium, waiting. In semi-darkness they made out the back of an oversized head.

"Garrick old son!" Arthur's voice boomed. "How's it going, eh? Any firm schedules yet?"

Garrick felt smug. Without false modesty he knew his proposals were good. If Arthur needed information, Garrick had the upper hand and everything was on track. The Deification of Chekhov was scheduled. With the official go-ahead, he'd ring Vee, who'd tell Roseanne, and everyone would celebrate. They'd make the London promoters sit up, and all the Morozoffs happy from Massachusetts to eastern Nevada. They might even cheer back in Moscow. But Arthur Ruddock didn't so much as turn round. A laptop lay on his knees, glowing like personal footlights.

"Has our Miss Corbel explained? I presume she's confirmed we'd received your proposals?" Arthur flipped down an adjacent seat, and pointed.

Garrick sat down. "Yes, but don't worry. I'm planning brilliant sponsorship deals. I've advertised for an assistant, and I'm seeing applicants shortly. So no need to worry. We'll soon have this town on the cultural map." He folded his hands and sat back.

Arthur twisted to face him. "Oh aye?" He shuffled his shoulders. "There's cold bloody draughts in this place. Can't you feel them?"

"It's that central heating. It needs urgent repairs."

Arthur stared. "Aye. And you're Director of Productions." He raised a hand before Garrick could speak. "That's your responsibility now. And as I was passing, I guessed you'd be awaiting my input. Finger on the pulse, local know-how, that sort of thing. Us innovators, we take all the risks. We bend rules. We push restrictions. But, oh dear, oh dear . . . once we forget local traditions!" He sat back shaking his head. "Don't you see? Folk are that conservative here. They're our consumers. It comes down to basic values. We're afloat in a shark-ridden sea where local knowledge is all." He sat back looking expectant.

"So first we start with Chekhov's 'Cherry Orchard'. Right?" Ticking them off on his fingers. "Then Chekhov's 'Three Sisters', followed by Henrik Ibsen's 'Master Builder' or Strindberg's 'Miss Julie', and . . ."

"Hang on, hang on! Think time of the year! Think man, think!" Arthur examined his knuckles. "What's instinctive is natural. Well?" Garrick's confusion seemed to annoy him. "Jesus Christ! Think Christmas! We're not bloody pagans in Norston. That's barely five weeks till Boxing Day, then you go live!"

Arthur snapped his laptop shut and grasped Garrick's arm. Thick fingers clamped into Garrick's raw shoulder urging him towards the stage

"A reality check, Mr Jones. Confronting the facts."

Starting at the orchestra pit Arthur pointed up, then around the proscenium arch, before panning full circle and back onto Garrick.

"At this point," Arthur said brightly as Phyllis materialised with two mugs on a tray, "Our lovely Phyllis usually brings me a tea."

He snaked the teabag out on a string, dropping it into the tray as Phyllis padded away, then he stood head to one side as if listening for something. From behind the fire curtain came muffled banging then counterpoint growlings of drills. Arthur gave a double thumbs-up.

"There! That's Manwess contractors checking the system. Now you can thank me in person. But first . . ." He caught Garrick's sleeve in the darkness. "Remember one thing. This ancient theatre. It's part of our 'community'," adding in inverted commas, "Our rock in times of massive change." His manner encompassed the whole universe. "Our traditional cradle of culture . . . Heritage, Continuity, those are keywords here. That's why yours is a pivotal, even a biblical, role." He drew Garrick closer. "So don't keep your plan to yourself. What've you chosen? Give us a hint." Arthur winked broadly. "People adore them transsexual sisters. They just love that lesbian paedophile prince! There's only one choice. Let's hope that's the panto you've chose? Am I right?"

Garrick could almost taste Arthur's moist breath.

Phyllis was still at her keyboard when Garrick stormed in like some cheap re-enactment. She'd seen it all before. Rex Schulman like some enraged drama queen, Bert violently kicking chairs, and even Danny and Reggie threatening strikes. She was their Resident Staff so someone had to maintain standards.

"But Cinderella?" Garrick kept on repeating, "Cinderella? Bloody Aladdin?" He could hardly spit out the words. "Puss in Boots, Robin Hood, Ali Baba, Mother Goose, Little Red Riding Hood and the Wolf, Babes in the Wood. He says you did Humpty Dumpty one year but everyone loves Cinderella the best!"

She nodded energetically. "Yes, we always get full houses. Every wee gel wants to be Cinderella. I know I did. And everyone loves the two dames. And they worship the lad who plays Buttons. We usually get in a singer for that."

"Sorry. That is not why I've been hired."

"Really?" She looked up in surprise. "But everything's here in your contract. I typed it myself. That clause about '*deferring to management's final decisions on schedules*'. You should always check the small print. You signed it. A contract is legally binding. Shall I print you a copy?"

Garrick saw she did not understand. His wasn't a bloody maintenance job. How come his Redemption had led straight into Hell? Anyway, Vee and her mother had great expectations and their blood was far thicker than water. When it came to the Morozoffs and Chekhovs, what mattered was Celebration

54

of Greatness and the assertion of Prime Human Values. How could these people understand that?

He remembered his father's obsession with laws and commandments, forever devising new, unattainable targets because Edwin insisted on literal truths, everything in black and white. Garrick recalled kneeling barelegged, praying to God to set easier aims. But first would come humiliation and anguish, like Cinderella now punishing Chekhov. Edwin had been dead four years but today they were closer than during his life. For a start he was easier to talk to. Now they debated on near equal terms.

But Phyllis was observing him. "Alright love." She gave a conciliatory sigh. "But pantos is when we make money. Once Cinderella's done, then bingo, the rest of the season's all yours." She gave him a long questioning look. "Honest love, your cheque's guaranteed. There's plenty who'd jump at the chance." She stretched a hand out towards him. "Come on."

"But you don't understand."

Phyllis's hand was slowly withdrawn. She flicked the cursor over her screen and gestured him to observe.

"Well look at this! It's your biographical details." She examined the monitor closely. "Yes, yours is a dead impressive CV. West End, Hollywood, Broadway, Awards." She whistled through pursed lips.

As Garrick watched his claims scrolling past, they looked more and more wild and outrageous. By hyping up qualifications with lies, he'd put himself on the line. But if they'd had these suspicions, why was he chosen at all?

Phyllis must have been reading his mind. "Well, maybe they just liked you?" Her long fingers hung momentarily over the keys. "Yes. That's the only explanation." She smiled.

For the first time he noticed those neatly trimmed, practical nails. Over delicate wrists slithered frail circles of gold. He caught a faint trace of a perfume; not one he'd have connected with her. It struck him she wasn't much older than he. As for that familiar fragrance? That distinctive scent? It seemed to affect him without knowing why. Associations ran out of control. He spontaneously pictured prominent nipples. Between those long sinewy legs were . . . he coughed and turned sharply away.

"You alright?" Phyllis was looking concerned. "Have you chosen which script?"

Why the hell should he feel guilty? He'd lied in a very good cause. During the lingering death of his mother, Edwin was always quoting the Bible, but if God were so good and all-powerful why let the innocent suffer? Why promise them lies? So, aged seventeen, Garrick withdrew two thousand pounds from the family account, and left. Clubland and showgirls went with the deal; sex and drugs in the same package. Everyone did it. Grass. Coke. Squats. Dipping and diving for years. He'd wanted to see Edwin punished, but Roseanne and Edwin would have been soul mates in hell. After all, it wasn't till Roseanne began asking questions and trailing through websites that Verity had any doubts. He felt a great surge of self-justification. His was the fate of all pilgrims and martyrs.

"So? Cinderella it is?" Phyllis's fingers were poised on the keys. "Well?" Her unblinking lenses bored through his bone and soft tissue; those eyes were hazel, their irises textured with grey.

Without warning, the door slammed opened. A black technician in blue boiler-suit and white helmet wandered casually in. The Manwess official began tapping at panels with what looked like a clipboard, as if the room were unoccupied.

"Excuse me!" Phyllis demanded, "Excuse me!"

The official noticed them. "Why, hey there!" His grin was as polished and bleached as new dentures. "I'm Manwess Gas! It part of total inspection." He indicated his identity card. "See. Legal obligations. As per official contract, as per Mister Councillor Ruddock. That's checkin' pipin', and tubin', pumps, connections an' junctions and so fort'. Our stated aim is, 'not disturbin' existin' occupants', an' so forth." He waved a large beguiling hand. "Know what I sayin'. Safety alway come first, so jus' you preeten' I not here." He unfolded a diagram then knelt to check panels with electronic devices. "Wish I was in show biz mesel'. Like rappin' an, that. There no glamour in gas. All it do is bubble out o'sea get pumped for mile on mile through massiff mains down load of tubin' an' spaghettis o' pipeline . . . on and on through meters an' macaronis in all sort o' conjunction." He gave a broad chuckle. " An' after all that? You go bloody burn it! It only old piping what holdin' this buildin' together!" The engineer unbolted a panel to reveal rusting valves.

Phyllis shrugged and sighed. Her fingernails clacked the first key, then rattled away like dry bones. As Garrick watched, 'The Cherry Orchard' appeared on her monitor screen.

As he moved through the echoing foyer, Garrick knew how Inuits felt when their sun slid below the horizon for months. All living beings had unfulfilled longings. In much the same way he was pining for Vee and his kids, but now his only solution was gone.

Aged about ten, choristers stole cigarettes and inhaled. That first taste of manhood raced through their veins. Right now he needed its sense of fulfilment but everyone must renounce something: his father insisted on that. Chekhov himself endured claustrophobia, sickness and exile, but at least Anton had seen its black joke. The Three Sisters, it said in bold type on the screen as Phyllis accepted his headline, but the victory wasn't his own. It was the great Russian playwright who'd triumphed, aided by those Morotzovs almost related by marriage. In the very throes of defeat they had won.

He paused beneath the brass chandelier and clenched both fists before pushing out into the street. The smell of burnt tar surged up to meet him. "MANWESS" in huge overconfident letters was painted on all the trucks and stuck onto windscreens, seeming to say "No Manwess employee need answer to man". Its territorial gains were coloured bright red on their maps. Its vehicles gathered like beetles to breed because this was the age of the corporate car, anonymous, polished and black. No corporate modesty here. However much Garrick fought, his nicotine urges fought back.

High up above him, the letters 'M A J E S T I C' were posted like slugs of oversized type, apparently nailed to the skyline. Ubiquitous pigeons circled and settled. As he scanned the theatre façade, over emblems and swags, cantilevered ledges, and inset carvings, upwards towards the twin turrets alongside the tilting 'T' of Majestic, Phyllis quickly ducked out of sight. Garrick was about to phone home when Phyllis emerged on the front steps behind him, swathed in her best woollen coat, handbag on arm, and pulling on knitted gloves.

"It's my consultant day. I'll not be long. I've spread out the candidates' details for you." With that she was off, her neat heels still clicking away.

The roar of a generator set pigeons off into free-flowing circles, scattering feathers, spiralling up around Garrick's tower, buffeted by rising gusts. This same wind tugged Garrick's own jacket. Its rising gale tore at tarpaulins, scaffolds and flags till it whined through the jibs of Eddie Craig's cranes. Pennants fluttered. Loose cables flicked at the wall. The temporary poster for Chekhov Players had started to peel, then with the first splats of rain he saw his name starting to run like the dripping of water wearing whole mountains away.

Back in the office his portable radio only chanted old hits. He was trapped in its niche when he should have been working in movies, not swamped with illiterate job applications, bogged down in Norston FM. Its jingles invited nostalgia in. "Buy now! Remember! Feel better". The joyous past glowed with suntan and sparkled with vivid blue water and Garrick had all his props here. He could still reconnect, frame by Kodachrome frame. But where was that shot of them flirting in front of a waterfall? It had been there on his desk. Stuff couldn't just vanish. He was on hands and knees scrabbling through wastebins when his desk buzzer went. He wasn't on call like a surgeon!

As usual Phyllis's instinct was right. Everything fell into place. He'd barely pinned Arthur's pantomime titles alongside selections of scripts, when there wasn't a choice. Forget Chekhov. Forget about his pilgrimage. Getting an assistant came first, pantomime or no pantomime. Did Verity need know every setback? Commandment Number One was 'Thou shalt be true to thyself'. Even if teaching drama in Norston wasn't his thing, who could say 'No' to hard cash when all their credit was gone?

Even as he began making lists, the old withdrawal symptoms kicked in. Up here in his turret, rising winds were compressing his brain. Maybe a gulp of fresh air would distract? He forced open the fire door and edged onto a narrow iron ledge.

The rusting balustrade creaked. Wiring wailed in the wind. Perspectives rocketed violently downwards. Corroding pipes elbowed back up as fire escapes zigzagged in reverse. He knew how the Ancient Mariner felt on his foc'sle ordering the storm to give way. Northerly gusts hauled heavy black clouds all the way down from the Baltic. You couldn't escape. It put this whole world into perspective.

Threadbare pigeons were riding north-easterlies which tore at flagpoles and roofs, while far below Manwess workers sheltered for smokes. Down to his right, building cranes pecked at demolished foundations. But no sign of a personal albatross yet. Away to the left, pile-drivers trampled everything out.

The scale was immense. He shrank to insignificance. Soon all this would be Norston Marina. It needed a gesture. Something had to be done.

In a fit of madness he gripped the bent handrail and spread-eagled one-handedly out suspended above the whole town. He didn't care. Adrenaline rushed in. The landscape swung side to side. He felt good . . . but then an irrational urge to hurl himself out into space.

If he jumped, he would fly! He'd astonish his children by gliding right down to their playground back home with the laws of aerodynamics suspended. Instead he'd have to sleepwalk until 'The Three Sisters' first night, when Garrick and Chekhov would get their rewards. If waiting meant a sacrifice, then Edwin would surely approve. He knew Verity and Roseanne would think he'd accepted defeat. It was best they didn't find out. Garrick would do what had to be done. He needed some simple, meaningful gesture. A symbolic statement. An encouraging token. Casting an oracle's vote? Maybe a straw in the wind? . . . Then the idea came.

Wedging himself in the lee of a buttress, he tugged the gas inspection slip from his pocket. It needed a contortionist's act. Balancing took immense concentration. Reverting to a ten-year-old he took the pink fluttering paper, creasing it diagonally, clumsily pleating, folding, refolding. His crude origami crushed squares into an arrow. This wasn't a printed checklist he held. It was an artist's emotional plea. He nipped the last crease with his nails.

"Manwess Gas Recommendation" (it read) "Urgent overhaul and replacement of entire system is vital, (etcetera, etcetera) . . . Signed, B.O'Casey, Regional Inspector"

He launched the pink paper dart into space.

Two girls crossed the Recreation Ground with Stacey stalking ahead as Abigail grew increasingly nervous. She always dreaded interviews. She worried about her freshly trimmed hair in high winds. She wondered about preparations. People's advice was mostly no help. Their so-called perspectives never made sense. She thought she understood why. Adults do not communicate. Right? Their words are different. They speak without saying much. They expect expectations, on about prospects, unemployment, careers . . . It's words, words and more lies. Despite Louise's intervention, Abby's first big appointment was due.

According to geography classes Earth is a blue, brown and white-coloured ball, spinning on its own axis in a track round the Sun, while the whole bundle heads off into unlimited Space. But Abigail wasn't impressed. She would have invented a more practical system. Space and skies ought to be neatly divided into simple crisp watertight layers. She pictured transparent balloons; neat little bubbles within bigger bubbles inside big balloons inside massive translucent spheres, one after another like neatly-fitting Russian dolls. Instead you had to accept what old people told you was true. This upcoming interview was one more way to keep them all happy, but Stacey was always dismissive while Abby's own mother assumed she would fail. She shivered and pulled her coat tighter round her. Somehow she'd made this commitment to Jilly Craske and ended up owing a favour.

That same icy wind which buffeted the Majestic, was tearing over Inchdale Park and down Lancaster Avenue, blasting the Recreation Ground on its way. It scattered water-vapour and dust, ripping last leaves from grey trees. The two girls kept to leeward, passing homebound mothers with fully-cowled buggies. Abigail was not superstitious, but today she'd avoided cracks in the paving, mentally counting her score while Stacey kept walking and talking as most of her words blew away.

Abigail gave appropriate answers and hoped for the best. ". . . Yeah yeah, an' my mum too Never no encouragement. Always changing her mind. She pushed and pushed to tart me up, then wants my interview cancelled. Why? Like, is she jealous? It doesn't make sense. It's blowing my mind." She almost stepped into a puddle. "Fact is, I'm only attending to spite her! Wouldn't you?"

But Stacey was pointing up at the sky, frantically tapping at Abby's shoulder.

"Look! Look!" she screeched. "What's that?"

Stepping from slab to slab Abby kept dodging the gratings. "I mean, she don't think I'm capable! Like I'm a dimwit or something." She studied a right-angled kerb. "Says I'm like, overreaching myself! What would you do?" But Stacey's eyes remained fixed on the sky. She said nothing.

Next minute she was heading upwind, arms outstretched, imploring. The 'It Girl' was shrieking. She jumped and screamed, stretching both hands in the air. Above her skimmed a paper dart buffeted on the wind.

"Quick! Or we'll lose it!" Stacey kept running, trampling lawns and dodging through bushes like someone berserk. "It's coming. Don't move!"

Abigail froze, pigeon-toed and aghast, as the paper dart headed towards her. Next moment it swerved then dived between gust and gully, banking, then plunging towards a building site. Stacey yelled and she screamed. All that trendy cool dissolved as the paper dart looped the loop on the currents.

Sometimes it hung on the air like a kite, next moment dipped, then it dived. It seemed to have a life of its own. It lifted and climbed before swooping down in a long sweeping spiral then banking in a half circle. Behind it scrambled a mud-spattered Stacey as mad and deranged as a hunter. Another gust caught it. It soared towards Eddie Craig's boundary fence. It climbed again in a long sweeping arc, then suddenly stalled and nose-dived towards Abigail.

Stacey dived forward, breathless and overexcited, screaming. "Leave it! It's mine!"

Except it fell at Abigail's feet. It simply dropped out of the sky. Abigail's instincts took over. She seized the pink dart before Stacey arrived.

"Hey! That's not fair!" Tears welled up in Stacey's eyes. "You bitch!"

The more she attempted to snatch it, the more Abby kept turning and turning around, shielding the prize with her body.

"Okay. Fair do's". Reluctantly Stacey gave up. "We share. Agreed?"

But Abigail waited. The balance had shifted. Whoever held this prize confirmed the new status even as Stacey spelled out the terms of their friendship. "Best friends" meant arm-in-arm, sharing lipsticks and burgers. It meant Finders-keepers. Division of spoils. It meant fifty-fifty on gossip. But Abigail relished the fact of possession. The fact was, it had dropped at her feet. Therefore it was meant for herself. A message from outer space or even beyond. Pinkness and softness suggested romance. But as Abby unfolded the creases, printing emerged on the back.

The paper was limp; the printing blurred. With every move her disappointment grew. Her fingers felt cold. An icy wind tore at their faces, with driving rain flicking raw cheeks. Then at the critical moment, Abigail flinched. She felt deluded and wrong. Without saying a word she spread the limp sheet upon Stacey's outstretched palm It reaffirmed their old interdependence.

Stacey's answering screech turned into a satisfied gurgle as she spread out the note on the bench, reassembling its patterns, excitedly deciphering words as Abby was walking away.

"Wait!" Stacey yelled. "Look! It's a gas bill or something!" She ran after Abby, waving it like a damp flag. "But what about that address on the heading? . . . Or didn't you notice the name?"

CHAPTER FOUR

CASTING

If he'd been later asked about first impressions, he'd have said "contradictory". "Genie appears through star-trap centre-stage," kind of thing, "And arrived soaked to the skin! A young woman, more of a girl; pale but striking, self-deprecating but confident" or something along these lines. Or was that too arch? Compared with other applicants she was too young. Just a school kid. Garrick saw that at a glance. Puppy-fat features, delicate skin blotched pink with cold, evasive grey-green eyes and neatly trimmed pale copper hair. To him she seemed relaxed and confident. Natural, alert and yet . . . . Even then he'd sensed something else for which he'd later try to find suitable words. "Too tinted porcelain' maybe? Fey? Elfin possibly? That frightening glow of pubescence? And definitely much too young and naive." Was immature the right word?

"Okay. Don't waste your time," his internal voice intervened, "Tell her outright you need someone older. Forget discrimination." And how could he as employer bog himself down? He had to be brutally frank.

"Welcome," he heard himself saying, "It's a pleasure to meet you Miss Roberts."

"It's Abby, sir," she repeated. "I call myself Abby."

He flipped through his notes and found Abigail Roberts crossed out in Phyllis's diary.

"But according to Phyllis, you've cancelled." She looked surprised. "Oh yes. It says so here," he insisted, "You phoned up this morning to cancel."

She was about to protest, then, of course, Abigail thought, it all came down to this. To hair! She trailed a hand through her tresses. Years of torment. Braiding, hair-slides, tie-bows, crocodile clips and her mother. It was Jilly Craske who had ended that hell, but Louise couldn't stop interfering. Was her mother her warder? Removing fridge magnets, packing trinkets in drawers, stuffing fashion dolls into cupboards, reading everyone's letters? Next she'd be checking her websites and friends. Now she was cancelling Abby's appointments and trying to block her career!

"Excuse me. I'm ever so sorry." By speaking softly she forced Garrick to lean forward. "That was a misunderstanding. It's all my own fault. You must've got thousands to see."

As their heads almost touched, he backed off. "Hardly. Not exactly a queue round the block."

Phyllis was due any moment. He'd have take the girl to his office, but as she followed him up, her nearness was oddly disturbing.

Garrick had lain awake till two that morning, then overslept. The first glimmers of dawn had produced a lemon-grey wash like premature visions of Spring. He'd taken the short-cut through side-streets where coffee bars, hairdressers, paper stalls, hairdressers, shops, and more hairdressers kept springing up. As he crossed the road outside "Crowning Glory", a Paradise Shopfitters van was drawing away. To avoid it traffic braked; a black saloon swerved to dodge Eddie Craig tipper-trucks. Garrick no longer cared about traffic. Soon he would have an assistant and all his pressures would cease.

He pressed auto-redial on Verity's number, expecting her answering service.

"Hi Gary?" she interrupted, "That you? . . Interviewing today? That all?"

"I thought you'd be interested."

"Sure, but none of us ever stops growing. We grow together, else we grow apart. Most of all, we're spiritual beings. So whatever happens, it's family first."

"Is that Roseanne again?"

"Leave my mom out. It's the kids. I'm very concerned about Rachel. No, not just Rachel. They start maturing too young." She gave a deep intake of breath. "The problem is Chloe."

"Who the hell's Chloe?"

"You see! You don't know. That's my point. She's Rachel's best pal. Her best buddy. More like kid sister, she says, but I'd already figured someone was teaching those words. I'm not repeating them, but if I say it stops kids staying kids, and that's . . ."

"No! You mean swearing? Sexual stuff?" He felt defiled on behalf of his kids. "My God! Where's Chloe getting that from?"

"From her big bothers and sisters of course. It's like mental abuse. Pre-teens, they know all there is to be known. Drugs, sex, whatever. It's sad. "

"In Lancaster gate?"

"That's how it is. I'll try a word in Jennifer's ear. She's their teaching assistant. Momma insists Jenny's the listening type. They've already discussed the Morozovs and Chekhov. Now Jenny's telling everyone. No, don't worry, I'll figure it out with the school. I'm running late, so give our dear, cousin Anton my love." She blew him a kiss and rang off.

He tried to take it in. He'd definitely write to his son and his daughter. He'd send them individual cards. He'd try to phone at least once a day. He'd risk extra credit for gifts, but one thing at a time. Planning too far ahead could be fatal, because arranging early auditions for Chekhov meant almost overtaking himself. Forget Uncle Vanya. The way things were going, the star would be a pantomime horse.

Outside the theatre were new cones and tape. Next they'd set up border posts and demand passports. Inside the main lobby, he found a Manwess official setting up theodolites. Another padded round, ludicrously tapping at walls and reading from an instrument. By the time Garrick had reached Phyllis's landing, he caught the murmur of voices, and stopped. He thought he'd heard Phyllis groaning? These Manwess officials were going too far. He turned the doorknob, pushed sharply, waggled, then heaved. The door remained shut.

"Phyllis? Phyllis?" He rattled the handle. " I need to get to my office."

He heard the clunk-click of the lock. Another wait, then there she was, thoughtfully smoothing her collar. Somewhere behind her a bulky figure was adjusting its tie in a miniature mirror. He stood like a walrus intent on a pinhole as Phyllis adjusted her glasses.

"Why Garrick! It's you!" She overplayed astonishment. "Thank you so much, we did get your note." The man in the background brushed himself down. "That note you left me last night? Well here he is. Your visitor's waiting."

A navy overcoat sprawled over a chair. A studded black briefcase lay beside the Financial Times. Arthur Ruddock seemed enormously pleased with himself. He sniffed as if he'd been snorting cocaine. The tail of his shirt bulged over his waistband.

"Ah! Jones!" Arthur thrust out a welcoming hand. "Lovely day! Don't apologise. Thought I'd drop by and check progress. I've got advertisers and printers to brief. The scene boys tell me you've made your decision." Garrick looked baffled. "You informed them yesterday. I understand something's decided."

"Such as what?"

Arthur glanced wearily at Phyllis. "Such as everything, Mister Jones. There's reputations at stake. Yours and mine for starters. That's why I've come extra early. Because . . ." He spread his hands and appeared to be waiting. "Well? Because of what?"

"Oh that. It's thanks to Miss Corbel's excellent advert," Garrick nodded towards Phyllis. "Not to mention her organisational skills. I'm interviewing assistants." Arthur and Phyllis exchanged looks. "I need someone who's perfect for Chekhov."

"Yes, good. I was coming to that." Arthur's gaze turned to the ceiling. "Thanks to lovely Rex Schulman, I've got some suggestions. He always used Lionel Parsons." Arthur gave a big toothy smile. "The kiddies loved his Ugly Sister best. Dames are the key as I see it. That's what Cinderella's about."

Phyllis was typing the name on her screen. "You want an availability check?."

Arthur was carefully buttoning his coat, then further adjusting his tie. He nodded, smiled, and turned to go.

Garrick exploded. "You're joking! You hired me for quality drama. Everyone on your committee agrees, so my decision's final. Anton Chekhov's 'Cherry Orchard' will be followed by his 'Seagull', then 'The Three Sisters'. There won't be any pantomime this year, not while . . ."

"Oh aye. Good try." Arthur gave a slow hand clap and sighed. "But my friend, our legal agreement? Remember? Your signature? Yes? Then our verbal agreement? Doesn't that ring a bell?" He looked back at Phyllis. "All as witnessed by others But you didn't wait for legal advice, did you?" From habit Arthur re-straightened his tie. "In your boots I'd buckle down and turn it to advantage." He paused and seemed to fill the whole threshold. "And as for your Curriculum Vitaes? That's Latin, and fully translated it says 'Don't push your luck'. Know what I mean? Over-egging the pudding. And think what bad publicity does. Lawyers lead to the bankruptcy courts." Arthur stretched out a hand. "Besides, we're all friends! This is work. You get paid." He slipped a big arm round Garrick's shoulder and walked him towards Phyllis. "Remember, after the panto the schedule is yours! But first . . ." He pointed at Phyllis's keyboard.

They watched capital letters tap onto her screen. 'CINDERELLA'. Arthur touched Phyllis's shoulder and nodded. As he strode out he gave a sharp whistle. Three figures appeared on the landing. Before the door slammed shut, Bert, Danny, and Reg had silently followed him down.

As Garrick ushered Abigail up to his turret, she noted his office was cramped. And they were alone. Exactly as Stacey had warned because Stacey knew about favours; she knew about the casting couch. She'd read magazines from cover to cover. She recognised celebrities. She'd wallowed in websites and revelled in pectoral muscles, secret tattoos, kinkiness, semen and blood on the carpet. Male Dominance was a video game. Add Aikido, Kung Fu, plus a bout of Karate, then everything is a scam, but in real life when she was needed, Stacey was nowhere around.

He offered her a seat at his desk. With knees clamped together she felt her neck and shoulders tense as Garrick laid out appropriate files. Finally he looked up from his notes, a finger poised over Paragraph One. Then slung his questionnaire aside. So this was that woman's daughter? A child of Louise? Of Louise Roberts? Of Club Arabica?

"Good to meet you Miss Roberts. Tell us what your interests are."

He liked to think he was trained to observe. Unconscious habits provided an insight. Add physical particulars: hair, teeth, makeup, fingernails, and most of all the voice. Experience helped but youth might actually have an advantage? The young would accept and adapt.

"We–e–ll," she lied, consciously suppressing her voice, "I love dancing and cleaning. Especially ironing!" While looking him straight in the eye.

He laughed aloud. He liked being thrown. The unexpected was very effective. That was a bonus. What counted was the chemistry, and being local she'd not be expect either a fortune or instant promotion. He'd train her to fit his requirements. First that bloody pantomime, then his great season of Chekhovs to come.

Abigail's fingers entwined till they locked. "Scuse me, but it's, like, okay to say Garrick?" She acknowledged his nod with a nod, and let the words tangle. "I don't mind where I work, see. Like, never mind the hours. London, Paris, New York, Manchester, Newcastle, Leeds or wherever. I don't mind. Really don't. Anywhere away from . . . you know . . . here."

She sounded faux-naïve but Chekhov himself even married an actress. That was young Dr. Anton Pavlovich for you! Garrick had not made that mistake himself. For Chekhov, Medicine challenged Affairs of the Heart (Like taking samples of sputum while his soul went into a spasm), but Chekhov was still an avid observer a hundred years after his death; suave in all his photographs, sympathetic and always observant. Before Garrick could ask anything else, she'd fumbled around in her coat pocket.

"Oh yeah." Abigail produced some crumpled rose-coloured paper, its pinkiness blotted and blotched. "An' there's this. Like, it just swooped out the sky." Warily he accepted it. "And look, it's got your name on."

This communication was clearly addressed to himself. A statement listing technical details; its dye had begun to bleach out but he recognised it at once. No Damascene explosions of light. No storms of dry ice. No two-way mirrors. Just a Manwess Gas report.

As he looked up, large flakes of damp snow started to spatter the windows. Perhaps sleet and snow would punctuate the rest of his life? It had snowed some thirty years ago as his mother's coffin was lowered in gravel-strewn clay? His father had never confronted the truth right up to the funeral oration, as if an ungrateful sheep had failed her overworked shepherd by yielding to cancer. Today this same identical snow proved nothing had changed, except the angle from which it's observed. Everyone went from cradles to graves via puberty, Income Tax, and National Insurance, through Zimmer frames to the grave. Now someone's career was in his own hands. A muffled phone started to bleep, faintly and patiently. It grew increasingly fretful.

Verity sounded surprisingly calm. "Hi Gary. Wow, contacting you! It's like swimming through batter, getting fricasseed in olive oil, then caramelised in boiled maple syrup."

Vee thought in tastebuds tuned to perfection. This way she'd created a comfortable lifestyle and complete satisfaction. Why, if she could sniff out a trace of ground pepper, couldn't she distinguish a financial scam? Maybe a hint of arrowroot here? The faintest whiff of fresh chilli? One single molecule of salt? Seafoods and shellfish, fungi or herbs? Yet there she was, reading him lists of new contracts and schedules without any sense of their danger.

He'd warned her that showbiz was showbiz. She'd not listened. He'd explained how remorseless it was, subject to markets and fashions. Now she was casually joking about handover meetings and fancy new management teams. Where would their family fit in her schedules? As for Mark and Rachel, he suspected their future included Roseanne.

"Aw come on Gary!" Vee was sounding outraged. "Don't exaggerate! My college plays ball, and anyway, momma's here now. The kid's'll be fine. An' my company's so excited. Hey, more to the point, what about you?

You've made our decision? Is it Three Sisters or Cherry Orchard? Come on, Roseanne's dying to know. She's telling all our friends on Long Island."

Garrick listened he mouthed, "Sorry!" to Abigail, pointing at his watch. She tiptoed across to the window, wiping it clear with her sleeve. Sodium lighting spilled over the street. She looked down and gave a quick discreet wave.

Vee was sounding perplexed. "Hello? What's with you, Gary? Speak up?"

He tried cupping the phone in his hand. "Everything's fine, but I'm in the middle of holding an interview and . . ."

Her hanging up did not help. Verity was cuisine-in-the-sky while he was palmed off with her Chekhov crusade. Didn't she know she had problems herself? Cooking was already passé. Her video series would never take off. She'd been conned and she'd be let down with a crash. Loving her was a problem, but when the moving walkway speeds up, you run damn fast Or jump off.

Other things would all work out, thanks to Anton Pavlovitch Chekhov, patron saint of survivors; third son of Pavel Yegorovitch Chekhov and his wife Evgeniya Morozova (whose name Garrick knew only too well). Their laughter was mingled with tears. 'Ivanov', 1887; 'The Seagull', 1896; 'Uncle Vanya', 1899; 'Three Sisters', 1901; 'The Cherry Orchard', 1904 . . . all brilliant plays. Anton's first meeting with Olga Knipper was reminiscent of Garrick's first meeting with Vee at the theatre ('King Lear', as it happened, in the West End). Their greatest achievements were Rachel and Mark. Their kids would love Aladdin or Cinderella but be bored silly by Chekhov. So, maybe in the same way as Garrick was reliving his father's mistakes, the kids should avoid repeating his.

As Abby looked down from the window, Stacey looked up and waved back. A few moments later, somebody tapped at their door.

Brinkhouse Center was crowded. Arthur was ill at ease. Bowling alleys were more typically Eddie. He felt underdressed in shirt sleeves, and naked without his wool jacket. He stuffed his crested silk tie in his shirt front. The rumbling of bowls and the clatter of tenpins annoyed him. The heating was too oppressive. (For God's sake, it was some 28°C, and around five degrees outside!). His belly was overlapping his waistband. He hated uncontrolled public exposure. Now he was starting to sweat. So much for public relations. He did not want to be caught out.

'Piazza Park' was not Arthur's choice. 'Amusements' were a misnomer and 'Ten Pin Alley' was hell. It had all the charm of a motorway stop. Unemployed youths in check shirts and leathers puffed cigarette stubs as pensioners plotted sedition in corners. This was no place for discussion let alone serious business. The rattle of skittles was punctuated by yells. Bending self-consciously forward on his right knee, taking aim, Arthur felt a sharp pain. The bowl spun from his hand and rumbled off down the long alley. His last three pins remained standing, then Arthur Ruddock collapsed.

"Whose damn-fool idea was it?" Arthur shifted his weight on the bench. "My poor bloody back! This in't no game for left-handers." And what, he thought, if local journalists saw him?

Kevin Bremner stared out of slats at dark snow. "At least it's better than freezing in boardrooms and talking about that damn theatre. The snag with you, Arthur, is you're not bloody fit."

"I've been around in my time."

"Oh aye?" Kevin was Eddie's close contact. "Can you give us their names?"

As everyone laughed, Gupta smoothed his moustache and leaned forward. "You can trust us, Arthur. What's the full score?" Then that high-pitched giggle of his. "You might have got sons you know nothing about".

"We're here to discuss the Marina. We need to co-opt some more names."

Kevin nodded. "Well Eddie's suggesting Sean Daly. He's got ideas for that theatre site. He's worked in Preston and Leeds so he'll bring experience. No objections? Right! Done!"

"Hang on. Hang on." Arthur steepled his chin on his thick, bony fingers. "I am proposing young de Vries .That's George de Vries, son of our Lady Peggy." All four looked taken aback. "Only as an observer of course. He's heir to half the land round here, and his mother's on our theatre committee .The point is, before long George will be running the trust, so I'm suggesting a purely informal arrangement. Officially he's underage, so nothing official, okay. 'Committed Onlooker' status maybe? A simple ad hoc arrangement bearing in mind his future position." He examined their startled reactions. "Listen. This lad's got business sense. We'd best have him aboard from the start." Arthur panned round their expressions, "We're in line for full 'city' status. We need youth. We can't stick to rulebooks when no-one else does. Trust me."

Stacey's arrival out of the blue took Garrick by surprise. It didn't seem appropriate. The interview was meant to be private, and he sensed she'd be a distraction.

"Scuse me, like, I'm Abby's friend. Hope you don't mind? It's lovely to meet you. Can we look round?" Stacey winked back at Abby. "Please? I've only ever been to a panto. And I'll not get another chance?" He thought she'd fluttered her lashes too. "Can we go stand on the stage? Please? That'd be awesome."

Once Garrick's interview was disturbed, a tour might be helpful. It might clear the air. Professional standards could still be maintained. There was nothing to lose by showing an applicant round. Of course he'd ask the girlfriend to leave. On their way downstairs he collected keys from Phyllis's desk.

'STAGE DOOR' it stated in red, 'NO ENTRY'. The heavy, steel pass-door guarded prohibited zones, and he felt he was flirting with rules. Even as he turned the key, the mechanism appeared to resist. But at a firm push, the door opened wide, then thudded shut behind them. He switched on the maintenance lights.

Out on the bare stage, echoes spiralled off into space. Its back wall crumbled like ancient ramparts. Behind it, the Norston Canal loomed only metres beyond: its crystalline outline merged into mildew and bricks, where

Celts, Romans, Angles and Danes were stacked into layer upon layer like archaeological detritus. Abby and Stacey exchanged disappointments.

They moved like trespassers, picking between contractor's tools. Darkness and dampness clung to the skin. The girls were bemused and uncertain as Garrick talked on and on about drama. As their attentions wandered, Garrick interspersed technical explanations with impressions of long-dead cabaret stars, but Abigail must have sensed weakness. She'd take on mock-Stacey accents, safe behind Stacey's persona. Who cared a damn about Chekhov, Shakespeare or Garrick? This wasn't Abigail's dream. Then Stacey pointed up into darkness and shuddered.

A rickety ladder skewed sharply up, disappearing into the flies. A trickle of snow blew through gaps in the roof as Coleridge repossessed Garrick's mind. High above them, coils of rope swung like a seagoing clipper hung with furled sails. This was a grounded galleon awaiting the tide, anticipating Westerlies. Its lines of perspective converged into rigging. Its geometry swayed. Spars and ribs creaked in anticipation. Decks slowly heaved in the tide. In the luminous shadows an ancient mariner watched . . .

Garrick began to explain. "Up there's what's called the flies. Those ropes were once manned by sailors called flymen. Men with great heads for heights. It's old marine technology, see. Counterweights plus sheer brute strength." And he laughed. "Sorry girls. Too dangerous for us."

But Abigail didn't laugh. The silver-white scars on her arms were provoked: she treasured their almost invisible mesh. With short clipped hair there was no going back. Like circumcision, adults slashed your childhood away. So she fixed her eyes upwards and started to climb. If healing could be so intense and profound, then danger had to be courted.

"Hey! Stop that! Come back!"

She could hear Garrick shouting; ignored him; kept climbing. Against better judgment he followed.

Rung after rung the two scrambled and swayed between quivering timbers, onwards and upwards, emerging in flurries of cobwebs through a rickety trapdoor. Below them, distances doubled and tripled. From Escher distortions Stacey looked up and screamed, suddenly trite and diminished, but the pocket-handkerchief-sized stage kept endlessly shrinking while above them a barely visible grid spanned the whole width of the stage. Ancient backcloths hung as becalmed as great canvas sails. Ghostly. Abandoned. Before Garrick could control himself, Coleridge intervened. This was a clipper adrift in the Arctic between waves and clouds, between fact and fiction. Gustave Doré's illustrations heaved with subliminal fears like the Ancient Mariner's mission. The slightest cough could blast them all out to sea.

Here Abby could be what she liked. An acrobat on a trapeze. A showgirl. A video star. Rows of counterweight sacks swung like corpses from gallows. Cobwebs shimmered in pencils of light. And far down below, Stacey was being upstaged. The climb-down meant literally returning to earth. No more fizz. No red velvet drapes, thigh boots, fishnet, or split silken panties. No silver-ringed nipples nor clitoral studs. No longer a video star. Gravity had intervened. The ground was immovable; the floorboards too solid. There was dust in her eyes and hair. She realised then what she'd done, but who cared?

She knew she had not got the job. It only meant telling Jilly Craske she had failed. No-one would be surprised.

At the top of Church Close, beneath Arabica's new decor, Louise Roberts was checking her watch. Melting snow had begun to re-freeze. Even outside her own club she felt ill-at-ease after dark. There had been riots here in the thirties with strikers chanting slogans, waving banners. None of that could happen again but history refused to stand still. The cotton industry collapsed overnight, all manufacturing folded, then housing prices rocketed until offices became loft apartments. Those once great factories like Hi-Fells Textiles, Slumberland, and Bolton Brakes, were decaying by the neglected canals. Only demolition was thriving. Everywhere Eddie Craig's spreading wastelands distorted local planning rules. If he could do it, others could. Louise was a venture capitalist too, so why was she finding it tough? It seemed that as the Earth warmed up, Manchester turned dereliction to cash, while Leeds spawned millionaire pads. As always Norston was bucking the trend by flirting with failure. Unless this boom was really a bust?

Louise was getting colder and angry. Wind-chill made waiting worse, and Celsius didn't help; Fahrenheit was never this cold. Her silver-trimmed Jules spangled dress was scarcely protected by a Lucio Semprini mock mink. She stamped in her La Fontaine Slingbacks and shivered. Her club's modest Neons glowed. This was the downside of glamour, but what people needed was off-the-peg dazzle. She couldn't even rely on her family; they'd always somehow let her down. Nor was Jilly much help. Being female in Norston meant banging your head against double-glazed triple-glass ceilings. But would muggers know her diamonds weren't real? Louise was wishing she'd brought her mobile because everything seemed stacked against her, Carlos included.

She'd married a good-looking nerd for his technological talk. He'd put his faith in electronics, convincing her to press the right buttons and everything would lock itself up. She backed into a recess for shelter. Carlos was no help. He could not provide security systems let alone advise their own daughter. As for his brilliant touch-screen alarm? It refused to let her back in!

"Security system?" she'd tell him, "It's shit! Your codes! Your lasers! Your sodding ridiculous keyboards!" All Carlos needed to do, was turn up as required.

She felt for her pocket alarm, as smooth and cool as an old-fashioned lipstick, as warm as a mini-vibrator. Its ear-slitting wail could wake a whole district. It was then she noticed a police car nudge round a corner and roll suspiciously past, its occupants twisting towards her.

She wanted to explain. She was Mrs. Louise Sarah Roberts anxiously awaiting her husband. And she knew very important people in town. For God's sake, did she look like a hooker? As she pulled her collar up round her ears, her mobile bleeped.

Abigail sounded drunk. "Mum? Where are you? I been waiting for ages. I can't wait any longer."

"What about me? I'm locked outside my own club. And no sign of your dad."

"But I got it!" Abigail screeched, "I did. I seen him. I got it!"

"Oh?" Louise looked frantically round. "Got what?"

Still shocked by her episode high on that stage, Abigail stood at the bus stop, clutching a takeaway coffee. Inside the local TELEGLO windows, banks of pictures moved in unison behind a heavy steel grill. Their images flickered in sync.

"Manwess Sponsored News. Energy you can rely on," proclaimed moving graphics across exploding fountains. Subtitles announced more factory closures, government statements, hospital changes, new council projects, and football sex'n'drugs scandals. The windowful of wide plasma screens repeated them ad infinitum. Abigail couldn't resist.

Cut Cut – Zoom Zoom – Wipe Wipe – faces and images came and went. As Abby watched, the screens turned into faces of clocks. Bong! Bong! Bong! went the silence. All the screens chimed in tacit agreement, then zoomed giddily into the Newsdesk. "Local News On The Hour". "Local News Headlines" the subtitles said as Abigail pressed her face to the grill. The square-jawed newscaster mimed a succession of lip-curling feats against visual clichés of Brinkside Gas before cutting to a full-screen face. Its caption read "Garrick Jones. New producer at Norston's Majestic Theatre" Except this wasn't the Garrick she'd met, but smoother and younger; its dark wavy hair curled at the ends, its eyes crinkled up

When Abigail reached 'Crowning Glory' she found Jilly Craske in a navy-blue suit, golden beads, and earrings like miniature chandeliers. Grains of powder clung to her lip gloss and dusted her faintest moustache.

"Well love?" Jilly studied her latest creation. "Let's hear the good news."

"But didn't you just see him? On telly? Just now?"

"Let's celebrate first." Jilly pulled Abigail up to the light and examined her complexion. "We're blood-sisters, right? Or hope to die." She tried not sound too triumphant. "I've got a vested interest in you. From now on, it's medicated creams and loads and loads of Vitamin C. No getting zits at that theatre!" She paused and grinned. "Like I said, it's part-shares together. Partners." She giggled. "Like I'm your sponsor and . . ." She stepped back, looking puzzled. "Well?" But Abigail remained stony faced, compressing her lips to a line as Jilly went pale. "You did get that job?"

Abigail punched the air! Both of them whirled around laughing, then Abby told of that paper dart in the blizzard, and both girls being taken backstage, and how she'd climbed up into the flies. How Garrick was great, but Stacey was scared.

"Hang on – who's Stacey?"

Jilly Craske's smile seemed to tighten then fade. She kicked away tufts of dead hair.

Her fleshy eyes narrowed. "You keep saying Stacey – Not her? – My Stacey?" She pointed at garbage bags squatting like somnolent pigs by the door. "Well, that's my little Miss Contract Cleaning. Is she your Stacey? That lazy cow?"

In the long silence, snow turned into slush and melt-water gurgled down drains.

"Anyrate, love, I've ordered a fancy new frontage. Yes. It'll have fully adjustable vents, special bonded safety glass plus Ultraviolet Filter 6. We'll need some big publicity then. That's where you come in. All you do is hand out my cards to the Stars, then you and me, we're partners. Our deal. They'll want their hair-styling here!" Jilly was loosening a notch on her belt. "It's special discounts for actors, but free to Big Stars, and I'll . . ."

Outside, a black Ford Mondeo straddled the No Parking lines, lights ablaze, engine racing, hazard lights flashing. The deep thrub of its multi-decibel bass shook Crowning Glory's discoloured windows and overrode the beat of the heart. Immediately Jilly snapped into action, bundling Abigail out.

As Jilly Craske scrambled aboard, the car's engine roared and tyres spun free. It swerved into traffic, leaving a trail of burnt rubber because Thomas knew people couldn't be trusted; his rivals, contestants, opponents! Speed was about taking risks, being proud of a thousand near-misses. Once in that car his senses were heightened. Life came in an amphetamine rush. Any change of perfume, different coat, even a brooch rarely worn; he noticed them at once. He knew how men like Garrick worked. He knew Jilly revelled in being flattered and groomed, forever testing his limits. He knew her like the back of his hand. Jealousy was physical pain. He stamped the pedal into the floor. G-forces tugged. With every change of gear he felt the Y-chromosomes fire.

The road surged beneath them. Rain bullets slammed at the windscreen. Jilly tugged at her seat belt, feeling waves of sickness. Secrets must always be kept and worrying symptoms ignored, so closing her eyes, she let Garrick fill her unconscious mind, escaping Earth's gravitational forces

Arthur's hippopotamus yawn was smothered with large podgy fingers. The sub-committee had gone into auto. Whiskey Macs hadn't helped. They should be discussing the theatre by now. What was needed was interlocking solutions, not quizzes and puzzles. It was bad enough handling Garrick. The rota was endless with most speakers missing the point. Even though the result was foregone, every idiot needed their say.

To speed things up he'd offered pre-packaged solutions. Based on research, these should have gone through on the nod. "Knowledge is everything," he'd told young George de Vries, "And absolute knowledge empowers. Remember that." On top of the Agenda he'd laboriously written in pencil, "Closure of matter before 6.30 latest." Only a simple yes-vote was needed. He yawned again. Then again.

Beside him George was drawing a long spiralling shape which ended in a forked tongue; a contorted left handed snake. This didn't need psychology. Arthur understood why. This world wasn't designed for left-handed people. Some physicist claimed the universe always moved clockwise, so prejudice was sown at creation itself. Hence dexterity was part of the language and sinister was a threat. A right-handed cosmos challenged both himself and George. Young George had inherited the rest from his mother, but Arthur could identify. He often remembered his first meeting Peggy just before the death of her husband. That was nearly eighteen years ago, and like everything else it happened by chance. Months later Lord Randolph collapsed while unveiling a memorial stone at a golf course, unaware Peggy was pregnant. Now the late baronet's name was carved on the theatre extension. He must have needed immortality badly.

"And regarding reopening that theatre . . ." someone said, and Arthur came back to life. "The Majestic needs a complete overhaul," Mrs. Scoular continued, "We all of us remember the work of our dear, lovely Rex Schulman with all his delightful innovations. I'm sure our new incumbent, the forward-thinking Garrick Jones will . . ."

"Point of order!" Like a flock of late butterflies, all their paperwork fluttered then stopped.

Arthur waved his Agenda. "Theatre Policy is not on this schedule. We are discussing Public Maintenance Grant. That's four acres of prime central site. So let's set a good example. We've got a young observer here today."

Awaking next morning, Garrick felt chewed then sicked up. Were there iced rocks in his pillow? He felt rootless and cold. Then he was again back home and there was Verity, lips puckered, so close he could taste her. As he responded, he became aware of flashing lights through paper-thin curtains. 'PATEL & Co.' 'BORKOWSKI'S BAR' and 'HUSSEIN BROS NEWSAGENTS'. Garrick continued to drift in and out sleep as slowly his room decomposed, then morphed into a glittering coach trundling little Rachel and Mark through forests of nightmarish finger-nailed trees. Then those faces; Phyllis and Arthur, like twin figureheads on a huge clipper ship carving through glacier ice as if . . .

"Ray-dee-oh Norston FM! It's your friendly station right here on the dial!"

Somehow he managed to scramble from bed. Yesterday had not been a success. Phyllis had said Arthur Ruddock would make all the major decisions. Policies weren't Garrick's concern. He should "reconcile himself to limited objectives". In other words, the panto came first. Chekhov was not on the menu. He'd signed all his choices away. That had played hell with his conscience. Should he tell Vee? Or wait till it was all fait accompli, then tell her?

"Darling, great news! I've got this fantastic deal. I get to do one panto, but in exchange, I get to do all of Chekhov. Great!"

Edwin had been ambivalent too, but that was Garrick's father's style. Hypocrisy redefined as high art: a teetotaller who classified vodka as a 'medicinal cure'; a pacifist using a cane on his son; a saint who could never resist a temptation? Chekhov's own solution was easy. By becoming a doctor he'd faced his own contradictions head-on. Not that this staunched the arterial blood which drenched sanatorium pillows. 'Physician heal thyself' But not without some outside help. Would Abigail fit the bill?

"Ray-dee-oh Norston! FM!" that goddam jingle persisted, "Start the day with your friendly station. Hi there! Keep smiling! Keep opp-tee-mis-tique! But first, Weather News on the quarter. Another grey morning with cold winds and showers . . ."

Bakers Row was fighting back with daily tramplings downstairs followed by slamming front doors. Garrick noticed a gleam of bright print on his doormat. A chilly breeze blew round his feet. Postcards must have arrived while he dozed.

Both his children had made their own cards. Joyous handwriting meandered over blank spaces. Rachel's green, cauliflower tree faced a bright yellow sun. Markie's London bus careered diagonally backwards in red. Their version of the American flag in purple and lime on squared paper was pinned on the wall by his bed. Previous drawings depicted trees with dozens of tiny green hands. He delighted in dubious grammar, their wondrously fanciful spellings, their hilarious observations. Best of all was Momma and Poppa holding vast sunflowers like peasant art. Chekhov would have approved. Today he'd have been over one hundred and forty.

Finally Garrick got through. Surprisingly Rachel answered in person. Too cautiously, he thought. Oddly formal and tactful. Their postcards, she said, were grandma's idea, adding they were just off to Knightsbridge, then to Piccadilly for lunch.

"And sure, momma's fine," she admitted.

"And Markie? Up to his usual tricks?"

"Uh huh. He's fine." In the background someone called out about taxis.

"Then what about you? How's dance classes, eh? Started piano lessons yet? And when's Half Term? It won't be long before Christmas."

"I'm fine too." She sounded patronising. "We all are."

"Darling, I miss you. I look at your photos and think, wow!" which failed to gain a response. "You must have some news, surely?"

"We–e–ll everyone's fine. And the food's fine."

"You're sure there's no problem? Is mummy very busy? With this new job of hers? Has she been to lots of meetings? All you need say is yes or no. I mean, I bet she's been working late every night? Poor mummy. Working all hours of the clock? Staying away? Overnight?"

"We're all fine." Each word was painstakingly chosen. "The home help's fine as well."

Home help? Assisting Roseanne? That was letting a cat out the bag. Censorship and brainwashing worked. He'd brought them up almost single-handedly, sharing their thoughts and their fears while playing the house-husband role. So, reading between the lines, every bugger was fine, including a helper he'd never been consulted about.

"Daddy. Are you coming home?" Rachel whispered, "When?"

He was caught on the hop. "Soon as daddy can but you don't have . . ."

"Sorreeee! Gotta go." With that she rang off, leaving him holding their postcards.

"Ray-dee-oh Noors-ton!!" crooned his speakers. "News about news! On the hour! First, a quick time check . . ."

Phyllis would at the office, and waiting. She'd know he was late. He had to get moving. Lukewarm water dripped from the green-crusted taps and seeped down the multi-crazed basin. The water was barely lukewarm. He'd just doused his face when there came that familiar rap on the door.

Half-naked, wrapped in his towel, Garrick peered outside. On his door-sill lay the free local paper. His bionic neighbour had presumably scuttled away on his metal extrusions. Garrick's wet fingerprints were spreading into the newsprint before he noticed the headline:

"Norston's Dramatic Renaissance," it said, "See page 5."

He thumbed clumsily through. Where were his picture and quotes? Instead the report referred to a new museum extension, the restoration of Beverley Crescent, and the funding of a local Youth Orchestra, as if the Majestic Theatre did not exist. However as first prize in their lotto, Garsdale Marts were offering, "A trip to see Lady Windermere's Fan in London's famous West End, with an overnight stay in a top Mayfair hotel". His own drama class advert should be on their back page as part of the Mercury's deal. So far he had not received one application. Apparently Rex Schulman used to cram students in by the dozen. But Garrick's advert was not there. He wondered what Vee would have done.

"Hi, you've got through to Verity Jones," replied the digitised voice when he phoned, "Please leave her a message after the tone . . ."

Not 'Garrick and Verity Jones' anymore. She had changed their joint message already. History was editing him out. He spoke straight after the bleep:

"Verity darling, hi. This is me Gary? Your husband? Remember? That prat who's up here in Norston? Think cherry orchards? Right? And sisters? An uncle? No? How about a seagull then? . . . Yes! You've got it! I'm that guy who used to prepare the kids' breakfasts, bath them, and push buggies round. Oh yes, and clean up whenever Scooby shat on that carpet. So, tell me, please, what's going on. The kids might be ill. You might be in hospital. For Christ's sake, Vee, give us a call. Love you honey." He blew a kiss and set off to face a new day of auditions.

Reactions back at Lancaster Gate suggested his message hit home. Soon Roseanne and Verity squabbled, then squabbled again. Now mother and daughter moped, while both children squatted in front of their plasma digital screen with sound at full blast as Burpo the frog was being swallowed by Slimmo the ravenous snake. Roseanne slammed the kitchen door. Venetian blinds trembled. Slimmo was joined by Dick Rat as Burpo was sicked up, unharmed. Rachel turned sound to maximum-plus, forcing Roseanne to shout.

"Hell's teeth, Vee! You give the guy every chance. It's our plan he's carrying out, thanks to you. Without us Morozoffs, he'd be where? Nowhere! No more achieving. No Chekhov. No status. He'd still be house-husbanding here in this kitchen."

Verity finished slicing the parsnips. "Sure, and I'm up to Here!"

"We can both figure out what he'd be doing! That doesn't have status! Least not in Massachusetts. Not in Connecticut and even less, Vermont. Folk have standards there."

Verity diced carrots, viciously chopping them into paper-thin discs and scooping them into a dish. "You don't understand. We miss each other."

Roseanne rolled her eyes. "Honey, have you ever known me be unfair? Sure he's got points, but did he lead you on? Or did he lead you on? You never saw that till me. Showgirls. Strippers. Lowlife jokers. Call that being creative? An artist? It's like you can't see what was staring you straight in the face. Two kids later, you reckon he's changed?"

"That's not fair. He's fully committed to Chekhov."

"Him? Bigtime theatre producer? Gary? Come on!" She gripped her daughter's shoulder. "You're the one sustaining this marriage. Aided by me.

And you and me's a team. I'm not some kind of stereotype. I'm the proto-feminist here, and that's why us Morozovs migrated to Boston. To celebrate Chekhov's ideals. Oh, and one more thing . . ."

Verity wrestled herself free. "You mean there's something else?"

"Sure. Why not? . Who first taught you to cook? Mmm? Not your poppa, stuck on his Scotch-Irish butt. May God have mercy on his soul. Blinnies and borsch are handed-down arts. You only get that through the blood."

Verity sliced away, reducing thick leeks to green roundels. "So that's why out I'm cooking all day, then always cooking back home!" She slammed the green coins in a pan and turned round. "Okay mom, I'm grateful to you. Okay? Satisfied?"

Roseanne watched the water boil up, controlling an intense satisfaction.

Garrick's daily trek extended no matter how much he shortened his route. Each day more contractor's vans and trailers parked round the theatre, with company passes wedged into windscreens. Apparently all parking laws were suspended. The Manwess occupation had turned into a fixture; a state within a state. And Vee still had not called him back.

Meanwhile pile-drivers battered Eddie Craig's site, and operators worked pneumatic drills. Not long ago steam-engines would have rocked these very same streets lined with mills and weaving sheds. These same granite sets would have rung to horseshoes, iron wheels, and metal-tipped clogs, but one din merely replaces another. Was he meant to hold auditions, let alone rehearse in this din? There were dozens of actors expected. He'd file an official complaint.

"Hi Meester Jones!" A boiler-suit topped with a Manwess helmet waylaid him. "We carryin' out more checks. Spess-ee-men samples," and he waved an electronic device, "Me an' Mr Kamara." The colleague waved back. "Him an'me from Montego Bay. Via Freetown, Africa, see. I'm Mister O'Casey. Remember?" The engineers held out welcoming hands.

Garrick tried to wave them away. "Sorry, I've got vital auditions."

"No problem." O'Casey maintained his universal expression. "We jus'employees. But Gas? Now, it known as 'volatile substance'. Like, combine 'im wit' oxy-gen in an enclose space an' you got real problems, okay?" He pointed out his ID card on its coloured ribbon slung round his neck. "An' like I bin tellin' your good lady, we got 'statutory duty on the public highway'. Out 'ere,". He waved expansively round. "All this constitute 'public highway', what wi' all the demolishin' and re-routin' goin' on, everyone cuttin' big holes in the tarmac!" He grinned. "Beside, we got rights in law not a lot o' people know 'bout. But tings soon 'appen, jus' you see An' till we meet again, be it in heaven or be it in hell, or some far-flung universe where yonder stars do gleam!" The gas board official carefully spread Garrick's palm, and gave it a welcoming slap. "Lucky for you 'bout the ground soil. It carboniferous limestone wi' plenty o'clay Else, hey man you got a canal down your vaults wi' twenty million litres of water!"

Phyllis was upstairs waving at Garrick. It seemed Arthur had failed to pass on any warnings or ask for suspension of works. A generator started to throb. Moments later, vibration increased. Pandemonium emerged from the stairwell, upwards through woodwork and bricks. The whole building shook as Public Utilities took their revenge. Excavations continued as foundations convulsed in the archaeological depths. On reaching Phyllis's office, Garrick watched as workmen rampaged below.

"Garrick? Oh Garrick. Thank God!" Phyllis was hoarse in the background. "Your . . . your appointments. They're here. For auditions! Yes, and someone from CTS Carpets Plus a special delivery? Plus who-knows-who arriving on spec!" She thrust phone and documents at him.

In these narrow circles news must have spread and mutated. Worse, he'd agreed to see any agents' suggestions. Net result: actors were arriving from every point of the compass convinced he was casting for Chekhov. No doubt Roseanne would be thrilled. It was just the renaissance the Morozoffs wanted. "The Apotheosis of Chekhov" And no mention of Cinderella.

Heading through the rows of dark stalls, Garrick saw dozens of hopefuls, feet up on seat-backs, crammed into dimly-lit rows, swathed in scarves, gloves, and overcoats, reminiscing about other great casting sessions. The Haymarket (vintage 1987). The Royal Shakespeare 1994. The National 1998. Her Majesty's 1999. The Royal Court 2001. The Duke of York's 2002. Now even more were arriving, all excited and hopeful. It was frightening. He thought of Verity floundering out of her depth. Critics would be ruthless. Soon she'd be flayed alive and dismembered. Columnists kill. She'd never cope when she'd always depended on him. She was a simple amateur in a tough commercial world. An innocent. He knew he'd have to step in to save her.

She was already having problems at home. She'd said she'd caught their kids watching videos down in their den well past bedtime. Girls in G-strings! Boys in posing pouches! A stripshow loaned by their school friends! There was enough smut in a pantomime script. They'd have Roseanne descend as the Puritan Backlash shocked by Europe's decline. She'd blame British culture and paedophile trash. Vee was accusing him too: he could tell by the sulk in her voice that he was the one who had failed.

At least for today, he'd have to be tactful. Ugly Stepsisters and frolicking Dames would stay in the wings. Once the cast had signed up he'd use the same actors for panto and Chekhov. It was as simple as that. Their carrot would be 'The Three Sisters'. They'd hear about the pantomime later. By holding auditions directly on-stage Garrick sat staring the orchestra pit in the mouth, examining its black velvety tongue, sensing its yellow bared teeth.

"Ladies and gentlemen!" he shouted, "Welcome! I'm Garrick Jones but you are all potential stars!" And everyone clapped.

Garrick meant to be fair. On the other hand, with everyone trekking to Norston and finding somewhere to park, forget Russian classics. Work was work. They'd sign whatever dotted line they were given, just as he had done himself.

First to perform was a gawky young comedian. Others followed, stumbling, mumbling, shouting, declaiming, as Abigail slipped in through the shadows and crouched out of sight to observe. She thought of those black and white kings in Jilly Craske's salon, and wondered. From Soap stars to Film stars, 'Celebrity' was in the air. Some recited whole speeches from Chekhov or Strindberg. No stand-ups. No gags. No comic pantomime songs. It felt like Championship Finals, and Abigail made mental notes to tell Jilly as one Shakespeare followed another. Then came a chunk of 'King Lear'.

The actress performing suddenly stopped in mid-sentence and stared .Everyone followed her look. Out of the dress circle darkness, big solid hands compressed thin air into slow handclaps. A bulky figure dragged itself to full height and leaned over the parapet rail.

"Hey-up!" Arthur called nonchalantly down. "Sorry lads and lassies, but am I missing the gags? Can't hear your punchlines up here. Cinderella's the show! We need some slapstick and honest, traditional smut! Thank God for the double-entendre." Then he was gone.

James Carr was well-known, undeterred, and supremely conscious of profile. Publicity shots emphasised an aquiline nose and long silvered hair. He seemed to materialise centre-stage, announcing a speech from Richard II, then slumped, as if all his tendons had failed. His sonorous voice left a dark stain on the air.

".And yet not so . . ." His voice came like echoes from dreams. "For what can we bequeath, save our deposed bodies to the ground?"

Abigail lurked at the back of the stalls. Jilly would have to hear about this. If a hair stylist could change your appearance with just a few snips, imagine what acting could do. It was weird. Biology classes reduced living to diagrams, but according to Stacey it was really about menstruation, body hair, dieting, headaches and contraception. But this? As Abby edged further forward for views of the stage she felt a tight grip at her elbow. A leathery hand clamped her mouth.

Out in the corridor she found herself face to face with Bert. He took her hand and formally kissed it. Carnivorous teeth trimmed his tannin-stained grin.

Bert signalled her to follow. "No offence meant, but we needs urgent help."

A heavy door thudded behind them as Abigail followed in shock. A narrow brick passage led to an arch, barred with a studded door, which opened onto a dark vaulted space captioned 'WORKSHOPS' and 'SILENCE'. A cardboard Lancastrian Rose swung from a nail. Ancient machinery jutted from red and white sawdust. Overhead chains cast multi-sourced shadows, and circular saws bared their irregular teeth like some X-rated movie. A time warp was closing behind her. Beside a crumbling dartboard were cutouts of mammary glands, their nipples heightened in Biro. Another nude crouched doggy-style, buttocks spread, vulva spattered with dart-holes.

Bert produced a large cardboard folder, loosened its red satin ribbons to release sheets of white cartridge with networks of gaunt graphite lines. Their geometry evoked his whole lifetime, his plans, elevations, projections. This was the practical logic of Euclid. He'd started aged fifteen. Together with the team they'd survived the flamboyant Rex Schulman. But here was Garrick, so where did Abigail stand?

"United we stand. Divided we fall. The law of the playground. Know what I mean? It's workers of the world unite."

As Garrick returned to his office after auditions, he casually chanced to look out And he blinked. New trenches had appeared overnight. Their territories were expanding; this was colonisation. A sharp rap at his door and Phyllis's head appeared. Her smile was barely skin deep:

"You've got rehearsals all next week, but Arthur says we can't afford to stay dark. His plan is renting out the main theatre. Stand-up comedians have booked from next week." Adding before Garrick could comment. "And yes, our whole committee's in favour and Oh, and another thing." Phyllis seemed to examine the flooring. "It's probably not important .but the other day I came across a torn photo, which I happened to put it in my diary for safety. Now it's gone. It's just disappeared." She shrugged. "And then today Someone dropped this in." She wafted a sealed envelope around like a bait. "No doubt a admirer."

It was addressed to him with printed full postcode. It looked official and formal. He suspected the council again. Inside he found an A4 sheet neatly folded in three.

"That Abigail Roberts is trouble" it stated, "She's too young to be trusted. For your own safety do not sign her up. Hire someone else!"

Stacey was trying to stay calm but the wind chilled every pore of her skin. Bars and clubs clustered Station Road where all the winds swing northwest from Iceland via Ireland, before being funnelled upstream. She edged behind a column and shivered.

Who dresses for gales? Who wears layers of jump-suits? Or thick thermal socks? So where's the advantage in doing two jobs? The only reason for skivvying and cleaning was it bought status, ready cash, and friends. But since Abby got involved with that theatre Stacey was losing out, like a light without shade or mirror without a reflection. And why share your billing when you could star in your own personal movie?

"Understan' my prop-osition! This ain't no im-position!" rose through grills from the basement and spilled out round her feet. She tried not to shiver but white satin ski-coats and knee-length boots were no help against hypothermia; even her nail extensions were shrinking. Stacey tugged up her collar. The music continued to taunt her. Downstairs, lads would be strutting their stuff, shaking dreadlocks and gold-plated chains, acrid with tobacco and beer. Abigail was missing all this, and Garrick was just an old man.

"Understan' my prop-osition! This ain't no im-position!"
Me an' you fit one po-sition! You's my bitch on one condition!
You come quick in my co-ition! Plenty plenty rep-etition!"

When at last Abby arrived, they walked down the luminous staircase through incandescent green hoops to the basement, linking arms. Mini-spots twirled like galactic searchlights spinning round magnetic black-holes. The dance floor rose up to meet them. Here you didn't need pills. Alcohol would ferment in the blood. This was a shared but internalised space. Anyone could be themselves.

"Don't fancy yours!" Stacey was pointing.

A line-up of spotty-faced boys gyrated as music pounded the eardrums. Stacey contemptuously pulled up her skirt, stretching the bra-top taut to her nipples. As Abby noticed Stacey's glittering hands, her own fingers looked suddenly naked. Beneath flimsy sleeves the scars on her arms started to burn as Stacey's aura expanded.

Jilly Craske was looking each way down the street, waiting as usual outside the salon, taking some refuge in shadows and hoping not to be seen. The Christmas streetlights started to swing, agitating long shadows. She hadn't caught sight of Garrick all day. Her billowing overall caught the wind, dragging her sideways, but still she kept her head down, afraid she was even more heavy. If this were the menopause, it was unacceptably early, but hopefully no-one had noticed. Other injuries showed. Things could no longer drift. It was time for a new resolution. She would rejoin the Friends of the Theatre.

Abigail would be overjoyed, she knew that. But Thomas? He was too obsessed with his honour, which meant she had to take risks. Surviving meant facing your fears. She took a deep breath as the darkness began to congeal and shadows solidify round her. As she turned to slip back in, she heard an odd sound. A shuffling? A scuffling sound?

She looked down expecting an animal, but saw two human feet squashed into muddy stilettos. Rising winds tore her expletives away. Caught in the sidelight she froze.

Abigail stared. The hairdresser looked like a cat in the headlights, her face distended, cheeks tautened, eyes puffy, and lips swollen. Before Abigail's eyes she seemed to withdraw like a sea anemone shrinking, then ducked quickly inside.

"No Gary, no! I did try to call back." Verity paced their St. George's Mews home, padding trails into new carpets, "But hey, it's not easy. I've tried. Most times I'm at meetings .planning recipes, deciding on menus, or . . . or . . ."

Little Mark in roller blades was carving furrows into the weave.

Vee clamped a hand firmly over the speaker. "Hey you guys! Don't make momma mad! Get out and play with your sister, okay!" She watched him trundle resentfully out. "Sorry Gary. What was I saying? Most times I'm out working, what with admin, or figuring organisation with Lucy. Or else, I'm out on the road."

By calling his cellphone she avoided embarrassing tangles with Phyllis: even the briefest of queries could stir up a few thousand years. No wonder George Washington quit. That's why she always celebrated Thanksgiving. Her mother was more impatient. She talked about "Gary's one act of atonement". Fulfilling a deal. Like she said, Capitalism was founded on risk, and Gary had so many sins to atone for.

Vee tried loosening the strains in her neck. "I mean, we don't talk, do we? We don't communicate. That's why it's always me calling you."

Whether or not it was strictly correct, it was the psychological truth because words by themselves didn't help; they had to mean something. You could talk turkey with cooks, but discussing kids or Roseanne with Gary, words were interchangeable. Two nations divided by one single language? Hell, that was so true. She let him go on till he paused to take breath.

"Like I was saying, I can't believe this is happening to me, little me. I got my own show! I'm not some kinda media saint. I never expected this much goodwill, or such love. Such caring emotion. I end up feeling a fraud, but you? Well it's okay for you. You've all-time greats on your side. You've got Chekhov and Ibsen pitching for you. You've got quality literature, Gary . . . But me? I've only got Mrs. Beaton."

"Yes, I hear you, Vee. But when they talk that stuff about 'love' .I mean, investors aren't academics. Those guys are dodgy. They've crocodile teeth, and they'll eat you for lunch. You don't seem to get it. It might be a scam."

"But I trusted you. I let you sweep me off my feet. Now you take such a cynical view."

"Vee, it's no fun up here. There's no heating. These buggers drive like maniacs. I'm just a poor pedestrian without so much as a single au pair! It's tough work."

Verity grunted. Gary was on the roll of a lifetime, allowed to be truly creative while she was no more than a craftsman, at best a college researcher. He couldn't resist a snipe at her mother as if she were some kind of threat? Though she was old and defenceless, but her Rostoff lineage led back further than Gary's and to much more distinguished roots. The Rostoffs were right to be proud because 'traces of genius ran in their blood'.

"Gary! I'm working my hands to the bone." From habit she tidied the room as she talked. "That video company's paying me thousands of dollars! With rights it could mount up to hundreds of thousands! Or more! Not counting cookbooks, websites, and all the usual spin-offs. I happened to need an au pair, so the company pays!" She packed toy guns in a box and clamped the lid tightly. "Not that money's important Except as a valuation of worth." She paused to let this sink in.

"Vee. Did I say I've been running auditions? Did I say I've been choosing my cast?"

She caught her reflection and saw an unfamiliar expression and groaned . "I'd audition for Anya myself. I'm very Anya, don't you think?" The reflection smiled in approval. "That's the Russo-American mix. There's a deep well of innocence. We trust a lot. I love hope. I love truth. I love love. I guess I've never grown up."

"Here we've got our backs to the wall." It was time to confess.

"Gary, sometimes cream curdles. Okay. Sometimes gelatines don't set But that doesn't stop us achieving. We don't make excuses in advance. You and Chekhov are my inspiration. It's that combination what gives me my strength."

"Yes but . . ." He took a deep breath before crossing the road. "Listen, I've something urgent to tell you." He protected his phone with both hands. "Things aren't quite not at all as I . . ."

"Gary, I'm so proud of you. You'll overcome that stuff, even if momma swears you'll pack in. You'll prove her wrong, but not for my sake or my momma's. The Rostoffs are nothing. It's you doing this. No, we're all doing this For you!" She could hear him breathing; in the background a police siren wailed. "Okay, tell you what. Let's do a deal. If you cast any big names in 'The Three Sisters' or 'Cherry Orchard', my producer is producing a chat show as well. I'll pass on their names. Okay? It's good for your show, and not only that, we're planning a guest slot for 'Cook And Let Cook' So maybe, just maybe, we'll get those guys onto my show? Is that a deal?"

On screen, a teenage Chinese chef was chopping chicken breasts sprinkled with herbs. 'Quik Wok' said the caption, 'Number 12 in the World's Greatest DIY Takeaway Snacks'.

In Verity's eyes, TV cooking was Drama; visual food was High Art. If he and his wife were competing directly, things could only get worse. When she rang off he disconnected all calls, taking the risk she'd hear about his changed schedule. A cool wind caught at his ears. Above him this very same sky stretched like a polythene dome right back to Lancaster Gate. Could he bounce his thoughts off its surface and connect direct with his kids. Why not? He was half their chromosomes. They shared a mutual code.

Agreeing to teach had meant getting a syllabus planned, so for once in his life Garrick was early. St. Giles's Church Hall was Rex Schulman's regular venue, therefore part of the deal. But Drama classes? With half the actors unemployed? And in such an overcrowded profession?

Garrick should have turned back, but he trudged on between crumbling memorials, clutching his bagful of scripts. Victorian values loomed from the drizzle. 'Step carefully, you tread upon my grave' a paving stone warned. Beyond, terraced streets stacked mile upon mile of blue slate. Was this where his audience lived? Among abandoned mills and factory sheds all intended to last? Their carding, spinning, weaving, and dyeing had been exported all over the empire. Now Eddie Craig's wastelands were too close for comfort.

Garrick had planned on arriving too late, but vacillated, then had second, third, and fourth thoughts, before resolving not to make any decision at all. He tried psyching himself for the lesson as water dripped off the Yew trees. Outside in the porch a Roll of Honour listed "Those who sacrificed their lives in the glorious service of God and Our Country in two Great Wars". Generations of Abbotts, Craigs, Dabinetts, Granfields, Ruddocks, Marsdens and Walkers, all bayoneted, machine-gunned, and gassed. As Garrick let himself in, a blast of cold air swept through the space. Everybody was already waiting. Louise Roberts rushed forward and seized Garrick's hand, hugging him in a clumsy embrace:

"Hello! Welcome!" She gestured the little group closer. "This is Garrick Jones. From the Majestic. As everyone knows he's taking over our dear Rex's classes." She gave him a conspiratorial grimace. "Now we're in his professional hands, because Garrick's producing our panto this year."

"But mainly the Chekhovs!" he added as everyone cheered, "And Ibsens. And Strindbergs. And . . ."

As more new arrivals kept coming he hoped they'd be paying hard cash, because after Lesson One few would return. Most of these were women.

One single exception was a young man who'd brought a comedy script, explaining he performed his own act. More latecomers came drifting in. At the back of the room, framed in a doorway, hovered a woman, pale and overweight. Large furtive eyes flickered from a pink fleshy face as Louise dragged the woman unwillingly forward.

"Garrick dear," said Louise, "Let me introduce my dear friend, Jilly Craske. We used to attend dear Rex's classes until. Anyway Jilly's a very keen amateur actress. She's our local expert on kings. A hairdresser who is very special to us. And as you know, my own daughter is your theatre's official trainee .Until she rejoins me to assist with my new club."

In the background he noticed the porch door half open: the trace of a shadow appeared to slip in. Then quickly vanish again. Receding footsteps faded away. From the banks of his stored mental patterns he instinctively guessed whom he'd missed.

"Bollocks, Roddy!" Josh had waited two hours outside the Church Hall to collect him. "I've replayed Combo's album four times!" The company vehicle cornered on two skimpy wheels. "I'm not your bleedin' chauffeur, man!"

Roddy grinned. "You know what a Hairdressers is? It's where women go to dye." He'd analysed verbal techniques, trying to sharpen his timing. "So how would you recognise an actor? If you don't talk about him, he don't listen!"

This was no conversation; just stalemate. Josh drove on like in those 'Drivemaster' finals. He was Scorpio in the Lifebuster game. Zhonk, zhonk! Whooph woomph! Points totting up on the windscreen). He was King Killer in 'Inter Galactics'. He was Remos the Giant in 'Race Against Hell' as in 'Zero's Human Torch Arcade'.

Roddy was nudging him now. "And why don't managers eat bananas? Because they can't find the zips!"

Josh groaned. This was typical Roddy, avoiding issues, making excuses, forever laughing things off. Soon they'd follow their usual solution. They'd clear two machines at Zero's, let battle commence and winner takes all. At Paradise Works, where they were called 'the unidentical twins', when it came to the crunch Roddy would always give way. Sometimes their friendship depended on this. It was Josh for instance who'd made their first contacts with Brinkhomes and Brinkside Estates. It was he who'd always chase up any leads while all Roddy produced was lame puns.

Even as Radio Norston thrub-thrubbed, Roddy shut his eyes to think his own thoughts, because Josh was over-literal; never understanding jokes; no imagination nor wit. Once Josh used to laugh. Now Roddy had to deconstruct gags like disassembly furniture, taking all his wisecracks apart. Explaining a joke was its death. Like sex you had to be in the mood. Once you only had to say "boobs" and Josh would keel over with laughter. Humour should be anarchic, corrosive, and black. "Tears of a Clown", said it all. Roddy revelled in darkness; the more masochistic the better. That's why his session with Garrick had failed. It had sapped all his hopes and left him with only old gags.

"Old accountants never die: they just lose their balance!" And dozens more. "A room full of marrieds is empty. Why? Because there's no single person in sight! Did you know a horse has six legs? Forelegs up front and two at the rear!"

As Roddy reopened his eyes, he was dazzled by oncoming lights. Josh kept braking, swerving, and swearing, wildly crossing and re-crossing canals, passing and re-passing landmarks. Dozens of junctions, one-ways, roundabouts, bridges, were punctuated by repetitions of road signs.

"Shit!" Roddy pointed out the back window, "We're back again on Cavanham Street, an' passin' that bloody hairdresser again."

Josh slammed on the brakes. Where'd his sense of direction gone wrong? However much he multiplied, eliminated, divided, and took averages, he always reached the same destination. He could picture those smooth freckled features with their prominent cheekbones and wild auburn hair. It was Abigail Roberts each time!

The van skidded and swayed. They smelled burning rubber. G-forces pulled. Beside him Roddy covered his face.

Since getting back home Jilly Craske was engrossed in accounts while preparing a meal and Thomas was especially withdrawn. Those typical sulks and strained smiles. Tonight this was hard to ignore. Meeting Garrick in person had made everything worse, like finding one's own Holy Grail then having it snatched away. Once Garrick had been merely a name, but when paranoia chooses its targets Thomas redirected his aim. Knowing this made her so nervous she'd gone home before the main classes began. It was a kind of cowardice, she thought, but every day she was brought face to face with that atrophy lurking in mirrors. It was always the same. In crowds she was wholly alone, and other symptoms increased. Doses of amphetamines helped, but to remain independent she needed support. A friend. An understudy, a stand-in was crucial. Now more than ever she needed Abigail's help otherwise she'd stay trapped in herself as events kept piling up, one on another, entirely out of control. That's why she'd left the class and rushed straight back to the Salon.

Not that this helped. Those Paradise workmen returned without warning, one tall and thin, the other dumpy and fat. It seemed very odd, but they had re-measured the place in a very professional way. Attention to detail they said. They assured her their brand-new facade would be a chic picture frame; a proscenium arch framing her hairdressing stage. It was hairdressing as theatre! Coiffure as performance! Styling as Performance Art! Her competitors would never survive.

As she heated a pre-packed moussaka, she inhaled its aroma. It seemed to build up in her throat. She suddenly felt bloated and sick. She clamped both hands to her mouth and slumped at the sink. In the next room Thomas was drumming his hands on the table, radio on in the background, trying to control his suspicions, proud of his attention to detail. Why today those particular clothes? That specific perfume? Those little knick-knacks? And as for packing small items of jewellery? Did she imagine he wouldn't notice?

This evening as she'd got into his car, he thought he had spotted the trace of a swagger. Maybe the subtlest flick of her head? Even a silicone pout to those lips? She had smelt different too; a fragrance he could not pin down but he knew whom to blame. Southerners didn't understand football. They were too thin-skinned and tight-lipped. He could read their subtext in her mind.

Autistic was Jilly's own explanation. Thomas was that kind of man. To him winning mattered. He'd race any car off the road, then blame her. That's why he needed her help. It wasn't his fault. Soon he'd be begging forgiveness. She knew could buy him off with a meal. Unpack the freezer. Let microwaves do the rest. This was the usual process. The dish had precisely 5 minutes 10.5 seconds to vibrate itself to the boil. The cat was impatiently pacing around so Jilly tugged on rubber gloves, opened a fresh can of Tibby, and was forking it into Zuzu's bowl when something did not feel right. Zuzu was arching his back, fur raised, tail erect. No music. No movement. No Thomas. Just silence.

She stood up, listened, and waited. "Thomas? Are you there?"

Something hit her before she could scream, scattering basins and pans. As she fell back, clothes were torn from her flesh, sleeves ripped away down the seams, her body bloated and bruised. Trapped against kitchen units, she watched him upending her briefcase, crushing sample shampoos and spattering lotions over the walls.

"Garrick fuckin' Jones!" He yelled, punching her when she screamed.

"Don't hurt me."

He kicked her, then again. She could not stop retching. A trickle of blood ran down her nose, its salty flavours filling her mouth as he waved Garrick's advert in her face.

"Is that where you've been? Hooker! Whore!"

"I cut that out for Louise's daugh . . ."

"Liar!" He pressed her head on the wall. "Do you pretend as I'm him?" She could smell alcohol fumes. "When I run that bugger down, he'll not be acting no more!" And thrusting his mouth onto hers, crushing her lips, wrestling her head, forcing his tongue down the narrowing cone of her throat.

All that came to her mind was the car. Thomas and his dominant car. She twisted round to the sink, and was sick.

CHAPTER FIVE

RELATIONSHIPS

When Abigail closed the back door behind her next morning, she stepped out into darkness. Then as her eyes adjusted she became aware of a grey phosphorescence. It was almost as if someone had been out overnight spraying aerosol mist on the lawn, then adding potato-chip leaves. They'd gone to such obsessive lengths as trailing pearlised saliva on plants, and having spiders' webs specially beaded. A single red rose was encrusted in crystalline sugar. Cascades of crystal sparkled from branches and twigs. Was this the very same force which posted that paper dart, landing it directly at her feet? Around her, suburbia shimmered and drowned. This was her 'Dawn-of-a-New-Way-of-Life'. The sky was starting to lighten. It sounded naïve but today she was starting anew.

Her alarm had buzzed at an unearthly hour. She'd crawled from her eiderdown nest with its trainers, knickers and laddered tights, its tissues, tampons and cotton wool buds, emerging into unheated darkness. Everything would have to change. First she'd binned her Barbie Dolls, showered, then dressed. It was time to recycle the rest of her life. While gulping instant coffees, she'd wondered what Garrick was up to that moment. Was he up and about? No one else was awake in their house. Both Louise and Carlos were snoring upstairs as Abigail slid a £20 note from her mother's handbag. Louise would never notice. Eventually both would awake, coughing, cursing, belching and farting as usual.

When "CLUB ARABICA" first opened, Louise Roberts claimed to be half-her-known-age. Abby had been mortified. Her own mother in shortie skirts, low plunging tops, and cutaway stiletto heels? In those final days at school, Abby suffered comparisons cruelly. A mum who behaved like a sister, coveting studs in her nose? Rosebud tattoos on her butt? Stacey's description was "cow dressed as calf". And Stacey should know! So why was Abby so different from others? Because they underestimated her, they'd undervalued her too. Unless there was some other reason? Perhaps she wasn't one of them.

Had she been fostered, cloned, or adopted? Even a fertilised implant? Or product of a one-night stand? Some biological freak who deserved compensation? She was no more than a letter in a DNA chain from school biology class. She was that Classic Recessive: lips like polyps, plasticised dentures, squinting eyes and colourless skin. Smiles were the fashion-accessory craze but hers was a mouth without definition. Mothers should not draw attention to themselves, nor take it away from their daughters. That was a fact. Louise took all the credit for Garrick taking Abigail on. Now she wanted his head on their walls as a trophy. Garrick would have to star at her club, and Abby was to close the deal.

It was Official Day One of Abigail's career. Within weeks it would be Christmas. She picked her way down the garden, taking shortcuts between twisted beanpoles, overgrown leeks, and brussel-sprout stumps. Feeling chills around Castle Mount, Abigail unlatched the back gate, and headed off down the alley. Ahead lay the future. The past had expired with her schoolbooks.

But how to break free? Be oneself? How when she'd glimpsed someone else in reflections? She'd caught sight of the omens. She had to preserve the new 'Jilly Craske style'. Appearances mattered. Actors could become someone else, anonymous and famous at once.

The brambled path led through conifers and holly via leafless sycamores into a small public park. At its summit, Old Castle Mound loomed, magnified through the mist. Here it was sacrosanct, silent, and free. Every sound rang out clearly. She whispered softly, enjoying the word, lips against teeth, repeating it louder and louder. "Fuck! Fuck! *Fuck!*" till cold air filled her throat and expanded the lungs. She was nobody's label. She was herself. She was free! She stumbled laughing uphill through layers of foam, like one of those little glass globes. You shake up the sphere and there it is: your life seen through snowflakes. But once you start climbing you have to go on.

From the summit the whole town unrolls like one of those classroom projects, all bobbins, cartons, matchboxes, loo rolls and cans, misted with strands of dry ice. She could pick out the towers of their theatre below. She could stretch out a hand, and touch. Perhaps Garrick was already at work? She imagined him in his octagonal office declaiming from Shakespeare, performing great acting feats. She could even pinpoint Jilly's salon where Stacey was mopping its dye-spattered floors at this very moment. She noted the ridge of the synagogue roof and dome of the latest new mosque. Westwards, the town hall, bus station, and office blocks became links along the Y-shaped canal whose surface reflected the brightening skies. Dotted along its silvery necklace lay church spires and chapels in sharp silhouettes. Somewhere Josh could be looking up too? Everything seemed within reach.

Suddenly a man emerged from the mists with two dogs. Snarling Alsatians headed towards her. In that moment her time-bubble burst, and she ran.

The early bus was cram-packed with shift workers, researchers, cleaners and temps. You caught it like a bad habit. It crept along, stop-starting, smelling of armpits tinged with cheap deodorant. Each junction brought a new gridlock. Each jolt displaced her assumptions. Hoardings had materialised overnight. A new one dominated the skyline. Surrounded by striplights, a massive framed window appeared to look out on a fluoride-white tower, which rose in dazzling perspectives blasted with Mediterranean sunlight. Developers promised a permanent summer. Forget Blackpool and Southport, a computerised vista of Norston showed gleaming towers rising from turquoise-blue waters, but The Majestic was nowhere in sight. As they passed Jilly's salon, Abigail noticed a contractors' van. Its timing was perfect. Coincidences could not be wasted. She leapt out at traffic lights, skipping through log-jams of fumes. Outside Crowning Glory, a familiar figure in white ski-top with fur-trimmed hood emerged, holdall over one shoulder. Hearing footsteps the figure spun round.

A furious Stacey flung back her hood. "Don't ever fuckin' do that again!" She stood hands on hips. "So? How d'you expect a cleaner to look? Like a bag o' shit? We don't leave us fashions behind us, you know." She reset her shoulder strap and prepared to lock up. "All I done is tested their hairspray myself." Stacey flounced her hair, then reacted to Abigail's silence. "Oh come on cow! It's 'perks of the job'." She shook her head. "Well? Your first day at work is it? Like, catch the boss early?"

"No. I'm here to pick up Jilly's business cards on my way in. Like I promised. For the actors," Abigail lied, "To hand them around like she asked."

Abby snatched a handful and ran. She gummed Jilly Craske cards onto lampposts, bus stands, and Manwess Gas advertisements, compulsively leaving a trail; a trail subconsciously designed to be followed. "Crowing Glory" was a campaign and Jilly was more than local hairdresser. She was fashion counsellor, lifestyle guru and messiah. And more.

Apart from the usual rumble of traffic, all was quiet in Lancaster Gate. Another cold bright day. A northeasterly airflow zapping the wind-chill to zero. Verity took early breakfast before waving Roseanne off on the school-run, dispatching wee children to classes like huddles of small refugees. Verity zipped latest scripts into her new Gucci briefcase before checking landlines, palm-top, mobile and pager. Without Roseanne and kids she could reclaim a diminutive moment, but sadly the term would soon end. She let her eyes slip out of focus. A major new project was waiting.

Back in Norston, Garrick was setting off late, feeling disorientated. Last night he'd worked through the David Pirie biography of Chekhov. That's after skimming through 'Commentaries on Ibsen' by Matti Riikonen followed by paperback extracts of Pushkin, reading till something past two in the morning. Somehow he'd scribbled postcards to both kids despite upstairs' loud sex. Then rogue prions intervened. The sensations of sweet-scented smoke. This longing spread from his lungs to his tongue turning his brain to warm jelly and wiping away all he'd just read.

How to decipher the motivations of characters that couldn't make sense of themselves? You couldn't expect revelations when you couldn't make sense of your life, but if drama were about love, violence, survival, passion and brute sex, that's also what fairytales did. They were warnings. Their themes were the loss of innocence, conflict, absurdity and vengeance, which led to remorse and the triumph of good. In just the same way his own life was intruding, jumbling past, present, and future. When he tried ringing home as he walked, Roseanne unexpectedly answered:

"Hi there! How's my son-in-law?" She started on a rising high. " And so early! And how's my great-great-great cousin Anton? I feel his blood through my veins every day. I had a great-aunt in Melikhovo, yes? .Where Anton wrote 'The Seagull' you know. That's before he moved South for his health. Today he'd get antibiotics, then a gene therapy course. When Lenin and Stalin arrived, we Morozovs got the hell out into exile."

Roseanne was eager to talk, but when Garrick asked to speak to his wife, Roseanne sidetracked him with chat about family welfare and inner city counselling. The cultural world would be watching his progress, she said. The entire extended Morozov family from Moscow to Maine would be waiting and praying. Everyone was depending on him.

He wondered how much she knew about Verity's venture. It was time to speak out. The TV business was full of devious scams and Verity's project looked like a confidence trick plus tax avoidance scam. Vee was far too innocent. She had to be warned for her own sake, he said, but Roseanne as usual bounced everything back on himself, wishing him well with The Three Sisters, saying how much she as a mother felt her daughter's deep pain. He realised then that Vee would not ring him back.

Ahead of him a parked black Ford Mondeo was up on the kerb, blocking pedestrians. Ideal for car bombers he thought and skirted warily by, but even as he stepped into the road, a cyclist only just missed him. It moved so quickly and quietly. Maybe this was his answer? A bike! He lengthened his stride and arrived at the theatre on time.

Phyllis overdid her amazement. She sat there quietly electric as if he'd materialised out of thin air. The fresh scent of Arthur Ruddock fluoresced in faint trails. She twitched her fingers, pursing her lips as if she'd been caught out, but quickly recovered.

"And how is our Director today?" She jumped up, handing him mail with some books. "There's letters need signing. And there's post marked 'personal', addressed to you."

So obviously Vee got his message. She'd had the good sense to reply direct to his office. He hoped she'd enclosed some notes from the kids.

"Oh Garrick Another thing . . ." Phyllis caught his sleeve and held it that split-second too long. "Excuse me, if I may say so Garrick, your drama class. Even dear Rex would've been pleased. Yes, impressed." She hesitated. "I'm so glad you took my advice. Most of us loved your poetry reading suggestion . . ." Implying an unexpressed 'But' while avoiding his eyes. "And yes, by the way our Mr Ruddock rang. He likes to be kept fully informed about schedules, budgets, and suchlike. Being a professional, he takes these very seriously. The two of you, such very nice men, it's such a shame. You might find you've got lots in common."

"Thanks Phyllis, I'll bear that in mind."

"And don't forget Peggy de Vries." He caught an edge to her voice. "A very traditional woman. She keeps a finger on the pulse, so to speak, as everyone runs round her son." She gave a wan smile. "Widows can be such manipulative creatures. Like Arthur, you'll love her Christmas soirée."

There it was again. That soirée. It must have deep significance because Ruddock kept dropping to it into discussions as if their timetable revolved around it. Garrick was tempted to ask more.

"And anyway, to be frank . . ." Phyllis continued, "And this is none of my business . . ."

But everything was her business, he knew that. She had restored theatre archives back through generations of Rex Schulmans, Aubrey Stokers and Randolph Waltons, right back to its Corn Exchange days. She knew every carton and box, each with its own inner life. The Theatre Museum was her own enterprise and must have demanded complete dedication.

"The choice of that that girl was entirely your personal choice." Phyllis looked up at the ceiling. "I never criticise. Except . . ." She examined the grain of her desk. "How can I put it? I wasn't here, and you . . ." She crossed to the alcove under the stairs. "First you must be needing tea?"

"Sorry?"

He heard her fill a kettle, flick its switch, the water energise. She snatched chipped mugs from a cupboard, poured scalding water and swirled tea bags viciously round. These she removed with a pencil, before slurping in milk from a carton. Then she returned.

"Now please don't . . . don't misunderstand me. I'm concerned about you. You need more experienced help. She's totally unqualified, that girl." She took a sharp angry breath, "But luckily she's only on four weeks approval And I do know the mother."

Garrick recalled those anonymous notes loaded with similar warnings, their childishness, pettiness, meanness. Everything fell into place. Then he noticed she had set out three mugs. Abigail was included.

"By the way," Phyllis added, "You're right about needing a pantomime script. I'll fax our favourite agent in Leeds. All you need do is tick the components. Mark a cross in the appropriate box. Long? Medium? Short? I suggest you pencil in the duration, allowing two intervals for the bar. Then, how much music? What style? How many characters, etceteras? You could mark percentage-wise comedy content, suggesting scene changes. Maybe rhyming couplets? And so on and so forth. It's easy. You make the choices. They supply the result. It's all done on computers and ready next day."

As Phyllis glanced at the clock, Arthur Ruddock stumped in, his neck bulging over collar. A fourth tea mug had appeared before Bert appeared seconds later.

Arthur was hot in the face. "Amazing. I happened to be run into our lads." He pushed Bert forward. "Our backstage staff have issues, it seems." He turned to Garrick. "Time for you to get them resolved." He folded his arms and sat back.

Bert held a sheet of A4 at arms length; his horn-rimmed spectacles slipped down his nose. As he read aloud Arthur loomed up alongside. The list of complaints filled both sides of the page. On completing his presentation, the stage carpenter read further points from the back of his hand. The subtext was clear. Bert's status was threatened. It was artisan versus artist; craftsman v. intellectual: men against women; northerners v. southerners; the age-old issue of youngsters being foisted on experts. No one mentioned Abigail.

Arthur intervened. "Good points. We'd better recruit a trainee for Bert? A dedicated apprentice who'd fit our tight budgets. Someone inexpensive. Cheap. There's hundreds who'd jump at the chance."

Phyllis began making notes.

Verity had not returned Garrick's call. Promiscuous feral pigeons colonised his windowsills. They fluffed up their feathers, busily cuckolding each other. Not much marital fidelity here. This was their sexual harassment centre; their pickup point, offering date rape for Christmas, with sex fifty-two weeks of the year. Again his phone intervened.

"Hi there," sang its camp tones, "We hear you're casting. You'll just love Daisy Scholes. You'll have to see her! We'll fax you a face. She's the new multimedia star. She's already performed in two promos. She's even prepared to do panto," it warbled.

Call followed call. Fax followed fax. E-mail came after e-mail. More and more offers came spooling in. Heavy packages came by each post. Messengers vied with deliverymen. He was bombarded with burlesque, vaudeville, cabaret and musical scripts. How many trees were sacrificed? Chekhov and Ibsen would not be dismissed. They were secretly amassing potential like adding fertiliser to sugar, fermenting explosive ideas. Then he remembered Vee's unopened letter.

The moment he picked it up, he noticed the writing on the envelope was not hers. Its postmark was local and marked 'Personal'. A single page slithered out. It had no address and no heading. Its misshapen lettering matched others he'd rashly destroyed.

"Abigail is not to be trusted," it read, "She will only drag you down. A friend."

Zhoonk Zhoonk Zhoonk In the middle of nowhere a helicopter came in to land. Whirling blades sliced the air like a venomous over-sized blender. A group disembarked, running bent-double, buffeted in their billowing jackets. Overhead, too close for comfort, chunks of atmosphere shot off in every direction. *Zhoonk Zhoonk Zhoonk.*

Verity felt her brain popping. This was combat mission stuff. Korea, Gulf War, Chechnya, Vietnam, Iraq. It was emergency services, air gunships and eye-in-the-sky all rolled into one for the sake of 'Fresh Country Venison Pie and Puréed Herb Potato'. Behind her the helicopter rose, its downblast scattering sandstorms and ripping the landscape apart. Through all this Verity heard a barely audible bleep. She crouched with her back to the barrage, the cellphone clamped to her ear.

"Yes?" she gasped, but her lungs were sucked dry by each twist of the blades.

Here she was, on a glorious morning pierced with winter clarity. A low-slung sun shimmered in lemon and gold. The skies were 360° blue. Gone was the greyness and dampness of London and now some bugger was phoning! As the team cowered in St Ebbut's courtyard, Verity could not help feeling renewed. Their orange Sikorski hovered like an inquisitive bug trailing its own personal vortex, before finally losing interest. As it skimmed away, leaves and straw continued to revolve in suspension, slowly, gradually sinking; dust back to dust, and ashes back into gravel.

"Who the hell was that?" Lucy demanded. "I mean, Jesus, Vee, that should be switched off. Frankly darling, there's warnings all over. It screws up electrical signals and Oh my God . . ." As the enormity struck her, Lucy felt faint. "We could have ended up in the headlines."

Verity took another deep breath. Cold air was invigorating, "Fresh from the freezer, unmodified, no additives, direct from mid-Atlantic". It implied Aga Cookers, spit-roasting, pastry-crust quail, and stuffed peacock pie. It knew it was pure. As they huddled alone in the middle of Devon, out of nowhere came renewed bleeping. The whole team glared at Vee.

She fumbled and whispered, "Hello. Who is it?"

Three hundred miles away Garrick sat grinning. "Hey there sweetheart, it's me!" He stretched his feet on top of the desk, blowing a kiss at her photo. "Honey, I miss you. You know that? Your picture's in front of me! I wish you were here in my arms . . . I wondered if . . . weekend for . . . we . . . that I . . . hoping to . . . but you're . . ."

"Just switch that damn thing off!" Lucy commanded, and emptiness reasserted itself.

Garrick's line was cut. He might as well have been phoning the Moon. It may have been coincidence, but just because you're paranoid it doesn't mean they aren't against you. As his father said: 'A woman can be read like a book, but not without recourse to the index'. Garrick wished he'd kept diaries, then clearer patterns might have emerged. He tried not to think of his children.

Glancing down he noticed a Manwess truck being loaded. As workmen removed snow-covered objects they left behind dark hieroglyphs. To him these seemed significant, but like the Ancient Mariner, Garrick failed to decipher a code. Only one message emerged: Vee was pissed off! She was a cook, not performer. And not until her new project bombed, as he'd warned, would he be proved right all along. The failure would give him a break to come clean. The sin of procrastination, that's all; merely Schadenfreude delayed and 'The Cherry Orchard' postponed. Everybody was playing a part and the pantomime had to be cast. Baron Hardup. Dame Maggie. Two Ugly Sisters: Asphyxia and Euthanasia. Cinderella. Dandini. Prince Charming. Buttons. Optional cat. Cinderella was the prototype virgin; the classic innocent victim, undefiled and unblemished. Casting her would not be easy. At least Trixie Waltham could sing and dance. Perhaps his new assistant could understudy for free. She looked quite the part.

Real lives could be typecast too. For instance, when Edwin George Jones met Amy Claire Harris, the attraction of opposites worked. Protestant sperm met Catholic ovum and Garrick had been its result. Then when his mother died young, she'd passed away so casually, buried with one bunch of flowers, a three-man chorale, and Edwin's protracted oration imposing the blame on his son. So Garrick conformed to his label. Adopting beads and sandals, he'd grown his first beard and smoked hash, then one drunken night he'd signed up as 'Production assistant' to a dance troupe touring the Mediterranean nightspots. There began his show business career.

Art could take many forms. Naked Eve gripped a live python called Adam between her bare thighs. Daisy sang nude from four metre stilts. Mirabelle swung naked on the high-wire trapeze. Chou-chou the contortionist's head appeared between her own bare thighs. And men cheered. They sold out every night with Garrick mostly pissed out of his mind'. But glamour was terminal too. Take poor Juanita, maimed in her one-woman knife-throwing act, or Lola the professional bride in her crown of glittering candles who died like Santa Lucia in cotton organza from 85% burns. Or Lisette Roualt who fell from high wire onto sawdusted concrete. All that seemed a lifetime ago.

He heard an almost subliminal tap. Defying all known laws of physics, atom by atom, a figure just seemed to emerge out of nowhere, letting the door swing shut behind her. Garrick waved Abby to sit, but she just stood.

"Phyllis said you wanted me," she said.

He thought again of those transitory acts: Sulky Suki, Little Lizzie Levene, Fire-dancer Marissa, and Chiffon the Filipino contortionist. All were little Abigails once.

"Is there a problem?" But Abby avoided his eyes

If symmetry were mathematical stasis then Abigail was immovable. Garrick dictated a short list of tasks. From time to time she'd lick her pen, staining the tip of her tongue. As the cuffs rode up on her wrist, he failed to notice the marks. Likewise those pictograms outside in the snow, their meanings melting away.

Hours on her feet in the salon made Jilly ache. The more tired she grew, the more hungry she felt. As if she weren't obese enough she was noticeably putting on weight. This wasn't helped by varicose veins bubbling up in her legs and gradually slowing her down. She blamed this on faux-marble floors. She needed some treatment. Perhaps she could offer Varicose Care as a sideline? There must be lots more ideas? Abby would bring in the clients, but Louise kept talking away.

Jilly tried to respond. "Mmm. Mmmm. Yes, love, I know." She continued running water into the basin. "Mmm Quite. Mind you, there's other strings I can add to my bow."

Louise had learned to keep her eyes closed. "Isn't that what I'm saying? It's 'window-of-opportunities time'. When there's a boom, folk spend. When things go bust, they spend even more! So when our theatre reopens, I'm inviting their actresses down to my club. The Majestic plus the National Press." Louise's eyes flickered open, then snapped shut as water cascaded around her and Jilly's suggestions continued to drift.

"What's more there's hot wax, lasers electrolysis, bleaching of fuzz Maybe pluckings with tweezers. I'd start with special discounts plus two-for-price-of-one ointments. Of course there's dandruff treatments, root tinting, hairpieces Not to mention psoriasis cures. And . . . and then there's extra extensions and wigs I could franchise the name Crowning Glory Systems? How's that?"

Louise didn't reply. 'I'm dreaming of a White Christmas' came over loud on the speakers. She could see Jilly was piling on kilos. Her pinkness compounded a physical torpor, loading the cellulite on. Jilly was too nervous. Over-sensitive even. That wasn't all. Louise's own problems also began in this very salon. They started on Abby's re-styling day because sexploitation was rife. Next day, the child signed up to that theatre. It wasn't meant to be like that.

"Anyway . . ." Jilly persisted, "I'd get Lady Whatsit to open my Clinic." Louise's head stayed pressed to the basin. "Yes, and add individualised booths. And . . . and new curtained partitions . . ." Still rinsing away. "I'll extend into lifestyles. Not forgetting the masculine market. But that'd mean moving of course. Bigger premises. Maybe a couple of floors?"

As Jilly leant over Lousie she sensed her ambitions melting away. Then out of nowhere cramps seemed to disembowel her again.

As Garrick thumped his desk in frustration, his papers took fright. Apparently Bert was handing out edicts, behaving like a full-time shop steward. An urgent pep talk was needed. Garrick ordered all staff to gather on stage.

On his way down, the house tabs were falling. Garrick noticed the auditorium doors were wedged open in defiance of fire regulations. He stopped to watch acres of worn ruby velvet came slushing down like wet blanket. It was oddly compulsive, that slice of brightness narrowing down to a slit; a rectangle shrinking into a stripe reduced to the thinnest of lines, moving slower and slower. Then that final flare, like the throes of a total eclipse. A slight shudder. Then absolute black. As the Fire Safety Curtain followed, it seemed almost profound. It said the show was over and done. As if the last cherry tree had been felled. But the rise and fall of that curtain was the most natural thing in the world, yet no-one applauded sunrise or sunsets. And no-one built picture-frame stages these days. He thought of his children and felt oddly moved. He pushed through the pass door as if he'd crossed a frontier, and strode out onto the stage.

Beyond him extended the great Russian Steppes and the mighty Siberian wastes, whose wilderness bordered vast arid deserts where sand grains pulverised sand. In its abandonment the wide-open stage was compelling. It enticed and allured. It was as if should he fall to his knees and invite inspiration like tongues of biblical flame. Thus are great prophets chosen. You move like a moth to its light.

Then he seemed to hear swelling music. Who could resist an overture? A tune? The tap of the toe? A click of the heel? It was if he were dancing through fountains. Dancing in the Dark! The click of his taps and the snap of his fingers. Fred Astaire without Ginger Rogers. The rhythm. The beat. For once in his life he had total co-ordination combined with the lightness of being. Even as he reached centre-stage, the music reached a crescendo. Then bang! A blinding explosion of spotlights! Music cut out. Utter silence.

"We was testing it, see," remarked Bert from the darkness. "Our new video system. So's make-up and cossies can watch." He pointed up at a camera suspended in the wings. "Closed circuit, see. T'all goes onto tape. By the way, we read your decision to cancel the Chekhovs and do Cinderella instead. Phyllis says as it's been announced on local FM."

"What!" As blood swamped Garrick's cheeks the prompt corner's glow flashed.

There, among switchboards and cue lights, a monitor was showing a view of the stage. Around it he saw "CROWNING GLORY!" flyers glued up alongside "CLUB ARABICA" handbills, like hookers' cards in a telephone booth And sensed the ghost of Rex Schulman.

He began wildly ripping them down. "We're not a bloody sales kiosk. Not yet!"

"Like it!" said Bert, "You'd make a great speciality act."

Arthur Ruddock avoided all talk of the theatre as he and Peggy de Vries strolled between landscaped hillocks and spinneys. Temple Storford was the hub of Capability Brown's famous Arcadian vision. Lined with ancient chestnuts and cedars, West Way stretched onwards and downwards towards the main house where intervening villages had long ago been razed, their shattered foundations deep underfoot like old graves.

As Arthur and Peggy headed downhill it felt oddly idyllic; a BioPic world complete with soundtracks of birdsong. This was a movie where time had no meaning. This was the Heritage Past. A carriage and horses could sweep through one hundred and eighty degrees. Plans for a wind-farm could not affect this.

"That's why we rely on you, Arthur," Peggy was saying, "We must give Garrick Jones our support. The Arts are so important to us." He took this as the royal 'we'. "And as for my Soirée, it's no more than a gesture. We owe them all some gratitude."

Arthur nodded. She always oversimplified. She lacked what he called 'political nous'. 'Universal Improvement' smacked of class and patronage. Emotions and reason were fatally mixed. Too 'metropolitan liberal' for him. She was benefactor of schools and numerous drug-addict clinics. The Majestic embodied The Family de Vries, commemorating the death of her husband. To Arthur's annoyance she talked as though she personally owned it. The fact was, both site and building belonged to the council supported by local taxation. Her family endowment barely paid for its light bulbs. She focused too much on that theatre, possibly at the expense of her son. Young George should be nurtured, cheered on, and encouraged.

Arthur felt responsible. Especially here. Whenever breezes drifted down from the fells, he could forget Liverpool, Manchester, Preston, whatever. At moments like this, time could stand still. Here nature confronted the winter and blasted oaks clawed at the sky like upended bundles of roots, as sheep compulsively fattened themselves up for the slaughter. It was all too idyllic.

Temple Storford's Palladian wings rise golden-grey amongst cedars and pines, its towers and pediments catching the light. Its eccentric assortment of styles represented his own personal conflicts; social, personal, political too. 'It's the art of the practical', a voice would remind him, "The old giving way to the new".

94

"Oh come on," she teased as they strolled beneath cedars. "You must have formed some opinion? The man's been here for weeks. Or were we mistaken about him?"

"I'm reserving my judgement. He's got new ideas."

She slowed to let him catch up. "Wasn't that the whole point?"

"People need entertaining not bashing over the head with a Chekhov! You've got to offer them tasters. Tempt them in slowly."

She walked off, leaving George like a bungee jumper in space. To her it wasn't a question of taste. The Three Sisters was documentary fact. The play could have been about her.

"And Garrick? What did he say?"

"Say?" Arthur laughed. "Only one thing. He had to agree."

"So it is Cinderella?"

"Of course. Force of argument, see. Entertainment, I told him, is the legacy of the de Vries." He heard her sharp cough. "And of course he completely agreed." She did not respond, "I suppose I see myself as a prophet. A local visionary maybe. I convert the unwilling."

"Our family . . ." she began but he knew the rest. "My husband was wholly committed to culture. Paintings, sculpture, music, but most of all drama. We owe that to Randolph. It was his vision of a New Global Centre to rival great cities like London, Paris, New York."

"And George? Your son? What's he think?"

Since the death of her husband, all their shared freshness had gone, and Peggy's vulnerability with it. Sometimes he'd recapture glimpses, but mostly for the past twenty years he'd watched her regress. A flutter of birds flew out of cover. Wood pigeons circled and soared. They walked on as high above aircraft scoured white diagonals, letting the stratosphere heal any scars.

"By the way," she remarked. "Won't that create a literal island?"

"Sorry? I don't quite . . ."

"That new marina. Churning up vast tracts of land. Re-dredging our lovely canal? Wouldn't that leave my theatre marooned?"

A plump spaniel came rolling towards them, the tail violently wagging the dog. It veered towards Arthur through the damp grass. Next minute Juno was jumping up, smearing his trousers, violently wagging its bum.

"There you see," Peggy said, "All creatures give off mixed signals. My son's such a schoolboy, yet, there he is, about to inherit this house and estate via the trust. By the way, my late husband wanted The Majestic renamed the 'De Vries'. Did you know that?"

"Georgie's a fine upstanding young man. Just like his dad."

"The age of majority doesn't test wisdom. All it does is measure years without as it happens, resorting to DNA tests. Has Georgie ever mentioned that? First comes my annual Theatre Soirée. That's one tradition I have made my own."

They'd reached Triple Paths Junction below the John Soane Monument, 'Cybele Enthroned With Two Lions'. The dog was breathing heavily now.

"Arthur? Remember our doing Lady Windermere's Fan? When dear Alec Guinness came up to Norston to star? And all those expensive hand-rolled cigars? And Rex Schulman directing? Dear Rex. They say Johnny

Geilgud played Trigorin in 'The Seagull' here too. That's over sixty years ago. Now that's why my Soirée's important. For continuity. But most of all for morale." She tapped Arthur's wrist. "As for poor Cinderella! That's what fairy stories do. They end at the wedding. Whereas in real life, as you know, we do not."

As they stood gazing back at the house, cool winds blew down from the moor

Garrick dialled Verity's mobile only to hear "This phone may be switched off." He was back with Frog Footmen and Elves and he needed a long-lasting nicotine jab. Once Cinderella was in the ascendant there would be no going back. Forget Russian Steppes, the breadbasket plains of Ukraine or the shimmering waters off Yalta. Forget Moscow, St Petersburg and Berlin. So much for the Olgas and Sachas, Nikolais and Alexeis. And so much for Chekhov's 'Seagull' or Ibsen's 'Hedda Gabler'. It's hello the pantomime horse!

He thought of Chekhov coughing up blood. His ultimate punchline was a Badenweiler spa, because to be a true artist you had to be dead. As in all the greatest comedies life itself provided the twist. So where did that leave pantomime? 'It's like cut-price Kabuki, but with none of its culture', someone said. So what would Roseanne make of its double-entendres? Its ludicrous puns? Its layers of sentiment camouflaging prejudice? The British understand. Their closet gentrification means everyone knows filthy jokes in advance, preordained therefore accepted.

"Gary, it's not even burlesque!" Roseanne's voice arose from his subconscious. "It's not vaudeville. Not cabaret. Nor operetta. Not farce. Not even pure drag. With all that cross-dressing, hell, it's like specialist fungi, okay? It doesn't relocate. Okay?"

He was sick of auditions already. 'Lionel Parsons as Dame?' he'd scrawled in one margin. Worse were pedestrian questions like – who fits the budget? Ricky Spark of The Spanners? Dale Waterstone? Cy Weekes, with dreadlocks and long lantern jaw? Armando Bloc, who'd played Othello in Stratford? Or Ranni Patel who'd gone from Shakespeare from Reggae? Or James Carr, who still fancied himself as a matinee idol? This wasn't Moscow Art Theatre, but here they'd all move straight from panto to classics; that was their trade-off.

"Oh yes it is!" booms the dame, waving her sequinned handbag.

"Oh no it isn't!" scream a thousand kids from all parts of the house.

"Then where is the villain?" yells Buttons

"Behind you!" scream a thousand kids, "Behind you!"

"Then his get-up-and-go must've got up and gone."

As for Cinderella, she was demanding her full score of victims. This was an Alice in Wonderland queen. Soon there'd be victims, exponentially growing, each one demanding their fifteen minutes of guaranteed fame. But once on-stage we all freeze! Somewhere among the synapses dialogue goes missing and brains congeal. By lunchtime he'd seen twenty-five hopefuls and needed a breath of fresh air. A single waft of nicotine had sent his brain into cramp.

"How wonderful darling. We'll let you know," he told them all, but everyone knew he had lied.

Back in his office he examined the photos lined up on his desk. His children closely resembled himself, or was he becoming like them? Those tiny amalgams of Jones-Pavel genes; their christenings, birthdays, outings, schooldays and Christmases, stretching right up to last month? He added two lumps of sugar to cold tea and only then did he notice. His mug had left a circular stain on a hand-written note, which must have been left on his desk. Conspicuously timed 'mid-morning', this message was crayonned "Urgent" in Phyllis's explicit writing. He held the notelet up to the light, but no secret message emerged.

"URGENT . Mrs Roberts phoned again!!!" was all it said, "Please call her back a.s.a.p. Also a Verity phoned? Says she'll ring back"

He dialled Verity. And waited and waited and waited . . .

By hiring a stage manager, Garrick hoped to put Bert in his place. So Bert seized on any technical details and wanted to patent the lot. For instance, the clever adaptation of pulleys for Cinderella's transformation scene was Bert's. Huge gauzes would swing from its hoops in the grid. This was a pantomime highlight. Controlling the man would be Fabian's job. Fire Regulations, Health & Safety checks, No Smoking signs, fire alarms, Fire Exit doors, sprinkler systems, meter readings, toilets for the disabled, safety barriers, etc. were all turned to Bert's advantage. Now Manwess Gas was claiming their arteries ran to the heart of the fabric for which the Law gave them full jurisdiction and inalienable rights.

"As for that Fabian bastard?" Bert shifted his weight from high up on a rung while adjusting his screwdriver grip. "But that little cow? My folk is Irish an' yours is African, right? 'Ard men as worked in mills. Endin' up on memorial slabs, poor fucking sods."

Danny shifted uncomfortably. "Shush man. Acoustics an' that."

Bert hand-drove another screw into the fixing. "This in't no totalitarian state. Not as yet." He dragged a beercan from his overalls . "An' that bloody Garrick's a fake." He popped the can until bubbles spurted and foamed. "An' what about our new little Miss Muffet? Her mum's an 'ooker what runs an organic brothel." He emptied the can in one gulp. "I respect myself, Danny, like I respect you. So how 'bout you start respecting your self?"

He crunched the empty can in his fist, then let go. It fell in slo-mo, bounced and bounded down to the stage. Bert produced another full can and held it outstretched. His laughter liquidised into giggles. Then he let go. The can hit the deck like an alcohol bomb. And Bert seemed to lose concentration.

Above at street level, the alley door suddenly banged. Footsteps continued, pattering down, small feminine footsteps on wooden treads.

Abigail came into a view. "Hiyah fellers! Need any errands?"

"You gotta be jokin!" High above them, Bert's ladder took on a life of its own. "Fuck off!"

Around him horizontals wavered; verticals started to narrow and sway. Even the grid seemed to quiver. He swung back and forth like an aerial ballet, tipping slowly, delicately backwards then sideways, a few degrees further each time as if rehearsed to perfection, and all the time cursing. She stared in shocked fascination as he traced semi-elliptical trails through several dimensions. Abigail seemed to hear full, choral music like a great Thanksgiving Mass. It tracked his aerial ballet, building towards the absolute faith of the Credo. A full orchestra combined with a million-pipe organ rose towards its apogee, before suddenly .plunging .plunging, and plunging.

An audience would have applauded as Danny ran helplessly forward.

Bert's body hit the stage with a thud, cutting the orchestra short, mid-crescendo.

Communications make fools of us all. Garrick decided he must have misdialled. No-one had answered. No recorded messages. Suddenly at the eighth ringing tone came a connection:.

"Hi?" said a woman's voice, low-pitched and husky, "Can I help?"

Garrick heard sniffs and a nose being blown. "Hello? Roseanne?"

"If it's Verity Morozoff you want, I'll take a message?" Roseanne sniffled. "Who is that?"

He might as well use semaphore flags. "Roseanne, it's me."

"And that's who?"

"Garrick. Gary. Verity's husband. Your son-in-law? Your daughter's wife?" He heard a soft grunt of acceptance. "Come on Roseanne, how are my kids? I hope they're not playing up."

"Fine. Sure. They're fine." After more snuffles. "They're just dandy." Her nasal breathing degenerated into a cough.

He heard children's voices raised in the background. "It'll be good to talk to them. You know how it is. I promised to phone. They must have loads of news." He could hear background giggles and clatter.

Roseanne snuffled. "They're doing fine." She coughed again.

"Having a cold is quintessentially British. That means you must be settling in." He heard violent coughing. "Anyway I'll have a quick word with Mark and Rachel."

"Right now they're showering. You want me to tell them you called?"

"They're not with you?"

"Gary, they're upstairs. Getting showered. That's the video playing."

"Okay, but don't forget I'm the one who's up here, slogging for Chekhov and all his descendants. I'm doing that as a favour. For you! Koromó! Chaika! Blood of the Morozovs!"

"I'll tell them you called."

This was déjà vu. He could hear the children quite plainly. He was back dating, trying to win over his momma-in-law but now Roseanne was fending him off. As he started to say his goodbyes, the line went suddenly dead.

Verity waved again. New arrivals kept pushing forward. Crowds of spectators had grown. Throngs of bodies, logos and graphics. Whirring, clattering lenses. A splattering dazzle of lights. Disembodied yelling and groans. She was leaving her first press conference accompanied by producers and aides. Her day had started at midnight. Now her smile was beginning to strain and her new shoes were determined to pinch. Still everybody kept shouting.

"Over here!" . . . "Look this way!" . . . "Give us a wave!"

Now her reflexes refused to comply. Basic nutrition was being hyped into showbiz, yet here she was, leading the trend. She tried to put the thought aside. While entire continents faced malnutrition, others transformed calories into layers of fat. Thanks to global politics, skeletal children with bellies distended would join flyblown corpses in pits while mothers and old people starved. It was so wrong. Very wrong But what could she personally do except give a donation to Food Aid? Someone had to publicise good food, and one single factor was driving her on. Garrick's assumption she'd fail.

Photographers caught close-ups of 'Food star frowning' and 'TV Chef gagging' as cold air and bright flashes combined. Pow! Pow! Pow! She waved again and everyone cheered. Her over-stretched lips and smile muscles strained as she answered everyone's questions. She remembered to quote major promoters like Sustenoso, Vitar-Pakk, Organello and others, as an automated walkway seemed to be sweeping her onwards, courtesy of Carl, Sandro, Gillian, Lucy and other crew whose names she'd forgotten. Her producers just loved her New England accent. They loved her throwaway wisecracks. Crazy guys cheered like she was a starlet. Next they'd be asking for close-ups of boobs. While one half of her brain was listing fresh herbs, the other half started to wonder if Gary would be impressed.

"Hi!" someone called, "How's it feel to be famous?"

"Who knows!" she twinkled, "Wait till you've viewed the whole show."

Introduced as "Daughter, mother, and wife," everything harked back to Croydon Town Hall where she'd first murmured, "I do". Then she'd scarcely known her man. She did now. Wherever fate was taking her, Gary was off some place else, but he'd be grateful one day. After all, wasn't it she who'd created his biographical details? She'd invented an opus peppered with classic revivals of Shakespeare, Broadway, Hollywood and other unverifiable facts. She'd made it sound so damn impressive Gary even believed it himself. That's why they gave him that job.

Lucy, Vee's agent, approved. They'd laughed a lot at the time. Now she was running the show. In fact Decorum Productions had rented a brand new hotel because that was the nature of fixers; everything fixed without taste. And so British. So far it had worked. Only one thing was missing; that one thing was her kids, but this was Roseanne's function right now. What else should a grandmother do? Verity still hated cut-velvet armchairs, gilt coffee tables with green-glass tops and crimson mock-Indian rugs. Every surface clashed. She complained.

"Alright, put it this way. The language is Dollars," Lucy explained, "'Cause that's what everyone talks! That's why I got extra brain cells installed. To deduct my sixty percent in advance and get it straightway invested! That's why we're all doing so well."

"Over here!" A suited male was pointing. "Your interviewer sits there. We'll pretend you're at home and this is your sitting-room lounge." He gestured expansively round. "None of your readers'll know that," then adding sotto voce, "Unless you'd like to give us a plug? 'Hotel Mallorca'. It's on the wine coasters, see." He stepped smartly back. "And here she comes now!"

The interviewer was guaranteed famous. Martina Yarrow sold womenswear space but Martina was no feminist choice. 'Bitchy' was Verity's word. Martina Yarrow easily filled a two-seater sofa, oozing competitive chill. Her handbag bulged like a reptilian egg-sack so Vee was expecting viperous questions. Instead Martina wittered on about viewing figures and syndication rights, between sipping white wine, waving both hands, and flashing her eyes. A cameraman lurked in the background.

As Lucy had said before leaving for London. "Honey, no sweat! Journalists love schmaltz and Martina's one of that pack. Throw her some candy! Add a few peanuts and popcorn for luck." But Vee remembered what Garrick had said and wished she could give him a call.

Martina gushed. "Hello Verity darling, I'm so looking forward to "Cook and Let Cook". Honestly, how do you do it? Calories? Vitamins? Trace elements? Permitted flavourings? I mean." She looked Vee up and down. "Me, I'm so so disorganised! I bet you keep your cherries well away from your bacon," and she winked.

Their conversation was liberally sprinkled with Martina's latest aphorisms bemoaning the frailties of woman, as though women's lib had not taken place.

"How do we girls manage? We need so much more than food." As Martina leaned over and patted her hand, Verity sensed where the conversation was leading. "Without a guy, I'm a tragedy queen." She waved be-ringed hands. "It's not in our feminine psyche. So how's yours, eh? The 'Mister Man' in your life? Is he is a big chef too?" Martina leaned expectantly forward.

Verity sensed being acutely observed. "Not exactly."

"No? Is that so?" Martina dragged out a notebook and waited, pen poised. "Not a chef? But he does have a name?" She grinned conspiratorially. "Yeah?"

"We–ell, he's kind of private."

"Aha. I seeeeee." Martina scribbled away. "You're separated? Divorced?" She moistened her lips. "He's not on some kind of a charge? You don't have to tell if you'd rather not." She leaned forward and winked. "Verity means truth, but you don't have to reveal private secrets. Everyone's got some stuff to hide, and you and me's both Yankees who'll . . . Hey wait!" Martina was pointing towards a table loaded with Brut Champagne Grand État. "Now that's what I call service." She gave a broad wink. "And all on the house."

Verity shook her head.

Martina gasped. "I can't believe you meant that!"

She scrambled to her feet, spilling her handbag over the carpet, then dropped to her knees, scrabbling for notebooks, aerosols, purse, cosmetics, spare glasses, batteries, phone, a recorder, and assortments of unidentifiable objects as Verity joined in the search. A tiny red light showed Martina's recorder still running as she popped the cork in one practised movement, and poured out two fizzing glasses.

"Ignore me," Martina sipped with eyes closed. "Just keep talking. Me, I'm a sponge. Everyone confides in me. So cheers!" And Verity began to relax.

100

The north end of Cavanham Street is fully exposed to east winds. As the early morning blew, Jilly Craske stood up, sat down, and prowled around in frustration. Everyone was on the make. Now her freeholder's agent had come testing walls, tapping partitions and waving dampometers round.

"It's there in the small print," he'd said, "Fascias are the responsibility of the leaseholder, otherwise there's a penalty charge."

Before daybreak her salon felt more like a cell. Many of her irregulars had booked for their twice-yearly hair-care, so when the shopfitters promised that renovations would take just one day, she'd postponed all appointments for forty-eight hours, switched off the heating, closed her eyes and relaxed, only to have cramps in her feet while her buttocks went numb. Light-headedness brought on euphoria mingled with surges of panic combined with an utter fatigue. Even her film stars looked frozen to death. Despite increasing exhaustion she'd refused to go near any doctors and risk their derision, but within weeks Christmas would catch everyone by surprise. By then she would have her new glittering fascia.

Paradise Shopfitters still had not arrived so she snuggled into an adjustable chair, curling both feet under her prominent belly. A portable black-and-white telly repeated old black-and-white films. A cookery show was insisting anyone's sex life could be souped up with shallots and ground ginger. But sex was never monochrome. Its spectrum was brilliant reds leading to purples and blues, gradually fading to yellows and browns, sometimes leaving traces of scars. Registered as 'accident prone' she had rejected counselling.

Watching chat show credits spin, a voice-over trailed a new series. "Cook and Let Cook!" She switched it off to watch Garrick pass. She needed her perk for the day. The roomscape was shrouded with dustsheets as if a death had occurred and Thomas still loomed as a threat. Lately he'd taken an interest in guns, calling them 'crucial utensils of power'. Yesterday he'd seen Garrick Jones in a journal and ripped the whole magazine up. She'd found its charred shreds in her bin, but that was Thomas all over. Only cars were truly human to him. People were lesser machines. He'd compensate with orgasms of speed. Each morning he'd give his pet vehicle its pat. This morning as usual he'd gone Formula One, racing down dual carriageways with cogs and gears screaming. He'd celebrated by playing Jagoff's new album full-blast on multiplex speakers, flirting with death and extremes which even she found exciting. She'd close her eyes, letting 'G' forces wring out her brain. She depended on getting that lift, but noticed whenever she got out of his car, it calmed down at once; its engine relaxed. Soon vehicle and master were purring together, their harmonies wholly in tune: Mondeo and Thomas, together, alone. She was the only intruder.

She must have dozed off. A large unwashed van was blocking out daylight. Paradise Shopfitters had arrived like noisy, everyday mortals and everything went into fast-forward. Hammers, chisels, drilling and banging. Soon she was in a wide-open cave exposed to a sudden onrush of air. Unless they hadn't noticed her? PVC sheeting was being stapled across a crude frame as Josh and Roddy unloaded replacement partitions. A generator was chugging away. Already the framework was shifting and creaking, its polythene bagging like sails. Isobars appeared to be flattening trees, but the builders worked on in a world of their own. Soon everything was blowing around. Then all her phones started to ring; first pagers, then landlines, one by one .She struggled to hear through the clamour.

"Hi Jilly? It's me!" she could hear Abby saying, "I was like, wondering, when your shopfitters were coming?"

"Listen!" Jilly held the receiver towards them. "That's them! And it's blowing a gale."

"Please can I have a quick word? Like, with them? . . . It's for Garrick. It's urgent. He needs some carpentry doing. He's relying on you to get him out of a jam."

"Oh is he indeed?"

As Jilly brushed away showers of sawdust and grit, a wistful smile twitched her lips.

On his regular trudge back and forth, Garrick swore to himself. He'd roughed out a cast "pending negotiations", which meant battling agents while Phyllis and everyone moaned. As if he'd not enough problems! They should be grateful for working at all, let alone starring in Chekhov, but with Bert in hospital he needed a construction manager fast Bloody fast.

He found Cavanham Street almost deserted. Shop displays were in a pre-Christmas sprint. One frontage was being completely renewed. Its neon and steel caught his eye. Its furnishings lay under sheets but on its walls were big photo-blowups in frames. The Peter O'Tooles, Larry Oliviers, John Geilguds, Gordon Popes, of this world were displayed in their prime Shakespearean roles. Above them, 'CROWNING GLORY' in neat polished chrome was partly obscured by tarpaulins.

His thoughts slipped back to Lancaster Gate, strolling arm-in-arm with his wife, their children alongside, everyone laughing and joking. Now when Roseanne headed off calls, his children must be wondering. Maybe they were missing him, sobbing inconsolably. Weeks could go past. What if their childhood were fraught with depression? Their teenage years bulging with stress? Looking beyond, he longed to see grandchildren born; to see them grow up. He felt a great flood of depression.

"I fear thee, ancient Mariner
I fear thy skinny hand!"

Something would have to be done. Family had to come first. He'd reached a decision when he heard a woman's voice. "Garrick! Garrick!" He hesitated that second too long. Lights changed. Traffic surged. Next moment, there she was; Louise pushing through late-nite shoppers, new ash-blonde tresses breaking loose from their lacquer; her silk scarf like a Japanese banner.

"Eee!" she gasped out-of-breath, "I thought you was going straight past me!" She swept long crisps of hair from her face. "Sorry! I'm due at my stylists tomorrow, thank God!" Standing on tiptoe, she kissed both his cheeks in an explosion of perfume. "When I saw you just now, I jumped out my cab!" She gripped his arm, backing him into a entry. "This is an omen, I thought. "

He thought straightway of Abigail. "Is there a problem?"

"Give over! Where on earth have you been? I've left messages all round." She dabbed her face with a tissue. "These days one cannot rely on one's staff. There's always some nasty machine in the way. But as Carlos says, The Lord God has pity. He tweaks events. My question is, when will you come to my club?"

Garrick showed his heavy briefcase and shrugged.

"Yes yes, I know," She waved away his excuse. "But it's Club Arabica. 'Café by day. Club by night!' It's the place to be." She leaned confidingly forward. "People love newness you see. Culture is definitely 'in'. They want to be fashionable, see. Specially round here. Not like my daughter's generation. And if she's giving you problems. But first Will you come to my club?"

"What? Now?"

She looked at him in surprise. "No no, of course not! I want to book you! Up here you're a star. And stars get to select their own date." As lights changed to green, she grabbed Garrick's hand and shook it? "Great, that's agreed! It's a deal. Get your agent to ring me."

On the spur of the moment Garrick had bought an escape. A late ticket to London. An Intercity Bonus Return. "Give your family a weekend surprise!" His conscience would take its revenge. As he paced the town's Victorian platforms his train rumbled in 'delayed by diversions caused by Manwess extending news pipelines'. His holdall was pregnant with last-minute presents but as Edwin would say, "It's the thought that counts". But Garrick had too many thoughts and no time.

He'd often rehearsed his homecoming scene; those Sistine Chapel moments when straining fingers would stretch out and connect. No father could ever be neutral and no parent stay detached. The émigré was on his way. He could vividly picture their joy.

"Missed you dad!" shout his kids, sobbing and laughing in one.

"My darling!" Verity sobs and admits, "You were so right. Showbiz is hell!"

Carriages were mostly pre-booked from Carlisle but Garrick managed to squat in a corner. A young woman thumbed through War and Peace. A bearded man with earphones slept. A West Indian couple read The Financial Times. Arrival at London was over two hours late after some poor devil had hurled himself under a train. However, by arriving without warning, Garrick was spared their anticipation. He resisted phoning from Euston. He was their special surprise.

On the Tube to Lancaster Gate, the closer he got, the more Verity came into focus. He pictured her tight little bottom, firm breasts and soft mouth. He'd get her bad news over with first. It wasn't Vee's fault her TV project had bombed. It was clearly some sort of tax dodge. The more accountants promised, the worse the resulting collapse. He'd recognised an obvious scam. He'd sympathise. Commiserate. Compared with her failure his problems were trite. Vee was a media victim, because everything was a gamble and audiences couldn't be trusted. Viewing figures ruled. Her catering college would take her straight back.

Then he remembered Roseanne .Even that could be worse. At least no-one had died. No cancers or motor-neurone disease. He skimmed the Evening Standard but place-names and even the typeface seemed changed. Apparently whole eras had passed and he was a foreigner now as if he'd adopted an alien scent. More to the point, would he recognise them? Growing and changing each day? .

"Think 'THREE SISTERS'!" he told himself. Not that bloody pantomime. Think Chekhov. Morozov. Think 'CHERRY ORCHARD'!" His marriage might be depending on that.

Walking from the tube to St George's Mews he felt like a prisoner released on remand. Whereas Chekhov escaped to the countryside, Garrick was escaping to town. His frontal lobes tried to un-install Norston. Damp leaves shuffled in dunes. A soft haze drifted from Kensington Gardens. Outside the Prince Regent Hotel Christmas lights blazed Seasonal Greetings. The moment he entered the Mews he felt a rush of excitement, and passing under that tall rounded arch surmounted by its Regency urns made him feel actually physically home.

He stopped to psych himself up. A cigarette or two might help? Vee was a creature of habit, so dinner was well on its way. A stupid grin overwhelmed him. Yes, time had stood still. Virginia creeper still clung like prominent veins to their walls; expensive cars huddled outside; a crazy cat shot out of nowhere. As he groped for his keys, saliva flowed, then the tears. He was still laughing as he unlocked his front door.

"Hellooo!" he called. "Hi! Darling, it's me!" A soft-porn video ought to create the right mood. "Vee!" He stopped on the stairs and listened. "Verity? Vee?"

All doors and windows were closed and electrics unplugged or switched off. Despite a Mont Blanc of cookbooks spreading like shale from the sofa down to the hand-woven rug, there were signs of hurried tidying up. This chaos had definite order as if absence were planned and prolonged. He settled down, knowing they couldn't be late because both children had school the next day. He put aside his video, and settled to watching news.

He awoke to a period movie. Cary Grant as some well-intentioned killer had narrowly missed stabbing his mistress. The heating was off. He stumbled into their bedroom and lay fully clothed on the bed, inhaling Verity's absence. He thought of phoning Samaritans Helpline, or calling Abigail out of the blue. Next time he awoke the coil of existence had untwined a further few twirls. It was all right for Chekhov. Anton knew everyone's motivations were complex because he understood people. It was there in his stories and plays how exiles returned and allegiances changed. It was easy for him.

Garrick unpacked his inadequate gifts. He scribbled ineffectual notes, leaving them on the hall table. Walking slowly around the apartment he registered every detail as if seen for the very last time. Then, collecting his baggage, he headed straight back to Euston.

Returning to Lancashire felt like defeat, or at the very least failure. Downing several large Beaujolais at Norston Railway Bar, his paranoia had fun. It suggested Vee's mother might be prime mover. She did not approve of Garrick. She was the classic mother-in-law aping the pantomime witch! But whole families didn't just disappear. And why would they spirit his children away? Roseanne was too obsessed with Internet records in Russian and her ancestral links to Massachusetts.

Norston had no such identity problems. It still retained its six-day-week. Its Sunday was the old-fashioned Sabbath; a muddle of faiths: chapels and a fancy Sikh temple, the acrid green dome of the Al Wahab Mosque; the crumbling stones of the Anglican church and the Victorian Synagogue. Here worshippers prepared for God's judgment while others peddled mementoes outside. As he sobered up, Garrick decided to drop in at the theatre and check for any messages. Nobody need know he had gone.

Retracing his original route, time seemed to fold back like arriving that very first time. Past and present converged as he dived down that narrow gulch of an alley he'd first entered just a few weeks ago. This was archaeology. It was like crossing an invisible threshold, revisiting geological eras. He tried to reconnect with that very first moment; a stillness combined with the flutter of pigeons. The sound of Eddie Craig's bulldozers sleeping.

As he clattered down the rickety steps he began to feel at home. The stairs were gloomily lit by bare bulbs but this was now where he belonged. He was part of Team Theatre. Phyllis's conditioning worked. First of all, he . . . next moment . . . he hung in mid-air like some comic cartoon.

Gravity ripped at his body. Nothingness rushed up to meet him. That high-pitched scream he could hear was his own. He started to tumble, over and over, grasping at handrails, newels anything, tumbling, sliding, bumping, snatching at fixtures and fittings. Abruptly, he crunched to a stop, hardly daring to move. Was he paralysed? Dead? He moved first one arm then a leg. His baggage lay scattered around him.

Garrick limped up the long winding stairs to his office. If he were injured he'd sue. Now he had no carpenter, everything needed repairs. He almost sympathised with Bert but as he lowered himself in his seat, it seemed that events would always obstruct him. Like the Ancient Mariner, he too was condemned to sail these polluted seas, always adrift. Never truly belonging.

"Alone, alone, all, all alone
Alone on a wide wide sea!
And never a soul took pity on
My soul in agony!"

He'd sober up and fight back. Only then did he notice a flickering light on his phone. He pressed 'Answer Play'. After clunkings and clicks he heard Vee's languid tones:

"Gary darling? Hi, I guess you'll try to contact me? No? Anyway, thing is, I've given up waiting. I'm taking the kids down to Bristol. We deserve a weekend break. You could try calling The Bedfield Hotel? Oh and Roseanne sends love to Chekhov So bye-ee from meee! From us all .And don't work too hard." She blew an audible kiss. "And think about us."

Back in Norston every step seemed to hurt. Baker's Row was lying in wait with familiar noises and exotic smells. Everything from Urdu to Hindi, Swedish to French, and Chinese to Japanese, subtitled with Anglo-U.S expletives. The great Dr Chekhov must have experienced similar medleys in pre-revolutionary Moscow. Pantomime would have been welcome, but Garrick's father turned such distractions to sin. The communal doorway was squeezed between a tobacconists and laundromat. As he inserted his key in the door, a barelegged girl in high platform sandals tugged his sleeve:

"You lonely?" she asked in a tremulous voice, then backed away.

In the entrance hall Garrick reached up and fumbled for mail on the ledge, but as usual found nothing. As he inched his way upstairs, he was steeply aware of his bruises. On reaching his landing the door opposite opened. A face appeared.

"Bin asking after you, has people." Those bloodshot eyes were restlessly squinting and blinking. "Bin folk asking questions," he whined.

Garrick gave a curt nod and double-bolted his door, but paper-thin walls transmitted the pains of intestinal plumbing. This was reality. Match of the Day echoed from over the landing. Next morning he'd have bruises to show. Now he needed ice-packs and rest. He thought about suing the council. To offset depression he switched on every light in the place.

There beneath the main hanging lamp and scattered all over his table lay his newly dismembered script fanned out like a vast deck of cards. Solitaire or Canasta? Who cared? This was another unplayable hand. He put on the kettle and made instant coffee.

"Enter Two Ugly Sisters, dressed in trainers and bloomers. They start doing aerobics on a range of training machines, while Cinderella polishes and cleans, running around lifting weights for them . . ."

ASPHYXIA. "Sister darling, aren't you impressed? I'm working away at firming my buttocks"

EUTHANASIA. "Really sister? You could have fooled me. I thought you were wearing a bustle."

ASPHYXIA . "How dare you? You're just jealous. Look at your thighs! Talk about liposuction. They'd need an industrial Hoover for yours! You look more like the Michelin man!"

EUTHANASIA . "What about you? Call those boobs? They must have implanted hot air balloons!"

ASPHYXIA. "Now, now! Little Cinders makes me sick! Look at her ! Bulimic with curves! That's a serious medical condition."

EUTHANASIA. "Yes! (She groans and puts a hand to her head). She makes me sick!"

Ideally it should be Michael Gambon, but Garrick could hear Wade Bluman too. And they'd laugh, the buggers, they'd laugh! As someone said, "Get the character right, then anything's funny!" Or do we laugh from sheer recognition, like catching a sidelong glimpse of ourselves? As his old man used to say, the only joke is Mankind. Except that wasn't funny. At thirty-eight going on thirty-nine, Garrick had scarcely begun to connect with himself, yet managed to lose touch with his wife. Once he'd been half of a couple, one quarter of a family unit. Now he was the absent fifth. That wasn't funny at all.

When the phone interrupted his thoughts, from the timing he knew it was Vee.

"Good evening," said a mid-Atlantic voice, "I'm assuming that is Mr Jones?"

He knew at once something dreadful had happened. "Who is that?"

"We've got urgent news," it continued, "Did you know, with Manwess Utilities you can combine your gas, phone and electricity bills into one single payment, and . . .?"

As he slammed the phone down somebody knocked at his door. Garrick promptly redialled Vee. When the banging renewed he peered out through his spy-hole. Seeing nothing, he edged the door open. The face from over the landing stared up.

The squatting man held up a package. "Some fella, like, rings me bell, Saturday."

When Garrick's phone started ringing again, he snatched up the handset:

"Sod off Manwess Gas! I'm complaining to the Ombudsman And the Minister. And the board of . . ." He became aware of a voice . . .

"Gary? Gary?" it repeatedly asked. "Did you just call?" Vee sounded calm in a dangerous way. "What on earth's going on?"

"I might ask you the same."

"Me? I left you a message to say we were taking a break in the country. A weekend's retreat from the world. Well? Don't I deserve that? One of us has to put others first!" He was stunned by her tone. "So mister smart guy? I booked the kids Monday off school. You could at least have called back." She was sounding unreasonably tearful. "But no. No gratitude there. You never so much as say thanks."

"Vee, darling, I'm sorry but . . .". What was she talking about?

"You're a damn-awful liar! You butt-hole! You goddam went and forgot!"

The line had gone dead but her words echoed on. Then something clicked.

The new parcel's label looked undistinguished. First class stamps. Postmark blurred. No obvious visible leads, but . . . he tore off its outer brown paper. Inside lay a smaller colour-wrapped package. No sender's name. He ripped open the next layer. Within this lay a gold cardboard box. Inside this, a silver wrap of animal softness. On opening this he found a bubble-wrapped shape. Wrapping followed more wrappings like a pass-the-parcel joke. Picking through the residue, he came across a tiny pearlised box neatly tied with a mini white ribbon, like a small egg in its nest.

As it flipped open, a coil of fine parchment unfurled. Something slithered quicksilver fast, as metallic and swift as a reptile. The 22 carat gold Rolex Imperator slid onto a patch of frayed rug. It postured. It seemed to echo "Cinderella", Scene Eight, end of Act II . The technological slipper was his. The timepiece was waiting, glittering, teasing. Its fit would be perfect. At any moment, it might dart away.

"To my dearest darling Gary Wishing you a happy anniversary. 15 short years! And two beautiful children! These are the fruits of my very first cheque, courtesy of 'Salle à Manger' and 'Cook and Let Cook'! With all my love, Vee," written in that neat round handwriting of hers followed by dozens of kisses. Inscribed in the watch case he read:

"To my darling Gary from Verity with all my love. Lest we ever forget. XX."

"Boom de-Boom! Boom de-Boom!" like many volcanoes erupting. "Boom de-boom! Yeaah!" the heavy bass thudded on. "Boom de-Boom! Boom de-Boom!" emulsifying bodies and brains.

Abigail too was dissolving to jelly. At two in the morning nothing existed but substances flushing through blood. How chemicals worked she couldn't care less. All she knew was, she and Stacey were perched on high barstools in darkness. The floor was a trampoline bobbing and whenever she tried putting thoughts into words, Stacey kept yelling her down.

"Stuff it, Abbs! Whingeing's for wimps!"

Clubbers stomped on as Abby scraped hair from her eyes. Her job at the theatre had failed: her work was not working; Bert was in hospital; Phyllis was objectionable, then Garrick had blotted her out. People undervalued her, Stacey included. If all she lacked was confidence, no other asshole helped. As for her mum, her only concern was to sign Garrick up for that club, like she'd already purchased her share. The distance between them had grown.

"Boom de-Boom!" Jolted by shockwaves, Abigail's wrists were beginning to itch, then to ache. "Boom de-Boom! Boom de-Boom!" Sound and vision fell into step, everything pulsing as one. Freeze-framed in flashes of colour, a black DJ in bright purple jump-suit with sunshades leaped from keyboard to sound-desk and back. Abby sat sipping her sixth Double-Skewler, bombarded by lights, watching bodies disconnect; a landscape of split-second stills; a future when anything happened; even worse, you got old. But what if she turned into Louise? The daughter becoming the mum?

Then the Karaoke began and Stacey kept yelling. No sign of Roddy or Josh. It couldn't have got any worse as Stacey dispensed her own mocking justice sending spotty boys packing. For her it was mature divorcees with million-dollar yachts or nothing. Abby withdrew but even in innermost parts of her brain she found herself cornered. "Are you enjoying yourself? Sure you want to stay?" and all in Louise's voice. Then when Stacey said she looked ill, Abigail stalked angrily off. Stacey reluctantly followed.

They emerged in a long smoky hallway, which opened onto a fire-escape where couples writhed. Stacey kept pleading but Abigail covered her ears. Everything was pulsating, squeezing blood out of dancers and pumping it off down the drains. Perhaps it recycled whole bodies? Here there were zombies, werewolves, and vampires and her whole head was exploding. There was something hallucinogenic about it. Stacey was shaking her arm.

She tried to check Abigail's pulse. "You okay? You've had a bad trip."

"No, not me. Just my soul."

"Jesus!" Stacey's eyes narrowed. "Next you'll be taking the veil!"

108

But Abby knew in such a world Cinderella was a flesh-eating monster leading a carnivorous chorus screaming for underage girls. A massive tsunami could sweep them away.

"Okay, I've had enough." Abby said calmly, "I've work in the morning."

Stacey's eyebrows flicked. "Work? You call that work?" She put her mouth to Abigail's ear. "Get real, lovey. What I call work is, like, cleaning out hairdressers' loos!" She pulled her skirt a notch or two up, legs apart, eyes closed, like a lap-dancing scene in some movie. "Know why you never score? You're setting sights at building contractors? Jesus!" She gripped Abigail's shoulders. "They're just fuckin' brickies!"

"No he's not. He's a carpenter!"

Stacey mock-yawned. "Like Jesus Christ, you mean? I'd rather have Garrick myself. At least he's a man who's got bollocks. But you. You're little Miss Mary Madonna, seducing God's bloody Angels. The virgin what's just seen the light?"

"You don't know that!"

Abigail took the Fire Exit stairs. Steel heels clattered down. Behind her Stacey laughed.

A gang of lads came scampering up from the toilets. As Abby descended, the steps rose to meet her. The guys continued upstairs.

Abigail looked back. He had not even seen her, less than an arms-length away, literally passing her by. Or was she invisible still?

As Stacey arrived, Abigail managed a smile, and was suddenly sick down the stairs.

CHAPTER SIX

PROMPTINGS

When Abigail approached the theatre next morning it was dark and still raining, but this is the nature of Norston. Less than four hours sleep hadn't helped. Nevertheless she'd obtained her National Insurance and had the compulsory row with her mother. She'd even caught a brief glimpse of her soul followed by the requisite hangover, leaving her brittle and cool.

At the top of Cavanham Street she noticed new hand-painted posters plastered across The Majestic's façade. 'Cinderella Coming!' they said, 'Keep watching this space!' as if pumpkins and mice would materialise any moment.

She skipped up its broad shallow steps. Foyer doors closed with a soft clunk behind her, obliterating traffic, builders, roadworks, Louise, and everything, as if an invisible airlock had shut. Savouring the stale dusty air, she very slowly exhaled. Ahead of her, from a shallow niche on the landing, the black-and-white photo of Garrick gazed out like one of Jilly Craske's kings. At least she had arrived on time, whereas last night her prospects hadn't seemed good.

Louise had been lying in wait. The moment Abigail entered the hallway she'd snapped like a trap. According to her, staying out late was the last straw, then she'd gone completely berserk. Hers was an Oscar-winning performance with nominations for Hysterics and Frenzy. She'd raked everything up. Truancy. Failed qualifications. Even her walking out of school (as if Abigail had been the only one to rebel). They claimed they'd been worried to death. When Abigail explained she'd simply been delayed at a bar by a migraine, her dad had reverted as well, just as Stacey had forecast. He'd

110

threatened vendetta, ignominy and shame, convinced she had been 'compromised'. Again, as Stacey had warned, 'families rely on control'. Like she said, it was tribal. Adults were shit-scared, because youth and sex brought their insecurities out. To that generation, kissing meant pregnancy or venereal disease. Sex wasn't just a physical act. The very idea was traumatic to them. There was something medieval about it. They could not accept growing up. Reaching sixteen with real legal rights was something they'd never be able to grasp. Instead Louise and Carlos had exceeded Christ's waiting disciples in their pacing and praying while drinking huge jugs of black coffee, then gone into slow motion panic.

It seems they'd been contacting hospitals, police stations, churches and morgues. They'd even called Panic Helplines. Apparently they'd been consoling each other with old family videos of 'Baby Abby splashing about in a pneumatic pond in the garden' and suchlike. They'd even admitted recalling exactly what she'd been wearing that day and precisely what had been said, as if to fix tiny details forever. Seemingly Carlos had offered up prayers, composing public statements mourning the loss of their beautiful daughter and pleading for her instant release. He was online to Child Rescue and planning to telephone Garrick when Abigail stepped into the light of their hallway. It was as if they had witnessed a ghost. Shock quickly gave way to hysterics. Then rage.

"My God! What time is this?" Louise had blocked the way. "You could've knocked years off our lives. And what about your appointment tomorrow? And what'll your friend Jilly say! If you upset Garrick, we'll bloody murder you!" Desperation distorted her voice. "Right, so that's it. You'll never make it. Now you're bloody out on your own!" Followed by almost physical silence.

After so many misjudgements and so many crossed lines, Louise had finally done it: cut the umbilical cord. Followed by instant regrets. When Louise began sobbing, worse was to follow. Both parents started begging forgiveness. Forgiveness from her! As if the whole world had turned turtle. Now, as Abby stood on the half-landing avoiding the photograph's unblinking gaze, Phyllis happened to glance out from her office, saw Abby, and tried to dip back.

"Hiyah Phyllis!" Abigail gave a vigorous wave. "Beautiful day!"

As Phyllis watched Abigail bounce down the office-block passage then dance out of view, she could not explain her unease. She looked nervously round. The very institution seemed under threat, however absurd that might sound. It appeared to her that whenever chaos was brought under control, new virulent forces emerged. Fresh generations arose like mutating viruses, leaving even the late, dear Rex Schulman passé.

Once Phyllis herself had joined as 'new wave'. In those days theatre was still much in vogue. Now Garrick had taken dear Rex's place, everybody was exposed. She and Bert would be next in the frame. At least she had some status still. She and Arthur were allies, he in his redbrick Edwardian terrace sipping neat whisky, glued to that massive video screen, she in her command post here. Her knowledge and experience made her immune when everything was temporary. The arrival of Abigail Roberts confirmed this. But who knew what their new man would do? When Garrick had first applied for the job, he was a total unknown alongside other applicants. On her own initiative Phyllis had gone to the trouble of checking his Curriculum Vitae. She'd found non-existent 'Seasons of Shakespeare', and productions of "Cherry Orchard" and "Hedda Gabler" at theatres she could not even trace. Perhaps, she suggested, those details didn't exactly square up? And wasn't his presentation too slick? Questionable even? Arthur's response had been unexpected. He'd not seemed especially concerned. He'd simply stroked his chin, nodded, and smiled. He'd almost seemed smug, and all of a sudden this Garrick fitted his bill.

"Arthur," she whispered, slipping off her spectacles, hoping the years would slip away too, "Coast's clear. She's gone."

"So what?" Arthur seemed irritated. "I'm on the Board. It's a regular meeting. I'm representing the council."

"Yes, of course I know that, but . . ." Arthur struggled with knotting his tie as Phyllis extracted the ends of his collar, smoothing the back of his suit. "What does Norston Mercury matter? Or that bloody Gazette? I've nothing to hide."

"Sorry, I didn't mean . . ."

"No no, of course not. But we depend on Lady de Vries. On her commitment to culture. She's our patron. We don't listen to gossip on Radio Norston."

"Quite." But Phyllis sensed something was not being said. "What I mean is, if I can assist . . .?" She helped Arthur drag his alpaca coat over his navy-blue pinstripes. ". . . in any way at all?" And she felt herself blushing.

"Thank you Phyllis, but what those culture vultures don't understand is, folk want entertainment piped direct to their brains. They want it intravenous. And raw! Accessible to anyone. We need to keep one step ahead." She was smoothing his overcoat with her bare hands. "But you, Philly, you're immune to such wheelings and dealings." He patted her head. "You transcend all that. And by the way, I'll give Bert your love. I'm calling in the hospital on the way home."

As his silver-grey Bentley slid away, the sky to the left was brightening. Phyllis clip-clopped around checking correspondence. In Rex's time, this had been her own little world; a confidential clearing house through which everything passed. She liked to stay in control, but as she moved a pamphlet out of the in-tray, loose letters spilled onto the floor; one addressed to "Garrick Jones Esquire, Director of Productions", and marked "Internal. Private", much in Arthur's archaic style. She held it up to the light and . . .

"Hi. Is Garrick here?"

Phyllis almost let go of the letter, but did not turn round. "Don't you usually knock?" She gave the packet a purposeful tap then thrust it into Abigail's hands. "And give this to Garrick." She noticed a small hesitation. "Yes? Was there anything else?"

"He's meant to be rehearsing on-stage, but . . ."

"No. Not this time." Phyllis folded her arms. "We're rehearsing at St Giles's Church Hall because the stage might be in use." She flipped two fingers as inverted commas. 'To earn its own keep,' so to speak, but don't quote me. I shouldn't burden you with this, but . . ." Allowing herself a secret smile, relying on the 'Peter Says' theory where any snippet quickly mutates into biblical proportions.

A miniature seed had been planted. The rest was female intuition. All evolution was based upon this.

Even as he entered the bike shop, Garrick gave way to compulsion, glancing again at his new watch, once more admiring its class; its numerals in 22 carat gold; the elegant sweep of its filigree hands dividing time into miniature fractions; its faultless engineering, its gold and platinum case. His wife knew him only too well. He was already late, but what was half an hour or so compared with ten years of marriage? This was Chekhov's centenary year. Time was wholly relative. The Majestic's gravitational pull wavered. The doorbell pinged, marking another small stage in his quest.

'Blue Mountain Byke Store. Pogo sticks and skateboards at discounts! 'No Interest Credit.' Gleaming machines filled windows and spilled out under awnings. City Bikes, Mountain Bikes, Rovers, Slaloms, Dual Suspensions, BMX. When it came to such practical details Coleridge and Chekhov were useless. As far as Garrick knew, neither rhapsodised about low-slung handlebars or aerodynamic specifications: nor centres of gravity, gearing, suspension, handlebars, weight, all to six decimal points. Should he go for carbon-fibre frames with tensioned steel spokes and poly-fibre aerofoil sections! Or was it multiplex gears with variable tensions? The limitations of literary culture were clear. Such realisations were painful.

A dreadlocked salesman in glossy white tracksuit and silver trainers hovered at Garrick's elbow, demanding to know the age of the child. Glimpsing a wrist encased in a few thousand dollars, he moved towards 'top of the range'.

"No thanks," Garrick said, "Just show me something sturdy and cheap."

The salesman was visibly shocked. "But kids got partic'lar tastes."

When Garrick explained he needed a second-hand bike for himself, the salesman dragged a black unisex from the shadows and gave it a wipe with a rag.

"Plus you'll be needing pump, screw-driver an' puncture repair kit, a waterproof cape, security padlock, safety lightin', insurance an' copy of de Highway Code? You not by chance needin' anyt'ing else?"

"Yes. Cycle clips. For my trousers," ignoring the salesman's expression.

As Garrick wobbled out into the traffic his co-ordination failed. With muscles and tendons at odds he scythed a sharp corner before turning uphill to the theatre: his son would not have been impressed. Bent down over the handlebars he pedalled and strained until he caught sight of Arthur's new pantomime posters. As Garrick wobbled and blinked at their supermart style, a black Mondeo was slewing up Huddersby Road heading for Cavanham Street, passing the theatre and carving up traffic in a continuous sheet of iced spray.

Despite being drenched and exhausted Garrick crossed the Manwess picket line, parking his dripping new bike in the foyer. In a rush of pheromones he shook out his cape, feeling a sense of achievement. He was renewed. Today would be lighter and brighter. His optimism would never be shaken nor would he be deterred from his task. Then he confronted his newly-framed younger self on the landing.

As Garrick entered her office, Phyllis could not help being aware of his watch. He held it conspicuously up to his ear before crosschecking the wall clock, which saved her from pointing out he was late. Instead she announced there was a collection for 'poor dear Bert' as if he were already dead, before explaining he had dislocated a shoulder, cracked a few ribs, and fractured two bones in one leg, 'poor dear love'. The management hoped he would not sue; the situation was painful enough. She explained that a certain Louise Roberts had phoned twice within half an hour, then added as an afterthought,

"Oh, and do you know an Elizabeth Scott? Norston Mercury? Also a Marianne Scobie? From the Norston Gazette?" She observed his reactions. "Have you time to phone them back? Or shall I fax your official statement?"

He shook his head. He had to get his priorities right. Before anything else Verity needed immediate thanks. Her gift had come as a shock. That parcel arriving by ordinary mail instead of registered post had suggested their usual symbolic gestures. Not this. It included a signed certificate plus official guarantee and expensive insurance. It had cost Vee a small fortune. And what if it had gone missing? He felt humbled. Almost ashamed. Tears welled up in his eyes. As he watched the second-hand spin round he felt almost guilty. It was hard to take in. This was a superbly engineered object, engraved with "Fifteen long happy years". It was a twenty-first century heirloom to bequeath to his kids. A modern memento mori. It was a tribute to love. He couldn't stop flipping his cuff, catching its sparkle, observing time moving inevitably on, putting his life in perspective.

Okay, so he'd been wrong. But with reason. He marshalled his self-justifications. No, the fact was he had forgotten. Forgotten, in spite of Verity's hints. Forgotten their anniversary. Bloody forgotten! He had been distracted, but he'd had plenty to be distracted about. After all, his Chekhov productions came first. Verity would understand that. So what the hell to do now? He'd have to send a reciprocal gift to commemorate their shared lives and celebrate their children But what? Electronic "thankyous" were useless. He needed to tell her he loved her, but until they could talk directly he'd have to rely on recording a message. But by the time he'd reached his desk, Garrick's cycling muscles ached. Then other muscles and tendons he'd not even known existed went into series of spasms.

As Garrick sat down to compose a response to his wife, Eddie Craig was enjoying late breakfast, having been up since five in the morning touring sites in the dark. Now Eddie was opening his post.

Today's correspondence ranged from accountants' bills to political crap from lobbying groups. Some he threw straight in the bin. Torn envelopes littered the rosewood desk facing his new Adam fireplace salvaged from Beckwith Grange. He scrunched another letter up. What environmentalists could not see was, that to improve you first had to destroy. Destruction had strict requisites. Its detail was the essence; it had to be planned with complete dedication. He studied latest catalogues between sips of high-caffeine, making notes as he went. As the Victorians knew, technology is an expression of faith.

It was all in these stiff glossy pages. Standard, de Luxe, Mobile, Multi-Wheeled, Tracked with Bulldozer Fitments, Fixed and Extending, and so on. Apparently anything could be flattened! Even the toughest reinforced concrete. He digested pages of specifications, relishing technical details. Oxyacetylene cutters now came in fashion-accessory colours with a range of pneumatic attachments. Bonus equipment came free with each purchase. Gimmickry was everywhere. He was still bemused when his phone started bleeping. He let it take a message as he kept turning pages.

'PERMITTED EXPLOSIVES' in double-thick caps had a section to themselves guarded with qualifications and warnings as if anticipating his plans. This was the modern hard sell.

"Introducing a classic new urban standard," it read, "The ultimate technology. Simple easy-to-use mouldable plastic, detonators included. Demolishes in seconds. A day's preparation, to safely remove a twenty-five-storey tower from the map all within less than one minute. Minimum technology with latest safety modifications. Think of work and man-hours saved! All you need do is truck the resulting landfill away. Easy as that! Visit our website. Send off for our video."

Time-frame stills showed chimneystacks melting into flat earth and electricity coolers like gigantic bobbins dissolving straight into sand. Talk about progress! Forget licences and registrations, high density centres no longer posed problems. It was almost disturbingly easy, destructive and constructive in one, but traditional craftsmanship abhorred shortcuts. As for Health and Safety laws, regulators distrusted science, and anyway archaeologists always protested no matter what.

It was never really that simple. With sacrifice came danger; the Old Testament blended with the Talmud and Koran, leaving him like Moses in a private wilderness donating his soul to the town. This was the temptation. First setting fuses, connecting the current and wires, leading up to the physical act of pressing the plunger himself then *Boo-ooom*! *Crrrunch*! Obstacles removed. Whole civilisations could be neatly erased, recycled and improved. Even Arthur Ruddock would be impressed.

Yes, they sparked off each other, did Arthur and he. Together with Brinkhouse and Brinksides they amounted to a dynamic team; a movement; a philosophy even. There was a Victorian optimism about it. Unconstrained progress would rescue the human condition and preserve humankind, so why should he worry? By global standards, this Garrick Jones was a minor distraction. In fact Eddie Craig was not sure why he gave the matter a thought. His mission was Urban Resuscitation. Not outdated drama. But once you started blasting, where would it end? With old institutions imploding? Norston Council included?

He gulped down the rest of his coffee, before phoning his site in Cavanham Street for a detailed report on how far they'd progressed this morning, dismantling buildings the old-fashioned way.

By the time Garrick got through to London, he'd dialled at least seven times. It was like being alone on a seesaw. Then to his surprise, a little voice answered.

"Hiyah dad!" it burbled, "It's me!" Mark was sounding upbeat.

"Hello son." Garrick chose to tread warily. "Did you know Daddy came home to London this weekend? But no-one was there So I missed you. How about that! Where were you? And how's mummy? She must be in a terrible state? All that hard work. And what with granny there too."

"Mom's out. So's nan. We been away filming an' that. An' had a great time! Triffic! And our hotel was great and so was the helicopter ride. An' we got loads and loads of food. And everybody kept on cheering and that! And people kept givin' me presents and candies, and Rachel got make-up then . . ."

He could not expect a little child to be aware of impending disaster. Through innocent eyes catastrophe must look like a series of picnics. Verity would have put on an act with helicopters and chauffeurs, but she wasn't cycling to unheated theatres nor having to battle with gas maintenance men. Soon she'd have to cut and run, but Mark would not have realised. How could he? Verity would have concealed her distress, but Garrick had tried to warn her. He knew it wouldn't work out, but even as she went into freefall, she would still be protecting their son. Girls however were much more aware. Sensitivity was hardwired into them. Rachel's two added years would make all the difference.

"So. Is your sister around?"

"Oh!" Mark sounded surprised. "Shall I get her?"

"Hang on a minute. This isn't half term? Why aren't you both at school?"

Mark's scorn was acerbic. "We got special dispemp-stations now Mom's a star! We don't go back till tomorrow." In the background Garrick heard muffled exchanges. "Shall I put Rachel on?"

"Lo daddy." Rachel sounded almost subdued, "We been in a hotel."

"Hi darling. Did you enjoy all that filming?"

"Mmm! We played in a big kitchen, and I made some pastry. That's all."

"Then it wasn't entirely good fun?"

"Oh, so-so People made such a fuss. Like they fluffed up my hair with a blow-drier an' stuff. An' school made us, like, promise to write essays about it. An' I got eversuch a lot to write. But I'm not sure I enjoy being famous." Garrick heard background whispers. "Sorry. Got to go. Nan's coming back. Some crazy cat tipped the trash over. Striped orange with a white tip on its tail. It's not local she says. Anyways, momma's off a few days buying us toys. Hopefully not cookies or candy. We've got such lots to do! We'll tell her you rang. Bye-ee! " He heard Mark chime in from the background.

"Bye-ee!" both shouted in chorus, and rang off.

Once again distance had struck with Vee going up as Garrick headed back down. Not even Anton Chekhov could help. Nor George Bernard Shaw. Nor Oscar Wilde. Nor August Strindberg. Nor William Shakespeare. Nor Richard Brinsley Sheridan. Nor status nor kultur. Not even the downmarket forces of farce. It was an inevitable process because he had casually lied to himself: perjured himself to impress. Now he was out on his own. He was stuck with Prince fucking Charming and that stupid cow Cinderella!

It seemed as if Vee and Roseanne were deliberately making things harder, colluding in Garrick's own lies, pushing him to further extremes. This meant his postponing atonement until he had actually started on Chekhov. Before that, Vee's project collapsing would solve Garrick's problems. She'd need him then as much as he depended on her. Until then, his family photographs created a shrine to living and life. Each picture had something to say. Only then did he notice. One was missing. That close-up of Gary and Vee side-by-side, heads together, laughing, almost filling the frame. He'd been sure it was there, but if people were stealing and cutting up photos . . . ? No that didn't make sense.

A bedraggled pigeon huddled on his window-cill, its head tucked under its wing. No billing and cooing. No last-minute mating. Theirs was a seasonal life. A lifespan in one calendar year?. In which case his 15 year marriage deserved celebration. Golden Anniversary? Silver? Whatever?

The cellphone caught him off guard. Its ring-tone hinted at Vee's distinctive inflections. He pressed it hard to one ear, allowing his glittering timepiece to reinforce every turn of his wrist. He manoeuvred the dial to catch any light.

"Gary! You turd!" rasped a deep familiar voice, "I got you another great offer."

"Rocko?"

"You need it spelling out? D – O double-L– A– R – S, an' that's you directing an' co-starring my namesake, Rocky Farino! Wi' sex-kitten Dianna Blaise! That's 'Billy Jo' the musical. Yeah man, it yours for the takin'."

Garrick knew others must have refused it outright. That was typical Rocko. Ibsen and Chekhov were peanuts to him.

"No no, trust me Gary," Rocko pleaded, "Remember Suki and Zee-Zee? Remember us touring? Cabarets all round the Near East. Okay! Don' say I don' never offer you help!"

When Rocko rang off, Garrick returned to his searches but still his missing photo was nowhere. Then, once his concentration was rocked, Suki and Zee-Zee began to recur. Those nights at the Blue Sphinx in Cairo. Dangerous and exciting. He'd been young and rebellious. He'd taken risks. Sex was exciting. Thank God there weren't any websites those days. All that slick erotica. And all their public perversions! By re-enacting provocative poses, including the full frontal action of Slinkie, they'd still be shocking today. Luckily he'd burnt all their pictures. He was down on his knees searching under the desk when he heard footsteps, light and distinctive, coming upstairs.

Outside on the landing Abigail stopped, holding an envelope against the light. As Garrick opened the door he caught her freeze-framed in a tableau vivant: the classic 'caught in the act' . As she froze in horror Garrick doubled up, laughing. He ushered her in and shut the door, amused to see she was blushing.

"So. What's this about?"

"Sorry, I – I". In chagrin she almost curtsied. "Sorry but Phyllis says as she's making a collection for Bert." She passed him the letter. "And like he's broken some bones, and won't be back working. Not till well after Christmas."

"Ah."

"That's why, you see. I've got this great idea. It's like, what with Bert being injured, we could be in luck. There's this carpenter I know and if we're everso quick . . ."

She explained about this brilliant artist who'd single-handedly built, constructed, and fitted the frontage for Crowning Glory, but Garrick had slit the envelope open and was reading:

"Jesus! This is bollocks, Abigail! Crap! It says we can't rehearse on our own sodding stage! And why's that?" He looked apoplectic. "Why? Because they're renting it out for 'Sponsored Talent Shows' and 'Stand-up Comedy Evenings'! Can you believe it? Comedians! Comics! Just when we need to rehearse."

"But St Giles Hall is where we rehearse. That's what Phyllis says."

"Oh really? What you mean is, they want to use our stage to make money. Anything for brass! Next they'll hold Karaoke nights, knobbly knees contests and transvestite strips, dragging our theatre's good name through the . . . ! And it's my name as well . . ."

He leant across to his bookshelves. She watched him flick across spines, anatomising, selecting. With great care he took 'Aho's Companion Guide To The Theatre' and fondled its weight in his hands before flipping through its dense-printed pages like a professor.

"Excuse a failed actor a moment . . ."

He raised up the book like a parson about to make a pronouncement. Then with a wild yell, slammed it violently into the wall. Together they watched it splay out slide down then slump to the floor, flutter a moment, quiver like a broken-winged bird before one final tremulous twitch. When he looked up Abigail was gone and everything had changed.

Teamwork pays, Roddy insisted. He and Josh gelled; a partnership dependent on trust. They were best mates; a duo that worked. Individual weaknesses were turned into shared strengths. Of course moonlighting did mean taking risks but as a semi-political act it struck at the very Company System. It undermined Capitalism. It turned theory into practical use. It was himself and Josh versus the rest, which meant more than financial reward. After all, why should company assets be left unused after-hours? Why should tools lie idle, weekends? That was criminal waste. Anyway, anarchy wasn't just about waving black flags. And Paradise Ltd wasn't all it seemed. It justified Realisation of Self. Or did it?

Roddy sensed reservations. At least he himself would always survive because wit was a dangerous weapon: he was honing it into an act. So what about the North-South divide and Culture's discrimination against them? It all came down to caste. It was racial; ethnic; tribal. Or didn't the Tory caste system matter? He'd recently noticed that Josh was only too quick to adapt. Little things had begun to add up. Despite knowing their shared exclusivity mattered, Josh was over-inclusive. Since that job in Cavanham Street a certain third party kept cropping up. Everyone knew no double-act ever worked as a trio. Every comic knew that. She wasn't in their bloody script, and Roddy was

118

not into three in a bed, so when Josh repeated Abigail's name, Roddy finally snapped.

"You fuckin' mad? You're not really thinkin' of takin' that job? At the theatre?" He raged like a thrice-thwarted gunman slamming huge timbers around. "Jesus. Takin' leave o' your fuckin' senses?" He found himself slipping back into Belfast, "You been like this since that fuckin' wig-maker's shop! Always so bloody unsettled." He hurled planks across trestles leaving Josh to re-stack them. "Where's your revolutionary fervour? Where's your sense of direction?"

"All I'm talking about is – like –" Josh repositioned a top-heavy plank. "Like it's nothing special. Except – except –"

"There's no fuckin' exceptions!"

Roddy slammed a last beam on the rack knowing the biggest joke was, it wasn't a joke. Truth was, Roddy couldn't trust Josh anymore, and if you can't trust your best mate, then even the loudest ovations signify sod-all but noise. Nothing stops satire. That's how creative comedy works. You bare bloodstained teeth at their laughter. You spit at them. You push back the bounds of good taste. Obscenity works. You make the public bite back. You swear. You insult them. Then when beercans and bottles get thrown, you know you've scored. Provocation gives strength and Roddy was strong, whereas Josh was always so eager to please. One day he'd find this Irish bastard ran his own comedy network beamed on every medium. Then Roddy would make them all laugh till they bled. The ghastly tastelessness of it! The utter unfunniness of it! The indiscriminate fury! The painful outrage of mocking your roots!

"The Irish Humpty-Dumpty? The wall it was that fell on him!" "The Dubliner who thought Cunni-lingus was an Irish airline .And flown by Pontius Pilot!"

He wanted to remind Josh what they'd planned: their shared ambitions; matching mortgages, side-by-side beach bungalows complete with swimming pools, sun-porches and roses, shared neighbourhood projects followed by community schemes, drinks down the local, walks up the Fells, strolls on the moors, golf down at Lytham, binding their whole lives together.

Instead Josh was yawning. "For Christ's sake Roddy, let's spread our horizons," And sounding so upbeat, "First stop, the Majestic. Next stop, Covent Garden. Then on to New York!"

Roddy watched as Josh packed his holdall with that same care and precision with which he polished each chisel and blade before stacking electric drills into holsters like infantry going to war. Their partnership was over. Finito. Like that. Josh had already deleted their past. Icon-Struction was terminally wounded and Paradise was one short.

"You still can't see it," Roddy said, "Can you? It's not you what's changed! It's her what's changed you."

Josh zipped up his holdall and held out his hand, but Roddy was looking away. Josh shrugged and walked out without looking back, then took the first bus into town.

At Market Square he took a shortcut between stalls, heading down a narrow back alley towards that very same door Garrick first entered just a few weeks before. This time it was unlocked and ajar. Josh tried to tune into

Abby's presence as if she might materialise. He continued down the rickety Escher-like stairs until he came face to face with Danny Utama. Danny stood, hands on hips with an all-encompassing grin.

"Hey man." Danny pointed down a brick passage. "We's waitin' for you, Josh. So hi!" They slapped hands. "Carpenter workshops is down dere. Everyt'ing ready for you, Bert says."

Josh looked around. The faintest breath of her perfume would arouse his total awareness.

Outside in the main street a morning mist hung on the air. Garrick was pointing up at the theatre facade. Phyllis followed his stare. He indicated lettering.

"Well?" he asked accusingly, and waited.

It had been dark when Phyllis arrived. Presumably somebody must have worked overnight. Assorted alphabets were distributed in random upper and lower-case letters across the whole fascia board.

"StAnd Up CoMICs AlL nEXt WeeK." stammered disjointed fonts.

"Well?" Garrick tilted his head from one side to the other. "What's that supposed to mean? Or is it code?"

If Garrick were accusing her, her only explanation was she had no explanation. Phyllis pulled her coat tight to her shoulders. Presumably when Arthur had made the decision, someone had done their best with a mixed bag of letters, leaving her literally out in the cold. No-one had consulted her and this was the result. To add insult to injury, she'd not even been warned. As for those Stand-up-Comedy titles, it proved that untested staff couldn't be trusted, and now Garrick was becoming unbalanced.

He was pacing around in a rage and repeating. "It looks like verbal Soduko. But with no bloody clues!" He waited for some explanation.

He felt completely justified. He was being sidelined into St Giles Church Hall. One exile was being piled on another. That was a test of anyone's ego. It triggered deeper suspicions and the more he'd tried to put them aside, the more his certainties failed. He was faced with so many dead ends. When minor inconsistencies looked like vital turning points, perhaps he'd got it all of proportion? He'd even questioned why he was here because wasn't it Vee who'd first spotted that newspaper advert for Norston? Not he. And how long had she known of that TV offer of hers? Since exactly precisely when? Could it have really come out of the blue? These questions refused to lie down.

But Phyllis was squinting, head to one side in the street, "On the other hand, it is very clever, isn't it. It makes the perfect talking point. It brilliantly catches attention like all Arthur's gimmicks. It's so modern and witty in one!"

In biting Scandinavian winds driven across the High Fells, the assembled company trudged towards St Giles's Church Hall. The Victorian building lay like a beached Anglican whale, its blue-scaled slates ridged with red dorsal tiles. As the little procession straggled between alopoeciac bushes and on through rusting iron gates, its Gothic carcass seemed to arch from the mist, encrusted with layers of past. This was the very essence of Norston. It symbolised the great era of ironworks and cotton mills, softened by a patina of age. 'Faith, Hope and Charity' was engraved into its carbonised stone. Its Christian message once undisputed was reduced to a pathway of recycled tombs, with everyone chatting and laughing, bubbling with expectations as Abigail followed behind.

At the porch entrance Garrick took a deep breath before turning the heavy iron key. As the door juddered open, Pre-Raphaelite visions erupted before him in a ceramic explosion. It wasn't what he'd expected. This Pilgrim's Progress was bold and vivid, crowded with evangelical patterns, crusading colours, and missionary style, designed to boost the mill-workers' morale. Nothing was tasteful or neutral. Gothicity had gone so berserk Vee would have been physically shocked. In the same way, 'Cinderella' was blocking the renaissance of great Russian drama.

Garrick paused in the entrance. This was his initiation too. His very first stab at directing. Already the schedule was tight, but hopefully by spontaneous triangulation his calculations should work. Adrenaline seeped into his system. Cinderella would have to go on. It was hardly Step One to redemption. So far there was no Cherry Orchard in sight, nor any Three Sisters. Even if these weren't the actors he wanted, nor even the show he intended, no-one seemed too concerned. They came with their pre-packaged lives chatting away about breakfasts, train times, dry cleaners, digs, hotels, films in production, and cheapest takeaway meals.

Garrick cleared his throat. "Welcome ladies and gentlemen. Welcome to Chekhov Players, The Majestic Theatre, and to Norston itself. I want today to be fun!" at which point his voice began to lose touch with his brain.

With pantomime still his unspoken word, Garrick kept talking. His captive audience murmured politely. Fabian Wass, his assistant director, casually waved from the sidelines, stubbing out a brown cigarette and popping a peppermint into his mouth, then pointed up at 'NO SMOKING' signs as if they were divine revelations.

"Up there. See. No bloody smoking. Remember the words of the Prophet." Then he grinned and everyone seemed to relax.

The hall was arranged for the read-through. Down each side of a long table were assorted benches like some medieval banquet. As Fabian tried to allocate places, Abigail ran around trying to help while Phyllis sat with notepad and pen, her laptop to one side. Nervous excitement grew as one by one, the cast rose to introduce themselves.

A large, jowly man at the head of the table began. "Good morning, ladies and gentlemen. I am James Carr." He bowed with mock grandeur, sweeping one hand through his thick greying hair. "I have the great honour of playing Baron Hardup, the classic anal retentive! Not that I'm mean myself. No, no, not at all So long as someone else pays for the drinks."

Garrick groaned. Those like James Carr with classical backgrounds would have their pantomime contracts extended, but no rise of pay (in the great Arthur Ruddock tradition). 'The Three Sisters', 'The Cherry Orchard', 'The Seagull', 'Uncle Vanya'. Maybe also 'The Rivals', 'Miss Julie', 'Master Builde'r and so on? A rising curve would bear everyone onwards and upwards. It sounded deceptively easy.

"Hi! I'm Trixie Waltham." Trixie stood at just over 1.5 metres, pink-cheeked, curvaceous and chemically blonde, with bosoms superbly enhanced. "Lucky me! I get to be principal girl. That's 'Cinders' to you." Her voice was high-pitched and girlie. " I get the bloody glass slippers at last! Just hope they're Jimmy Choo slingback stilettos, that's all." She nudged her slumping companion.

Pippa awoke with a start. "Oh yeah. That's me. Pippa White The only black transvestite in town! An' like, I get to put on drag and be an utterly charming Prince Charming. Everyone's principal principal boy! Mwaw Mwaw!" She slapped a large olive-skinned thigh, "But Lordy knows how I'll cope with those Three Bloody Sisters But I'll maybe white-up if it helps!" Followed by laughter and whooping.

"My friends." Lionel's barrel chest rang with Shakespearean tones. "Good morning. I happen to be Lionel Parsons. I once played Laertes in Hamlet at The Majestic some thirty seasons ago. But different times, different manners. This time I appear as Dame Maggie, wicked stepmother, with a certain tendresse for . . . for whom I've not yet decided! It's either me or these wall-tiles. One of us will have to go!"

He sat down to more laughter and signalled his companion to speak.

"Hi everyone. Name's Orlando Marcel. This'll make a nice change after twelve months as Knut Brovic in the West End with our dear James here. At least playing Dandini proves I'm very versatile."

"Yes," whispered James Carr, "So we've all heard."

Garrick was thinking that Chekhov would have coughed blood and departed by now. More names came and went but Abby saw only parades of capped teeth, contact lenses, dyed hair and surgical facelifts. She blamed Jilly Craske for this insight. Being 'Stage-struck' risked total disillusion.

A small shrivelled man was waving for silence. "Ay up! Ay up! As you'll know, I'm Reggie Buck – and talking of catchphrases, I'm a right'un! Yes?" No signs of reaction. "Get on with you!" He winked with one eye, then with the other. "You're right. It's me. I done Palladium panto six times. Get on with you! Yes, I'm like a bad habit. The gristle what sticks in your teeth! You lucky people, you! I'm playing Buttons, so let's hope he won't win! Tee hee, that's me! I'm a right'un!" Reggie switched off his grin, and sat down with a furious scowl.

Before his buttocks touched the chair, a black actor with Eddie Murphy styled hair jumped up. "Hi folks. Thank you. Thanks .Truman Goss is my baptismal name Sometimes known as Fats. But heaven knows why!" He patted the spreading bulge of his stomach. "I play Asphyxia, first ugly sister, and I'm glad to be here." He bowed towards Garrick. "With all you classy legits."

A hefty man like a basketball player going to seed, was already up on his feet:

"Hi. I love your great little country. Me, I'm Wade Bluman. Your token Yankee, okay? Conforming to the stereotype. Maintaining the cultural mix. As it happens, I been researching your traditional English-style panto. To us it's vaudeville mixed with burlesque, but I've never yet played a transvestite. Like this is strictly transsexual stuff?" He seemed to have expected a laugh. "Okay okay, no homophobics. But we don't get this back

122

home. So I welcome the chance to play Euthanasia. And hey, what a great name! Fats and me, we make a great contrast as twins, him being five-two, and me well over six foot, four and threequarters. I guess that's the joke, because if we're meant to be twins shouldn't we . . . ?"

"Thanks," shouted Garrick, "There's tea and coffee down the far end."

Abigail slipped into dogsbody rôle surprisingly quickly, pouring lukewarm liquid from chipped vacuum flasks and replacing plastic cups. Everyone wanted a drink. Orlando secretly squeezed Abigail's hand, inadvertently pressing it into his groin. James Carr stroked Abigail's noticeably ringless fingers. The more she observed them the more her certainties started to waver and feminism seemed to make sense. She dreaded the thought of barbed whispers and fingers aimed at herself, but some weren't even aware she existed. Trixie accepted a coffee without looking up. Others demanded more sugar or milk. She soon became invisible. It was time to listen, observe and compare, sorry for some and envious of others, absorbing their uncensored chat. This she'd later copy into her diary, adding colourful detail for Jilly. Her friends would shrivel with envy. This way she'd fulfil her part of the bargain while seizing a chance to promote Crowning Glory and recommend Jilly Craske. Stacey's warnings had already begun to recede.

"We're depending on you, sweetie," whispered Lionel, giving her a conspiratorial wink, "We'll need a decent prompter with all this balderdash!" and patting Abigail's bum, "We girls!"

Garrick smile was beginning to hurt. He needed to perfect his performance and firm up his plans, but most of all he needed more time. Only Vee knew who he was trying to be because Garrick himself wasn't sure. Freud had got everything wrong. Instead of revelatory vision all Garrick could see was a vast cosmic plughole sucking everything and everyone down. Where were those great universal truths? The features of classical drama? Cinderella did not fit that perspective. He noticed Abigail getting attention as she floated amongst them, and felt impatient without knowing why.

"Hello my love. Is Abby, short for Abigail?" Carr was asking, "It has an Old Testament ring. Like Naomi, Rebecca and Ruth. All very beautiful women." He kissed her soft hands, imperceptibly sliding a hand down her thigh.

"It's Abby," she said firmly, "Short for Abby," and pulled sharply away.

James Carr liked the unexpected. It stimulated interest. 'The Art of Conjunctions' he called it, where no-one exists in isolation, and everyone's lineage stretched back millions of years. 'The more people live, the more they have past,' was his motto. Observing Garrick apparently 'on the defensive', James asked himself, 'Why so?'. He told himself to 'Observe and deduce', because having once played Sherlock Holmes he'd felt an instant rapport. Duality came with the job. You had to manipulate to succeed. Charm was part of his training.

"Why Garrick old chap!" James Carr gripped the director's shoulder. "Lovely to see you,"

He looked Garrick straight in the eye, noting his speed of responses, body language, unconscious reactions. He'd learned to register pitches of voice and tot up the symptoms. Such characteristics revealed more than intended. Each mannerism combined towards a total effect and Garrick rang unfamiliar bells. Something didn't ring true.

"Loved my audition. Delightful." James shook Garrick's hand. "But maybe I wasn't quite at my best, but . . ." He punched Garrick lightly and grinned. "No. Only joking! Now tell me I'm wrong, but didn't we meet in some other existence? Maybe a long time ago?"

Garrick shook his head firmly and turned to move on, but James caught his arm.

"But the name?" James was frowning. "Mind you, I wasn't christened James Carr, you know. I'm actually Corinth Braithwaite-Woods related to the Life Peer of that name. But James Carr sounds so much better. By the way, look at those two ugly daughters of mine. Can it be right, for a father to fancy his girls? Between you and me, that blonde daughter of mine, she's got a magnificent arse!"

Verity was backing out of her taxi. At exactly this moment her cellphone bleeped its new Lohengrin theme as if it had hyper-susceptivity-timers. She stumbled, slipped on loose gravel, nearly ending up on her knees in the rain. Such timing meant only one thing: this had to be Garrick! She let it play on while retrieving her case, then wiped the mud from her sleeve.

She cut Wagner short. "Hi."

"Darling!" Garrick sounded delighted. "How you are? I rang for a chat."

She snatched the receipt from the driver, adding five pounds for a tip. "You mean, aside from the fact I'm up to my elbows in shit?" She waved to the departing cab. "And never mind my whole schedule is drifting. And I'm out of fresh herbs, plus I'm getting soaked to the skin . . . and being pursued by researchers? Aside from all that, everything's just hotsie-totsie!"

"Look, I'm sorry if . . ."

"Don't give it a thought. My crew's eating high on the hog! Everyone's like 'Wow, what is this?' Our backers have gone stratospheric. They're scheduling another series, plus I've been promised a raise! Yep, I got to admit it's all pretty amazing."

Garrick was uncharacteristically silent.

She waited. "So that's my news." Her cab had vanished into the mist. "How goes our Cherry Orchard, then? Momma's so impressed, you know that? She never figured you'd do it. Come to that, nor did the kids .We're really impressed. Everyone thought you'd find a way out or dumb down. I said, no sir, my husband will stick to your guns. No dumbing down! It's Chekhov or nothing! Momma's so absurdly proud to be Russian. Sure, maybe a couple of generations adrift, but hell, she's learning that back-to-front alphabet of theirs, and . . ." Verity thought she heard echoes and splashing of water. "Gary? Where on earth are you?"

"I wanted to say that I miss you, you know that? Your confidence. Your wise advice."

She hesitated, shielding the phone from the rain. "Well . . . thanks."

"Anyway I'd better go. I'll call you back. Right."

No he damn wouldn't, Vee thought. Not if that's all he could say. She pressed the Off button, and stumbled up the puddle-strewn drive as Garrick left the urinals.

After introductions, the read-through started with much nervous laughter. As James Carr pointed out, provincial audiences lacked metropolitan taste. After years of touring West End plays, he was a student of urban decline. With one glance at Norston's run-down estates surrounded by demolition, James could gauge his audience. He rated it barely three out of ten. That's way behind Halifax, Preston, Warrington, Salford, or anywhere South. The new script was no better: a paste-up job, knee-deep in rhyming couplets and groaning with tooth-aching puns. Even Reggie Buck complained you'd get more applause from a neatly placed fart. On top of this, the climate was deeply depressing. Abigail wondered whether to tell Jilly how James had confided that Norston's canal was a sewer, and its multiple stores were out-of-date rip-offs. The town itself was his idea of hell.

"Only joking of course," James had added quickly, "We're nobodies here, so who am I to comment? My only task is to provide some minor distraction." But she knew that was not what he meant.

As rehearsals progressed, Abigail kept a lookout for Josh. He could have dropped in and said "Hi". After all who had got him his job? Lionel and Orlando were recalling great Pantaloons and Columbines from Commedia del'Arte traditions, as others recited uneven careers, listing in detail their roles and achievements. It was everyone looking for allies while swathed in an aura of deep-fried tobacco, Fabian Wass took illegible notes. In dusty polo-neck and spattered black jeans, grinning through smoke-tinted teeth, Fabian resembled a movie cartoon. "We Celts," he would say, "We red-heads!" promising Abby steady advancement if she could give him full satisfaction.

Then came that grating voice, rising up and down several octaves. "Prince Charming's Ball?" That's Reggie stopping rehearsals, patting Pippa's substantial rump and waiting till everyone's eyes fix on him. "I mean," he says, "What's this about a Prince's Ball? Eh?" He looks Pippa up and down, his bulbous eyes bulging. "This 'ere particular prince don't have no balls! So why don't us call it 'the Prince's Boob!'". But nobody bothered to groan.

Instead every punchline was argued to death, with every phrase a battlefield and motivations more disputed than Hamlet's or Lear's. From sheer repetition boredom soon began to set in, driving Trixie to desperate knitting. When lunch break was called Abigail dived for the door. .

"Hey, Abby." Garrick intercepted her at the porch. "I hope you don't mind, but if I need some wise some female advice . . . ? The woman's point of view?. If that's not taking advantage, of course? Could you help? Please?"

Jilly Craske too would have jumped at the chance.

Garrick gazed out across skyscapes of clouds stretching like Arctic oceans from horizon to horizon. Was his office drifting? Or was it the skies on the move?

'The fair breeze blew. the white foam flew
The furrow follo'd free:

We were the first that ever burst
Into that silent sea.'

The Ancient Mariner would have known a Force Nine was approaching; a squall turning into a tempest, from one single cloud no bigger than a man's hand, at which point folklore becomes superstition. Coleridge knew what it meant confronting the unexplained and unknown. Moments later skies cleared as if Garrick had imagined it all. Everywhere was hand-painted blue. The mists had dissolved. Vee had been right. Panto was hardly an intellectual challenge! 'Just learn the lines and don't bump into the scenery' was everyone's motto. You could perform dumb, deaf and blind, so long as Buttons waved to the kids and the Dame kept exposing her bloomers. Everything would fall into place once the show started its run. Then everything would change again when the Melhikovo Estate came to life and the human soul could be freely explored.

James Carr would make an excellent Lopakhin,"like one that on a lonesome road, doth walk in fear and dread" and with his lopsided grin. As Chekhov knew, you had to smile or you'd string yourself up, because words were such double-edged weapons. That's why Garrick kept Rachel and Mark in the front of his mind when asking for Abby's considered advice. When he had encountered her in the front lobby, he'd tried to put her at ease, even removing his expensive new watch and dropping it into her hand for effect, but she'd only seemed disconcerted. She had not sensed the interaction of metals, nor admired white gold, yellow gold, platinum, nickel, silver, with jewels like soft slithers of ice. Yes, he'd handled everything badly. Like when he'd shown her its engraved inscription she'd been embarrassed. A well-meaning gesture looked suddenly clumsy. Vulgar even. He'd needed her discreet advice because young women knew about trends in the way Phyllis did not. With Abigail's help he'd select the right gift for Verity .and work out how to pay for it later. Instead Abby had returned his watch without comment, dropping it into the palm of his hand.

"But aren't I lucky? That was gift," he'd explained, "Can you believe it? A gift. I wanted to show you because you're a woman with taste. I mean, what if someone wanted to buy you a present? As a token, say?" She looked bewildered now. "Any item of jewellery, I mean. Something a woman really desired?" He looked at her expectantly. "What'd you suggest? Any ideas? I need a sense of direction." She seemed to study the lay of her knuckles, spreading her fingers, individually inspecting each nail as he waited. "Look, if you'd rather not . . ."

"Oh, I don't know". She steepled her fingers, pressing the joints almost back. "Okay. Say, like a brooch? Or or maybe, like, a really nice ring?" She was eager to get away. "Yes. If you want to say something, you can't go wrong with a ring."

As he wheeled his bike down the steps, he thought about her suggestion. Manwess workmen were loading sawn tubing like cast-iron spaghetti, bearing old central heating away. Forget choosing gifts. Like living and dying you cannot avoid these contractors. With 'NEW COMICS' posters now plastered across their theatre facade, how Vee would react? It did not suggest any forthcoming Chekhov. He tugged his ski hat over his forehead and pedalled out into the headlights as red lights turned green and traffic snarled into movement. Instinctively he'd taken a glance at the watch, ending up in the wrong lane. He pedalled frantically. Swerved. A van cut him up. An Eddie Craig truck blasting fumes boxed him in at a junction. As he tried to manoeuvre, a black car cut through on the inside, almost clipping Garrick's front wheel. The thrust was followed by vacuum pull. As Garrick wobbled, vehicles around began to speed up. A white Transit van forced him into the kerb.

Wheeling his bike down the pavement he happened to pass a small jewellers. Its tactful windows glittered with small discreet charms hand-crafted in 'environmentally tested, organic, child-friendly gold'. That's the least Vee deserved. What would Abigail think? His pressed his forehead onto the bullet-proof glass, peering through metal grills. Down amongst rings, necklaces, brooches, he spotted a panel of luxury watches. There was his crunch. The Rolex Imperator itself in limited edition. Its diminutive label said in 5pt lettering £39,650. As security cameras focused, red-eyed alarms grew suspicious. He smothered his wrist with his cuff and moved off.

Stacey was waiting for Abby in her own personal part of the spectrum. Her outfit fluoresced in the shadows. Metallic-mauve lip-gloss challenged bluish-red blusher. Electric-blues swapped discords with orange. Purple eyeliner combined with false lashes to give a startled expression, but by the time Abby arrived Stacey had waited enough in the cold.

"Huh! So a contract cleaning's not a career in your eyes? Maybe, but it fucking-well pays! So? How do I look . . . ? Don't bloody go into raptures!"

She strode off down the colonnade, long-legged and prancing. Steel-tips clicked on terrazzo. The Brinkhouse modernised Arcade gleamed as they passed. Its cast-iron glowed with gold leaf. Its refurbished stores and boutiques made Abby felt drabber and drabber. Once she and Stacey had so much in common. Now with her latest scars starting to itch how could she even begin to confide? At the turn to North Arcade, suddenly Stacey stopped dead. Abby cannoned into her.

"Right. Give us it straight." Stacey stood with folded arms. "Who's the guy? Is it Him?" Abigail shrugged. "Listen cow, you was meant to be keeping a diary. You promised Jilly you'd tell what he eats, does, says. Wasn't that the deal? Or are you screwing him?"

"Stacey! Garrick's been married ten years." But Stacey rolled her eyes. "No really. He loves his wife. She just bought him a Rolex. It's their anniversary, and . . ." Abigail could picture that watch as it slithered from Garrick's hand into hers. "And it must've cost a small fortune."

"No!" Stacey gasped. "That's classic! Next step it's divorce!"

"But he's only asked for advice on some jewels."

"Jesus!" Stacey grabbed Abigail by the shoulders. "Why didn't you say?"

Abigail found herself being propelled to beneath the central glass dome of the original Edwardian shops. "Restored by Brinkside Renovations" it said. Beneath the multiple gilt chandelier the countdown to Christmas was reaching crescendo.

"Stacey! Dear girl!" a man's voice was calling, "Have you been waiting?"

A middle-aged man in camel hair coat had emerged from the jewellers behind them. The shop windows were layered with midnight blue velvet, and speckled with flashes of fire. He pointed up at the big hanging clock. His flowing black hair was flecked with distinction. Stacey gave a smug smile.

"Hiyah Sanjay. This is my best friend Abigail what I told you about. She's an actress." Stacey nudged Abigail. "So, will Sanjay give Abby that discount?" She winked discreetly at Abby. "Be a darling? Please?" She puckered her anemone lips. "Aaah thanks, sweetheart. You're everso generous. Thanks."

As Sanjay's eyes locked onto Abby, his hands slid around Stacey's buttocks. .

On their very first day at The Majestic, Trixie had cross-questioned Abby. Now, after reading 'Stage', 'Variety', 'Theatre Times', 'Drama Today', 'Board & Breakfast Monthly' from cover to cover, Pippa and Trixie double-checked their overdrafts, contacted agents, scrutinised credit card statements and topped up supplies of birth control pills. Trixie was too conscientious. Nothing could be left to chance. As the Union Rep. she'd learnt the hard way that new environments could not be trusted. This meant adopting inspection regimes. Anyway, as a professional she distrusted the comedy circuit. Amateurs she called them; The Booze and Drugs League, Testosterone on a High. Actresses were circumspect because whatever their genes, everyone ages. And dies. No exceptions. So having methodically checked out the loos, they'd gone on to investigate dressing rooms earmarked by Fabian Wass for Cinderella and Prince Charming .You could not check too far in advance. Lives could be saved by aerosol sprays.

Down below stage, the dressing rooms were as cramped as punishment cells. Everything looked thumbed and worn, tinged with a sulphurous tincture of gas.

"Panache!" Trixie had purchased an extra-large Panache Antiviral, paying with her own cash. "Panache! Panache! Panache!" She sprayed toxicity liberally over fixtures and fittings, marking future territories and leaving them germ-free exuding chemical roses. "Panache!" She aimed again at the seat. "That's birth control with a vengeance! Death to any misplaced sperm!" She threw her head back with a big throaty laugh. "Remember that dildo joke, when . . ."

She caught sight of Abigail in the doorway. In their expressions Abigail recognised forces as strong as her mother's. That same annoying attention to detail. That folksy familiarity. That disturbing jollity which screeched 'middle-aged middle-class'. Trixie was flipping her ragged blonde tresses as Pippa bent close to reflections, massaging any potential wrinkles. As they crouched, examining strands of frayed hair, Pippa caught sight of Jilly's trade-card jammed in the side of the mirror.

She held it up triumphantly. "Hey! Look Trixie! Hairdressers! Thank God!"

Abby's suppressed her discreet satisfaction that Jilly Craske would finally be pleased.

128

As Garrick licked the envelope glue, rendered carcasses came to mind. Likewise that trail of detritus behind those demolishers' cranes. Here in this radio black spot he was often reduced to primitive pen-upon-paper. His solution was to send postcards with printed-circuitry themes. He liked the idea of digital ditties to celebrate Norston, or Happy Birthday's repetitive chant. As Chekhov remarked, provincial Russia was a cultural wasteland whose Holy Grail was back there in Moscow. Garrick saw the parallels. The past was an all too familiar place. Ten years they'd exchanged wedding vows: that did not seem so long ago.

Their wedding was in Hammersmith London UK, not Wayland Massachusetts as planned. The redbrick church had been arching, empty and bitterly cold. He recalled signing the register and nearly misspelling his name. He'd been glad at that moment his parents were dead. But Verity was elegant and poised. She'd shielded him from her New England contingent whereas Roseanne kissed everyone, openly laughing and weeping, regretting they weren't in an Orthodox Church. He remembered Vee's father announcing, "Not so much losing a daughter as gaining a son," as if to convince himself.

The wedding party was over-attended and noisy, but the menu exposed Verity's talents; her genius even. She wasn't just a glamour girl swayed by Garrick's delusions. She'd personally organised a New England-style feast complete with multi-tiered cake iced in extravagant detail. That would be the prototype for her emerging career and all those banquets and dinners that followed, including her famous cookery school. Now she was being seduced by false prophets who'd risen high in order to crash with a bloody great bang.

He'd chosen a greetings card which when opened sang "Love, love me do. You know I love you!" in a merciless loop in response to Verity's 'We live. We die. But this is a Rolex forever!'. His problem was a reciprocal gift without admitting he'd forgotten the date. In his defence the office calendar only recorded one item. "Remember Lady V's Company Soirée" in Phyllis's writing heavily underlined for the future, to which Garrick scrawled "NO!" in red letters. No mention of the Dress Rehearsal that very same day,

To afford a suitable present for Vee, he would accept Louise's offer. He would perform at her club. He might suggest a monologue? Or read some Shakespearean sonnets? Perform a famous oration? Then he'd casually ask for a fee solely to guarantee his professional status. Then he'd renegotiate his overdrafts before any credit ran out. However, buying jewellery was not his strong point. It was essential to get some advice. He was just going out when Sod's Law struck. Landlines lack any respect.

"At last!" answered a husky contralto.

"Louise?" Garrick grabbed pencil and paper for notes.

"No, sorry, not guilty. It's me. I'd heard you've changed your mind. Arthur said you would." This voice had an unfamiliar edge. "Yes Garrick, it's me. Me." She sounded world-weary. "Elisabeth Scott? .The Mercury? Arts and theatre critic? You wanted some publicity? So as we've this tie-up with Norston FM plus a local Liverpool station . . . ? I'm at 376942, extension 15, and waiting. When you're ready for an interview, call me back. Okay?"

As Garrick feared, whenever his authority faltered a subtle anarchy spread. While he craved his nicotine fix, James Carr, Lionel Parson, Trixie Waltham, Pippa White, Reggie Buck, resolved hierarchical problems with carefully targeted laughter. Somehow a consensus emerged and rehearsals kept plodding on. A dance added here. A song cut out there. Bits of 'business' everywhere. Not that Reggie Buck helped, always in trouble with learning his lines. Any lines. He did not trust the printed word

"Too bleedin' artificial!" he'd claimed, and as for prepared scripts. "Too fuckin' rigid!" But hadn't he heard of ensemble?"

Reggie loathed formal structure. Only ad libbing could keep a spontaneous feel.

"No! Look, this is my act, matey! It's all about this . . ." He opened then closed a soft hand while winking at Abby. "Getting and holding them! Because this is the nature of Buttons", he said, "A cheeky-chappie pageboy-type whose only aim is big bloody laughs."

Encamped on the fringes Lionel was slowly imploding while Orlando Marcel and James Carr heatedly discussed 'The Three Unities', making them sound like a pop group. Lionel's rictus smile bulged into soft fleshy grandeur wobbling with spasms of spite. He laughed and patted backs, but everywhere he saw critical subtexts and venomous propaganda.

Garrick's frustration was showing. Where was everyone's sense of proportion? This wasn't Chekhov, Ibsen, or Strindberg .It was Cinderella, for God's sake! Cinderella the panto! Humour was a volatile gas bubbling out of solution, so when the laughter came, it exploded. Instead with James Carr in monologue mode, wit sounded like Management Speak. They had barely touched on that scene between Baron Hardup and Cinderella; between father and daughter, blood-ties versus politics, when Garrick remarked it was too bloody slow. Trixie belched quietly. James Carr clapped a hand to his forehead as if suddenly seeing the light.

"Aaah yes! Of course!" James exclaimed in mock shock, "Our director means it's too much like Chekhov." He seemed to offer a grudging respect. "Yes Garrick my dear, you are the absolute expert. Professors Leonid Andreyev and Nikolai Sanin are mere nothings. You always know just what to say. From my own research I know you're a very great scholar." He half-bowed again. "Unlike ourselves, Garrick's an expert on the Boyars, the Smolnyi Institute, and on Grand Duke Alexander, Grand Duchess Elisaveta Feodorovna, the Mennonites, the lot. Let's see, when is Anton's Name Day? It's there on the tip of my tongue." The silence extended. "Oh well, what's a date compared with a lifetime of literary knowledge?"

As Abigail leaned for a runaway pencil, tight denim stretched into the groove of her buttocks.

"Thanks Jimmy." Garrick got an encouraging laugh. "Well while we're on dignity and philosophical truths, how about that stunt work of yours? You know, all that prat-falling business where you get your arm caught, yeah? You get kicked up the arse. And your pants drop down round your ankles, yeah? And then you fall flat on your face?"

Garrick would date future tensions from then, but Abigail joined in the laughter without knowing why. She was the Assistant's assistant. Invisibility came with her job. She'd not studied problem pages for nothing. Besides, Cinderella wasn't just fairytale stuff. Everyone's symptoms were there. Lonely housewives. Family squabbles. Teenage angst. Everyone confessing their pain. She'd witnessed girlfriends' preoccupations. What mattered was love and romance, but what never made sense was their absolute longing to get themselves married to sport stars or bankers. So why let men into their knickers, get themselves pregnant, then dumped? Cinderella would head the same way and only a miracle save her.

This would not be Abigail's fate. No way. Exiled in a draughty church hall, she rarely if ever saw Josh. She ran meaningless errands between bouts of brewing tea, and that was the heart of the problem. What to tell Jilly Craske? About knitting, vegetarian cold cures, and cut-price pizza vouchers? Reduced to dreary anecdotes, in a moment of madness she went as far as to promise Jilly that Trixie and Pippa would personally visit her salon.

As her diary narratives grew wilder, Josh's image started to fade. She'd noticed Garrick becoming more appreciative too. He was obviously pleased with her work. One evening as she tramped to her bus stop, she became aware of someone falling in step.

"Do you fancy a drink? To break the monotony, eh?" Garrick asked, "We both need a break."

It sounded so predictable she almost felt relieved. At the same time she hoped he wouldn't hark back to those jewellers and ask for more fashion advice. That would be taking advantage. As they picked their way between parked cars and bollards, the sky suggested an overnight frost as the first pricks of starlight appeared.

If Star Signs were omens, Garrick was glad he'd devised his own concept of 'Chance'. After all, it wasn't sheer luck he'd caught up with Abby. One simply opened doors and waited. For instance, the very day his first wife buggered off with that bipolar, photographer guy, Verity came into his life. In a single Entrepreneur Networking Session she'd guaranteed Sylvie's memory wiped. Looking back, Vee seemed the inevitable choice, yet she must have been thousands to one.

According to his father, everything was preordained according to moral rectitude points. Therefore depending on God's will, you either fell in love or caught TB. As if Chekhov deserved to drown in his own blood? Perhaps he'd not scored enough bonus points?

The Red Lion's sub-culture of Sushi & Chips in t'Basket combined with blue haze. It invaded their No Smoking corner and Abigail was looking tense.

Garrick dabbed away rings of wet beer. "I must admit I owe your family some thanks."

"Oh yes?"

Family? – Abigail wasn't just under the subheading "Roberts", submersed in their identity, and ranking less than Louise. She felt already demeaned.

"Yes. Because I have you to rely on," he persisted, "You and your friend Stacey. And her tame jeweller of course."

Ker-Boom! *Ker-boom*! Karaoke had come to her rescue. It was all so typical. An out-of-hours employee was being used and abused. A tuneless chorus began belting out "Girls just want to have fun" as Abigail' eyes locked onto performers. It wasn't for her to organise discounts to benefit Garrick's stay-at-home wife. She wasn't jealous or possessive but it wasn't her job to save anyone's marriage or provide jewellers' catalogues. As Garrick ordered more wine and kept pouring, Abigail began to feel quietly self-righteous.

"Sorry, but I think I might be pissed!" she murmured, swaying side-to-side and adding as the music cut out. "An' if I wanted a present ,a gift, me, I'd always go for the ring!"

Her words were left on air as someone loomed up beside her. Or was it a trick of the polarised light? A too too solid shoulder came into view. A shiny blonde curtain swished across Abby's blurred vision.

The voice was hoarsely contralto with traces of Leeds. "Garrick, what luck! I know you won't know me by sight, so I'll introduce myself." A glittering hand stretched out across Abby, "As it happens we've already spoken today."

Lizzie Scott grasped Garrick's hand. Her chunky rings pressed into his fingers. Her glance back at Abigail said 'Everything's noted'. She watched the two stumble away past the gaming machines, observed by the omniscient CCTV.

As Jilly Craske's partner waited his turn at Indianapolis X, Thomas took note. For someone who lived with eternal injustice, life was a torment whose quota was never fairly allotted. In his total world 'Death Bug' competed with 'War of the Worlds'. Evidence had to be kept in reserve.

According to guidebooks Norston is the ideal-sized town. Not too big and not too small, its outskirts dotted with mill owners' mansions and suburbs. Estate agents love it. Despite its past industrial phase, recent booms had passed it by. Manchester, Halifax, Huddersfield, Leeds all have inexplicably thrived, as did Liverpool, Preston, Warrington, Birmingham, Sheffield, Leicester and Derby. Even Norwich, Luton and Milton Keynes. Even Southampton, Plymouth and Cardiff. Everywhere. Anywhere. An infectious property virus was already sowing new seeds.

Louise yawned under the dryer as warm air fluffed through her hair. "Jilly love, folk up here are snob. But with sod-all to get snobby about. So I offer them something classy and highbrow plus food and liquor thrown in. That way they'll happily pay through the nose and that's why as I need some exclusives. Because Garrick Jones rates 'exclusive' up here."

Jilly nodded thoughtfully. "So's that where your daughter fits in?"

Louise ignored Jilly's question. Club Arabica was her last throw of a dice. She'd calculated the odds and planned all her menus, having first stumped up a massive down-payment thanks to a recent aunt's death. Not so much a mortgage as a sodding great gamble, she'd said, but when you throw statistics up in the air no-one knows how they'll come down. That's why Louise needed endorsements. She needed big names. And Garrick Jones was there on their doorstep and top of everyone's list, the Added Snobbery Factor. He was bound to get instant attention.

"Mmmm. Same with me and the salon." Jilly sounded distant. "Everyone has to have gimmicks."

"So lovey? Be honest, what d'ye think?"

The wait was long and considered. The fan whirred away but Jilly's mind was elsewhere.

"You see I've investigated colonic irrigation." She felt Louise jolt. "Or I could maybe build an extension out back? Or add on a sauna? Tanning studios even .What do you reckon?"

Jilly needed much more than a gimmick. She depended on Abigail spreading her name round that theatre. Publicity mattered. When her theme was showbiz Jilly needed a regular boost, so Abigail's updates were vital. Lately the salon had felt like a treadmill. She didn't like to admit it. Today she was shattered, depressed and frustrated. Admittedly she was overweight, but diets never seemed to help. Earlier she'd sat in her clientele section flipping through old magazines. One centre-page spread featured a brand-new cookery show, 'Cook and Let Cook', but when half the world suffered from malnutrition or AIDS, who needed patisserie? Who cared about chefs? Celebrity ought to mean style but as usual those featured meant nothing. Jones was an unmemorable name and Verity sounded passé.

As for calorie counting, unexplained bouts of elation sustained her. She trimmed, backcombed, permed, shampooed, conditioned and highlighted regular clients, and that was the crowning glory of hair. From melanin to keratin, it grows and grows and grows. You could read a whole lifestyle from one single strand. Again she felt inexplicably queasy. She had to sit down. As always when scared, her thoughts always led straight back to Thomas, together with the rest of her fears.

The headwaiter hovered. Media diners were worst. Journalists were a provocative lot and their loud badinage was punctuated by laughter.

Verity had begun to sound shrill. "Oh come on, guys! Don't be so goddam dismissive. Flavours matter. Really. How'd you cope with no sense of taste. Imagine that. Right?" A few of them nodded and smiled. "Come on guys, I'm serious."

Or couldn't they see taste was the prime among senses? Sweet, sour, bitter or salty? It was down to receptors on tongues; our taste buds really, really, mattered. Think papillae, add saliva plus a sense of smell, and the palate's a coalition of organs amounting to something deeply subjective, even hypersensitive, affecting everything we do. She added that bone china helped because everything tasted better off Wedgwood, especially when cooked by somebody else. That made them all laugh. But she meant it. The science of flavours was pretty damn tricky without a precisely accurate gauge. Sensations were all in the mind. Hence napkins and silverware varied the flavours. A floral centrepiece had its effect. With a cold you could lose half your sensations and sometimes barely taste damn all. She hoped they were taking this in.

She herself had been lucky. Her talent came down through the Morozov line like musicians' perfect pitch. Both her kids had it too, which made them intolerably picky. Sadly, she added, her husband Gary did not. Everybody laughed and cheered.

"No seriously. Fact is . . . " she persevered, "Seriously, eating is fifty percent in the mind. I mean, when you're stuck in a desert, a grub or an insect can taste pretty good."

She was getting to like this for a lifestyle. 'The Royal Hotel' enjoyed multi-star classification. Its Banqueting hall was baroque. Here she was feted. She was a star and this was a feast. New courses arrived. Glasses were filled and refilled. They treated her not just as an expert, but as entertainment too. Whatever she said got applause, so much so she'd begun to feel quite Messianic, pointing out how all living creatures had to be fed and some crops were more worthwhile than others; their vitamin content, metals, trace elements, and so forth. Even with genetic modifications. This too got an unexpected ovation. She must have hit a G-spot there. You could sum people up by their responses to food, she explained. You didn't need a diploma for that. Again everyone thumped on the table and laughed. Applause got further applause. It was okay for Gary, she thought. Relationships muddied the palate. To him eating was a bodily function same as his approach to sex. A man who screwed the same way he ate! That was key to his psyche. He took the whole world for granted, including herself. Her generous gift of that watch changed the game.

As the next course arrived it looked superb, but even as she opened her mouth something felt odd, inexplicably wrong. The texture was lumpy and dry to the tongue. And what were these ingredients? Nervously she moistened her lips. Where were those other sensations? Everything tasted of hydrolysed cardboard. Chewing became a purely mechanical process. She felt herself break into sweat. She inhaled then exhaled. As for any aroma? Then when she tried to close her eyes the murals began to intrude. This was alternative culture. After a day's filming 'Cooking with Woks', 'The Feast of Diana' depicted multiple couplings strewn with flowers and ripe fruit. There too was 'Pomona handing grapes to the Cupids' with a lascivious smile as tasteless as the food in her mouth. She felt the blood drain from her face. Beneath these vast chandeliers, murals continued their mythological orgies, feasting on nectarines, pineapples, oranges, grapes without inhibition.

"Verity?" Someone was sounding concerned. "You okay?"

A waiter was topping her wine. She took an experimental sip, rolling the liquid around in her mouth. She felt it swill between tongue and palate. But nothing. No taste. This wine had no flavour. Nor did anything else. She tightened her cheeks and managed to swallow. Was it psychosomatic or was it a symptom of something? Brain tumour perhaps?

"Verity?" inquired their chief sponsor licking his lips like a Satyr. "Do you get these minutest cardamom traces? In our pommes de terre a la crème magnifique?" He waited expectantly. "Also, that whisper of garlic in the truite majestueuse? And maybe the slightest sensation of nutmeg? And thyme?" He looked extremely pleased with himself. "One of your own tips, I believe?" He produced a small magazine cutting. "'An expression of humankind's deepest sensual requirements', as you put it. And if I may say so, superbly expressed!"

He stood up to address the whole table. "My friends, we have here a Major New Star who brings spirituality to food!" He raised his glass. "Here's to us all! And a series! Let's hope they commission a USA version."

As they were happily toasting themselves, Verity noticed the chandelier shimmer, its icicles melting, its crystal drops magnifying the spectrum. It began to rotate in a spiral, spinning away into space .As she rose unsteadily, her pallor stopped table-talk in its tracks.

134

"Sorry you guys. Won't be a sec!" and she lurched away.

'Stoned', they were probably thinking, 'Women can't handle drink'. But no-one intervened as she padded out, one hand to her mouth. Not having her cellphone she found a wooden cubicle as pert as a confessional box, intending to ring Rachel and Mark but found herself dialling Garrick instead.

As usual his phone was switched off. This time she needed to teach him a lesson.

Rehearsal schedules were in the Stage Manager's hands, but for all his backslapping humour Fabian Wass was letting things drift. Frustration was growing. James Carr's sidelong glances became openly directed at Garrick who struggled to integrate scenes, and Garrick as usual tried to shift blame. In his view, any decent lieutenant should impose order, but Fabian failed because no-one disliked him enough; they took his schmaltz at face value. All except James Carr, which wasn't surprising. To Garrick's suspicious eyes Fabian's Curriculum Vitae had looked dubious from the start. So why had he hired him? The birds of a feather syndrome, he thought. Fabian probably wasn't even Irish, but Verity would have seen through that aura of stale tobacco and Guinness. Unless that was his roguish attraction? Garrick couldn't investigate further without undermining himself.

By now they ran on majority votes. Everything was so bogged down compromise was compromised. All traces of satire had been reduced to low groans. Even Roseanne would have approved. Reggie was right about that. He said it needed "a bloody good kick in the bollocks" then a burst colostomy bag, adding some well-aimed lampoons, and cutting that Chekhovian bittersweet humour James and Lionel admired. Either that or wake up one morning to find you'd been quietly castrated. Meanwhile James Carr turned his attention on Garrick, quoting non-existent mutual friends, testing him out. Professor Thisovitch, or Doctor Thatovitch, and 'The Art Theatre' Moskva, and James's talk of Soviet theatre with its theories of 'Socially Relevant Drama'.

"Is he taking the mickey?" Abigail whispered.

At first Garrick played along but if Abigail noticed, then others had too. She wasn't so dim. The more he observed her, the more his perceptions were changing. She could see through a devious old ham like James Carr. Garrick reminded himself that despite those first anonymous warnings, Abigail had been his own personal choice. His judgement had been justified. The politician in him felt reassured and with it a growing respect. She'd be his local sounding board. A Norston contact was vital. It made perfect sense. He and Abby would make a great team but three would make an unbeatable trio? Louise, Abigail and Garrick himself? Appearing at Louise's club would seal the alliance and . . .

". . . You see," James was raising his voice, "You see, my Baron Hardup's essentially 'sub-Molière'. That's to say, anglicised from the French in a pseudo-Eighteenth Century pastiche. It has a literary derivation, going right back to classical roots." He mimed twirling moustaches, bowed deeply, then painfully straightened up, to laughter. "And so you have to ask yourself, was there a trace of self-mortification in Hardup's attempts to aggrandise his second wife? An element of self-denial perhaps in rejecting his genuine daughter? And thus denying his own genetic descendant? .In which case was Buttons some bisexual, even asexual creature? Hormonal problems? Arrested development even? That's the dramatic dilemma."

"Oh bugger that!" yelled Reggie, "E's only there to get laughs!" and silently Garrick agreed.

Yet, when they replayed the scene, the paradox was it had subtly developed. James's low formal bow had metamorphosed into a grotesquely startled half-curtsy making Reggie's vulgarity seem almost tragic. Somehow the timing was perfect, Garrick was forced to admit. Despite rewriting chunks himself and Snopaquing out unfunny gags, it worked. Now he'd emphasised Dandini's double-takes, the Sisters' new patter song, and the Ugly Stepsisters pas de deux. Give people a catchphrase and they'll laugh out of sheer recognition. It wasn't exactly Strindberg or Chekhov, but it added appropriate corn:

Buttons (turning to leave): "Farewell. I must be going off."

Dame Maggie: (sniffing and pulling a face) "Yes. I wondered what that was."

"Once I used to think I was stupid," Buttons announces, "But thanks to lots and lots of research, I know for certain I am!"

Whenever real life intervened, the problem was always Roseanne, the classical mum-in-law cliché. She might insist on Verity divorcing him, but his kids would love the show – They'd know Lionel Parsons in his Dame Maggie manifestation (a latter-day Dan Leno or Herbie Campbell) was unmistakably a male bedecked in woman's clothes. No complex dilemmas of gender. Nothing transsexual about it. And the Prince was a far-from-lesbian woman rescuing a dithering pal. Then there was barefooted Trixie herself; winsome but feisty, mutating from room-maid to Pop Star then Minor Royal in a single shoe-fitting session (with not a single GCSE while shovelling peas off the knife to her mouth). This was the traditional world of "Oh yes we do!" versus "Oh no we don't!" complete with knockabout banter, verbal raspberries and spontaneous farts.

As Cinderella began to take over, Chekhov receded like dying embers glimpsed through a primeval forest, and Garrick regressed to a hunter lost amongst wolves. Even the church hall mutated. It turned into cumbersome dinosaur ribs drifting through massive expanses of ice. These images kept finding ways to return, always reinventing themselves. And his mental firewall was letting them through.

Thoughts of his children still intervened. Their latest notes enthused about face-painting sessions. Apparently they had been out for popcorn'n'pizzas with gran because momma was incredibly busy. To compensate she'd bought them electronic games. Then Granny paid for swimming lessons, then arranged a sleep-over for Rachel's friends; organising Thanksgiving parties and sponsoring Mark's first Judo lesson . . . no-one mentioned Garrick's musical cards. Nobody thanked him for greetings. Nobody asked how he was. 'Ask yourself if you are happy, and you immediately cease to be so.' It seemed to him 'The Cherry Orchard's' emotional roots were being systematically starved, despite Vee believing he was working himself to the bone fulfilling her family ambition, while being sustained by Roseanne and her expatriate circle. Wait until internet rumours

136

got round! Even worse than this, he still had not chosen Vee's anniversary present.

The fact was, the more Cinderella took shape the more he'd been distracted, and the more he had started to care. Yet when the day's rehearsals were over, everyone rushed to get out. Shades of the factory whistle, he thought. Would they be like this if it were Shakespeare or Ibsen?

Gradually out of a grey opalescence a plan began to emerge. After recent frosts, an unexpected mildness had loomed out of nowhere, drifting up northwards from Spain like opening a great oven door. Clouds like overweight sponges exposed their soft underbellies stained Gazpacho pink and Garrick could taste Cordoba's dust, its vineyards, paprika, and olives. A typical Verity trick. She'd sold him the South, inducing the flavours of Chekhov's Ukraine, the Borscht, the Blinis, braided breads and savoury torts. Her theory was that life had evolved from those plains, thriving on fresh food and good sex; not necessarily in that order. He could almost bite into spiced breads and pimento. He gathered his papers together that night, conscientiously switching off lights. Dusk had begun to surge in. Condensation dripped from cold glass and radiators creaked as they cooled. He watched Fabian Wass disappear into shadows waving a six-pack of lager. The Church Hall was locked up for the night.

He heard voices chanting. How would The Majestic cope without central heating? Its Late-Nite Comedy fans would freeze in the laughlesss expanse. He knew their show would run at a loss and slap Ruddock down a peg or two. This seemed a suitable time to drop in. As he wheeled his bike past the theatre, gaggles of youths lined the road, crowding metal barriers, discarding windcheaters, cagoules and parkas, seeking the last rays of the sun. Hundreds of others were jostling for space.

Garrick watched disbelieving, as more kept arriving. According to his new Rolex, there was half an hour before the doors even opened. Soon this queue would wind round the block and sell out. He turned towards the peace of the towpath where waterlogged leaves dappled the glassy face of dark water. First he had to phone Vee, but most of all he needed to think.

"Hi. It went well today, didn't it?" a voice whispered and echoes acquiesced.

There she was, Abigail in grey padded coat and soft sandy hair, outlined against semi-glazed water.

"Thanks, I – er – yes, but comedy's all about timing and . . ." He went into professional mode. "That's what takes the rehearsing . . . but what I don't understand is how is it cheap local stand-ups can fill a whole bloody theatre? No, I mean seriously, why?" She looked bemused. "Or am I out of touch? Is that it?" She looked vague. "Okay then, answer me this. Is that what they really want? Crudity? Aggression? Is that the nature of humour today? Upending stereotypes and conventions. And yes, I guess, puncturing Establishment pride. Rebellion isn't constructive, it's . . ."

"I like walking here." She gestured vaguely. "It's a bit . . . very quiet."

"Aha . . . The sun's rim dips. The stars rush out. At one stride comes the dark," he intoned, "That's from 'The Ancient Mariner', By Coleridge? You never read that at school?"

"We only did cooking. I failed."

Conversation ceased. The skyline turned into shadow. It was odd how sometimes nothing gelled. At other times everything made perfect sense. At rehearsals Abigail saw the significance of action; each gesture; every twist of a wrist or flick of a heel. You could read whole characters into slight hesitations, and every 'inflexion' expressed deeper meanings. They said acting was an extension of truth, now she had nothing to say. Or was it Garrick that didn't make sense? Unless, was Stacey right? Stacey with her rosebud tattoos. She'd gone to great lengths to explain about men. Their kinky ways, their freaky obsessions, their waterbeds and black satin sheets. It was hard to imagine. Stacey had tried it all; everything, anything, she said. Oral sex, vibrators, whatever. The images preyed on one's fears, but if men couldn't be trusted how could women have faith?

"You've done a deal with my mum?" His confusion emboldened her. "Like I'm for sale?"

"Good God, of course not. It's not like some contract's been signed."

As she turned and ran, he saw her silhouette crossing the footbridge. As if on cue, street-lamps popped into life spattering sequinned reflections. The water looked static and viscous. A malleable crust swayed over fathoms of silicate gel where larvae and corpses lurked between reproduction and death. A moorhen flew up in his face. A rat plopped into the water leaving slow ripples. Two youths came clattering loudly over the footbridge as one by one windows lit up and street signs flickered to life. God's Great Lighting Console he thought. It was almost too brilliantly staged. In less than two years this would be Brinkhouse's 'Garden of Eden'. Glittering octagonal towers would vie with hexagonal multiplex blocks, genetically engineered to expand. The Majestic alone would survive.

As Garrick pushed his bike through the dark he thought he'd imagined a cough. A cigarette flared. Muffled expletives. Long echoes. Soft footsteps. On reaching the road Garrick leaped onto his bike. Moments later, a black saloon rolled silently out of the shadows and turned in the same direction.

Freewheeling downhill towards Club Arabica, he hoped to catch Abigail up. There were things he intended to say, things he should have said, things he wished had stayed unsaid. As he approached the club entrance, Louise appeared like a centre-stage cabaret star, beaded in scarlet, a deep carmine shawl round her shoulders in a darkly satirical moment. A dark vehicle swished slowly past then rumbled away as she waved.

"Garrick! Darling! What imaginative timing! And arriving by bike'! This means you've decided! I can't wait to celebrate!" She broke into that familiar laughter.

If only she'd known she would have had cameramen ready. This was already a photo opportunity missed. When he seemed to hesitate she dragged the handlebars from him, delivered his bike to the doorman, then guided him on through plasticised palms into the tightly packed hall. To his relief there was no sign of Abigail. A table was marked 'Reserved'.

"All you have to do, my dear Garrick is talk and I'll listen. Tonight it's all on the house."

She was sublimely happy she said. A modern reformer amongst the philistine world. Few people here understood abstract art, let alone culture. Especially Eddie Craig and Arthur Ruddock.

138

She lowered her voice. "And yet I feel so lonely here Because, as you know, culture's not fashionable yet. Sadly no thanks to my daughter. My own flesh and blood. We shield them, don't we. That's a parent's sacrifice." She inclined towards him. "I'm so glad you dropped in. What will you be performing for me? I can't wait to hear what you've planned."

Pedalling back to his digs, Garrick wobbled the final few metres, running straight into the wall. He lugged the bike up front steps to the hall. No sign of post. No messages. No postcards. Nothing. Here letters meant Final Demands and received suitable treatment. Perhaps Vee's letters had been trampled underfoot? By the time he'd dragged his bike upstairs and was trying to insert a key in his door, his co-ordination had failed. As his bicycle slipped with a clatter he caught it from rolling downstairs.

"Aye aye!" A balding skull, its features diagonally blanked at mid-nostril, peered round a door. "Been ridin' that? Or some dolly?" The whole head emerged. "Theatricals! Always bleedin' pissed!" His broad wink lacked any amusement. "Shaggin' I'll bet. That's why them women come askin' for you. Oh yeah, too bleedin' true! Bangin' us doors. A tarty bitch wi' loads o'fuckin'damn nerve." Garrick turned his key in his door. "No lad, serious. She come again today, askin'. Flashy young dolly. Askin' bout you. An' she . . ." He mumbled on inaudibly.

"Me? She asked for me? By name?" Garrick wondered why Abby should call.

But those eyes were evasive. "Why? Because I'm first top o'stairs, see. Social Benefit? Income tax? .Debties? Drug squad? Whatever But if you don't know . . . !" The wizened head disappeared briefly. "Aye, an' this come today."

As the thin wrist emerged, Garrick grabbed it, tensing his foot on the door. Like a trapped lizard thin fingers writhed. Bones seemed to crunch. The voice rose to a gurgle as Garrick's grip tightened, forcing the envelope forward.

"Very young was she?" Garrick tightened his grip till the sinews knotted like cords. "Sandy-haired was she? Pretty? Sixteen or so?"

"Dark hair." The voice quivered with pain. "Plenty o' leg. Snoopin' management type." As Garrick's grip slackened, the man groaned. "An' a microphone snug as a bug 'tween 'em boobs. Asked enough fuckin' questions!" Bloodshot eyes crimped into a sneer. "Friend o'yourn, then?"

Garrick gave a sharp tug at the door, trapping the skull as it screamed.

Later as he lay in bed his thoughts slipped back to Lancaster Gate. He could neither stay awake, nor fall asleep. Soon there'd be clematis buds in the mews and daffodils at the back. He pushed the grubby script aside, its typeface splayed like graffiti. He stared at the painstakingly scrawl on the reverse of a purple somnolent cat:

"Dear dad. Are you well? We are well. Scoobie is well. How are you?"

He was missing out on their lives. Trivia mattered; silly games, learning to cycle, learning to swim. Judging by photos enclosed, his children were rapidly maturing. Their expressions seemed more self-aware with their new hairstyles, fresh confidence, different clothes and those few extra inches. All within weeks. And that wouldn't be all. Such was Roseanne's Chekhovian duty she would be instructing them in Turgenev, Gorky, Tolstoy and the Cyrillic alphabet too. She'd make sure they learned by heart the Morozov Ancestor Tree. The really sad thing was Vee; she would never succeed in the media world. It was too misogynist and she wasn't the type. The odds were stacked against her. When her show was finally cancelled, Roseanne would be looking for someone to blame. He knew who that would be.

Roseanne had never trusted him. He could not survive her expectations. Divorce might be on their cards? He'd never sleep now. Darkness was too invasive. An ambient light glowed off net curtains as he twisted and turned. Those letters had sobered him up. Would anyone care whether he'd worked on a Chekhov or panto? Looking down through net curtains, the shabby street gained a strange glamour. Caught unawares it could look almost beautiful even at two in the morning. He crawled back to bed .But there it still was; Abigail's tremulous smile. And Abigail's unblinking eyes.

That Bleep-bleep! Bleep-bleep! did not fit with his dreams. Diving over cold lino, he expected a drunken wrong number.

Verity was sounding slurred. "Gary! Hi! At least I've gotten hold of you! At last!" She smothered a giggle. "Oh shit, I'm slightly, but only everso slightly, whoops yep . . . 'fraid so . . . zonked to the teeth on Champagne!" Garrick checked the time again. "But I just had to tell you. Everything's pure fairytale! My recipes don't even count anymore."

"The bastards!" It confirmed his worst fears. "It's what I expected."

"No, no. I mean just cooking's no longer important. It's me. My personality rating's 'alpha one plus' And that's tops! Okay blame 'focus groups'. Seems all of them love me! Previews rated me at 90% approval. An' that's just unheard of! It's wild! Now there's talk of me fronting new shows."

"Where the hell are you?"

"Me? *Heaven! I'm in heaven!*" she sang out of tune. "But I knew you'd be thrilled. Hey, and wait for this. Their main presenter's got some psychic condition so they want me to stand in for him! On a chat show. While he takes six months intensive. Isn't that news! And it's all thanks to Lucy! She's like top agent and media consultant in one. They've commissioned a follow-on series with chat shows in the pipeline. Lucy says, cash in while we can, because in another twelve months, cooking'll be out of the loop."

"Darling, listen. First of all I want to say, this wonderful gift you've sent me. I can't thank you enough. It's too much. It's just too beautiful. Superb. A work of art and . . . and I miss you so much, and and . . ."

Vee began emphasising her lifelong commitment to Chekhov, dear Chekhov, and how vital his plays were, and how thrilled she was that Gary would bring them to life. She did not seem to have heard him.

"But Vee, I may have misled you . . ."

"Come on Gary." She talked excitedly on. "What's a gorgeous Rolex between friends? It's my 'substitute kisses' And I've got a job offer from Paris. Another from Frankfurt. One from Palm Springs. Like I was being franchised out. Like I'd been cloned and mass-produced. Then all that Wow Moet et Chandon Wow And some lunatic's planning a movie! Real moving movies! Wide-screen, action-packed with car-chases and stunts." She waited for Garrick's reaction. "Hello?. Hello? Have I lost you?" Wrapped up in his bedspread Garrick slumped wearily sideways, clasping his phone as it died.

CHAPTER SEVEN

TIMINGS

"Yeah. I'm into shopahol, me!" The orange wig bobbed up and down in a circle of spotlights, sometimes backlit like a halo. "No, no, I mean it. I'm a convinced shopaholic!" He gave a V-sign to the crowd. "Bastards! No! No! I mean, have you heard about these new sex supermarts? Flavoured dildos? Get a sperm bank free?" A few bewildered titters. "And ever noticed them birds at the tills?" He pointed into the audience. "Yeah, you with them beer-bottle specs! You never noticed?" Some sniggered, some jeered, and Roddy felt a great vindication.

They thought they were smart, paying to be entertained. He almost despised them. That was the trouble with commerce. It loved corny crap if it bolstered their egos. But awfulness appealed to him; it worked. Its deadpan unfunniness was the core of his humour. Antisocial, vulgar and mocking. It was satire of satire, parody of parody, the opposite of wit. That's why it was funny. Like those boring pantomimes it celebrated the triumph of crap.

"Anyrate, I'm not scared of death. I just don't want to be around when it happens. But it'll get you lot before it gets me." And he wanted that to be true.

On-stage his imagination ran free. Josh had succumbed to fairytales appeasing middle-class values. Josh had sold out. For sex. Obsessed with that ginger-haired Barbie felt like a knife in the back. Here Roddy felt free. He could be racist and sexist and iconoclastic. His sneer could scathe a whole theatre, daring the buggers to laugh.

Garrick had meanwhile slipped into the back on a 'know-the-opposition, check-out-your-competitors' basis, keeping well to the shadows, astonished at how packed it was. The humour did not seem funny. No target was spared: the old, the sick, foreigners, women, and the mentally ill. It challenged and outraged him. But how many of these would turn up for Chekhov? Or had even heard of him? Or Shakespeare? George Bernard Shaw? Let alone Oscar Wilde?

". . . Yeah," Roddy was saying, "Double and bust!" Miming voluminous breasts, splaying his lips and popping his eyes. "Yeah. I know! I've boobed! An' talk about service! Service? You load up from this superstore, keen to nip out without paying, then this bird, she asks to see what you've got!" He seems to be miming mounting a bike. "You get it out and ow! That's painful! She pushes it under a laser! 'That'll be ten quid,' she says 'Gift packing is extra!'" Somebody tittered but nobody laughed. "Trouble is . . . you're all thick as shit."

This got a few piercing whistles. At last Roddy sensed their first waves of revolt. It came like the first grunts of stampede with twitching shoulders, shuffling legs, then a low moan like an approaching monsoon, and he knew he was hitting his targets.

"An' that's not all. This mate of mine, a tall skinny josher. He gets this crush on this bird. She says, 'Help help. Please, I'm still a virgin.' 'That's great,' he says, 'can you fake an orgasm too?'" Roddy thrust out his pelvis, one hand to his groin, the other raising two fingers, and leering.

Somebody threw a beercan, followed by catcalls. Others booed and began hurling bottles. Many stayed necking and chatting. In the back row Garrick squirmed as agitators started to spit, then stamp. Body-heat boiled into steam. Rhythmic clapping swelled to a roar as Roddy jeered and swore back. In that unwritten contract between victim and mob, public stonings would follow. Something hit Garrick's head. Adrenaline brought added danger. As missiles spattered around the performer, people were openly laughing. This too was part of the fun. This whistling, chanting and fury.

This was the show keeping him off his own stage. Council's finances came first. His 'middle-class middle-aged' label had stuck. If exile were a draughty church hall, was he the lifelong émigré? He who'd once been up-and-coming. Whose youthful follies were catching him up. As his father would say, 'Only be true to thyself!' But first you had to know who you were.

On-stage the comic was shaking a fist, turning defeat into triumph. A carton hit him full in the face. A trickle of blood ran down his cheek. With a jubilant one-fingered gesture Roddy strutted off followed by bottles and cans as Garrick slipped away in the night.

Every morning Phyllis had to energise still-sleeping keyboards as keys kept rearranging themselves. QWERTYUIOP played anagram games. Again it mis-typed "Cimfere;;a" Thank God for 'Spellcheck' she thought. Behind her Garrick was raising his voice on the phone.

"The point is, Arthur, why are we stuck in that so-called Church Hall?" His voice had risen a pitch and now he was thumping the desk. She knew Arthur would not be pleased. "Jesus, it's soulless, depressing and sodding inconvenient!" She watched Garrick helplessly clenching a fist. "No, I don't care where Rex Schulman rehearsed. We're the official lessees. The Chekhov Players." By now he was frantically punching at air. "No, no. We've been pushed out to make room for some crude, simplistic shitty babyish . . . " He waved around for adjectives and failed.

The working day juddered to life. Street decorations dripped condensation combined with carbon-monoxide. A sullenness hung on the mist. By the look of it, Christmas would not be welcome. All round the theatre Manwess was busy digging more holes and dredging new misshapen trenches. Unable to contact his family, Garrick felt he was banging his head.

"But the point is," he persisted, "I've hired distinguished West End stars who are prepared to stay on to do Chekhov. Otherwise 'Cherry Orchard' is out!"

"You said it. Not me." Arthur was losing patience. "Listen! Pantomime is what 'heritage' means. And that means we rehearse over there while running our current show here. The council wanted 'Charley's Aunt' or 'Lady Windermere's Fan' or . . . No, 'Laughalong!' is what puts bums on seats. Right. Simple as that."

"You call that lot comedians? They'll smash the place up."

"Maybe. Maybe not." Arthur tried to sound patient. "In times of uncertainty all entertainment's a gamble. But someone's got to pay for them busted boilers. That's fact. Anyway, we can't afford to stay dark. What's a few naughty jokes for kids with too much cash?"

"Then go and see for yourself And that Roddy Bluebird? He's bitter and twisted. Our whole reputation's at stake. Ask Lady de Vries."

When Phyllis heard Garrick quote Peggy de Vries, she knew he'd trampled sacred ground. From her post at the keyboard she saw Garrick flounder and tried to imagine the rage.

"Yes, but . . . think about Brand Image then?" Garrick was still clutching at straws. "Cultural status? All I'm asking is, how can the world's Greatest Classics follow such . . . crap?"

Garrick turned towards Phyllis, inviting approval, but she typed on, preoccupied with her fingers flicking over the keys. The vital finger was bare. There ought to be garnet, a Gemini stone signifying divided souls. She wondered what Arthur was saying.

"How? Eh? How?" Arthur's voice was distorted with anger. "If you ask me, Mr. Jones, you're out of order! I represent Norston Council what represents the whole people. And I'm a democrat, me. Now let me explain..."

Garrick set the phone aside then sat back. Phyllis watched him exaggeratedly yawn as Arthur continued, reedy and distant. She noticed Garrick examine his watch as Arthur continued unheard, but Arthur would get his own way in the end. Eventually Garrick put the phone down.

"Oh dear," she murmured, "As bad as that?"

Garrick gave a rueful nod . "Yep. I've blown it."

"Oh, I don't know. It could be worse. Arthur's a full-time survivor, but you . . . you're a serious artist and anyway, anyway . . ." She returned to a flurry of typing, aware of miss-hitting keys.

Garrick's thoughts had returned to Masha, Irina, and Sophie Prozorov, those three inevitable sisters. Like Vee's own Morozovich forebears, Vee would identify with their longings. Garrick missed her in much the same way as Chekhov missed Olga while she was performing in Moscow. Similes and parallels. The dilemma of men living up to their wives. It rang too many bells.

"Ah, just one other thing," Phyllis murmured, "A small thing really. I've been meaning to ask." Which made it sound significant. "How's our new stage carpenter? Settling in, do you think?"

He looked surprised. "Why?"

He'd taken him on at Abigail's recommendation. He wondered what Phyllis was trying to say.

She knew she was beetroot again. "Oh nothing, nothing. Together those two are so very effective. Abigail's on his same wavelength, that's all And closeness helps. In many ways."

She returned to her a notepad as the door slammed and Garrick's feet trampled downstairs. As Phyllis adjusted her cuffs and composure the telephone started to ring.

As Church Hall rehearsals continued, Pippa and Trixie cornered Abby in private despair. As Trixie said, it wasn't just fashions or styles: her hair was a mess and her nails badly needed attention. On top of that she was putting on weight. And as for her teeth and skin . . . ! But Pippa felt even worse. Why, she demanded, couldn't Cinderella be black? Why always Essex blonde? She ran long fingers through tightly crimped hair. The real fly in the ointment was male because men reduced women to ciphers. They never examined their souls nor invited women's opinions. This was in their DNA: misogyny muddled with fear.

Abigail's foreboding was eased by knowing Jilly Craske's business cards lay in both actresses' handbags, complete with Crowning Glory's full details, because Trixie had gone to the trouble of checking the salon's address. As Trixie said: ageing was stacked against women: their designated dressing rooms were crap: the toilets were falling apart: the heating was a disaster. And Garrick was no bloody help.

"So sort it out for us, darling. We're up there in one week."

So, when Garrick strode into the dressing room earmarked for Cinderella, he saw a reflection. A three-shot. A triple portrait. A tableau vivant. If this were film, he'd have shot it. Abigail was showing Josh the No Smoking sign, pointing out the dodgy shelf, broken coat pegs, loose door-latch and wobbly mirror, as noted by the actresses.

Josh was fixing the mirror. "Essential maintenance, right?" he said without looking round, "I'll soon get it done."

Garrick reacted. "And what about our scenery? And where are your bloody designs?"

"It's them gas engineers. They're ripping out old radiators and leaving all the crap to me. Take a look at what's left of that boiler."

"Sorry but I need designs. Traditional. Stylish. That's borders with backcloths and wings. We need to discuss it."

Josh finished the shelf and started packing his tools. "Okay. No problem." He nodded and grinned, "I'm working on sketches. I'll drop them round. See what you think."

Abigail watched him go. "Sorry. It's my fault."

Garrick put a hand on her shoulder. "Of course not, Abby. You're trying to help. Everyone's fighting their corners. That's human nature. I'm afraid it's all part of the job. At least Phyllis was impressed by you . . . No

144

really, she said so. You're doing a wonderful job, and I'd hate to discourage your zeal But if there are further maintenance problems, you should refer to Fabian first. Or myself. Do you see what I mean?"

She nodded. Or was it like Stacey had warned? Was Garrick like sort of staking a claim? He'd been confiding about his home, his kids, his isolation in Norston, his discovery of Lancashire, his love of the North. But was any of that really true? He'd told her their conversation inspired him just by the physical action of talking, whatever that meant, but Stacey pointed out they'd never once talked about Chekhov or work. Just himself, and never his wife. Even then, Abigail couldn't help feeling a tiny bit flattered. When Jilly Craske heard, she'd be jealous. To her, he was another King.

Garrick had begun to suspect he was losing his grip. Soon he might have to crack down. "The smallness of life shows in the smallness of vision", James Carr kept saying, and Garrick thought he was the target. Perhaps they laughed behind his back? No actors had confided in him but Abigail was popular. She enthused like her mother: she rhapsodised too like Louise. She was chatting to Reggie, Orlando, and others, running errands, marking their scripts. Soon James and Lionel were flirting with her. She'd volunteered to help Fabian Wass, perhaps even secretly fetching his drink? With Pippa and Trixie, Abby was one of a trio. When everyone voiced their opinions through her, was her allegiance to him? Or was the real problem Josh?

Too many distractions! Garrick felt like a schooner dismasted at sea, blown on the winds and beset by the Ancient Mariner's tale. He felt already compromised. He'd bought a pack of cigarettes smothered with warnings of Cancer! and Death! Dropping the unopened pack in the trash gave him a temporary high. Verity would approve, but pantomime was Heresy. To him it was only a means to an end. Any attempts at compromise failed. He'd tried involving the cast. He'd asked for suggestions, but none of that worked. Unintended Consequence did. In any resulting hiatus, Trixie would further develop her role.

"Wait, wait! Say, what about if Cinderella's gets a vacuum cleaner? Yeah?" Trixie mimed the actions, "And keeps tripping flat on her face? Or hey, maybe she's secretly into Kung Fu? Yeah? Then keeps falling over?"

Nor was there any shortage of gossip. Abigail's anecdotes grew. She noted Reggie's catch-phrases and Lionel Parson's motivations. Their subplots. Lapses of memory. Self-doubts and hysterical laughter. Then Pippa was always demanding her prompt. Every actor wanted a say, but rising above this sea of distractions, Garrick kept sailing on. "Verity, Rachel and Mark" he would repeat in his mind. "Verity, Rachel and Mark! Verity, Rachel and Mark," over and over again like a mantra.

When it was tea break again, James Carr called for silence. He produced another thin book.

"Now, this little paperback puts Cinderella in context, 'La Cenerentola', the girl who lives in the ashes. Italiana, you see. Pantomimo! From Harlequinade, descending from mimed Roman farce. That's why Pantomine doesn't exist in the States. It's a strangely British tradition. The aristocracy reduced by land reform and agricultural change. Add industrialisation combined with urban growth . . . all of which hits our good Baron. Hence poor Baron Hardup. Undermined by emerging classes and deficient banks. So never forget the social dimension. I strongly believe in doing research. So remember my friends, it's about more than social class. Our Cinders is no working-girl. She's the baron's first daughter. The child of a previous marriage whose mother probably died giving birth. The social comment's implicit."

Pippa was looking perplexed. "Is that why I'm playing in drag?"

Garrick pounced. "Not at all. I congratulate James. He alone brings these philosophical contexts. Like Aristotle and Freud. I mean, there's a whole tragic-comic dimension. Political psychology works. We can use it." When James Carr gave an appreciative bow, Garrick continued. "So in light of this, let's have James's big belching scene. Then him blowing his nose Then Pippa's thigh-slaps again? Then that business where James goes arse-over-tit, followed by Reggie's best raspberry fart Then that bit where James gets kicked in the bollocks and howls in the course of high art."

Sometime then the mood must have changed. Despite constant rain and contractors' chaos, friendly rivalries sharpened. Abigail noticed tension increase until James Carr seemed slightly unhinged, constantly shadowing Garrick, almost literally treading his footprints and breathing his breath with always that dentifrice smile. 'Poncing around', as Reggie called it. James announced he had been learning large chunks of Chekhov in Russian. Abby saw him one afternoon with Arthur Ruddock, both bent over textbooks, murmuring agreement. Neither noticed her there.

While Garrick was bogged down in schedules and details, his memories chose random events, like that day back in London: the day he'd first met Verity in Leicester Square. She'd asked for directions, this bright cookie girl, but he'd misheard 'bookshop' for 'cookshop'. On that day everything changed. When she'd claimed to be a trainee chef, he'd plumped for being 'Top Theatre Director', adding on the spur of the moment he was planning his very first movie. It hadn't seemed significant then, but he'd mentioned a playwright at random. The name was up there on the billboards. 'A SEASON OF ANTON CHEKHOV'

"A movie? Wow." She was very impressed. "Did you know about Chekhov's mom? She was Evgeniya Morozova. That's us, back on the female side. Like great-great grandma, whatever. From some place near Lugansk way back in Tsarist pre-Soviet times. Now isn't that weird?"

That's how coincidence works. He'd invited her to lunch at Fortnum & Masons next day. She'd seemed impressed by the food. It went from there. On the basis of mutual trust they'd set up home and got married in months, no questions asked. His own parents had been dubious, so the wedding was simple and quick. Not long after, his mother lay dying: she left her husband with multiple guilt. Later when Edwin came to die too, he must have had it rehearsed. Always damn quick with his morals, quick to the pulpit, over-quick to write to the press and so much the frustrated actor, he'd invited everyone round. And everyone came. Maybe this was the source of it all? Drama ran in Garrick's blood? Like snatches of verse, its rhyming couplets came back like an indistinct chorus.

Vee had found a culinary lecturing job while he'd dipped and dived to invent a career. Then came the babies. That's BTK and ATK (Before The

146

Kids and After The Kids!). He'd opted out of dancing troupes and Exotiques, kept to the peripheries, head down, earning a living in printing. He'd stumbled on while Verity took the elevator straight for the top. You set yourself targets. You plan ahead. Only then do you start to look back.

As Garrick felt through his pockets at tea break, looking for his mobile, he came across a pamphlet. On his way in, passers-by had been leafleted. 'NORSTON, ATHENS OF THE NORTH' they read, 'Phase One: DEMOLITION' which featured shots of Eddie Craig, Arthur Ruddock, and Lady Peggy de Vries. This opened into a decorative map showing multi-storey stepped towers plus a huge glass pyramid. These dwarfed a greatly widened canal and marina on some indeterminate scale. The theatre itself was omitted. A massive tower block stood in its place.

Fabian was counting and re-counting his orange-stained fingers. "Jesus!" He made a final count looking shocked. "Jesus! James's is right! In just a few days it is Christmas!"

It was as if it had only just dawned. Time had been leaking away. All conversation ground to a halt. In the shocked silence Fabian produced a worn diary and began scribbling notes and reminders:

"Time's little enough to buy prezzies or cards," he moaned, patting James Carr's back, "If you hadn't mentioned . . ."

"No, no, not at all." James Carr sounded world-weary. "What I meant was, there's not enough time for rehearsals."

Out in the washroom, Garrick was pressing his phone to his lips. "Hi darling! It's great to hear you." Then an unexpected rush of emotion . . . "But how's our little babies, then? I miss my two little angels. I miss them. I miss them so much."

"Gary?" She sounded incredulous. " Rachel's ten and Mark's eight for godsake! Come on!" She laughed just like the old days. "They loved your greetings cards though. Your musical offerings, right? Microchip Mozart. The idea was sweet." He sensed reservations. "But nursery rhymes? I mean! Hey! Gary, they're nearly eight and ten! They've grown up. Remember? As momma says, they're at that emotive age." Before he could protest she'd dismissed it. "Never mind. Filming's going great bucks!" Abruptly her whole manner changed. "It's six episodes for starters, plus there's a whole bunch of options. We did Thai Cuisine last week. We'd spent the whole budget on finest spices, best seafood, organic herbs and lemon grass with exotic fruits out of season. It went a real wow! The camera crew wolfed the damn lot! Ah yes, and I met the Thai Ambassador plus Sir Damian Shale .Propositioned by a Lord! That was crazy. But fun."

This was not that same Verity Jones who'd undergone fertility clinics. This was the new version: cooking roulades in public, lionised and canonised for baking Victoria sponge; for stir-frying spring onions with prawns on a bed of perfumed rice. This was the real drama. Neither Chekhov nor Ibsen.

He could picture the posters:

"TONITE! STARRING VERITY JONES"

First, take 2 cloves of garlic, finely chopped. 50 grams of drained anchovies. 175 grams of chopped and pitted black olives. 1 fresh chilli, deseeded and chopped. Add 1 heaped tablespoon of . . ."

But who bothered to cook when they could microwave snacks? Cooking was a luxury craft like flower arranging or pastels, a hobby for enthusiasts. Even he could see that. There were too many cooks and few signs of a broth. No doubt Vee would be a One Day Marvel, repeating recipes slowly for those who'd just retired. At her invocation, puddings would be expected to rise and jellies instantly gel. She might inspire her own cult. Her shrine could be crammed with dried herbs. But somewhere, at a pituitary level, Garrick knew otherwise, because the truth was that millions were starving. Literally. Millions were born to die in parched lands, their water polluted, bellies bloated and skeletons huddled together, suffering biblical famines. As the planet crowded up, every calorie counted. And what if the whole climate changed? Where was Edwin's Loving God in all this?

"Tell me how's our 'Cherry Orchard' coming?" Vee was asking, "That's what everyone's wanting to know. And momma wondered if . . ." Then click.

One moment a connection. Next moment Norston was cast adrift and Fabian was handing him tea. A road drill shattered his morning. By mid-afternoon oxygen would rarefy and darkness seep into the brain.

Back at the hall he found actors sipping tea. It seemed so normal, this tea and biscuits, chatting about mortgages and health; so very ordinary that Garrick renewed his unease. Anton Pavlovich would have understood, racked with illness and doubts. That's where the playwright's greatness lay. He scrutinised human preoccupations with wit and understanding. You needed to be a doctor for that, which pre-supposed some forensic involvement. A stage-play was nothing on paper. But in translation? Without actors to breathe it to life? Wherever that Afterlife was, Edwin would pass instantaneous judgements. He'd been a Shakespearean man.

"Dammit, look," Trixie was moaning, "My hair needs fixing. I feel like cold shit!"

Pippa nodded feelingly. "Me too. Let's book a coiffure."

Lionel was pursing his lips. "Yes. We all feel very strongly. And though I play the Stepmother ugly . . ." He flexed his broad shoulders. "It goes against my whole aesthetic." Then slipped away for a smoke.

Stacey's bedroom celebrated excess. It revelled in luminous outrage. Now she was tearing the last Ricky Tone nude from her walls because the old Stacey was gone. This was her new reference point. She'd adapted to pattern-on-pattern and texture-on-texture. It was lurid, loud, and over-dramatic, papered with Lexus Timone, and cluttered with everything trendy. Stacey was a one-off and no-one else came in her room. It wasn't intended for Abigail's taste, this fluffy-pile lilac carpet scattered with discarded clothes. That blue plaster Madonna bound and gagged with gold chains. Those bras and knickers hanging off handles, sweaters bulging from polythene bags. The nests of anklets and stockings, with boots and shoes interbreeding.

Abigail searched for somewhere to sit. Abandoned false eyelashes colonised corners of unredeemed jumble. Bottles, jars, and canisters, leaked

148

mysterious compounds as Stacey lip-glossed away, leaving Abigail free to talk theatre and Garrick:

"... Anyrate, like I said, I reckon my mum's right." Stacey's eyebrows shot up. "No really, Stace. She is. You've got to be moral if you want men's respect."

"Crap!" Stacey's kick demolished a landscape. "Crap!" Her newly refurbished lips flashed vicious and gleaming, glittering, crisp, disconnected. "That's crap."

Abigail hesitated. "But you . . ."

"Sod the bloody Majestic. Get real. Success is only down to one thing." She took Abigail's wrists, her face hard as Kabuki and smooth as rice powder. "Abigail petal, it's simple. Either you fuck. Or you don't."

"You never listen."

"To you?" Stacey nodded along to the music. "It's psychological blockage. You're frit. Like maybe you've been abused then forgot?"

Sphincter muscles narrowed her throat. "No!" Abby shrieked. "No."

"There! Victims always deny it. So it'll have to be counselling next, then electric shocks to the brain. Sometimes they drill teeny little holes in your skull." She flashed a quick grin, before dusting her cheeks with a large sable brush. "All I try doing is help." Stacey closed her eyes to soft bristles before dabbing her face in the mirror. "So come off it, Abbs!" She took Abigail's gaze to be envy. "Never mind. I'll teach you make-up. Experiment. It's easy. Have fun." Abby looked away as Stacey tried to connect. "He hasn't taken advantage? Your boss? You're not . . ."

"No!"

"Aaah. Poor little tart." Stacey stretched towards Abby, her fingers straining to touch.

A fist smashed into her face! As Stacey staggered and fell, Abigail slammed every door in the house. Bham. Bham. Bham . . . storming off down the street.

Abby could not shake off her mixed feelings next day. Friends were the worst. You never knew who was acting. Not even those you knew best. She was no longer so sure about Garrick.

Garrick himself must have slept well. He awoke feeling fresh. Pale traces of daylight began sketching traces through darkness. Blocks of multifaceted towers mirrored blue and white flecking into composite skyscapes. This was December with hints of July. For once he had managed quick calls to his wife, and even had a word with his kids, so with Verity's Rolex still burning his wrist he knew his run of good luck would continue. With so many favourable omens he'd try window-shopping en route into work. Few opened early. Those jewellers that did, refused to 'do deals'. Everything pointed to Sanjay.

Thank God for Louise Roberts, he thought. At least she had accepted his plan. He'd perform a monologue chosen for its suburban appeal. What Louise called her 'target audience'. The devil however would lie in the detail.

Or as Louise put it. "My aim is to provide enough culture to pay off our mortgage!" Then her loud outrageous laugh. "Yes, because everyone is improving ourselves. That's Club Arabica. Folk pay to feel good and don't care if they don't understand so long as it works. Like I always stick to Versace. Gold cupids, curly columns and scrolls! It screams 'style' in a blackout. That's class guaranteed, no matter what Abigail says." She leaned across and lowered her voice. "And talking of her I want to be totally honest Because sadly my daughter She lacks my perception. I don't want her letting you down. There! Now I've said it!" She snatched up a notepad. "Now what's the poem you've chosen?" She carefully wrote down his choice.

Soon Sanjay's gold and platinum bracelet would be his. Even if public performance were risky, his wife's spontaneous rise would lead to her equally spontaneous fall. When the crunch came he'd be there. No more shared lives at a distance. They'd be together again.

"Hi?" came the voice on his cellphone, sounding more transatlantic than ever. "Who is this?"

"Hi darling. It's me. I've been thinking. Why don't you come up to Norston?" He waited a beat. "And stay the weekend?"

"Oh yes? And when's that exactly?" He sensed a shrug in her voice.

"Next weekend! I'll rent a hotel. Five stars at least. So say yes."

Her response was drowned in a babble of voices and muffled asides; "No, not now Simon, I'm on the phone." Then she came back loud and clear. "Well Gary, you know how it is and as it happens . . . Like I was saying, as it happens . . ."

She took an extra long breath. Only then did it dawn. She was trying to think up excuses.

"Gary look I'm pretty damn sick of hotels and food. But, but as they're giving us a break . . ." She was offhandedly turning him down. "So I figure. Hell Why not?"

Out on location, a sea breeze scoured the esplanade, whipping up froth. Verity nodded, her distracted expression unseen. Garrick mentally replayed what she'd said as a Westerly hammered the beaches with storms of polythene bags. Around her all Eastbourne shivered. A film crew huddled, backs to the weather. The barbecue spluttered. The Steadicam caught the first spots of rain. Verity smiled, then everyone started to run.

The two ugly sisters, Asphyxia and Euthanasia, were practising with home-perms, their heads encased in huge plastic bags, building towards Trixie's tear-jerking ballad; "No-one nowhere loves me, yeah!" The pianist poised at the barely tuned piano as Trixie took a big gulp, then stopped with mouth open-wide. All eyes turned to the prompter.

Abigail was reassessing her life. Was she meant to switch off her brain when events were so interconnected and identities all overlapped? She knew exactly how Cinderella felt, identified so completely it hurt. When everything jarred you asked yourself who you were? She could be doing what Trixie did, only better. In fairytales heroines always won in the end, so what if . . .

"Hey you! Prompt!" Trixie was frantically snapping her fingers. "Shit". She tried to flip words from the air. "Abby! Wake up!"

At coffee break Abigail joined the habitual smokers outside, coat wrapped tightly around her. The least Josh could have done was to text her. From the blackened Church Hall she looked across a wind-torn oasis, beyond which stretched the war zone where Eddie Craig laid waste to the future. A single gnarled cherry tree was counting down its last days as the Somme and Passchendale loomed. Sheltering under its branches, Garrick tried not to inhale.

Abigail pushed through overgrown shrubs, finding herself on a granite-sett street surrounded by flattened foundations. An abandoned highway from nowhere to nowhere. Yellow strips fluttered like prayer-flags on strings.

"Abby?" someone said, "That you?"

Through broken hoardings a figure emerged. It was not the Josh she recognised. His hair was crisp and clean; face recently shaven; black leather jacket polished and shiny with Cargo jeans direct from the store. He was waving a cone of metalised paper as if he'd been lying in wait. But how could he have known?

"Lucky I've caught you, eh?" He vaulted the fence. " Peace offerings."

He brandished the crushed paper cone in her face, but as she ducked, scents and colours burst out. The package exploded with yellows and golds. Next moment Josh was gone, vanished as if he'd never existed. Thick black smoke now trailed the whole landscape, obliterating his existence, its pungent smell like dead bodies.

Garrick was taken aback. Her gift was so unlikely it must have been consciously planned. Its outburst of yellows, creams, oranges, reds, engulfed him. Blossoms fluoresced from the dark. Their perfume went straight to his head. What was she trying to say? Apart from a portrait of Chekhov taped up next to a print of Melikhovo Lodge, his office lacked personal traces. Okay, a photo or two, but Tiger Lilies were favourites of Vee. So how could Abigail know?

He'd underestimated her. Abigail's bouquet changed the whole mood. He sniffed the lavish aroma, running a finger over a petal. Back home in Spring, lilies scattered their deep-staining pollen until rooms would pulsate with those rich musky scents. St George's Mews became an indoor garden. Now in this same fragrance both Vee and Abby were inextricably fused deep in the primitive brain.

Phyllis rammed the bunch in a jug of fresh water. "Floral tributes, eh?" She thrust the jug back in his hands. "Who's died?"

Huddled in the passenger seat Jilly Craske was subdued. Most mornings they'd race into town, but now the rush-hour traffic was jammed. Thomas obsessively revved up the engine. Norston was indifferent: too big to know neighbours and too small to remain incognito. Competition drove everyone on, and Thomas raced to close any gap. When he suddenly slammed on the brakes, it jolted her forward.

"Thomas?" she asked in a small voice, "Lovey . . . ?"

They had slowed to a crawl outside the Majestic with Thomas's head half out the window.

"That bastard!" He pointed up at 'GARRICK JONES' in thick solid type on the billboards.

Icy winds cut into the cab. "Er, Thomas . . . ?" She raised her collar and waited in vain.

As the seat belt cut into her body, a substitute self eased any pain. 'Curvaceous' was their code word for fat. 'Full figure' meant obese. Each day she'd decide on that new ultimate diet. Whatever the physical world, she'd survive. Her endorphins always kicked in.

"Thomas love . . . ?"

The car's response was to detonate vapour, emitting more and more toxins, violently carving a swathe through the traffic. It swerved and braked, teasing destruction by split-micro-seconds. Strapped into seats as tight as small coffins, her rush of adrenaline extinguished all concepts of death. Road-rage was Pure Art, It redefined life as 'A Spasm'. As ever she was glad to get out. While she was crossing towards her salon, he skidded away with the reek of burnt rubber, and was gone.

"Morning pet!" her shampooist called, "Traffic been dreadful again?"

The girls had opened without her, but as she entered their bright new facade she felt exceptionally gross. Her bodyweight seemed to drag. She felt bloated and heavy. Background music was sounding off-key, and all she could hear was the mechanical straining of pistons and grinding of interlocked gears. She even felt sick at the smell of shampoo.

"My! You've missed such excitement!" Amy and Veronica were shuffling foot to foot, nudging each other. "We've booked in two stars!" they chorused, "Yeah. From Cinderella! An' like you said, we've cleared all bookings till lunch."

Jilly Craske had to sit down. The hairdressing world would have to take note. The Gazette and Mercury would jump because everyone read Elizabeth Scott. It should be projected on clouds or flashed across the Town Hall. Jilly wanted to scream. She could foresee such a dazzling future she began to feel almost weepy. With celebrity endorsements she could become Head of Makeup, or Chief Cosmetician to Trans-Planet Movies? It was time to leave Thomas behind .But Amy was pointing and waving.

"Look. It's them!" Veronica hissed.

Photographers and film crews should have been waiting. But no. Not so much as a camera phone. There should have been a red carpet with Jilly Craske in glitzy tiara showered by floating pink petals. Instead all she saw were two silhouettes approaching her armoured-glass door. As Jilly took her position, smile at the ready, two thirty-somethings wearing padded tops and tight pants slouched in with high heels and fluttering scarves. Ordinariness followed behind them. The anticlimax took Jilly Craske's breath. Before anyone noticed, Trixie and Pippa were seated, all capped teeth and white fillings, face-to-face with their well-trained reflections. Soon they'd be fully relaxed, glad to detail their lives as Jilly Craske kept egging them on.

"Acting?" Pippa explained, "It's all about faking. It's pretending to be someone else. Like back home I'm lying awake nights, pondering It's who am I? What am I doing? How much do I owe, kind of stuff? " She giggled. "You get to that age. Then it gets to you."

"As for men! They're no bleeding help," Trixie chimed in, "If my boyfriend said what he thought, he'd have nothing to say! But with my first husband, we were happy for years. That's till we met! .But weddings are lovely, honest. Marriage is fine. The only snag comes with the living together!

That's why you need a couple of husbands. Keep one in the wardrobe for spare."

"Aye, an' you know what that called?" Pippa gave a toothy grin, knowing the routine always worked. "Well, Bigamy is marrying two But Monotony's when you stick to just one." And everyone fell about laughing.

Jilly tried to steer conversation back towards Garrick, like which shampoos he used, the music he liked, the books he read, the kind of women he fancied. Celebrities could all have false teeth and cheap wigs, face-lifts and nose jobs, quadruple heart bypasses and triple brain transplants. She wondered how they would have reacted to Abby.

"Abby? She's got one thing I'd die for. That's youth."

"Too bloody right," Pippa added, "I'd not say 'No' to a nice youth myself!"

"Me neither," Jilly thought as water gurgled in whirlpools down basins and waste pipes, reiterating the spin of the Earth.

Extractor fans clattered and whirred. Somewhere a car alarm sounded. The click click of scissors. Vibration of traffic. Then like the last frames of a movie, they expected the credits to roll.

"Now gentlemen, remember, it's investment as provides reimbursement. Luck doesn't come into it." Arthur Ruddock stood back from his lectern. "It's what we promoters call 'guaranteed chance'." He paused to pan round. "My Lady And Gentlemen." He spread out his large stubby hands. "Here we are on the brink of a future where none but the brave deserve the fair. What with public pressure, it's us who's taking the risks. But have we got the confidence? Can we keep our nerve?" He paused for effect while glancing back at the clock. "The question is, can we?" The audience shuffled. "Are we up for investment?" He waited again.

He was chairing more and more meetings urging Brinkside Associates to invest in The Majestic short-term. He'd lobbied Cavanham Estates and talked to shareholders in Netsky Simons and Comrie & Cant, but Eddie Craig seemed to be canvassing Manchester projects while Norston Council kept backing out. Legal delays were not helping. When no one responded, Arthur Ruddock answered his own question.

"Right. That's a yes! Yes, of course we can, Eddie! We can't go wrong! And why not? Because that's what sponsorship means? Look at your maps. Page twenty-eight. There. Look. Everything's in your favour. First, it's not in some conservation zone. And according to our surveyors, it's architecturally invalid. Its foundations are inadequate too. Add to that, entertainment's gone electronic. Plus the site's got redevelopment value. Plus it's going for a song! So draw your long-term conclusions! You buy the Majestic." He spread out his arms towards major investors. "All agreed? It's just to cover a few meagre months."

But Eddie had other things on his mind. The Majestic still suited the hammer and chisel approach but 'Re-Evaluation' was his latest buzzword; he nodded to agree with himself; even noblest crafts dated. Nowadays with explosives and timers a multiple tower could 'whoomph' at the press of a button, but Eddie was aiming for literal and maximum impact before the whole market crashed. If fifty floors could pancake into a sandwich, the Town

Hall's twenty-five susceptible floors were no challenge. That site was ideal for small-scale experimentation.

Unaware of concurrent proceedings Garrick worked on in his office. Right now he needed a smoke. It wasn't enough to be churning out gags. Soon there'd be journalists ferreting round. Perhaps he'd rename Cinderella "Part One in the Apotheosis of Chekhov". But Vee and Roseanne? They'd not understand. It would sound to them like betrayal.

James Carr had got everyone twitchy. They took comfort in costumes, wigs, and props, raising such awesome questions as whether Cinders wore ear studs or naked lobes for Scene One? Followed by diamante for the grand ball? With chandelier danglers for the finale? Garrick sat cracking his knuckles and gritting his teeth. He wanted a sweeping impasto. He wanted more guts, but having lain awake for nights he was slowly becoming more shattered. It wasn't for him to calm itching scalps or untangle tresses. Let Crowning Glory deal with such great human dimensions. Hair was their bloody job.

Jilly's was a balancing act. Since revamping the salon's facade others quickly followed suite while Louise claimed Club Arabica was busy pulling in crowds. Now there was talk of financial recession. Without theatre gossip or Abby's showbiz scandal, Jilly feared she would quickly lose out. Despite the actresses' unpublicised visit, it could still be too late. As coloured streetlights blew with the sleet, she'd noticed Garrick was passing less often. Somehow she had to cling on because Abigail promised, and no one should abandon their dreams. No one could dodge Christmas.

She tried gluing Garrick's portrait to mirrors, furtively kissing her fingers then pressing them onto his lips, hoping connections would flow. But nothing. Then came a new wave of sickness. Once business was over she switched off the main lights to wait in the dark. Thomas was atypically late. She must have dozed off.

A bang! Outlined against streetlights, hair dishevelled, black leathers catching the light, there he was aiming his hand like a gun. Next moment he's ripping Garrick's face down and shredding him all over the tiles. Thomas swore. His fist smashed her teeth against lips. The impatient Mondeo awaited its master's approach. Tyres spattered the gravel.

Jilly came to with a start, feeling swollen and bloated. As they pulled onto their forecourt, security lights blazed. Thomas had already gone in. Their front door lay open. His silhouette bobbed on drawn curtains. She found him with hands piously folded, seated at her best polished table, in her best armchair. Beneath overhead lighting his eyes were like skeletal hollows. It was high theatre. High camp. A mock 'X'-rated movie. The play must have already begun.

"You and that Abigail bitch! She's Garrick's little pimp. Passing dirty messages! That makes you guilty too!" He took a mock-legal stance. "That's a sin. Confess!"

"Please. I'm not well."

He'd begun to unzip his leather jacket. "You knew you'd be punished. And anyway . . ." He'd started to roll up his shirtsleeves. "You love it. Look at you! Bulging! Letting yourself go. You and that sneering soft-fingered

Garrick. His fornicating hands up their knickers . . ." He gripped Jilly's body. "Their their fat swollen breasts and fat bums and . . ."

To his satisfaction she had started to whimper. He bundled her up narrow treads and over loose carpet. She stumbled ahead, coughing, moaning, as if mounting a scaffold, completely fulfilling her role.

"Yes, you want to be caught. You like being punished." She strained round to face him. "Yes you do! That's your little game. Playing the lead in your drama. You and that shit Garrick Jones!"

For that she had to be punished. Punishment without fear or favour. He knew she deserved it.

Arthur Ruddock was chairing another appeal. Sponsors and charities loved him. General assemblies, dinners, lunches, speeches and minuted meetings multiplied in his diary. He may have suspected their motives but this evening there was too much at stake. The drip, drip, drip of routine punctuated his life. First the Call to Order. The Reading of Minutes. The Presentation. The Keynote Speech . . .

". . . And as you know," he concluded, "'Cinderella' will be our Council's fortieth and most popular panto". The committee seemed to sigh as one. "We've the world-famous Garrick Jones directing Starring Lionel Parsons . . ." He consulted his notes. "And Pippa White, Trixie Whatsit and James Carr and . . . and many others of note. So as a reward for support, I'm offering you all complimentary tickets. That means, it's all on the house!"

"Hear hear!" they chorused, mentally apportioning seats to their families and clients.

Brinkside's usual formality lapsed as 'Dress-down Friday' seeped into Norston, but Arthur stuck to club-crested ties, advising young George de Vries to do likewise. "No new craze ever lasted," he'd said, "Just dress the part, George. Play to win."

George as usual demurred. He couldn't be anonymous. He had to conform. Reminders were carved into every plaque in town. The De Vries Music Society, Drama Group, Unmarried Mothers, Poets, Political Refugees, you name it. It was there to be franchised. Glasses of Burgundy helped. First his mother had sold out to the theatre. Now it was all soirées and Chekhov ... with Garrick Jones only the latest arrival. Nevertheless, the conference suite in Norston Castle Hotel felt so relaxing that even George's nerves calmed. Arthur remained as protective as ever, advising and fussing around, but when Arthur provided left-handed scissors and so-called left-handed pens, that seemed too over the top.

"Not at all. We've got this in common," Arthur would say, "You and me. Cack-handers both!" Tapping George's left hand. "And your mother's a wonderful woman. She and I. I knew your father of course, but I've known her since since before the late Lordship died. In the great days of amateur dramatics." His lips allowed the brief ghost of a smile. "Like me, she wants you to take your rightful place in life."

George shuffled his notes. The subject kept coming up.

"Yes, you and me," Arthur said, "We speak our minds too. We've so much in common." He took George's silence as grateful acceptance. "No no, not at all, I don't expect thanks. Kindness don't come into it. It's what we can do for each other. You've inherited class and I provide experience. Right?" He gave a broad wink. "Together we make a bloody good team."

George dreaded speeches as much as he loathed his mother's soirées. When Family Trust lawyers had set his official majority date they'd launched a time-coded missile. His father always insisted, "Death is only Nature's way of telling you when to slow down," while he'd kippered his lungs with Navy Cut Extra swilled down with neat Irish whiskey, indulging his 'Stage Door Johnny' ways. Father and son had nothing in common, yet from somewhere George had developed strong mercantile values, with Arthur quietly bridging gaps and being a mentor as if he'd been there from the start.

Tonight George would take his first seat at a meeting. Soon he'd be heading his own family trust. 'Temple Storford Estates' with its anachronistic hundreds of acres. Buttoned into a hand-tailored suit, this was George's personal countdown, his own rite of passage. Ahead were those combination-locked vaults pre-set with his birth certificate code.

"Er, ummm . . ." George cleared his throat. "Gentlemen, thank you for allowing me this opportunity to address this meeting of of Brinkside Developments. I am proud to step into the shoes of my father."

Eddie Craig continued reading a booklet while opening a mineral water. *Fizzzzz*! Water effervesced into glass as Eddie unfolded a centre-page plan. He brandished a pen then began blotting out buildings, zapping them out like a hit man.

Pow! . . . Half Cavanham Street *Pow! Pow! Pow!* Away went most of Royal Street. Then Market Place blitzed. The Majestic Theatre was purged in one last frantic scribble.

Once events speeded up, they could not be diverted. Thomas was breathless and dazed. He bent over their mattress, bed sheets coiled in tight knots, and tried to awake from a nightmare. Ghosts of repetition ran wild, reflecting every possible angle. Jilly was avoiding his eyes. She groaned but said nothing. Just groaned. No acting. No stuntmen. Just grinding three-dimensional pain. She groaned but said nothing. Her passive acceptance only provoked him still further. Transgression had to be punished! This was their burden: their shared retribution. Honour must be obeyed.

He'd sworn it would never happen again. Never. Not ever. He wasn't violent by nature, therefore no way to blame. She hadn't responded. She'd goaded him on. Despite his attempts at remorse, the bedside lamp cast cautionary shadows highlighting strewn clothes and spatters of blood on the linen. Catharsis worked. Sometimes you had to do bad to do good. Everyone knew where the blame ought to lie. Even if it hadn't been Garrick, she would have found someone else.

He fetched packs of ice and wet towels, packing them around her. She was sobbing and retching and pushing him off. This was becoming a pattern. Now she'd be sick again several times. He could hear her sobbing up there in the bathroom. His hands were still shaking as he poured several stiff doses of brandy. When he turned the doorknob to enter, the bathroom was locked. He angrily rattled the handle. In the long silence he was suddenly scared. Then enraged.

"For God's sake! Open up!" Hurling himself at the door, again and again, throwing his whole weight against it, not hearing her undo the latch.

This time he hit the door at a run hung in mid-air as it gaped, cartoon legs revolving, then crunched with a '*BLATT!!*' on the edge of the bath before crashing against the hard basin. Trickles of blood melded with hers on the tiles.

Jilly felt quiet and detached. She observed it all like a performance, as if marionette strings had been cut leaving him sprawled like a foetus, a malformed child, writhing in its agony. She picked up her long trimming scissors, closing them tight to a point, watching him squirm. Most of her wounds were internal. Others were well out of sight, but the ache was acute and intense. She touched the sharp tip of the blades.

His threat was barely audible. "I'll kill that bastard. Fuck Garrick. You'll see."

His words bypassed her brain. In the cold white merciless striplight, she leaned over him. Each scratch and bloodstain showed up dark mauve as she sliced. He started to uncontrollably shake.

"Shush," she whispered, her wet hair dripping over his face, "Shsssh."

'Morning in the Bowl of Night, has flung the Stone that puts the Stars to Flight' . . .

Poets had got that dead right, Garrick thought. Even Norston was starting to mellow. With every new day his prospects improved. Now he could stand on the rim of the future and watch everything fall into place, but as he approached the church hall with a spring in his step he heard laughing and shouting. He stopped at the porch before going in.

A ball was being booted around with no concern for stained windows. Even James Carr, even Truman and Reggie. Everyone was joining in, laughing like kids in a schoolyard. Garrick had nothing to lose. Cycling had tightened a notch on his belt. His stubble was becoming a beard. He felt every bit "The Director". As he charged in, the ball ricocheted back and forth and scrimmages flowed with the tides. As Garrick picked himself up someone shook his hand. Others slapped his back. Now he was part of their scene. This was acceptance. Pains and bruises would fade.

Then it was back to Scene One, Act One, and as usual Fabian was on the book, hair wild as ever, issuing prompts whether wanted or not. Lionel and Orlando swapped gossip. Trixie and Pippa were reworking moves and James Carr was ready to pounce, and everybody questioned decisions. Now Garrick regretted listening to Phyllis. He should not have lent Abigail out. It left him exposed. The church hall seemed empty without her. Continuity mattered. He'd ended up taking the flak. As James Carr rambled on about The Brothers Grimm, Garrick's attention span faded.

Down in the theatre's foundations, Abigail scrabbled on hands and knees, bare-fingered sorting out archives, picking through old programmes like the strata of past generations composting down in these cellars. She was here on Phyllis's orders clearing out underground stores, but why store anything here?

It felt like a punishment task designed to keep staff in their place, disinterring the dead, sorting out the ancient deceased. Who had they been?

157

Gloria Pennywell, Dominic Bright, Elsie Taylor, Jack Elwes, Soraya le Brun? All smiling like juvenile masks. As years of canal soaked through the bricks, layers of paper compounded. Pages were crumbling apart scattering fungal spores. She could actually taste the decay. Then more and more names. Noel Coward, Lily Langtree, Moya Winn, Laurence Olivier, even Shakespeare, Ustinov, Marlowe, right down to an Agatha Christie. She came across a Grimaldi and Edmund Kean. Even a real 'David Garrick 1717– 79, Director of Drury Lane Theatre'.

History meant nothing but she ploughed on, unearthing the past. From time to time she'd hear footsteps on-stage overhead and catch snatches of indistinct chat. Once she thought she heard Josh whistling, but didn't that bring bad luck? With numbing hands she unpacked another thick folder. More crumpled faces emerged. She recognised some. Nigel Wright, Dinah West, and Suki Skoo (Once big names on children's TV). She noted their pulpy formaldehyde faces. These bunches of uptight pubescents were so bland they looked like old snaps of her mum. Page after page. Show after show. Then she stopped She stared . . .

There it was. A shot of "James Carr in Breton Follies. A daring revue by Ben Croft". She held it up to the light. Yes, it really was him. A very young James Carr, unclothed and uncensored on a leopard skin in front of a faint Eiffel Tower, making eyes at the lens.

Garrick began to feel better. As he watched Pippa rehearsing her dance it brought to mind his own touring days seen through the glow of North African skies. He'd been young and rebellious. He'd wanted to shock. And he did. But he'd learned from his sudden success, and from its equally sudden collapse. Lessons had to be learned, but learning imposed limitations. Take Lionel's attempts to learn lines. He only recalled a self-edited version which changed. Soon he'd be mangling Chekhov, but whereas Chekhov would probably groan into his borscht, here in this draughty church hall Lionel was magic. He transformed a bulky sweatshirt and jeans into a fully flounced frock complete with three-quarter high heels, multi-tiered wig, and size 24 bosoms. There was a grotesque fascination in that.

Put James and Lionel together, and there was the ideal double act. Their kitchen scene with its rolling pins, pastry and slapstick moved like an elaborate dance, its pirouettes backed by a rollicking Durham brass band. This had to be choreographed to the nth, but tempers were getting increasingly short. It was simpler for Vee. 'Take 83.6 grammes of this, and 204.4 grammes of that, mixed and baked for seven minutes fifteen seconds at exactly 256.35°.'. She never had doubts. Her judgements were instant and clear, so all the more reason to prepare for her visit. Knowing her fiercely critical tastes, he'd check out hotels and seek local advice. His marriage might depend on this. Abby once more came to mind.

"No, no. Let's cut all the rolling pin stuff," Garrick suggested, as the pastry scene ran into the buffers.

Everything came down to timing. This meant pressing psychological buttons, but pressing them in the right sequence. Presumably the formula lay in one's cortex, waiting to be accessed, only requiring appropriate triggers.

But when the scene restarted with James in an outsize chef's hat, there was Fabian, diving in and out supplying new props, getting laughs.

James Carr would not be upstaged. He pushed Fabian roughly aside.

"Fabian sweetie!" he sneered in rasping falsetto. "There's only one problem. You're Irish!" A ripple ran round the room. "This hybrid Art of pantomime It's the domain of us British, because we love compromise and confusion." Then he was off into one of his well-rehearsed off-the-cuff lectures. "We take Italian comedy, mix it with French fairy tales all mangled up with music hall. Because laughter's the primary refuge of tears."

Fabian stared. James peered over metal-rimmed glasses.

"Yes, Victorian panto was wholly inclusive. Ask Lionel. From knife-throwers, fire-eaters, conjurers, jugglers, tightrope walkers Tigers in cages .women with pythons Sword-swallowing Sikhs, circus horses, elephants, midgets dozens of clowns, and semi-naked acrobats throwing rubber dumbbells about. That's what we should be aiming for. Contemporary inclusiveness. Reviving the quintessence of true melodrama in this so very post-electronic age. Don't you think so, Garrick?"

James Carr gazed up at the windows of saints and glowed in their silent applause. Garrick turned on James Carr.

"Bollocks, James. Melodrama? Rhetoric? Do Plato and Socrates tell us a thing? No! Philosophy sucks! It's all bollocks! We're not academics. We're here to entertain kids who'd rather suck lollies in front of a video screen, like my two. If this means you dropping your pants or farting to order, okay, then you'll do it for laughs!"

James sighed. "Honestly Garrick love, with due respect, all I'm trying to say is the 'transformation' scene is about deeper psychological truths as in all fairy tales, that's all. It's about metamorphosis. It's pumpkins into glittering coaches. Girl into woman. It's metaphors in the Freudian sense. It's about our sexual fantasies. About our own aspirations, your dreams. Surely Jung underlines this sense of the id and the ego? Ask any psychiatrist. Yes?" Garrick's Rolex continued its countdown as Verity's visit ticked ever closer. His checklist increased in proportion. Hotel rates, room service, cleanliness, reliability, etceteras, etceteras, but most of all, cuisine. His fingers desperately pressed at his lips, reviving old nicotine tastes.

As usual Garrick was out in the washroom when his phone rang. Wedging the phone between head and shoulder while trying to turn off the tap, he tried to sound upbeat:

"Hi! Darling! At last! I've been trying to catch you."

"Really?" The voice was Louise. "How fortunate. You remember us discussing your one-man show?. Well, I've been wondering. Have you done much preparation?"

The question seemed loaded. She must be about to back out. He dried his hands on his jeans. With no agreement in writing he'd no contract to insist on. His former misgivings vanished and £ signs flashed in his eyes. He couldn't book Verity into cheap bed-and-breakfast, that was for sure. It came down to good faith. A verbal deal was still a deal. He wasn't some pawn in a feud between Louise and her daughter. If this were bluff and counter-bluff, he'd try bouncing it back.

"Yes I have, as it happens." He managed to lie surprisingly coolly. "You've been my top priority. I've spent hours refining and rehearsing my act." He'd expect some cancellation fee, she must understand that. "I can fax you my script right away, if you like?" He'd put her on the bloody spot. "I've spent hours on research. It's a world-famous poetry classic." Now he would pull the whole rug from under her feet. "So if you were thinking of bringing it forward Okay, that's a deal!"

Yes, he thought, that's game, set, and match! He'd demand compensation. He gazed up at the tall lancet windows and waited. He almost heard her rearranging her words.

"Garrick, my dear, you must be psychic. You've just saved my day." His brain slid into reverse. "Bring all you stuff with you tonight, eight o'clock, Club Arabica. And bring your script. I may have a little surprise." She mwah-mwahed kisses into the phone and was gone.

She'd set him up. He leaned against the nearest wall. His palms had gone moist and his fingers were damp. She was bringing it forward. He wasn't prepared. His impulse was to call straight back, listing prior engagements, but James Carr's baritone voice interfered.

"Garrick, old love, how about doing the ballroom on ice? You couldn't get cooler than that!"

Abigail had returned. At the far end of the hall Fabian had organised flip charts. These appeared to indicate 'days per artiste' in proportion to 'number of lines in the script' laid out like a management spreadsheet. Naturally James had taken offence and stormed across to intervene. Trixie caught his arm, while Pippa signalled to Abby:

"Hey everyone! Come over here. We've got perfect proof little things matter!" She took the packet from Abby.

Pippa pulled a photograph out. A bony young man with prominent ribs postured naked against a frayed leopard skin. With pelvis thrust forward and wreath round his head he smiled with thick lubricious lips, self-consciously raising a goblet. 'Breton Follies' the caption announced, 'Erotique Revue, 1970. Introducing Jamie Carr'. As James spluttered and choked, Garrick saw a scrap flutter from Abby's pink rucksack. As he caught it, it flipped, revealing a sun-tanned Garrick and Vee smiling through unmistakable lip-prints.

As he slipped it into his pocket, Fabian Wass waffled on about scheduling costumes and sets, referring to Josh as if he were a new Cecil Beaton. To Garrick, Josh was only a chippie, young, slim and over ambitious, who behaved like God's gift to women. Didn't he understand times had changed? In an era of pixels and wrap-around screens, the idea of painted hardboard trundling round on blockboard wheels seemed utterly, totally mad.

Trompe l'oeuil backcloths painted on canvas? Clumpy cutouts dropped in on ropes? What was needed was a computerised system, noiselessly hydraulic. That's what kids expected. Palaces rising from oceans, cottages turning to forests. Storms, floods and volcanoes materialising in front of their eyes. So why not cherry orchards too? Birch forests, lakes and fountains? Dachas, villas, palaces? Lean-to sheds and elegant shaded verandas? As a profoundly impractical man who couldn't knock nails into planks, he was depending on someone dynamic, someone fit and functional, someone he could wholeheartedly trust. Someone who wasn't Josh.

As Garrick sheltered under the porch with his bike, pedestrians scuttled like Lowryesque phantoms. The darkness flickered with lightning. Vee's gift to him was his benchmark. He'd over-extended his credit, but choosing a top-class hotel was essential. He might try and waylay Abigail for advice? He might also ask how she'd acquired one of his personal photos. Then suddenly the skies opened up.

"It is an ancient Mariner
And he stoppeth one of three,
'By thy long beard and glittering eye,
Now wherefore stopp'st thou me?'"

Its repetitive rhymes were invasive. He had the slim volume there in his pocket. He gave it a comforting pat. Thanks be to rhyming couplets! Maybe that batty old seadog and his death-wish albatross arose from a poet's psychosis, but Garrick could win with Coleridge's help. Louise had called his bluff, now he'd have to talk her into giving him time. He'd phone her at once.

"Phone her? You think you've rationalised everything out?" The voice intervened from the back of his mind. "You're deceiving yourself. Not to mention your wife." His father must have subverted his conscience. "Grow up, man. You're too self-centred by half!"

Immediately Garrick's conscious mind struck back. "You! You're just my neurosis As for dragging in Vee, that's cheap paranoia. Next it'll be Roseanne, then our kids. So keep my kids out of this!"

"Gary, Gary, come on." The voice whispered. "It's not so much your intentions as judgement I question And what if you're misleading yourself?"

"Sod off!" Garrick said aloud. At which his hypothalamus switched off.

Abigail was well ahead, bobbing along with such bounce her ponytail swung in time with her backpack like the incarnation of zing. His pulse rate soared. The whole of life was her catwalk. How could she know that somewhere ahead the Ship of Lost Souls was steadily tacking towards her? As skies started to clear, Garrick pedalled, then freewheeled ahead. Soft tyres passed over tarmac in an almost frictionless whirr.

"Brrrring Brrring!" went the bell, "Brrrring Brrring!"

As Garrick approached Club Arabica, Louise must have been coiled up and waiting. She emerged from the doorway. A black trouser-suit with ultra-high heels gave her a top-heavy appearance offset by a silver-gold bouffant. Botox had ironed out former wrinkles. Her eyelashes fluttered like wings. Her lips seemed as puckered and glossed as a drag queen. She brimmed with tears as she hugged him before stepping back, observing the man, then the bike.

"Well, at least you're a man as cares for our planet." She clutched at his elbow. "But does it care a damn about you?"

Mortality rode at his shoulder: he knew that. Dangers accrued like water on stone, blurring what Ancient Mariner verses he'd learned, because

161

cycling in traffic was risky. Passing trucks like monstrous icebergs sucked bikers into their slipstreams. Fleets of Manwess vans wove in and out. Everything missed by a hairsbreadth, so surely his odds must have narrowed. He insisted on chaining his bike to a lamppost.

Her ornate rings crunched into his fingers. "You and me, we've got an intuitive sense." As they entered the lobby she lowered her voice. "Mind you, tonight's been a minor disaster. I'm not blaming Carlos , though it's entirely his fault. Tonight we've got foreign tourists. So guess what?" She caught his dawning expression. "Dead on!" Louise snatched his overcoat, handing it to an attendant. "Tonight's act cancelled last minute. Now you're our celebrity guest."

Louise kept a tight grip, leading him to a small table beside the small stage, seating Garrick to face her. Was she expecting him to perform? Coincidences didn't happen by chance.

"Garrick my dear, I can't tell you how grateful I am. Arabica may be small, but it's us artistes as keep our community going. And my friend Jilly agrees. Jilly the hairdresser lady?" She waved towards other tables. "That's why I'm so glad you could make it. My own daughter refused to work here. You're very brave to take her on. I hear you got enough warnings. They expect instant stardom these days. Anyway, now's our big chance."

Before he could protest she was dragging him into the spotlights. Well-nourished diners banged tables and rattled their glasses to whoopings and clappings. Once they'd smelled blood, Garrick thought, they'd cheer the next disembowelment, applauding each decapitation. But the spotlight was swinging away. Louise was excitedly pointing as two figures emerged into glare. Pippa and Trixie sauntered out between tables, in overcoats and scarves. Pippa blew Garrick a kiss, her black stilettos clicking terrazzo. Trixie gave a broad wink. Suddenly they slipped off their topcoats, revealing tight glittering costumes topped with ornate Jilly Craske wigs. Sequins sparkled on Lurex. A drummer materialised, softly tapping a beat as Pippa settled down at a piano with Trixie beside her

"Good evening, Norston!" she yelled, skimming a finger over the keys, and everyone cheered. "We're dedicating tonight's performance to 'Cinderella' And to the Chekhov Players at the Majestic Theatre." She led another burst of applause. "And to our great stage director, Garrick Jones!"

This wasn't Chekhov. Nor Ibsen. Nor Igor Stravinsky. Not Shakespeare. Not Strindberg nor Arthur Miller. Certainly not Coleridge poems. And yet the audience sat spellbound, entranced, as their voices swooped and dived through the octaves. Garrick sipped compulsively. Could one sip of Merlot, a tiny drop of Chardonnay, or the waft of a South American butterfly's wings induce mighty floods in Tibet? But Louise was insisting on answers.

"Resht ashured," he slurred, "My preparationsh For the 'Anshuntent Mariner shycle They're . . ." Where was the thread of his words? "You'll sheeI guarantee promise my absolute trust. The Anshunt Mariner'sh great, and and . . ."

A blast of cold air. Ice seemed to pass through the building as the main doors were flung open. By the time Abigail reached their table, Louise had gone red in the face. Like the classic drunk, Garrick saw several dimensions at

162

once. Was Louise really Abigail's future? Or was this Abby reflecting her mother? Their likenesses multiplied, superimposed, distorted into one blurred double-vision. Abigail was frantic

"Mum, it's Jilly Craske! She's been took ill."

Louise looked from Garrick to her daughter to, then slowly, patiently back.

"Being innocent isn't naïve. You couldn't be expected to know." She took her daughter's hand and held it. "She didn't want others to know, but grown women do. It's something we feel. Do you see what I mean?" She smiled and gave a Abby a hug. "Tomorrow, I promise, I'll give her a call."

Wobbling homewards through sleet, Garrick quickly sobered up. Tonight he'd seen Pippa and Trixie perform, but weren't they contracted to him? Yes, he had been impressed. Very impressed. He envied their effortless instincts, their energy and confidence. Most of all their applause. So despite the conditions, he decided to return via Cavanham Street and pass that hairdressing salon. "She's your greatest fan," they'd all said, but wasn't there something voyeuristic about making a detour to see your own pantomime adverts? Except nowhere looked quite the same.

It looked and felt unreal. By sodium lighting Victorian frontages had turned into stencils projected on gauze. Office blocks were cubes of ice and scaffolding floated on styrene foam. Street lights cut into luminous circumflex cones, dissolving then reassembling again. He wondered how Vee would respond. Their reconciliation would demand a high price: Roseanne would see to that. Now her daughter was a 'Celebrity Cook,' she'd reassess Garrick's comparative value. The stock Russian clichés: failed travelling student, failed manager, failed agent, failed consultant, and even failed alcoholic! As Roseanne once pointed out, "Marriage can cramp women's souls. We are the mitochondrial bond. It is we who prolong the Morozov blood. Biology knows women are the human race."

He'd not thought through Vee's invitation. What really mattered was Chekhov. That's why she'd sent him here in the first place. He must keep her away from the theatre, make sure she kept out the town centre, and asked no leading questions. Their hotel had to be way out of town.

Turning into Cavanham Street he braked, skidded in slush and nearly broadsided into the salon. Feather-down flakes floated from aerial pillows. Sleet turned to snow then back into icy drizzle. Roadways shimmered like shallow canals as downpipes disgorged and drains overflowed. This was no Russian winter. No crisp Tolstoy moment. Lancashire was not Moscow But if he closed his eyes, he could picture dry-frosted tracks between silver-thin birches like xylophone notes on the eye, transforming grey slush into Siberian snows. A balalaika strums from a dacha. Chiming icicles accompany swishings of skates. The tinkle of sleigh bells. The crunch of iced snow. But as always, real life came clobbering down; it offered a pantomime coach trundling across an uneven stage.

The salon itself was in darkness, all its signs turned off. As Garrick dismounted, large wet snowflakes came swirling around. He wheeled his bike up close and tried to peer in, but saw none of his pantomime posters. A hand-written note was taped to the window:

"Due to ill health, the proprietor will be away till next week. We thank our clientele for their great understanding."

As rain drummed against rickety windows, his room felt unexpectedly cosy. After sixteen attempts to book a hotel it was now close to midnight. With every line engaged his frustration grew. As time drained away, Verity's expensive, generous, elegant, unstinting, anniversary-celebration, gold watch became a constant reproach. He needed to buy a conciliatory gift. To afford this he counted on Louise and her nightclub. So where would this leave Coleridge? And the Ancient Mariner's tale? It left him with no more excuses, thanks to Trixie and Pippa. He'd underestimated them. In return they'd put him to shame. They were a duo. He was a dodgy CV.

He lay fully dressed, staring at cracks in the ceiling. His journey home had taken him seemingly hours. His clothes were still damp. His mattress was stuffed with deep-frozen potatoes. As ever his thoughts returned to his kids. He could visualise them aged three, six, and nine. Their baby faces were quickly supplanted, overlaid, and restructured: their unblinking smiles were laid out on his desk. He knew they would be missing him. And what would Vee be saying? What would she tell them? Would she undermine him? Plant insidious thoughts? Paint him as an absentee who'd cruelly abandoned his kids? Roseanne would always back her up. Admittedly there'd been times when he'd shouted. Okay, bloody sworn! But for their own good. And if he'd ever hit them, that was for the best of intentions. They knew that.

In a space between two frames, he propped up the still-crumpled photo from Abigail's bag. 'Garrick and Verity laughing straight into the lens'. It had been divided by a sharp crease intended for ripping apart? It seemed to be significant.

He prowled the room in gloves and scarf before slumping out on the bedspread. He watched long trailing cobwebs catching the flickering light. Marriage had changed his whole life. He was happy. He could not deny it. Outside the temperature fell to -3° Celsius. By his Rolex Imperator SX it was twenty-past-two in the morning when Garrick slipped into light sleep, spread-eagled on top of his duvet.

CHAPTER EIGHT

POLITICS

The seasons could do their damnedest but Arthur Ruddock always enjoyed Temple Storford. Even on a late afternoon it had a timeless Englishness. Compared with downtown Norston the air came bracingly fresh off the fells, which is why Victorian industrialists quickly moved here. The bourgeoisie escaped factory slums they themselves had created. As these up-and-coming fled the down-and-out, the richest built brand-new gothic estates.

Today the district was full of such piles, with swimming pools added. Temple Storford itself was one such 'National Treasure' in which Arthur like everyone had his own stake. Here he could walk to echoes of Elgar as if to a Pomp and Circumstance march. He understood those industrialists' yearnings as he strolled alongside Peggy de Vries; she in her tailored jeans and Home Counties tweeds, check scarf and suede boots, he in his usual suit. Arthur was on duty representing the theatre committee, which Peggy's late husband had chaired before him. His overcoat flapped in the breeze. His city shoes crunched on the gravel. With a bracing chill off the moors, ice crystals scoured the once silver-blue skies. Here time had no meaning. Talking seemed irrelevant. Both felt only twenty years young but the old contradictions would not go away.

"You know, it's – what I mean is . . ." She tried rephrasing her thoughts. "I've recently Anyway I've begun feeling old Which may be sad, but that doesn't make it any less true. And don't say I haven't changed. We both have." He looked about to object. "And don't tell me it doesn't matter. I can't evade my duties. You see, George is so very dependent. It's hard enough being a mother and father as well. Disciplining one moment, then comforting the next." He tried to speak. "Yes yes! I realise you've tried to help but in many ways he's still just a boy. This means . . ."

"But together we . . ."

"I appreciate that, but these days 'coming of age' is mere legalese. Nevertheless . . ."

She quickened her pace. Entering the portico Arthur as always found himself catching his breath as if they'd stepped back a full two hundred years. Forget council intrigues and planning departments, he was here "regarding the forthcoming Theatre Soirée", which meant ignoring those pastoral hillsides and traditional woodlands centred on this formal façade. Its Roman pediments and Jacobean wings seemed carved direct out of stone. Soft golden stone. That was the Temple Storford effect, extending for room after room. But no double glazing. No saunas. No sun decks. No lifts. Not here. He thought everything needed an urgent upgrading.

"By the way, did I mention?" Peggy was untying her scarf. "We're refurbishing the original kitchens. It's my last act as Head of the Trust. Restoring them to full working state. I'm hoping for cooking demonstrations. Maybe this Spring. Visiting chefs and suchlike. What do you think?"

Arthur wondered if George was consulted. The boy had never mentioned it.

"Oh yes, and we've reconditioned our old butter churns. Yes, and restored an absolutely brilliant apple-peeling machine." She smiled with rapt satisfaction. "Also, I've found someone to mend our ancient clockwork spit We'll be having National Trust members right up to New Year. Then a short break until Easter After which, we're rebuilding the stables, repairing the Italian cascade, then reinstating the fountains Or have I already mentioned that?"

What Arthur loved most was the Georgian library; its peeling leather-bound books; its huge brass chandeliers and busts to Virgil and Homer. It made him feel good. Same with the Jacobean hall and its great trestle table cut from one single oak, assembled on site three centuries ago. Who cared about kitchens? He loved absorbing atmosphere, imagining himself as Lord of the Manor pacing the parquet, smoking a classic clay pipe. If he ever got the chance, he'd decide what improvements to make. Structural priorities first. It would mean planning a practical schedule.

"And naturally," she continued, "We'll be using the main hall again For my Soirée." Peggy was waving vaguely. "Say, maybe sandwiches? Pies? Sausage? Dips? And of course a large bowl of punch. As you know, actors are always hungry and thirsty. I've continued the family tradition of inviting the pantomime cast. That means masses of flowers. And Champagne Because the new season is so very special to me." She turned for Arthur's reaction. "Your new man seems very different too. We need his new broom. And Chekhov should take us upmarket for once. Don't you think?" And she waited . . .

But Arthur's thoughts had strayed to the paintings, especially the John Sargent portrait of Herbert de Vries. He could identify with that. There was a nose of distinction. He and young George shared similar traits. Arthur continued scanning the faces, rating their relative features, unconsciously feeling his own. From Peggy's expression he realised he'd been asked a question, and guessed straightaway what it was. He tried to sound reassuring.

166

"Don't worry, planning consent's been agreed, and our architect's models are double-locked in the town hall extension where people have to ask permission to enter. Anyway demolition's already proceeding and . . . and . . ." She was looking at him oddly. ". . . And anyway, people don't know what they want till they get it. Offer them a marina and there they'll be, buying boats."

"We were talking about my Soirée," she snapped, "And our new Season." She produced a bunch of magazines. "So where is the publicity? Not here! Promotion is our lifeblood. In particular when it comes to such classics as our dear Anton Chekhov. How is his 'Cherry Orchard' going for instance? Or his 'Three Sisters'? Garrick Jones is so full of ideas."

"First things first. The pantomime's booking already."

"Our theatre's future's guaranteed? Is that what you're saying? The preservation order first, then our big season of culture?"

Arthur gave an ambiguous nod. She was still a beautiful woman. Attractive enough to bring all those memories back. Invented meetings; illicit stayovers in London. The fun. The excitement of youth. Then when her husband died only weeks after George's birth, all of that changed. To think that within months the lad would take over. All Arthur needed to do was to wait, because George was a very apt pupil; a chip off the old block. Who knew what secretly ran in his genes?

Peggy was enumerating lists of soirée arrangements as Arthur listened to the crackling fire, thinking how well he would suit such a house . . . He sat up with a start. What was that about Georgie? Asking now would give him away. Peggy had already crossed to the window. She switched on the lights. He realised then it was dark.

"I'm so relieved that's all off my mind." She gave a deep sigh. "Thank you. I hate feeling guilty. I'm glad it's out in the open at last." She turned back from the window. "That awful sleet is turning to rain, so you won't need to stay overnight."

Following their appearance at Club Arabica, Trixie and Pippa gathered a curious group at rehearsals next morning. Wade Bluman, the tall Ugly Sister, sat alone in the toilets furtively sipping a brandy. Out in the main hall, a hungover Garrick continued to pace up and down, willing his phone to connect.

James, Lionel and colleagues were gathered round Pippa and Trixie as the duo sang replays of their act. When Trixie performed an impromptu high kick everyone cheered; even Lionel. Pippa announced they'd be known as 'The Seraphim Twins' from now on, and seemed to be on a zonking great high. Black was beautiful and she was in full ovulation! No cellulite to speak of. Firm stomach muscles. Not a single varicose vein. No contact lenses. No problems with teeth. Together with Trixie, her prospects had literally changed overnight. As Trixie explained, an invisible current crosses those footlights. Once applause enters the bloodstream it's addictive; you snorted life like cocaine. They planned to hire Jilly Craske as their stylist because it was she who'd made them feel good with themselves. Next would come breast implants, colonic irrigation, and maybe a Botox treatment or two. After that came the whole world!

"By the way, has nobody heard how Jilly is?" But she got no response.

As Abigail handed round rewrites, James Carr still anguished at finding his past in their archives while Pippa and Trixie fizzed with excitement. When Pippa suggested adding their duets to the show, Garrick demurred. What with a belching Cinderella, a thigh-slapping transvestite Prince, a Fairy Godmother with migraines, and a Buttons who farted, there was every stock character and every predictable cliché. Garrick wanted to strangle the lot. He glanced across at Abigail. She was always so placid and normal he found himself observing her, always calmed by her presence. This wasn't stalking, he told himself, only closely observing. Verity would understand.

At lunchtime Abigail headed outside. Greyness dripped in long grass. Her skin shrank tight as latex, constricting the blood and provoking unwanted compulsions. Even as she fingered the flesh an invisible blade etched delicate shapes whose exquisite geometry criss-crossed nerve-endings and veins. Under this whiteness seethed layers of fat. She could surgically cut her distractions away. As she pushed through overgrown yews she saw a hunched figure alone on the bench. So that was how he reacted to pain? Garrick was secretly licking his wounds. He was like her. He suffered too. She edged down beside him Then noticed the mobile phone clamped to his ear.

"Bastards!" he muttered, "That sodding Castle Hotel! Always bloody engaged! No bugger answers!"

"I suppose you've dialled the right number?"

"Yes of course. There's Inbuilt Memory Functions. Redials are automatic." The number came up on the screen. "There. You see."

"But have you tried dialling from scratch?"

He dialled again with exaggerated care, announcing each number before holding it up to her ear.

"Good afternoon, this is the Norston Castle Hotel." came a bright voice.

After the ballroom scene was blocked out, Garrick stayed on to sign Phyllis's letters. Later a minicab manoeuvred right up to the theatre where "Gas Danger" warnings had been newly propped up on the pavement. Across the theatre facade its 'Laughalong!' sign was now topped with a grinning clown's face.

The cabbie wound down his window as waiting cars hooted behind. "One of you's Garrick Jones?"

Garrick caught Abigail's her elbow. "Consider this as overtime."

"You'll drop me home on the way?"

The driver watched narrow-eyed through his mirror. "Where to?"

"Castle Hotel," said Garrick.

Abigail leaned forward. "Via Castle Mount Road, please. Drop me at the Moat Street turn."

The cabby glanced into his mirror. "Short route? Or scenic route?"

They must have crossed several junctions, swung through roundabouts and entered Castle Mount Road. Just then a black Mondeo skimmed past, flashing its brake lights like bloodstones. As their taxi slewed to avoid it, they clipped a bollard before narrowly missing a tanker. They finally mounted the

168

kerb with a thud. As Abigail reached for Garrick's hand he took it and squeezed. The downpour had thinned to a drizzle. She could feel him against her, surprisingly warm. She closed her eyes as the driver cursed, then they raced off down side roads. Turn after turn bobbed behind in their wake.

Located at the motorway exit, The Castle Hotel marked the latest stage in the town's rings of tired suburbs. Eucalypti jostled with Leylandii to camouflage its industrial past. Theirs was a deliberate statement, no further proof required. Brinkhouse Developments ran through it like letters through a stick of rock. Brinkhouse, Brinkside, Brinkhomes, and Brinkmanship were its trademarks, cast in bronze and repeated in prominent statues. Brinkhouse hotel celebrated a brand-new facade. Here guests encountered their sliding reflections in walls of black mirrors, reminding them just who they were.

A dinner-jacketed doorman hovered. His boot-polished skull clashed with his luminous shirt. A porter emerged out of nowhere, escorting them through, but Abigail hung pointedly back.

"'Scuse me," she whispered, "I noticed the Ladies back in the foyer. Won't be a sec!"

As Garrick waited, each move of the hands across his watch's engineered surface emphasised his commitments. Each pulse, each jewel, each turn of its miniature cogs and each drop of its minute escarpment all added up. It totalled ten years; one wife, two children, and a pension scheme demanding repeated investment. TEN years. One-zero! Ten years? It chose not to mention his gathering debts.

As they entered the Dining Room with Abigail in worn sweatshirt and jeans, the doors swung open on sensors. A twin-headed gold eagle proffered The Menu. It was all appropriately Tsarist. From sheer superstition Garrick still carried 'The Cherry Orchard' around in his briefcase. Would Chekhov have understood Verity's claim that food should be worshipped and blessed? The Maître D' with grey beard and full tails moved balefully forward to greet them. Three places were set. Abigail wondered who else was due.

To Garrick's surprise she seemed completely at ease. He would replay all this later and wonder. Having selected a vintage Margaux St Germaine, Garrick offered the tasting to Abby. She took the glass with long slender fingers, her double-jointed elegance as sculptured and fine as a dancer's. She swirled, sniffed and sipped, approving the wine.

He raised his glass. "Let's drink to us both, and to the Chekhov Players . . ."

"And to poor Cinderella! Like when the show ends what happens to her?"

Not far away, masked by the columns, Eddie Craig's party was taking their seats. His onetime brother-in-law Arthur was accompanied by a big man in glasses. It was obvious Norris was holding court:

"No Eddie, it's easy You drill. You insert. You link to a circuit. I press the button. Boom!" Norris examined his nails. "You apply for the licence. We do the rest."

"Oh aye?" Eddie slowly unfolded his napkin, repeatedly smoothing and nipping the creases. "And the cost of insurance?" He looked around. "Arthur? Who pays?"

"Put it like this. What if some bugger gives you a million for nothing?"

Eddie suppressed a yawn. "I've already got a million."

Arthur grunted. "All right then. Another million."

"I've got another million."

"Think big empty spaces." Arthur drew shapes in the air. "The whole site's available. There's over ten years work."

"In that case . . ." Norris produced a laptop, setting it up on the table. "Here's my schedule You pay us to set your explosives. Then . . ." He mimed an explosion and laughed. "Forget Cinderella! Forget Garrick Jones."

Arthur was not being pushed. "But not till I'm ready. We've no final agreements, let alone public consultations or planning approval. As Eddie well knows, at this, our pre-consultation stage there's political aspects. There's also a Board of Trustees."

Eddie was ripping a page from the wine list and starting to draw on the back.

He pushed it over to Arthur. "These are my latest proposals. I've submitted them to the Ministry myself."

Arthur smiled stared, examined, then instinctively shielded the sketch with his hand. "Hey! My plans!" He waved the paper. "My plans. They're copyright. You've copied them!"

"Maybe great minds think alike?" Eddie's smile was seraphic. "According to our calculations, this particular blotch should represent the Majestic. Okay?" He pinched it out with a snap of his fingers. "No need to confirm or deny." He screwed the page into a discoloured ball and threw it away.

As Garrick sampled hors d'oeuvres, each self-winding movement emphasised Verity's heartbeat. She was ticking away at his wrist, and taste was all in the mind.

"You do still mean to do 'Cherry Orchard'?" Abigail suddenly asked.

"What? As you of all people know, that's what I'm here to do. But if you mean the pantomime? I've got no choice. It's what I'd call our introduction. Yes, a prologue. A pro-prologue." He warmed to his theme. "It's a first step towards the great Chekhovian heights!" A ringing tone came into focus: without checking he switched off Vee's incoming call.

Abigail nodded. "I think I understand Cinderella. I mean, there she is, slogging away. A dad who reckons she's useless. But, like, she's got dreams. Brilliant dreams. Except everyone dumps on her. Same with poor Trixie. Broken home an' all that Alone with masses of people all round her. Those stepsisters don't understand. Nobody does. Only that dim pageboy of theirs So when out of the blue she gets sponsored to go to this ball. And meets this man of her dreams? Even if it's a woman in drag Well maybe it's all fairytales, but everyone deserves a chance . . . and anyway . . ."

She had the odd sensation of being observed, boring into the back of her skull. As she swivelled sharply round, three smartly dressed women were leaving. Elizabeth Scott stopped to look round, took everything in, and next moment was gone.

Garrick signed the bill. Thanks be to credit cards, he thought, but time was fast running out on his watch. If he wanted to work for Louise he needed peace between mother and daughter. First he'd send Abigail home in a taxi. Then he'd reconnoitre hotel rooms before confirming his booking.

"Don't worry," Abby said, "I don't mind coming and looking as well."

At each floor their lift opened to reveal an identical featureless maze. This was world of soft-centred containers intersected by galleries, elevators, stairwells and lobbies, linked with padded corridors and hundreds of de luxe apartments, all pre-packed and delivered complete to the very last doorknob. No two suites were alike but all hummed to the very same wall-to-wall music. Their young attendant ushered them in. No switch stayed unswitched and no handle unturned; everything from curtain controls to ice box and Jacuzzi.

"And this," he said, "Is the central control. Digitally sensitive with full attenuation. And this, the main control handset operating television monitors, hi-fi, DVD, CD, Internet connections, with thermo-digitising systems, telephone, lighting and cyber-dimmers, heating. Note also the bed Double-King size." His eyes slipped round to Abigail as if seeing her for the very first time. "Feel the delicate hand-woven covers." The sheets billowed out like parachute silk, seductively floating and gleaming. "Feel."

This wasn't so much a bed as a stage. It answered the questions of Cinderella's fate. A stadium of a bed. Garrick would share this arena. Share it with his wife. Abigail's fingertips warmed to the touch. As their guide was extolling trouser presses, hand dryers, and iced water dispensers, she flipped a Crowning Glory card onto the bedside, then slid another one under the covers, hiding others wherever she could. Jilly's cards would spread like a virus. She felt a great sense of elation.

"Of course I have to emphasise," their guide was saying, "This will not be your actual room but all our rooms have these top-of-the-range specifications."

Garrick slipped a folded banknote into the man's pocket.

Abby regretted sending that email, but sometimes honest intentions backfired. Of course Stacey had no regrets. She acted shocked, incredulous, even offended. Everything was okay to her. Everything came down to sex. Everything had connotations. You couldn't expect understanding from her.

"No, but I saw you with him!" Stacey was defiant. "If you didn't want me watching, why tell me? Weren't I supposed to be impressed? Little Miss Maid o' the Mountains? I saw you looking cow-eyed and drooling!"

Abigail fought off the tears. "You spied. You spied"

"Who texted me? I call that an invite!" Stacey pouted mockingly. "Oh Garee! I'm so crazee about you! But you wanted witnesses, right?"

They were back in that playground, Abby in pigtails, thumb in mouth, skipping to anyone's tune. Stacey in flounces drumming out the beat with her heels. Two little girls, tooth-and-nail humiliating each other. As always Stacey over-reacted. Jagged nails and metal-tipped heels. As always Abby retreated then sulked. Stacey always had to win. Whenever Abby retreated, it seemed an admission of guilt. The laughter always pursued her.

Garrick too had been forced to retreat. First light the touch-paper, stand well away, then watch the flames fizzle out. Deciding on a hotel was an achievement. Verity might not agree. Despite the drone of generators and rattle of road-drills, Garrick heard that ringing-tone. It punctuated his life.

"Hello?" he replied, "Who is that?"

Then a voice, almost a whisper. Tiny. Uncertain.

"Dad?"

"Mark? How are you?"

Even if that sounded banal, distance caused enough problems. You don't burden your child. Chekhov and Ibsen would have known that. Not too emotional. Never intrusive. No sentimental cloying for them. But when it was Garrick's own son? His own flesh and blood? That wasn't a problem. Not until now.

"Hi." One banality followed another. "How's school?" he asked, "How's momma? How's Rachel?" His defences began to collapse. "I've missed you, you know that? I've been getting texts, but . . ." With the back of one hand he wiped at his cheeks. "Tell daddy what you've been doing."

"Swimming," came the matter-of-fact voice

To his amazement tears blurred his brain. "You've been out breaking the ice?"

"'Course not, silly!" Mark's laugh was scornful. "It's indoors. It's got a heated pool And I'm in class two and I'm going to work for my lifesaver badge."

"The main thing is, are you happy?" But Mark only ummed. "You don't sound too sure?"

"Well . . . it's Rachel. She's driving me bonzo."

"Noooh! That's not fair!" Rachel sounded nasal and sniffy. "Everyone's caught it! Except little clever-clogs here!" He heard Mark's cry of pain. "Wait till he's coughing an' sneezing. They catch yucky things down that pool." The pause was filled with her sniffling. "Gran's down the shops. She's buying sweetcorn what gets in your teeth an' we've got to call her Roseanne."

"Rachel darling, I want you to listen." He tried to imagine her reactions. "If anyone tells you daddy's cleared off And he doesn't care anymore . . . then they're fibbing. It's lies. They're not telling the truth." He paused to let it sink in. "Does anyone say that?"

"'Course not."

"Always remember who washed you and dressed you. And put you to bed when mummy was working?" There was no response. "And who bought you toys, and . . . and . . . anyway, what matters is, I'll soon be back home. Then Me and mummy, we'll . . .

"Nana's back. I can hear her."

"Next time, I want to hear about all you've been doing. Everything. Every single little thing And if you've got any problems Any problems at all . . . you must ring and tell me and I'll . . ."

"Bye," Rachel said, but the line was already dead.

As rehearsals unfolded, he'd come to believe he knew what he was doing. 'Keep pedalling', he told himself, 'Keep pedalling'. With the hotel finally booked, he could turn his attentions to Verity's present. The Ancient Mariner was his salvation. Thanks to its easy-rhyming verse, he could perform well enough for a fee, then Sanjay would do him a deal. The very same tide would reinstate Anton Pavlovich Chekhov, letting 'The Seagull' take wing, then all his problems would be solved overnight.

So Garrick dipped and dived. Jilly, Trixie, Pippa and Louise all followed their working routines. Lionel indulged in grandiloquent camp. All sharing the same cosmic spaces, walking the same sidewalks, treading the same paving and stairs, slinking through the same shadows, ducking and weaving as if they peopled some vast shopping mall, together but all out of sync. At the same time Manwess Gas continued to burrow through subsoil, drilling past cables and ancient foundations, excavating geological strata, tunnelling deep into Earth. Soon they'd be breaching the magma itself. As Eddie Craig's trucks carted the old town away, the theatre was left like a solitary outpost in Norston's post-urban wastes.

Louise served 'Club Arabica's' best cappuccino thick with white foam and coated with pure bitter chocolate; their Ultra Blue Mountain Special. She leaned forward anxiously, stretching out a braceleted arm.

"Tell me. I can't bear the suspense. What are you proposing?"

"Aha." Garrick sipped and swallowed, ecstatically closing his eyes, still holding his script facedown.

She smothered an urge to snatch it and read. It was bad enough not knowing, but inviting local bigwigs meant she could not take risks. Every penny invested was vital. Every penny belonged to the bank.

Cash was on Garrick's mind too, but as caffeine began suffusing his system, thoughts of currency quietened his nerves. This could be his big chance. By just one single performance Verity's gift could be guaranteed. And as a freelancer, who knew where this might lead?

The auditorium was crowded. On-stage a Chinese cellist in jump-suit and silver trainers was interpreting a Ravel serenade. Louise beamed around at her diners, blowing sea anemone kisses. Garrick could be her new guru. A star. With Garrick she no longer felt menopausal but almost fashionably sylph-like, whereas Jilly Craske had become strangely obese. Louise did have her suspicions, but some people never want to be helped.

She gripped Garrick's elbow, backing him into the cloakroom, hemmed in by topcoats and scarves. "Quickly. Tell me what you're performing for us." And wished she'd held an audition.

"What here?" He cleared his throat. "And now the storm-blast came And he was tyrannous and strong." And so on . . ."

"Yes but . . . but what is it?"

"He struck with his o'ertaking wings,
And chased us south along."

His voice was soft and subversive; insidiously baritone.

"And along did cross an Albatross:
Through the fog it came
As if it were a Christian soul
We hailed it in God's name!"

Louise backed up against mohair and gasped. "My God. I bet you didn't write that yourself."

"Hi. Hope I'm not interrupting?"

Elizabeth Scott could materialise out of nowhere.

Louise's features froze. "Garrick my dear, this is our local reporter. From the Norston Mercury." Then moved like a fight referee, her bodymass intervening, hustling the columnist off.

Though Jilly's scissors kept snipping, her concentration was fading. She ached with exhaustion; her whole body bulged. Strands of hair slithered malevolently through her fingers. All these new conditioners! All their acrid chemicals! Shades of Medusa, she thought, as conditioned reflexes toiled, but as fast she could decapitate tufts, these short snakey grubs multiplied into venomous vipers! If there had been any justice, Jilly would be in Hollywood, restyling big Stars, not perched like an outcast here on the rim of recession. Seeing Garrick Jones pass by every morning was small compensation. Now, if hair were an art, then hairstyling was sculpture: its layers of epidermis coated hard bone kept extruding keratin like pasta. One follicle was much like another. But add that psychosis called 'fashion' and Louise was both her model and victim. Jilly could chop out those tresses. Slash! A naked patch on Louise's scalp! Another slash. Then chop! A deep cranial pit! That'd stop her endless achievements.

". . . This is why health's so important," Louise continued, "You've only got one body, love."

Jilly's pain was her own. Thomas tried to control, but he'd never intrude on her innermost soul. Nobody could. She guarded her internal distress. In a strange way this released her. She could float like a hot-air balloon. She could blow on the wind hermetically sealed from the world. She was free to shadow spontaneous lives while keeping her anguish contained. But still Louise kept chatting away, listing her latest contacts and arty new friends: Lilliana Pollard, Anoushka Brown, Dianne Smythe, scattering names like fertility rites.

". . . Funny thing is . . ." Louise was saying, "In spite of all that, our Abigail's fine. But I'm the one that's gutted . . ." Louise kept her eyes tightly shut. "Hey! You've not been listening! Nobody does." Jilly kept trimming as Louise timed the long pause. "Like I said, it's about Garrick Jones! I'm showcasing him for the press at my club." The scissors stopped. "But that's between you and me. Right? It'll be The Ancient Mariner's Tale but that's classified. And you're invited. Now what do you say? Isn't that wonderful? Eh?"

As Louise twisted exultantly round. She caught sight of Jilly bent double, face contorted and pale.

Anton Pavlovich Chekhov. Born 1806, nearly ten years before the battle of Waterloo in the small Russian provincial town of Taganrog. Went off to Moscow medical school. Moved to Yalta on the Black Sea, the Russian Cote d'Azur, where he rubbed shoulders with Gorky and Tolstoy, writing famous short stories before hitching a lift back to Moscow, then writing those magical plays. Taganrog shared the dilemma of Norston, its post-rural decay at the mercy of Manchester and Liverpool. This was a sub-Chekhovian cosmos, where an idealised London replaced Chekhov's prototype Moscow.

Garrick had gone one step further. As if Cinderella weren't bad enough, he'd promised Louise he'd already learnt those hundred-and-one verses of Coleridge's "Rime of the Ancient Mariner". He felt he'd personally sailed seven seas towards the South Pole, through hell and high water. The text danced in front of his eyes, but the real world would not keep its distance. Its boundaries were paper-thin. He heard the wall thudding behind him, increasing in tempo, then came loud gruntings and groans.

"The Sun now rose upon the right,
Out of the sea came he!
Still hid in mist, and on the left
Went down into the sea."

It rhymed like weekend doggerel, but he'd got out of the habit of learning. He blamed Samuel Taylor Coleridge. Everyone was to blame, because while time slowed down, seconds just flitted away. His new watch was proof. Its function was to remind him she had remembered while he was the one who'd forgotten. He covered the text with his hand:

"The ice was here, the ice was there,
The ice was all around:
It cracked and growled, and roared and howled
Like noises in a swound!"

He felt a thin chill from his ill-fitting windows and shivered. The room was carved from an iceberg. A deep-frozen, permafrost draught blew direct from the Arctic. It would have been easier to make some excuse to Louise and resign. Instead he retired to the bathroom, and sat on the edge of the bath.

"The ice was here, the ice was there,
The ice was all around!" He intoned.

His voice distorted clattered back. Disjointed syllables ricocheted. Instantaneous echoes replied. Everything mimicked his efforts. For this he blamed his left frontal lobe. Or was it the cerebral cortex? A police siren wailed in the night.

"At length did cross an Albatross . . . An alba . . . Albatross! "

His tongue was out of sync with his lips. "Another fucking albatross, messing my consonants up!" Midnight or no, he on longer cared. "A shitting, great, beady-eyed bird. It's crapping all over the oceans! An oversized, humourless seagull pecking at corpses? How did it ever get into verse? And without even checking out if it bloodywell rhymed?" A bright blue light flashed over the ceiling as the room remained apathetic.

"Through the fog it came: as if, as if, as if . . ." But that flashing blue light was persisting, persisting . . ."

It was way, way past midnight, his Rolex insisted. He heard a crash downstairs. Then clattering feet up the stairs, the thud of a door battered down. Wall-fittings shook, pipes rattled, panelling quivered and someone was screaming. Next the ker-bump ker-bump of something dragged downstairs.

He gesticulated into his mirror, declaiming in a hoarse whisper:

". . . And I had done a hellish thing,
And it would work 'em woe;
For all averred, I had killed the bird
That made the breeze to blow.!"

Again the siren ripped into echoes, then the flashing blue faded. Garrick's buttocks grew numb. His feet were ice-cold on bare tiles. It was true. Life wasn't some sort of audition, that latitudes counted, and distance did add enchantment. He missed the comfort of Lancaster Gate but Verity was too far away. She flourished; she even cooked to applause. He wondered if she took this for granted. How could she know that he desperately loved her, and that without her he was missing half of himself? He longed to speak to his children. Then somewhere close at hand he seemed to hear a child inconsolably sobbing. It could have even been next door. But it was closer. Far closer. The sobs became gut-wrenching howls. He sat in the darkness and listened. Parents had to respond in a crisis. No-one got their childhood back. Clamping both hands to his ears he made the fateful decision.

He awoke feeling refreshed and set off with a spring in his step. The sky was a blend of lemonade-cocktails with dashes of blackcurrant. From Bankside Heights to Bradford Road, everyone's postcodes were touched with a crystalline layer. The sugary glaze on parked cars was still crisp. Powdered ice blew from high wires. Icy steam trailed from extractors. Generators spewed purple fumes. A Manwess truck slewed over black ice, just missing the theatre itself.

Verity's last postcard had rhapsodised about filming in France and Mallorca but looked forward to their weekend in Norston. "Miss you!" she'd scrawled, adding plenty of X's. So far, no more notes from the kids. Not even a text.

"The ice was here, the ice was there, the ice was all around". That was so true. He freewheeled through slow traffic, feeling a sense of achievement. Cold air sliced his cheeks and made his eyes run. He was narrowly missed by an articulated truck then almost hit by a bus. He wished he'd purchased a cycling helmet. Cars honked and mo'cyclists swore but soon he'd have hard cash in his hands. Every verse equalled disposable credit.

"The ice was here, the ice was there,
the ice was all around . . ."

Verity would need soothing and care. She adored the extravagant gesture.

"The ice was here, the ice was there,
the ice was all around . . ."

He'd choose a suitable gift and leave a deposit, ask Louise for his payment in cash, then pay off the balance next day. Even if talk was of The Earth getting warmer, compulsive rhythms and nightmarish images cut in. The ice the ice. The bloody ice! More verses came in fits and starts.

"The ice was here, the ice was there,
the ice was all around . . ."

Last night he'd repeatedly dreamed his kids were adrift on a black, sinking hulk in the darkness, frantically waving. Around lay drowned corpses, tangled and slimy. From behind his soundproofed glass he'd hammered and screamed, unable to help. Before his eyes they'd drifted between mountainous icebergs then disappeared into a blizzard. He'd hurled himself at that glass, again and again and again. Then awoke in a sweat of damp sheets.

Coleridge must have been high on drugs when he wrote; an addict hooked on narcotics; the classic opium junkie, which grew from a single laudanum drop into a permanent fever? Garrick pedalled harder, zigzagging through Heptonstall Square as tiny faces filled his vision, replicating like virus, propagating themselves while blotting out everything else. Mark and Rachel, Rachel and Mark, reproduced hundreds of millions of times .His passing image flickered back from shop windows as he passed barely a hairsbreadth away, his mind firmly set on his children. That's when he had the idea. It came out of the blue. Golden Anniversary? Or Silver? Ruby? Diamond? Cardboard or Glass? Whatever? Surely celebrating ten years must have its own special emblem?

By the time he'd reached the main intersection, traffic was log-jammed at lights. He found himself in slow-motion, fragile and overexposed. An Eddie Craig tipper truck swung to the left. Into this backwash of carbon monoxide, Garrick felt himself being drawn, half aware of a presence, a blackness, a looming existence, its gravity sucking him inwards. He seemed powerless to resist. The Laws of physics were briefly suspended.

As Garrick gripped his handlebars he clipped the kerb, then started to topple. Before he'd hit the ground, the shiny black car had merged with the traffic . . . then everything must have gone blank.

As he wheeled his battered bike shakily towards the church hall, Garrick heard laughter. Brash communal laughter, and . . .

When he came round again, he found himself slumped amongst cigarette stubs where desperate actors had huddled to smoke in the porch. As his brain started to clear, his bruises started to throb. Some lunatic had wanted him dead. Melodrama was loose on the streets. Or had he survived for some reason? For a higher more spiritual purpose? His old man had devoted whole sermons to forgiveness and penance. Few people got a second chance.

As he stood up he could hear muffled laughter then cheers as he pushed at the door. It felt like catharsis. He could forget Russian drama. He was back to those two Ugly Sisters, one Dame, a Baron Hardup and his very worst dread, Daisy the pantomime cow. There was no sign of life in this landscape of floorboards representing a stage. Coloured outlines were sketchily furnished with crates and steel chairs, but the hall was deserted. Assorted props lay like discarded weapons after some catastrophic defeat. He could hear further outbursts of laughter? Someone was impersonating a strangely familiar voice. He picked his way to the back room. As Garrick appeared he noticed their startled expressions.

Reggie Buck pointed at Garrick. "Jesus laddie! Who won? The wall?"

For the first time Garrick noticed gravel and blood on his clothes as everyone stared.

Reggie produced a battered medical chest marked with a crude red cross. "Make way for a licensed First Aider. Let's glue you together, sir." He spoke in that oddly familiar accent Garrick had heard in the hall. "Okay sir. What belongs where?" He winked and everyone giggled and smirked.

"We've made second brew," shouted Daisy's back-half, "Unless Garrick'd rather have milk?" He flicked up a heel, started to moo.

As Garrick joined in the laughter he knew how much he belonged. They were his team. He was accepted and all their commitments were shared. They were his 'Chekhov Players'. A fellowship. A social interaction. If Art were all about Truth, then Truth was a single-cell virus. No one was immune. Here he was welcomed, not just because he hired and fired, but almost in loco parentis, rather like being their father. He thought again of Rachel and Mark. At this moment, he loved everyone with a deep, almost sexual love. And wasn't this what creativity meant?

He was feeling light-headed as ointments and First Aid were applied and Reggie talked on in that peculiar voice. In this Garrick's moment of total acceptance, he embraced them all. Even the two who combined into one bovine monster, plus an outsize udder, four rubber teats, and a repository of every bum-slapping, tit-worthy, anti-feminine joke. Misogyny on two pairs of legs. But something wasn't quite right. Reggie's impersonation jarred. Garrick could not quite explain why, but as laughter faded he thought he sensed a chill in the air.

In this moment of confusion, 'The Cherry Orchard', 'Three Sisters', and Seagull felt so close he could hear balalaikas and see peasants high-kicking. Then the strains of refined polonaise. He understood the Ranevskys' dilemma, their sadness, nostalgia, and poignant dreams. Sometimes their lives felt more real than his own. Liuba and Leon, Lopakhin and Boris, Anya and Varya, Yasha, Dunyasha. And then again Masha, Irina and Vershinin, because everyone was an exile from somewhere and everyone had to have hope. Was London his Moscow and Norston his Yalta, or was it the other way round? Manchester and York were even more glamorous beacons. He had wasted his past and his youth. It was time to move out and rehearse on the stage

He noticed James Carr making big dramas of yawning, with caustic asides in that peculiar voice; that oddly familiar voice. He recognised its rhythms. That was the joke. Those mannerisms too. But why?

All at once it dawned. They were Garrick's own.

Garrick thought things would improve straightaway once they'd changed venue: that everyone would burst into life. He should have stood up to Arthur before. Abigail was no glove puppet either. Sometimes you had to be yourself. Relationships would have to change. But where did acting end and living begin? And where did living end and acting begin when a single nicotine grain was a threat? As deadlines approached everything came into sharp focus.

He could clearly feel timbers warp and pipework rust. He could hear the crunch of subsidence, even digestive tracts of dry rot. He was aware of every water molecule as it seeped in through the subsoil dissolving all geological time. He overheard alliances changing, relationships creaking, and passions convulsing round him. On stage he was exposed to gales blowing in from the Urals. Just out of sight lay birch forests, dachas, frozen rivers, and howling wolves in the forests. Beyond lay St Petersburg, Moscow, Paris, and Rome. The only limits were in the imagination. He surveyed those once-empty seats as if they were packed and applauding. The world was his stage, and if he held breath he could feel the whole planet turn on its axis.

For two years he and his strippers had tramped nightclubs in the Middle East and Europe till demand outstripped supply. Those tight little breasts and pretty waxed V's. Those were the profitable years of his youth. Then along came ascetic Islam and with it global billionaires. His best girls ran away with old men, leaving Garrick with just enough nerve to call himself Theatre Producer. He printed suitable trade cards and got listed in directories. And it worked. Verity had been so impressed she'd married him without asking questions. Roseanne was very different. She was the formidable mother, the archetype mother-in-law. She and her Ivy League husband were busily endowing Research Institutions. That's until Vee's papa died. Then genealogy struck with a vengeance and Roseanne began her research.

After the Morozov project she started to investigate him. Then came revelations, followed by certain admissions, which led to his swearing that oath. Why should he care about Pushkin or Chekhov? That was purely emotional blackmail. Nailing himself to the spot meant if history were a single great tide, then Garrick would always be swimming against it. At least Edwin would have approved. A 'Journey to Tarsus' implied some Divine Revelation, which so far Garrick had missed. Then overnight 'The Cherry Orchard' and 'The Three Sisters' turned into unshakeable aims.

"And remember this is the literary North!" Peggy de Vries had enthused, "And Chekhov's one of us. A born and bred Lancastrian. Like Wordsworth and Shakespeare."

"'Scuse me, shall I mark up the script?" Abigail was asking.

Those half parted lips. That glint of white teeth. Those nostrils and lashes. When Garrick smiled she'd responded. A chain reaction of smiling. She as her usual mixed-message self. Only pain ever proved she was living, but when those auto-neurones kept firing, their ambivalence started to grow. She smiled. He smiled back. He felt he didn't need to explain.

"Actually, I'd value some advice. Your recommendation. Local knowledge, that is."

"To choose that jewellery, you mean? Yes of course."

"You guessed! You're a woman with taste."

"Okay, I'll give Stacey a call."

"Stacey?"

"Yeah. She's the one with the contacts. She's crazy on spending. She's our window-shopping queen! I mean, she'd get us a deal, 'cause it's her special vocation."

"I'm going to work on the script. If you need any help ask one of the guys."

In the world of subsidised theatre, Garrick depended on others. On Fabian for a start. Fabian had odd-jobbed through life but that was any stage manager's burden. The fun had gone from the job. Onstage rehearsal meant clearing everything up for the following 'Laughalong!' crowd. For that lot he wouldn't forgo a small drink when there were others to help.

"Sweetie-pie, give us a hand." He thrust a stage plan into Abigail's hands. "Get Josh to help. It's his plan, and I'm not well." Then scuttled quickly away.

She knew Josh wouldn't help. In just a few days he had changed. Now he almost ignored her. Maybe he was blaming her? Maybe there was somebody else? Humiliation combined with despair. She reverted to childhood, crawling round on hands and knees, scaling graph paper onto the floor.

Norston has great aspirations. As Garrick kept hearing, history is part of its name. Forget the pretensions of other great towns, Norstonians first invested in steam and built the world's earliest railways. Their Irish navvies churned millions of tonnes of dark earth as hundreds died in its furrows. Celtic blood mixed with black soil to build these waterways, only to see them clogged up like sewers. History keeps repeating itself with subtle new variations. Build again, then knock it down. At those very same co-ordinates where Arthur Ruddock proposed to build his new "Albana Marina", stood the town's first theatre. If inward investment is what voters wanted, The Majestic ought to become The Beacon of the North, shining down onto southernmost decadent London.

As Garrick continued his tour below stage he was certain Rex Schulman never came here. The further you went, the lower the ceilings. A faint orange glow subverted the shadows. Dressing rooms shrank into closets, which dwindled to minuscule cells. Such was the power of exclusion that wherever the 'Laughalong!' cast pinned their names, the Chekhov gang had scribbled them out. "Mene mene tekel upharsin," the moving hand scrawled before being rudely scrubbed out.

He pushed another dressing room door. Roddy's name was chalked on a panel. He knocked and walked in. Pinups and ashtrays smothered every surface. Weeks of Crowning Glory leaflets were wedged up round mirrors like prostitutes' business cards. An orange wig lay among throwaway cups and pizza boxes, recalling Roddy's farcical sketch about workmen replacing shop windows, his homage to Marcel Marceau. Garrick remembered how no one had laughed.

Back in his office he practised reading aloud. It seemed barely moments ago surveyors were measuring fractions of fractions while continents drifted and mountain eroded to plains. 'The Ancient Mariner' was merely his start. Soon there'd be darkness, and were it not for the ambient glow you could have counted every star. This was 'Ancient Mariner' weather leading to meteorological stillness and gathering fogs which foreshadowed his Samuel Taylor Coleridge Day. Louise would be waiting. He did not need to psych himself up. Soon he would perform it live. He might later add 'Under Milkwood' to his canon?

> "The moving moon went up the sky
> And no where did abide:
> Softly she was going up,
> And a star or two beside . . ."

Sometimes panto still intervened. His rewritten scene satirising the Mayor almost worked. It gave the casting some extra edge because councillors cried out to be mocked. Nikolai Gogol knew that.

> "And now the storm-blast came, and he
> Was tyrannous and strong:
> He struck with his o'ertaking wings,
> And chased us south along."

Standing at his window he felt as brightly exposed as a target. Orbiting satellites could zoom in with telescopic sights. Hitmen could be anywhere. They didn't have to have reasons when road-rage already rampaged the streets. At this very moment those comedians' groupies would be chanting like football fans. Would these masses ever hold demonstrations for Chekhov?

> "I fear thee ancient Mariner!
> I fear thy skinny hand!
> And thou art long, and lank, and brown,
> As is the ribbed sea-sand."

An alarm went off in his brain. With little time for the shops he raced downstairs two steps at a time his Rolex continued to pace him. As Garrick emerged in the street he saw Phyllis's silhouette caught in the cross-light as a large polished black Bentley materialised from the shadows.

Below cast-iron arches of Brinkhouse Arcade, Stacey was impatiently pacing, her white fur collar fluffed, her angry lips gleaming and dark eyes heightened with Van der Weldt Grey. Iridescent necklaces glowed in the lights. She let Abigail kiss her, while giving Garrick a wink, glancing from one to the other. Nuances always intrigued her. Expressionless faces provided the perfect blank canvas. This time she'd been in at the start. Now her mind could run riot. A couple? A pairing? Just having it off?

"The point is," Abigail was saying, "We've not got long. Like we'd like to see Sanjay's selection. You know rings . . .or . . .? " And gave a 'whatever' shrug.

Stacey basked in reflected delight. "Hey gal! Why didn't you say? That's just great!" She pulled Abby closer to her. "My Sanjay's everso romantic! Loves spoiling people, know what I mean? Sponsoring pop concerts, wrestling, boxing, cage-fighting Anything."

As the women walked ahead, arm-in-arm, bottoms in sync, Garrick's optimism grew. Verity would be impressed if she knew the care he was taking. It proved how much he was putting himself on the line, because when you hit borrowing limits any transactions were tricky. Here he'd the help of Abigail's friends and Louise, thanks to be to the Ancient Mariner! But when he tried to recall a few verses, 'Jingle Bells' suddenly blared from loud speakers; a mechanised reindeer nodded in time; a tattooed man held out bony fingers. 'Save the homeless, sir,' he urged, 'God bless you, please'.

"It is an Ancient Mariner,
And he stoppeth one of three,
"By thy long grey beard and glittering eye,
Now wherefore stopp'st thou me? . . .

"Please, please, do come in." Sanjay half-bowed at the door of his jewellers, stretching out to shake Garrick's hand. "I'm staying open solely for you, Mr Garrick. Purely at Stacey's request." He spoke with smooth public-school vowels. "You see, I am genuine lover of theatre."

Garrick noticed the ornate gold ring on his hand. Sanjay exuded composure in his striped shirt and hand-painted tie. Beside his tailored presence Garrick felt scruffy. He gazed uneasily round. Green glass and ebonised panels enclosed spotlit displays as exclusive as any great exhibition. Every showcase was filled with perfection but none of the items were priced. Each basked in insularity and status. If you had to ask the cost you could not afford it. Sanjay had noticed Garrick glancing nervously round and recognised the celebrity syndrome. Publicity was their lifeblood and fear.

"Closed-circuit cameras is it?" He patted Garrick's wrist. "Don't worry. Believe me sir, we guarantee full anonymity. Absolute and total. No-one need know you've purchased a thing. Not till the photo-opportunity moment! No no!" He gave Garrick a playful slow-motion punch. "Only joking!" And steered Garrick towards a spotlit display.

He unlocked a small cabinet and slid elegant fingers over its gilt-handled drawers.

"Can I direct you to these particular items? Finest cut diamonds. Multiple carats. Purest white. Chipped out of South African mines. You choose which." He began sliding out black velvet trays lined with glittering hologram stars. "But for you As a personal gesture . . ." He held them teasingly up to the light. "And being as you're Stacey's friend, I'll deduct fifteen percent." He looked over at Stacey, who blew Sanjay a kiss then winked at Abigail," And as it's for someone we know . . ." as Stacey seemed to edge them both on.

Garrick was becoming uneasy. He saw multiple zeros rounding up every digit. His clothes seemed to draw all the moisture and salts from his body as he noted the rising cost of each jewel. Did they imagine he earned Hollywood fees?

Sanjay was smiling benignly. "And with an important name, such as yourself, we give you a special personalised box. It comes stamped with gold leaf, wrapped in aromatic paper, and topped with a neat silken bow. If you like, we deliver with servants in turbans, accompanied by a small Hindu band. No no, only joking! That's unless you insist! But seriously, to us, all clients are millionaires and get treated as such." He glanced at Abigail while laying more rings on his counter. Now sir, do I hear you appear on TV? Is it a soap? Should I know which?"

"Look, I'm in a bit of a rush."

As zero hour approached, he feared the Ancient Mariner's curse. One shouldn't kill one's albatross, then hang its remains round one's neck. More trays began to emerge, each more sumptuous than before. Million pound antique diamond chokers emerged from a safe. Emeralds, sapphires, rubies, emeralds, opals, agates, amber, jade, and miniature pearls in multi-strand coils, with Sanjay offering use of his eyeglass.

"My greatest pleasure is pleasing my friends. However, if it's a purely matter of choice?"

Gazing desperately round, Garrick caught sight of a coral and ivory necklace. Its readable price tag had instant appeal. For Vee it would be the gesture that counted.

"Now this." Sanjay was opening a long leather box. "This is less than two hundred years old, and once belonged to the local de Vries family at . . ."

Garrick pointed at the coral. "No wait! This is perfect! Perfect!" The price-tag fluttered alluringly out. "It's so stylish. It's got that quality. It's so ideal I'll leave a small deposit, and pay cash tomorrow."

"My dear fellow," Sanjay took a long deep breath, "No deposit required."

Louise loathed hanging around. Rex Schulman had never kept anyone waiting. Why couldn't Abigail phone? It wasn't hard to press a few buttons. It was her job to make sure Garrick was prompt, but no. You sacrificed your life for them. Suddenly whole aeons were gone and they'd turned into pampered adults. No child ever respected her parents.

As Louise paced up and down, bra-straps cut into her back and panties pulled tight in her groin. As if discomfort weren't enough, her hormones were countermanding each other; hot and cold flushes in rapid succession. Already diners were packing her tables and latecomers scrabbling outside. She'd not be surprised if people were taking bets on her mystery guest. It had all got out of hand. Out in the kitchens Carlos was making his typical chaos; clattering saucepans; gruntings, cursings and swearings, bubbling, fizzing and steaming, and sweat.

Louise was waiting out in reception when Garrick dived in the back door. He found himself ushered straight down to the basement. Next to the toilets the smell of stale urine was mingled with sweet disinfectant. His dressing room was cramped but ritual would calm his nerves. Number one, gargle. Immediately his tonsils stiffened and his tongue swelled like some alien presence. Number two, clean teeth. Toothpaste squelched into stripes of spaghetti, and peppermint swamped his cerebral cortex. A battered extractor fan chopped up the solidified air, shredding the Ancient Mariner's tale.

"Garrick?" Louise called down from above, "One minute thirty seconds and counting! Good luck!"

As Garrick stumbled up the narrow stairs a wave of body-warmth struck him. He felt reassured. Words were his security. He would read direct from the page: that would be easy. A pleasure. No problem. But as he emerged on the dance floor, he stumbled, lost all sense of direction and stopped. He heard a roll on the drums, followed by Pow! Pow! Pow! Blinding spotlights dazzled him. From out of the darkness Louise led a protracted ovation. Garrick basked in the moment, clasping both hands above his head like a boxer. Then the clapping faltered. It faded then died as bewilderment began to set in

Garrick was alone in the wastes of the Arctic. In that one moment he understood death. A follow-spot trailed Louise to his side. As she approached, aromatic mists swirled like a high-octane soup. It set off a chain of reactions. This was Abigail's distinctive perfume laced with hint of cocaine. He knew it at once. A rush of excitement intensified his sensations. Louise led him centre-stage like a long-lost friend.

"Welcome to Club Arabica!"

She offered a delicate cheek, half-closing her eyes. Abigail's perfumes became overwhelming. Female scents and female lips. Abigail and her mother. They shared the same scent! As he embraced her, a sudden roll on the side drums. Followed by a crash on the cymbals like music-hall punctuation. Was this some kind of suicide pact? Was he meant to jump through some bloody great hoop?

Louise began backing away, fixedly smiling. "Ladies and gentlemen, I I want you to welcome the great, very great . . . Garrick Jones!" A smattering of applause. "And tonight he's performing The Ancient Mariner by Samuel Taylor Coleridge."

So this was it, he thought. 'The Rime of the Ancient Mariner' weighed anchor, set sail, and the sea began to take over. He adjusted his script, then slammed the book shut! In a flash of transfiguration, words came so softly the audience was straining to hear. Like buoys on a seascape, the audience pitched and rolled. On it bobbed Pippa and Trixie, with Lady de Vries and her son. And was that Lionel Parsons? James Carr, Reggie Buck and the rest? Rocko? Verity? And Rachel and Mark? Everyone he knew? The still before a great storm? He had this crazy compulsion to wave. Not waving but drowning, he thought. He could make out the hairdresser from Cavanham Street. Also Stacey with Sanjay. But was that really Eddie Craig? And with Arthur Ruddock beside him? This was the Ancient Mariner's tale, an allegory of frustration. It felt like the curse of survival without any hope of redemption. Here Edwin's son was the clown. It was Garrick the Jester, comedy on a Nietzchean scale, becoming his own alter ego.

"It is an ancient Mariner,
And he stoppeth one of three.
By thy long grey beard and glittering eye,
No wherefore stopp'st thou me?"

Rhymes and rhythms flow like the sea; like tides and waves; like bards telling tales or Shamen reciting wild visions. It struck like hard liquor straight at the brain. No more clinking of glasses. Garrick could hear his own voice like a stranger's. The commonplace seemed specifically minted. A language all of its own.

"The Wedding-Guest sat on a stone:
He cannot choose but hear;
And thus spake on that ancient man,
The bright-eyed Mariner."

Somewhere above, an albatross floated, wheeling and turning, fanning its feathers into immaculate curves, gliding and circling through networks of halogen lamps.

"In mist or cloud, on mast or shroud,
It perched for vespers nine,
Whiles all the night, through fog-smoke white,
Glimmered the white moonshine . . ."

His brain kept diving ahead, skimming the waves in slow-motion, plunging into time-frozen spume, scanning decks and rigging as if searching for something. For what? Then he caught sight of Mark. And Rachel too. Just as they'd been in his dream, out there on deck, as pale and frail as skeletons. Old nightmares recurred. Masts and rigging solidified into ice. But somehow he kept mouthing the words, pounding to each mini-climax Then setting off again and again, building up and up unbearably . . .

"'God save thee, ancient Mariner,
From the fiends, that plague thee thus! –
Why look'st thou so?' 'With my cross-bow
I shot the Albatross!'" . . .

So much for meddling with nature, extinguishing cultures and species. In an endless universe of Black Holes and Galactic Collapses, total extinction was moments away: seas into deserts and mountains to plains. Here Love and Death combined like Syphyllis and Aids. We start by feeling immortal, then age. What would Chekhov have made of what Gustave Doré depicted so well? . . . Blame Coleridge and his opium dreams!

"Her lips were red, her looks were free,
Her locks were yellow as gold . . ."

He was poised on that final cusp, dragging sentences out, milking every moment.

"Her skin was as white as leprosy,
The Nightmare Life-in-Death was she
Who thicks man's blood with cold."

Out there on the ship's deck, a figure like Verity was shrouded in cordage and rigging, swathed and hooded, as black as a widow, and pointing. Was she dragging his babies away? Then who was the other figure? The skeleton as seducer? .Or was this really Abigail? Her eyes as green as jade ice?

"Day after day, day after day,
We stuck, nor breath nor motion,
As idle as a painted ship
Upon a painted ocean,"

Really believing these words came direct from himself.

"Water, water, everywhere,
And all the boards did shrink;
Water, water everywhere,
Nor any drop to drink."

Familiar quotations seemed uniquely transformed, leaving Chekhov behind in their wake. At that very same moment, in a film studio somewhere, Verity was demonstrating crêpes brulées and moules à la marinière. She was free to surf each fashionable wave, while he found himself sustaining a drama right to the end. All that was left was the hint of a question.

". . . A sadder and a wiser man
He rose the morrow morn."

The lights blacked out and Garrick dived for the Fire Exit. As he emerged in the street, a hand caught his sleeve and held tight. Elizabeth Scott edged into view as if from a black-and-white movie, hair rimmed with shimmering light. She stood blocking his route, holding a microphone up to his face. After all, it was she who had caught Garrick dining with minors, and "Norston news should be making the news", as Ray Seaton once said.

When Abigail had been left at the jewellers, she'd vowed not to attend Garrick's show. Men are such bastards. When Garrick asked for Abby's advice, Stacey knew men never said what they meant. He was obviously sounding her out. As she'd explained, the gift was really intended for her. An old trick she said and Abigail was convinced. Especially when Sanjay quoted that TV commercial where 'Older Man' invites 'Unsuspecting Girl' into 'Scriabo the Jewellers' and buys her a diamond-chip ring. "One of Life's little gestures" went the jingle, "Every woman deserves one". Sanjay explained how the custom was for a man to buy his girl a love-token, or how else would jewellers survive? The trick was to secretly test the girl's tastes, and this was what Garrick was doing.

When Abigail ran off she'd planned to never to see them again. Dramatic gestures were needed. She had to pay everyone back. Then winter darkness struck without warning; its huge celestial shutters came slamming down. As she sheltered under Braewood's portico, street lighting popped into faint fluorescence. Then came more rain. And more rain. She headed as usual towards the canal. Sometimes it was her best friend. Sometimes its stillness ran as dense as iced soup reflecting fluorescent purple, but now its surface refused to reflect her. Its bottomless trench ploughed the Earth's crust, carving through town and bisecting its bricked-up remains. She began stamping to restore circulation, blowing into cupped hands, knowing she might never face humans again.

When she eventually approached Club Arabica, babbling spectators emerged. Out in the foyer Louise would be busy outshining the rest. What's more she'd risk anything to spite her own daughter, be it liposuction, face-lifts, surgical implants or genetic rejuvenation regimes followed by hormone injections, sexual restoratives, followed by manicures, pedicures, and all-over massage. Anything. Everything. Her mother was more like a pantomime dame. Worse even than that, she was her rival.

Garrick escaped from the nightclub, evaded the reporter, then kept walking. Drizzle was cold on his cheeks. It was best to leave failure behind. Perhaps he might not get paid but that was a risk he would take. He concentrated on toecaps and puddles, convinced that by not looking up he would be invisible. What could not be seen did not exist. He had to escape as fast as he could.

Abigail trod carefully too, padding the same stretch of road. In every patch of asphalt she saw indecipherable patterns. If she kept to unswerving bearings she knew she'd be safe in the world. Viewed on CCTV both their trajectories narrowed, then closed. Geometry cannot be distracted. The climax was inevitable. They might even have brushed like the wing tips of moths. But passed unaware.

As Abigail drew nearer, a tottering figure blocked out the light. It stumbled. Its high heels scraped on stone slabs. Dark glasses clattered into the gutter. A body crumpled onto the kerb. In the sodium glow Jilly Craske looked swollen, bloated and pink, her bulging eyes like overripe plums, but still with that carnival grin; dazed but quietly exultant, wiping away the tears.

"Brilliant, love. He's brilliant. Just brilliant! But . . . "

She nodded towards the far side of the road then scrambled up on her feet.

A black saloon waited partway up the kerb, its hazard lights flashing.

Garrick had overslept. Rehearsals did not go well, although none of the cast criticised him openly. The Ancient Mariner seemed like some half-recalled nightmare but déjà vu was already fading. According to Phyllis, Garrick's phone had been ringing all morning but he'd refused to respond. Best to switch everyone off. With second-hand gossip sometimes escapism worked, but nothing was helped by actors with colds causing the day to run later and later. The way the day was working out, he dreaded confronting his wife .Then, at midday, an envelope was delivered by hand, direct from Club Arabica. To his utter amazement it contained his full payment in cash, plus bonus greetings from Louise.

He gave everyone the afternoon off and raced back to the shopfest arcades, where he caught Sanjay off-balance. Saved in the nick of time thanks to The Ancient Mariner! He never thought he'd say that, but it gave him an even better idea. Symbolism mattered. He'd choose the perfect metaphor. Her Rolex was surgically linked to his system, but his choice of gift would be just as substantial. His would truly embody their Love. Metaphors really did matter; nothing too trite; simplicity and utility combined with classical mass.

"No need for cash, Mr Jones," Sanjay had said, "We offer excellent credit," looking shocked by the sight of bank notes. "But thank you. Any friend of Stacey and Abby is mine."

Gift-wrapped it looked so impressive and now he was ready for Vee's arrival.

He'd arrived extra early. Since his first visit new spotlights glittered off multiple crystals, and dozens of orange trees paraded in earthenware tubs. When invisible speakers relayed updated Vivaldi, all must be right with the world. Surely Vee would be impressed. She'd always underestimated the North. Garrick paced around, waiting, but whenever he checked the time, he came face to face with Verity's exquisite taste. The Castle Hotel still ignored him as he paced up and down.

"You alright sir?" A suspicious porter suddenly appeared at his elbow.

Why hadn't Vee phoned to warn she'd be late? Had there been some accident? Traffic jam? Diversion? Now he was being observed, or were they keeping suicide watch, assessing his terror potential? They'd swiped his credit card, shaken his hand, and given him a questionnaire to complete before handing over the key to his room. Now he was seen as a threat. The gilded Christmas tree swathed in its gold-lamée fronds soared like a mutant. 'Seasons Greetings' flashed over the entrance as digitised Musak hummed 'The Best Suki Solomon Carols'.

It seemed carols began in mid-August, the first Santas were observed in October. There followed Christmas, Easter, Epiphany, Mid-Summer, several Bank Holidays, Annunciation, Candlemas, even Halloween and Guy Fawkes, before back to Christmas again. He had quite enough time to reflect on Reggie Buck's laborious jokes, and Orlando Marcel's attempts to build up the part of Dandini. The bloody show wasn't entitled 'Dandini', for God's sake.

"You're so lucky sir. We'd only one room left tonight," they'd told him.

It wasn't until he'd pushed open the door that the full coincidence dawned. It was the very same room they'd inspected. Room 112 with its all-encompassing bed. He remembered Abigail's open-mouthed awe. Now he continued to pace up and down patting the elegant box in his pocket, envisaging pile-ups surrounded by fire-tenders and ambulance sirens. By the time most of the guests had arrived the hotel was winding down for the night. Remaining staff watched as Garrick repeatedly straightened his collar and tie, still pacing a trail on the marble.

At last he heard a car drawing up. He raced out to the forecourt to greet her. A muddy Porsche gave him a flash of its headlights, revving its conspicuous wealth. The young driver leaned out, sleeked hair shining black beneath canopy lights. He waved Garrick over.

"Hi there! Sorry guys. I'm meant to be somewhere right now." He spread a map across his steering wheel, adding. "I'm running late. Guess I've missed the junction."

"Depends where you're heading."

"Oh shit. What time is it?" Garrick showed him his watch. "Thanks mate." The young man bent over his map. "My sat-nav's failed. Can you see? Is this place anywhere near?" As Garrick leaned into the window the driver pointed at it vaguely. "Sorry mate, what time did you say?"

As Garrick pushed back his cuff, something flashed. Polished metal. Sharpened steel. Reflections. A blade! In a one single movement the man clamped Garrick's wrist, then accelerated away, swerved through the gateposts and out. As Garrick fell to the gravel he missed the car's registration.

He stared at his wrist. An invisible line seeped miniature globules of blood. Only a paleness marked where Verity's gift had been. His Rolex Imperator was gone.

CHAPTER NINE

TEMPTATIONS

Above the rumble of traffic came the sound of deceleration. Two luminous pinholes punctured the mist. Twin cones of light cut through the evening and swung into the forecourt. 'Woman in a hurry!' it said. Verity flung open the door and stepped into the glare of the canopy lights.

This was her moment. It marked a new chapter, not least because Gary was achieving potential at last. Her camelhair jacket set off her new twin-set and pearls. She trailed a hand through carefully groomed hair. In her experience hotels responded to style. She had a special expedition planned, after which she was free to enjoy. Hopefully Gary had everything fixed, but with him this could never be taken for granted. Their marriage had nearly foundered on that. As the chill air struck she searched out a closed-circuit camera. She focused a smile on its lens and finally she got some reaction.

The doorman appeared. "Good evening madam. Yes?"

"My bags are back here in the trunk. And yes, I am booked in."

An attendant arrived out of nowhere and agreed to park her hired car. Soon others in bow ties and waistcoats competed in carrying bags. She ordered these to be left in the foyer and looked around vainly for Garrick. Men were not reliable, the British no more than the rest. Some of her friends were into their second divorce but Gary was over-obsessed with their kids. It had taken ten years of marriage for him to make a romantic suggestion. Should she credit Chekhov with that? Or her own powers of suggestion? When it came to the crunch, theirs was a celebration of what? A wild affair subsiding into conventional marriage? Mutual acceptance. A mid-Atlantic alliance? At least her poor momma had tried. The soul of Crimea may be diluted and with it the blood of Ukraine, but as a widow she could at last fulfil herself. She would have been happier still if her daughter had married an oligarch prince.

Gary hadn't been straight from the start, that was the problem. Big in entertainment, he'd said, and they'd both kind of clicked. Her own career was booming so when the kids came along he'd slipped into househusband role, sacrificing his high-flying career. Maybe that was a warning? At the time she'd felt guilty. She'd been so sickeningly grateful the pleasure went out of her work. It wasn't till two kiddies later when colleagues posed questions she realised how little she knew.

Roseanne couldn't help interfering. According to her, no man could be trusted. There was always a hint of the Caucasus there: always the Morozovs merged with the Chekhovs. God bless the old family tree! "I'm Russo-American," she'd say, "With extra Moral Majority genes", so when genealogy struck, she was hooked. Roseanne set off on internet searches, poking through virtual archives. That way she'd hoped to track Garrick's path through the entrails of showbiz: that way she'd ferret him out.

And there it all was. Roseanne was triumphant. Cheap girlie tours, dubious niteclubs in Christianless places, cheesy high-kicking routines and alleged 'misappropriation of funds'. No West End hits and no Hollywood movies. Names and dates fitted. It all added up. He'd acquiesced so easily because he'd had nothing else in his life. That was a bit of a downer. Now at least he was earning his keep. Roseanne called this payback time. "Told you so", she'd kept saying.

The young porters hovered, smiling and fawning. She slipped each a fiver and off they flounced leaving Verity drained. It was not for her to hunt Gary down; it was for him to come and greet her. Life was too short for motorway stops, but all the way down she had never ceased thinking. A recipe might spring to mind. Some major fad could be waiting. She couldn't afford to switch off. Now she needed freshening up. She slipped off to the washroom leaving a porter guarding her bags.

Garrick remained out of sight, still feeling shocked. Traumatised even. He needed to compose himself. He'd been publicly mugged and had never resisted. It had needed a suicide gesture. He should have hurled himself in front of that car, allowing its wheels to crunch over his body. In contrast, Verity arrived in style. Hollywood downplayed. Designer Chic with a conscience. This was her unsuspected twin, alike but so dissimilar. The unknown unknown. Somehow the distance between them had widened.

Despite first-aid his wrist was still swollen. A Band-Aid tugged at raw skin. Worse still, closed circuit cameras were 'off for maintenance reasons' so no one had witnessed events. Without any visible proof the hotel was reluctant to call in the police, implying he'd been negligent, treating him more like a crook than a victim. Double brandies hadn't helped, and Garrick rubbed shabby shoes down the backs of his jeans and ruffled his overgrown hair. He would have to tell her what happened. But not now. Not yet. From where he stood she glowed like an MGM starlet, looking half her age. This was no visiting chef de cuisine nor Lecturer in Dietetics. She looked younger and brighter than Abigail or their dancers.

Once in the washroom Vee had slipped off her shoes, relaxed, and felt better. Most of her sorority were into their umpteenth divorce. The good old

Class of 65. The Allegheny High School set. All on Maintenance, all with pre-nuptials sorted. Here however she'd learned the hard way. In Britain it was best to conform, or get labelled Yank. She laid out her rings on the washstand, rinsing both hands in the basin, letting the fingers relax, wondering what Gary had bought. Maybe a bracelet? A necklace? Hers was a very competitive world. Gary had a lot to make up for.

A haggard young woman emerged from a cubicle, coughing. Vee automatically shielded her rings.

The woman leaned confidentially over, breasts spilling out of her blouse:

"Shouldn't leave them around, love. There's muggers everywhere."

Verity dabbed herself dry, adjusted her lips, freshened her complexion, gently re-lacquered her hair, then reverted to thoughts of her kids. At least they were safe with her mother. No doubt they'd get a bellyful of the Romanov Czars, but that entire world was long gone. The Cold War was over. The USSR no longer existed. The children were too young for such stuff, but to momma, blood ties came above anything else. Dynasties grew from deep roots, implying Vee had abandoned the faith. Like, how come she'd not christened Rachel as Raya? Or Mark been baptised Mishka? In which case she wondered why she'd not been baptised Vera herself in a full Russian Orthodox service? That was a question that hadn't been answered.

Outside in reception, Garrick was plumped on a barstool confronted by landscapes of bottles. For the first time he noticed a group of signed photos. One was recognisably Rex Schulman. Another must be Eddie Craig. He furtively sniffed at an ashtray and surreptitiously pined as Verity emerged from the cloakrooms.

"Hi!" she shouted, switching into total charisma and throwing herself in his arms.

Even at the moment they kissed he felt he'd been cast as Familiar Stranger. Theirs was a public performance and this was a retake too many. It seemed to her too that Garrick had changed. Was it the 'Cherry Orchard' effect? Gary had been 'Chekhovised'? Caught the melancholia? But without the perception or wit? Or was it more of an Anglican chill?

"You're looking really great," Garrick insisted, "Yes, really. Terrific."

He didn't ask about her journey. He didn't enquire of the children, nor ask after her mom. She also noted he'd not mentioned the watch, nor her letters or cards. He almost seemed preoccupied. For God's sake, she'd rearranged her whole life to be here, cancelling trips to Geneva and further bookings in Munich and Paris. On top of this she had just driven miles on British roads. Here there were no Interstate Thruways and drivers were ultra-aggressive. She'd been cut up by some crazy black car on the bypass, then almost slammed into head-on by a Porsche only a mile down the road. Next time she'd take a Manchester flight then rent herself a chauffeur.

"Okay," she said, "Where's our room?"

Two eager young porters came rushing. Garrick lowered his head and hoped no one would refer to his previous visit. The elevator barely reacted. Split seconds later they were on the first floor following an unending curve which seemed to go on forever. The Senior Liaison Assistant hurried ahead, unlocked the door and ushered them into Room 112.

Vee studied herself full-length in the mirror, fluffing her hair and slowly regaining composure. It was not easy to be just herself when she'd got out of the habit, so when Gary came over and stretched an arm round her, sliding one hand to a nipple, she pushed him away.

He heard her testing the hand-basin taps, toilet, shower, then bath, no doubt awarding them points. He began to re-examine his wrist. He was lucky the arteries hadn't been slashed. When she emerged, wrapped in white towelling complete with the hotel's tower motif, he noticed she'd lost weight. She looked amazingly svelte and refreshed. So far she'd not mentioned the Rolex, thank God. This was no time for confessions. He hoped it was fully insured.

"Room pass the test?"

"This robe's American cotton!"

"Naturally. We checked that out." And straightaway regretted the "we".

Verity was inspecting the bed, followed by phone, hair-drier, icebox, TV, trouser press, mini-bar, kettle, before flopping back down on the mattress, hair swirling out like a dark polished halo. He switched off his cellphone, cutting all links with the world.

"Jesus, Gary, I'm pooped." She closed her eyes and lay silent. "Things I do for global culture! And all for the sake of our tastebuds. Okay okay. I know what you're thinking." She stretched out those long slender legs. "I mean, 'roller-coaster' no way describes it. So maybe my Karma's unsettled. What I need is spiritual peace. Peace, perfect peace." She lay, eyes closed and lips parted. "Main thing is, have you missed me?"

"Don't ask." He knelt on the mattress beside her. "We can lie here all weekend. Just you and me, together, alone. No cooking. No Chekhov." She started to laugh. "And best of all, no kids!"

Her eyelids flashed open; her knees snapped shut. She buried her face in the pillows.

"Honey?" He took her hand and kissed it. "What is it?"

She snatched her fingers away. "You have to ask? I mean Where am I when they need me?" She wiped her eyes with her sleeve. "Pursuing careers Like I'm evading my duties, stifling my own deepest instincts. And that is so unnatural Most times I feel so so guilty I'm serious, Gary. Dumping on my mom, poor momma. Poor babies I mean, Jesus, what a time to start having a conscience! And now . . ." She wrapped herself in his arms.

They lay side by side facing the empty video screen, comforting each other.

"Darling, we've got to put ourselves first."

"Hell yes! We're here to celebrate, yes And all we can do is . . ." She snatched up the remote and hammered it into the pillows.

The empty screen suddenly burst into life, blasting from twenty-four speakers. A spaceship unloaded alien beings. She pressed the control. The picture blacked out. She flung it hard at the wall. Gary was removing his shirt, undoing every button, now unfastening jeans, tugging them frantically over his feet. As he leaned towards her, tensions dissolved. Next they'd entwined in the sheets, curling up into contortions. Skin emulsified against skin; warp into weft. He forgot the pain in his arm and knew he was in love with his wife. A simple and conventional love.

Then out of somewhere, a previous presence imprinted itself on the room. Moving like invisible shadows its ghost came to visit. Garrick sensed its all-seeing eye. As sheets strained and the velveteen headboard hammered the silk-papered wall, Abigail's spirit gazed down, and with it shades of Coleridge and spirits of 'Kubla Khan'. At the moment Vee cried out, time jumped a few notches, then all the clocks resumed. A ventilator fluttered to life. The mini-fridge murmured. As Garrick and Verity lay in the darkness every sense was magnified, deafened by their own breathing.

She rolled onto her stomach, feeling suddenly drained. "It seems ages. Too long."

At least her Film Unit helped her. Almost a substitute family. Extended camaraderie. Professional friendships. All that was some compensation. Sometimes it felt like Gary took her for granted. It wasn't some kind of balancing act, but he'd not gotten round to her generous gift. Not even a mention. His body language said it all. And she'd gone to such effort.

"Gary? If it's not me, then it's gotta be you!"

"Me?"

"You, Chekhov, and Norston. You're all so shacked up together. I feel like I'm butting in on some party."

"But I've thought about you and the kids every . . ."

She scrambled out of bed, avoiding his deflated body. The crumpled sheet had imprinted itself on her skin; a texture like tribal markings. She jumped when he touched her.

"No. You're freaking me out. You goddam forgot!". His not wearing her gift was offensive. "Anniversaries may be purely symbolic to you . . . ! But that was my first advance. My very first cash from my very first show."

He held up his wrist, dramatically pulling the dressing away. She didn't respond.

"A collector's timepiece they called it," she said.

"You won't believe what happened but . . ."

"Twenty-five carats of clockwork!"

"Vee . . . Listen! I don't know how to put this. I should have been more suspicious"

"What are you trying to say? It's fake? "

He took a deep breath. "No! I got mugged." He thrust his bare wrist out. "That's what I'm trying to tell you. I got bloody mugged!" She looked uncomprehending. "Right here, outside this hotel. Yes, there. In that forecourt. Some maniac in a racer."

After her initial shock Vee took it all surprisingly coolly. What was done was done. At least no-one was dead. She vividly pictured that little red Porsche she'd almost hit just a few miles down the road. Everything fell into place but it wasn't for her to feel guilty. Gary was the one who'd messed up. Anyway, guilt was a double-edged blade. She'd learned a lot about that. History could cut both ways and history repeated itself. Families put that in

194

proportion. Her grandfather shot in rebellion, her father defrauded, and now her husband knifed. It looked like she'd been drawn into some pattern. Repeating old affinities? Seeking sympathetic genes; subconsciously making her choice. All their men had been reckless, as if carelessness was a deliberate choice, appropriating its own DNA? She could believe anything now. Chekhov's own landscape had been riven with change leading to a great revolution, but Norston was meant to be safe.

Garrick too had begun to reflect. A still small voice reminded him of premiums paid without claims; lots of practical details. Valuations, late payments, everything fitting the pattern; one debt compounding another. One moment he'd been wearing her gift like it was part of himself. Next it was gone. That wasn't all. There was Cinderella's demotion of Chekhov. Now was the time to come settle up and come clean.

"Darling, I . . ."

"Okay okay. I take some of the blame. I guess I took risks with the post. That kind of luck couldn't hold."

"But Vee . . ."

"Has anyone called the police?"

He nodded. She slid an arm round his shoulders.

"Great. Then leave it to them and get back to Chekhov. That's why you're here."

Here it was without prompting. His cue to confess.

"Look Vee, I've been thinking."

"Who? You . . .you're joking."

She started to smile. Garrick's mouth twitched. Then the shared laughter; laughing and crying; living and dying in one, when he felt her body go rigid.

"Gary?" Her fingers clamped into his shoulder. "What if it gets out into the tabloids?"

"Why should it? Anyway, all publicity's good. Isn't that what they say?"

"No Gary, no." She pressed a finger into his lips. "One thing I've learnt is, once it starts there's no turning back. It's who you meet, what you wear, what's your brand of vitamin pills. Think what they'd do with a mugging."

"But out here?" Then implications started to dawn.

"Yes. What I'm saying is, we take one step at a time. First, that watch was inscribed, plus there's a serial number. I mean, I don't want to star in a crime wave with forensics and stuff like the movies."

She thought of her sponsors if the press raked up Gary's past. Her mother was right. Those troupes of high-kickers. His belly dancers and strippers. They'd guarantee headlines. "Cook and Let Cook" would be griddled before ever hitting the screen. No doubt they'd include Rachel and Mark, then drag in Roseanne. And hit the whole Morozov tribe.

"There's a bright side to this," he was saying.

"Like what?"

He'd played the part of Garrick so long she wanted it to be true. Now he was fumbling around in those big pockets of his, then going down on one knee.

"For you. A small compensation." The small, blue vellum-wrapped box was tied with a flurry of ribbon.

"What is it?"

"It's magic!"

Instinctively she weighed it up in her hand. It was unexpectedly heavy. She held it up to her ear, shook it then examined the ribbon. Expectation was part of the fun. She'd underestimated him. In her heart she knew just what it was. There was something sensual, almost sexual, about it. He knew her tastes exactly. He knew her delight in fine jewels.

With one sharp tug she untied the ribbon then tore the wrapping away. Out slipped a large jeweller's leatherette box. Inside was packed with gold mica. She delved with the tips of her fingers until she felt something hard. With manicured nails she peeled away layers of tissue. Suddenly like a constellation of spotlights, crystalline facets exploded like spectra. Like the dawn of creation, that moment seemed to expand and expand ever outwards. Vee seemed suitably stunned.

He kissed her. "Isn't it great!"

She stepped back and sat heavily down. "What is it?"

"It's finest quality crystal. As you see, a limited edition. It's got its own certificate, numbered, signed, and guaranteed 'Pure Lead Crystal'." She looked numb. "Yes. Original hand-cut Bavarian glass, with only three thousand made. The gift of the decade they said."

When vows were exchanged, she and Gary were equally, perfectly matched. They'd made the selfsame commitment; a fifty-fifty investment in life. Her choice of gift was meant to enshrine all those years. She could see its imprint still there on his wrist.

He unfolded the vellum guarantee. "I ran a quick Internet search. Ten years of marriage makes this our Crystal Wedding! So this is it A cut-crystal ashtray."

"So when the hell did I smoke?"

The pause seemed to last, then continued.

Alcohol seeped into their bloodstreams. Videos merged with each other. Their room overlooked acres of car park. Through loose-woven drapes Garrick could see the main road with headlights winding past the old castle mound like blips on a semichrome screen. This was suburbia without destination, as disturbingly bland as any of Hopper's Metroland landscapes. Next time Garrick awoke, Vee was kneeling on the carpet, semi-naked, gleaming in the half-light, hair coiled up at her neck. He relished the ridges and curves of her spine as she crouched, opening her portfolio, apparently going through papers. She meant to put faces to colleagues? Including maybe some fancy locations? Snapshots of their children too?

Triumphantly she held up a page. "Take a look at this! If cookery's a passing trend Like boob-tubes and bobbysox So what? Filming's cool. When no-one's got time to cook these days, I'm like their go-between. My agent gives me a couple of years at the top. That means we're all depending on you, Garrick Jones, to bring some class to proceedings."

"Like how?"

"How?" She picked up a print. "First take a look at the sheen on that pasta. See these ginger chip cookies! The texture! And how's this for Tuna Bake? You can almost smell the Parmesan. So much work went into this. Then what if the press gets news of your theft? Think what they'll say. We'd be the news. Another celebrity mugging! It'd ruin our Christmas promotion. 'No adverse publicity' it says in the unwritten part of my contract."

"You're joking."

"No I'm serious. It's major. It's family viewing. Episode One is on Boxing Day."

"You mean hush it up? When that bastard stole our watch!"

Someone had knocked at the door.

"Don't answer it!" She snatched up her robe and disappeared into the bathroom.

Through the eyehole Garrick could see a wide-angled brown, balding skull. Why did he have to see life through a prism? This someone was holding a passkey. As the visitor leaned into total distortion Garrick released the front door. The manager almost fell through.

He quickly regained his composure. "I do apologise. We usually respect a privacy sign But this is urgent, regarding 'events', shall we call them?" They heard Verity running the shower. "Regrettably, it's from the police. They're short-staffed, see, owing to football hooligans, night-spots and such." He handed Garrick a printed slip. "Here you are, sir. All contact details. What they're suggesting is, you go down to Central Police Station, make your statement, and give a full description tomorrow."

"Tomorrow?"

"Tomorrow A.M. That way we'll all be covered. Norston's a very civilised place with a generous counselling service. Regrettably, we've no witnesses here, being as our surveillance was disconnected owing to maintenance problems As you know, we're having that fixed. So, by way of apology, we offer you each one free lunch in our restaurant. If you need further help, the name is Karami."

As the door closed, Vee re-emerged, hair in a towel like a turban.

"Right now I could do with a stand-in. But thinking about it, what lasts are the classics, the Chekhovs and Shakespeares. Not ordinary mortals like us."

She held the ashtray up to the light, refracting facets over walls, bed, and curtains, through seemingly thousands of prisms before dropping it into her bag:

"That's why everybody envies you, you know that? Your Three Sisters, Cherry Orchard, The Seagull My producers, my crew, they all do. I'm just a passing Celebrity Star, but you're the 'paté de foie gras with trumpets', like my line producer says. Even my mom's impressed. We're all proud of you, Gary. You know that."

He knew there was nothing to say, especially when she couldn't see her own danger. Producers only commissioned a pilot, never intending a series. Avoiding tax was their game. Maybe nothing would ever get aired, but when her crunch inescapably came, they'd swap mutual failures and share a laugh with the kids. Then things could go back how they were.

"By the by, did I say? The network commissioners? No?" She took a deep breath. "Well they just love my show! God knows why. It's not great art. It won't last, but . . . but Lucy says . . . she says, 'Go for it!' So I did. And I've got a huge raise, and I'm signing for two additional series. And that's just for starters! It's millions plus a bonus I'm fully signed up!" She sucked at a finger, looking outrageously coy. "What I'm getting at is, with my new schedule, my mom and the kids, I need a manager. A personal full-time assistant. Someone who's close to me. Someone I can totally, utterly trust . . . now do you get it?"

He was staring out into darkness, his eyes drifting via streetlights, bright scribbles of neon, and blocks of Varilux windows, wandering out of control towards where Abigail lived, barely half a mile away.

By one o'clock in the morning Louise Roberts was nervous. Teenagers needed a microchip implant or intravenous pager, so when Abigail still hadn't come home, Louise began frantically ringing around. As a last resort she tried Jilly Craske. No voicemail, no Ansaphone, no Thomas, no nothing. When best friends don't confide, something has to be wrong. Since Abby's first visit to Jilly's salon she had started to change: more withdrawn, standoffish and even aggressive when she ought to rejoice. Louise would have been be glad if somebody cared about her, not sulked about getting advice. You take your exams, get the best grades, only then did you get the hell out, not walk off mid-term. Despite her mother's efforts Abigail had gone ahead and chosen The Majestic and Garrick.

Louise had taken risks herself last night. Yes, they'd got cheers, but Garrick's nightclub performance evoked carcasses swinging on ropes, corpses curled up in hammocks, and ships of skeletons packed to the gunnels with death and disaster. Luckily locals had raved and applauded, some even demanding repeats. Starring him she could sell out again and again. When he was to blame for her nightmares that was the greatest contradiction of all. Was Abigail aware real life would feature romance and rejection, but self-hatred came in the pack? Its terrors would have to be faced. And that was all Garrick's fault. His Ancient Mariner flashbacks arose like ghosts of the drowned. The undead emerged from the holds of a ship like sufferers dying from AIDS.

Still waiting by their front gate in the dark, Louise was cold and frustrated. She'd swallowed her pride, phoned, and caught Stacey revising for her Diploma in Hygiene. Stacey claimed she'd not seen Abby all day. As more hours passed, Louise's nervousness turned into dread. Twice they'd come close to alerting Emergency Services. But waited.

Soon even Carlos was anxious; their house felt like an oversized shell. The night was disconcertingly clear with only a sliver of moon. Out on those streets, real human beings were trafficking real women and children. Others plied recreational drugs like a pharmaceutical gala. She'd read about glue sniffing, acids and meths. Soon there'd be knifings and shootings in Norston. Carlos sat tight on the staircase as Louise continued to prowl. A man should be scared for his daughter. Honour would have to be served.

Louise tried ringing the theatre again. "Thank you for calling," it said. "The Majestic Theatre is closed at the moment. No one is here to deal with your queries. Please call again between the hours of nine and five," in Phyllis's metallic voice.

Louise and Carlos slouched at their metal-topped table, silently blaming each other. His greying moustaches visibly drooped as wall clocks clacked the seconds away. They swore that if Abby were spared, they'd make it up to her daughter. She could have whatever she wanted.

They woke up with a start at past two o'clock and Louise understood desolation.

She shook Carlos. "Right. One last check then. Then we call the police!"

A tipping point had been reached. They knew they were wasting their time. Abigail's bedroom door lay ajar, as abandoned as the Mary Celeste. It seemed years since they'd actually entered this room. Who knew what organisms bred in its dust? It was Abby's memorial now; a memento mori frozen in time. It felt like the tomb of their hopes. This tiny uninhabited space would be dedicated to her, no detail changed. As Louise entered, Abigail's wind chimes rang in the draught, suddenly jarring, discordant.

They fumbled for the light switch, half-blinded with tears. Then, as their eyes adjusted they saw a shape in the sulphurous glow. Beneath a Romeo poster Abigail's corpse lay fully-clothed on her bed, sprawled like an overdose victim. Her tendons had tightened; flesh had shrunk to the bone. Freckles disfigured a bluish white skin. Damp hair clung to the skull, the mouth hanging open and shapeless, as red as a gash. As Louise screamed, the body moved.

Abigail blinked in the light, her features still puffy and white.

Clarity only came when they'd gone. Minutest details became glaringly clear. As she kept her eyes tightly shut, spotlights picked out Abigail's thoughts as she moved through computerised pictures interacting with dreams. Was she asleep? Or awake? Her brain was on some virtual circuit, gliding through passages, galleries, stairways and rooms, apparently knowing just where to head.

In a flash there she was. Room 112, the Norston Castle Hotel, just as she remembered it. She relished all its decorative detail. Its wall-to-wall pale velour. Its well-padded headboard. Its woven damask with gleaming silk pillows. Wide plasma TV/computer, icebox, trouser press, water-cooler, mini bar, telephones, stationery, lush fitted wardrobes, etceteras, and en suite bathroom with power shower and swirl-effect bath, right down to those nuts in cellophane packs, those complimentary chocolates. She could walk around, touch, taste, and feel in three dimensions.

This living, virtual world was punctuated with Jilly Craske's calling cards, like some animal spraying its territorial scent. Printed cards were everywhere, marking out Abigail's visit. But something else kept intruding; movements, sounds, and thoughts that she fought to dismiss. She clamped her hands to her ears; spinning round so quickly she almost fell over, then stopped, took aim and zoomed in.

Two bodies lay in that bed. Two naked bodies entwined. Thrashings and pumpings, gruntings and moanings, thrustings and bumpings and grindings. Garrick was with his wife, in full view of anyone's thoughts. It was filthy, vile, and obscene!

Alone on her own narrow bed, Abigail flailed, feeling her body double with spasms. She wanted to retch. Her stomach welled up in her throat. She started to gag. Ghosts would not be exorcised! Crouched in the dark, she drove nail scissors into her forearm, fumbled, and sopped up the blood with a tissue.

As Garrick lay comatose, snoring, Verity awoke with new vigour. First rays of sunlight picked out Victorian spires and the theatre's twin turrets beyond. From its location high on the hill, the Castle Hotel looked out across clear winter days. Hints of light frost were stirred by soft easterly breezes. She showered, padded round and got dressed. Downstairs at breakfast, smiling diners greeted her, everyone piling their plates with huge portions. She was sipping fruit juice and munching a minimal muesli, finalising her plans, when Garrick arrived, pink and raw from the shower.

"Morning!" she called, "Isn't this just glorious!" But his only reply was to nod. "And so clear. And so dry!" She laid several pamphlets out on the table. "Guess what. I've got our itinerary scheduled." She gave him a peck on his cheek.

One thing she'd learned: twenty-four hours represented a single location. That's how filming worked. Her guidebooks were packed with suggestions. Sites for her forthcoming nation-wide tour were marked with hand-written slips. By concentrating on details she had eclipsed all yesterday's crisis.

"How about this?" She thrust a brochure under his eyes, flipped through the pages and pointed. "Today we're starting right here!"

Temple Storford lay at her fingernail point. To Garrick's mixed feelings, at least she'd not asked to visit his digs nor shown much concern for his work. Despite all their trauma she was as cheerful as ever. Not once did she mention his crystal anniversary gift, even avoiding his last night's attack. She'd planned their 'day out' without once dialling home, behaving as if nothing had happened.

'Temple Storford. A country seat in the classical style epitomises great British traditions,' her catalogue said. He casually flipped through the index. Grand Tours. Slaves and Plantations. Marriages. Deaths in childbirth. Bored elder sons. Corrupt younger sons Alcoholics. Bankruptcies. Betting And all the usual Aristocratic Affaires. This was their first day together and sightseeing was the last thing he'd planned.

"And look at this." She opened a double-page spread. "They've got these great original kitchens And Gary, listen 'Temple Storford has fine period kitchens, rebuilt and equipped to latest contemporary standards by Lady Agnes de Vries (1834. 1892) at the end of the nineteenth century. Superbly restored by the present Lady de Vries' Isn't that astonishing? And our expensive researcher's not even been there! This'll be my personal coup, no sharing the credit. That way I'll get direct say in production."

Her schedule was fixed in advance. He knew straightaway he was trapped. In much the same way Roseanne had inserted the Chekhovs into his annals and Chekhov would be his auto-da-fé. On this the whole family honour depended. No panto was acceptable. They'd not react well to 'Cinderella'. So maybe now was the moment, no matter how he'd got here? Things happened, that's all. Then from out of his vague retrospection came the ghost of a passing suspicion.

"By the way." He casually stirred his tea. "When did all this happen? Originally, I mean?"

"Sorry? What?"

"This offer of yours? Presenting this cookery programme? When did they first suggest it?"

"When? You want dates? I don't know. I'm not a walking calendar."

"But when? Before I applied to come here?"

"Gee! I'm not a diary!" She gave a bright, dismissive laugh. "I don't date-stamp events. Anyway, so what? Come on darling, I can't supply digital read-outs." She began packing her guidebooks away. "I guess I knew theirs was a major proposal. I mean. I'm not superstitious, but maybe I chose not to flaunt it right then. Not till I was sure. Nobody jumps till they're sure."

That was enough for him. An oblique confirmation. After all, it was Vee who'd actually come up with the plan for a Chekhov. And it was she who'd urged him to grasp the nettle, no matter the risk, or how short the notice? In fact, wasn't she the one who'd cut out that advert? Or was it even her mom? The plot-line was becoming clear. It had more damned twists than a movie.

He felt a surge of paranoia. Yes they had booked his Norston interview for him. They'd organised it right down to timetable checks, presenting this as his way of salvation, like Chekhov replacing religion. It offered a quick absolution. Or was mistrust there in his nature? Likewise sons disowning their fathers, deceiving, or being deceived by their wives? And would this be transmitted to Mark?

Verity was tapping her watch. "Come on honey, we're late. I'm off to get ready. Meet me outside at the car." She gave him a kiss on the cheek

He caught her in the entrance hall. The main display was wall-to-wall carols. Sprigs of holly burst from every available surface. Bouquets of mistletoe bristling with beads and red ribbons hung from brass chandeliers surrounding an oversized Christmas tree, which dominated the entrance. A family was leaving with children and luggage, stacking their goods in a pile. A dog sat chewing its lead.

"Let's not go out. We need time together."

"But that's exactly what we'll have! Storford is too good to miss, and I'd be killing two birds with. Anyway, you just love nosing around. Point is, we need new slants for my show and this could be my ideal location Plus I'd steal a march on Susanne Anyway, women directors! They can be bitches with other women."

"But . . ."

"You're not keen on Victorian kitchens? Okay, okay." She raised both her hands in submission. "First . . . first we'll look round your beautiful theatre. Come on, let's go. You can show me around your set for Three Sisters. Is that a done deal?"

He pictured the Majestic's façade. She'd see the 'Laughalong!' And Cinderella adverts. In this asymmetrical world, Manwess was mining the Earth's molten core while Eddie Craig scavenged its crust. Pantomime ruled and Garrick was living a lie. Unwittingly he had set himself up.

"Nope. First things first. I'd rather see the kitchens with you. Whenever else would I get such a chance?"

"Then Uncle Anton must be good for the soul. It's the Cherry Orchard effect." She pressed a provocative kiss on his mouth. "Okay sexy, we'll tell the kids all about it when we get back. Let's go."

"Good morning, madam, sir." The early desk staff were formal. "Welcome to a brand new dawn. You weren't disturbed last night I trust?"

Verity cast a quick look at Garrick. "In what way? Exactly?"

The clerk leaned confidentially over. "Some local, how shall I say, theatricals? In the Halifax Bar Right under your room. From the Majestic. You can change suites if you want." He referred to his screen, then his attention shifted to Garrick . "And did Sir sort out his particular problems? Sir will be around? The management are revising security issues And the police are making formal enquiries, this morning. I've been advised they'll need to consult you regarding the taking of statements. That is regarding the theft of a watch."

Verity intervened. "No problem. My husband will co-operate fully As best as he can. Regrettably we've prior arrangements." She extended her finest dentifrice smile. "Right now, we're running late, so tell your managers to keep all the messages for our return. Okay Gary, let's go."

As they turned to move, a young woman in cleaner's smock tugged at Garrick's jacket and pointed. This was his penalty. The price of local fame. This is what press exposure did.

"Sorry!" He waved her away. "I don't sign autographs off-duty."

But the girl almost curtsied to Vee. "But aren't you like.in the news? Famous?"

Verity backed off. "No. I don't think so."

"Sorry yes, but you are!" the girl corrected. "I seen you in Seasonal Features, New Year's special. The Sun and The Mail." She thrust a menu into Verity's hands. "Please, put 'To Jacinta with love'. Then your own name. Please miss? Please. I don't mind whoever you are."

As their hired Chevy squelched away, a police car arrived and parked in the 'Disabled' bay. Two plainclothes detectives got out and wandered languidly into the Castle Hotel.

Verity took the Daleside route by Olde Castle Mount, turning at the Motoscoot junction heading towards Temple Storford. As they passed near Abigail's home her presence reasserted itself. Garrick half expected police sirens behind them. This morning he'd found two Crowning Glory trade-cards secreted in one of the drawers. Maybe others lurked in acts of conscious sabotage. By taking this break from rehearsals he'd be avoiding such problems as how to make Cinderella look an ingénue? Trixie was hardly the type. Then that bloody pastry scene? Flour and water like nuclear warfare! All bums, tits and baking powder! You couldn't be refined about farce. Its formula was fixed and eternal.

As the dual carriageway rises in an arc above the broad Fluvor plain, its gradient takes you higher and higher. Below them, faint cutouts of buildings rose through a mousse of pale mist where everything seemed to be melting. A few remaining factory chimneys rise like stalks in the valleys. Below the escarpment, countryside stretches in every direction. This was all his catchment zone, this in-between-land interspersed with small towns. Would they flock to see Anton Pavlovich Chekhov from here?

Verity stamped on the brakes. Road signs announced Brinkside Asphalt's latest resurfacing project, diverting traffic into one lane. As they crawled forward Verity cursed and Temple Storford seemed to recede. Low clouds trailed fingers of rain through the distance. As soft wooded pasture dissolves, Sollihurst Gap is the fault-line. At Saddletop Junction the earth's crust appears randomly tilted. Windswept moors are dottled with bracken and sheep. A National Trust sign points towards "Temple Storford". The by-road twists around outcrops of rock.

Josh was stumping the lanes beneath Castle Mound where middle-aged middle-class build walls round their lives. The Roberts might see themselves as "upwardly-mobile" with crap about 'Poetry, Progress and Art'! Pretentiousness may be an art, but there was nothing comic about it.

It was time to sort everything out. Despite his clear invitations Abby pretended not to respond. Perhaps in her eyes Josh was a labourer, not a serious artist? A backroom technician? A nerd? But not one of the Garrick Jones' luvvies. Josh had already broken with Roddy after his builders' yard jibes when she'd been the main butt of his humour. Now Roddy was laughing aloud and alone, Abby had written Josh off. He who'd just had his hair trimmed, and invested in tailored twill trousers, new suede jacket and shoes? How ironic was that? That's why he needed to put her in some kind of context.

As he reached the top of Mill Lane, low sunlight flared briefly, then faded. A rising wind blew any footsteps away. Cobblestones pressed underfoot as he passed recycled warehouses. "Brinkhouse de Luxe Apartments" signboards proclaimed. A Sikh in Norston United scarf; a woman walking two poodles; a burqua'd figure flapping as black as disguise; all gave him swift looks. He was not invisible but irredeemably rooted in earth: not stalking but walking, then holed up in his black-painted bedroom at nights.

He'd zigzagged through 19th century terraces, through countless Coronation Streets, crossing racial and cultural ghettos. Sikhs, Bangladeshis, Jamaicans, Punjabis, Muslims, Hindus, and sprinklings of Orthodox Jews. Dogs barked behind fences; pigeons fluttered and flocked. Abigail would be waiting whether she knew it or not. That freckled pink nose. Those trembling lips. Those wisps of copper-toned hair. His inbuilt radar homed in on her person and he knew in his heart that she cared.

At Castleton Road the neighbourhood changed; scattered bungalows looked as if they'd been dropped from the sky and compressed. Then came lines of semi-detacheds. Conifers and crazy paving ran riot. The avenue ended abruptly below where the castle's outer defences rose like burial mound subsumed into a community play park. Above these fortifications black clouds continued to roll. A strange morning umbra spread like an unpredicted eclipse and everywhere barometers dropped. It was as if a dark wing passed over the sky, confusing the streetlights, disrupting their brief hibernation.

Nothing felt familiar, though Josh had visited it hundreds of times in his mind. He thought he knew it back-to-front, but this was her antithesis. Like himself she did not belong. By checking house numbers he found a forecourt furnished with fibreglass nymphs and oversized Arcadian urns. He tried to imagine her there. Was Abigail posed in the warmth of her bedroom, naked in front of a mirror? Was she feeling her body and maybe even thinking of him?

A loud clap of thunder. Splats of black rain. Bloated clouds bursting. When lightening hit, a steel pylon crashed and Josh's mental screen blanked out. He dragged his hood down over his forehead and scurried back towards the main road. He found a bus shelter packed with pensioners, shoulder to shoulder awaiting the 17 bus into town.

Temple Storford House borders its man-made lake surrounded by parkland created by Capability Brown, planted with cedars, pines, and avenues of chestnuts and limes. As you drive through Lodge Gates, a cattle-grid grumbles a drum-roll of greeting. To Verity this felt like a paean of welcome. At the end of this vista, looms the great house itself like a composite architectural essay seen through damp mists. There it was. Just like a painting.

"Pure Englishness," Verity thought. "Jacobean fascia with Georgian additions and flurries of Regency Gothic". Ideal for that opening wide-shot and alone worth their visit to Norston. Off the top of her head, they'd fade up on a wide-angle lens (to set the location), then mix through a montage of rooms direct to the kitchens? Maybe opening captions could run over this?

The closer they got, the bigger the edifice grew. Its scale was deceptive. It was everything Garrick admired yet distrusted. Not till they emerged from their car did a day, which began as unseasonably mild, lose any restraint. Clouds blew like volcanic dust. Bay trees and bushes rolled with the punches. Verity clutched Garrick's hand as they joined the next guided tour shuffling into the main hall.

A punctilious guide with an NCO voice strutted ahead. In the centre stood a vast open fireplace, framed with marble pilastered grotesques like a memorial chapel. A long trestle table ran the hall's length. According to the commentary, this plank of solid oak had not been moved since construction in 1672, cut from a single tree on the estate and assembled on site, complete with four matching trestles.

"Right. Now it's on to the kitchens." The guide strode ahead. "And please everyone, mind the steps! It's half an hour to hospital!" Everyone laughed as required.

Verity pushed to the front as they entered a set of big rooms vaulted with heavy wood fanlights and panelled with louvres and glass. Verity felt her first thrill of excitement. White enamels reflected white light. Handmade white tiles added an almost swimming pool feel. Passing reflections slashed rhomboid panels across limewashed walls in a wildly theatrical gesture. This was real and authentic; a whole culinary lifestyle. It was 'Cooking the Victorian Way' And so much scrubbed pine! With utensils, graded, stacked and labelled, tier upon tier like armour. They'd love this back in the States. Salt-glazed earthenware, polished brass, and china like pure Beatrix Potter: rows of dried spices in ornate glass jars: jars of pickles, bins of assorted flours. This was a salted, boiled and pickled cuisine, complete with real-life preserves. She turned round to comment, but Gary had gone as if he'd slipped out again for a "nicotine fix". Just as she'd feared, he'd reverted.

The guide fended off more and more of Verity's questions. He demonstrated mechanical jacks and clockwork spits, pointing out slaloms of ladles, aware she was starting to corner attention. Everything from graters, flatirons and trivets, to bellows and fry-pans, colanders, graders and sieves. Copper pans like polished gongs. No he didn't cook, but everything here was authentic! And yes, Lady Peggy insisted on that. In fact some demonstrations were supervised by the lady herself. And yes, all food was estate-grown and organic And yes, yes, yes! Of course the bread ovens worked!

He turned to charts of carcasses displayed like colonial maps. A riot of basting, pickling, boiling and roasting, so vivid she could hear the animals slaughtered. Chopping blocks and salting trays. Huge basins of lard. Ribs and haunches like torture. Hand-cranked Buchenwald images infiltrated her thoughts. She sat on the nearest bench and felt faint.

As she did so, a woman in a Burberry checks was staring. Soon a little group gathered. A British babushka tugged Verity's sleeve, took a quick photo, then turned triumphantly back to the others.

"What did I say? We thought it was you!" She seized Verity's hand, and the group applauded. "We're so looking forward to your next show."

As they were driving out of the park, loaded with postcards, guidebooks, brochures, and photos, Garrick explained how when he'd slipped out he'd seen a man looking like his theatre boss. But Arthur Ruddock meant nothing to her. Then just as they were approaching the exit, a Range Rover emerged between trees and lazily swung into their path. It stopped dead with no signals. Garrick braked. Tyres slithered and squealed on loose gravel as they swung past. As distance stretched out behind them, Garrick could make out George de Vries and Arthur Ruddock unrolling maps, then pointing back at the house

Verity shuddered, "Behaving like they own the damn road!"

Back at their hotel the receptionist called them over. Their pigeonhole was overflowing she said, handing thick wadges of letters to Vee who dragged Garrick aside.

"Jesus! How come this lot's addressed to me? No one's meant to know I'm here!" She turned on the desk clerk. "Now listen to me. I'm anonymous, right. I've made that quite clear."

A manager intervened. "Apologies, but I happen to know that one's a note from the police. They come back twice expecting you. I told them as you'd planned to pay them a visit. They'd found that red car, abandoned in Liverpool. Nicked of course." He anticipated Garrick's next question. "And no sir, sorry sir, not retrieved as far as I know. It's probably been sold on for drugs." The manager looked sympathetic. "Me too, I'm on your side. I'd have them assholes castrated!"

One large brown envelope was addressed to Garrick, rubber-stamped "Official". Two others were filming schedules for Vee, which she thrust in her bag, without comment. This left a single envelope addressed in longhand to "Garrick Jones, Director of Productions, c/o The Castle Hotel" which did not fit in. He quickly slipped away to the loo and tore open the hand-written letter:

NORSTON MERCURY
incorporating THE LANCASHIRE STAR,
62-65 High Street, Norston

From the desk of Elizabeth Scott:

"Dear Garrick,

Remember me? I am very persistent. This is by way of reminder. My contacts tell me you are staying here this weekend. Lucky you! You did promise me an interview. What is more, you guaranteed to ring me back. What happened? If you have changed your mind, we shall pursue other sources and not trouble you, but at least I tried to give you your side of the story. I cannot say fairer than that.

I put this in writing so you will have it on record . Look forward to hearing from you by return. But if not . . .
Love from Liz. "

Verity saw Garrick folding the letter and frowning. As elevator doors opened behind her a group of Italian tourists emerged dragging luggage on wheels. She pounced.

"Not another final demand?"

"What?" Garrick seemed startled. "Oh this?" He casually ripped the envelope up and tossed it into an ashcan. "It's hotel spam, that's all," but crunched the letter up in his pocket.

She had not been prepared for Norston: not paparazzi with microphones primed and cameras on auto-focus. Crowded elevators came and went all round them. People spilled in and out. Some looked at her and waved.

"How come everyone knows who I am?"

"I've set you up?" He put a comforting arm round her. "Is that what you're saying?"

"Just coincidence, right?"

Then that shiny glass ashtray! What the hell was he thinking? It put her marriage into perspective, making the Christmas tree in the foyer seemed lurid. Wasn't it meant commemorate birth? She thought of her children alone and could not suppress tears. Gary's work had become the distraction.

"Look, I didn't choose to get robbed." He sounded so disengaged. "I'll make sure the regional press doesn't hear. It won't get reported. Okay?"

She shook her head and walked off, and he knew when he was beaten. Later they'd sit on the bed and phone home to their children. But first he would let her stew a few moments, so he wandered across to the bar.

No matter how much he kept shaking his head, walls refused to stay upright, and verticals nudged horizontals. The bar seemed to fill the whole space, but when the floor started to sway it proved one couldn't rely on one's senses. The gossip was that some lunatic had got mugged by attempted suicide bombers who'd stolen some identity. Then there was talk of celebrity tarts in the district. At each repetition everything became more grotesque. Then the atmosphere changed. Voices were lowered and scribbled notes exchanged. He'd heard Eddie Craig's name several times, along with Brinkside and Brinkhouse, always followed by moments of silence followed by other familiar names. He had not arranged a time to meet Vee, but time must have been suspended, because however hard he stared at his wrist it refused to respond.

As he hurried out to the foyer, he came face to face with a young porter pushing a trolley of luggage like an accident waiting to happen. As Garrick reeled, the porter continued as if nothing had happened. It was then Garrick noticed. That new matching luggage? So ultra-distinctive! Complete with nametags and belts! These were Verity's cases and this was the oldest trick in the game!

He lunged and kneed the man in the groin, upending the trolley, scattering cases and yelling to uniformed doormen. Big burly men moved quick as dancers, pinning Garrick's arm up his back. Security guards emerged from the woodwork and wrestled him to the ground.

"Oh-oh. I'm sorry guys." Verity was as soothing and calm as ever. "Looks like there's been some misunderstanding. What's technically known as 'crossed wires'!" She rounded on Garrick. "They're taking my bags to my car. I've had a change of plan." She flipped several banknotes to the groaning young victim. "However My husband will be staying on. Look after him please?"

She turned towards onlookers and knew she had to respond. "You see, it's about being a parent. It's about loving And not dodging pain." She sensed they identified strongly. "Kids are extensions of ourselves in a truly generational sense. That's why I've got to leave this beautiful town." She blew kisses from the palm of her hand, "I do love you all!". And whispered loudly to Garrick. "Don't forget, it's my first TV trails this weekend." She tapped meaningfully at her watch. "So, don't you miss them, okay."

Spectators gathered, applauding, as she signed their last few autographs and left. As her rear lights disappeared the fact began to sink in. She really had gone, and time had begun to unravel, tangling itself into knots. He was bruised and alone and booked in for the night. Then out of desperation came a wild idea, materialising from nowhere, and Garrick quickly began sobering up.

Of course Vee was right. Having paid for their room, he might as well stay. It was that simple. He could read scripts in bed with breakfast included. Besides, further research was essential. Actors could sense hesitation and any lack of preparation showed. The pressure was on, but the irony was that while he was going highbrow, Vee was trading down. Polarities reversed. Their graph-lines might even have already crossed. She was the one who'd be starring on everyone's screens as he withered away on the vine.

When he called the police they made sympathetic responses but insisted he dropped in a statement to please his insurers, and help their efficiency targets. In that case he'd nip quickly back to the theatre and collect appropriate books. But by the time he'd reached The Majestic he was missing Vee all the more. He paid off the taxi. The night sky was icily clear, its blackness sprinkled with diamonds. You could never escape the environment here. A rising wind spiralled the turrets, tearing at flagpoles. His office felt even more claustrophobic, while far down below, swinging street lamps exaggerated that scar on the vista marking Eddie Craig's steady advance

One by one Garrick collected relevant books and was ready to leave, when sentiment overwhelmed him. He knelt and kissed each family photo. Even as he switched off the light, all these realities changed. Millions of raindrops played hell with the spectrum, satirising the cosmos. Slowly random patterns defocused, re-forming into a recognisable shape with wide-open eyes, freckled cheeks and soft smiling lips, because brains are hardwired to formulate faces.

So there she was. Abigail staring straight into his soul.

As he walked back he recited 'The Ancient Mariner' to himself like a mantra, watching his feet hit the pavement.

"The ice was here, the ice was there,
The ice was all around:
It cracked and growled, and roared and howled,
Like noises in a swound! . . ."

At some point an autopilot must have cut out. Next time he looked up, Club Arabica was steadily moving towards him. When verses became incantations such was the power of cheap couplets that poets demanded revenge. This was a carefully laid Coleridge trap. Louise had not only backtracked on his follow-up bookings, but the Albatross Curse was gliding Garrick back to the scene of his crime. He lowered the umbrella over his face. Glass beads drummed on taut fabric. He thought he heard someone calling, but it might have been a trick of the echoes. He quickened up. From somewhere came scampering footsteps.

Abigail clamped a bag on her head as she ran. "Hang on!" she was yelling, "Hang on," then snuggled up under cover. " Hey! Why didn't you stop? That Mercury woman was really knocked out by your readings. Didn't you hear? Everyone loved you. You'd even got Jilly in tears. Says it reminded her more like a movie it was so trendy-cool. Next thing she'll sell icebergs with albatross trimmings. I bet your face'll be next up in her shop."

She noticed Garrick's briefcase. Why wasn't he at the hotel? And where was his wife? And why was he walking through town? But Coleridge rhythms drowned out the rain as Garrick tried to switch off.

208

"And soon I heard a roaring wind:
It did not come anear;
But with its sound it shook the sails,
That were so thin and sere . . .

". . . And the coming wind did roar more loud,
And the sails did sigh like sedge:
And the rain poured down from one black cloud;
The Moon was at its edge . . ."

Despite his instinctive resistance, he was unexpectedly touched by her fervour.

"Abby," he was saying, "I've just had a thought. Why don't you come for a meal? You see, my wife, Verity She's had to dash home to London. Family matters, I'm afraid." He grinned reassuringly. "So what do you say? Just to keep me company? To maintain my morale?. After all, you are my assistant. What do you say?"

They watched cooling rainwater fracture into liquid glass then swivel away down the gutters. If gravity worked like a warp in the mesh it reflected the shape of a car. At the edge of his vision it hurtled towards them, but nothing could happen by chance: what Coleridge would have called Fate.

As Garrick snatched Abigail back, the vehicle aquaplaned past, slithered through red lights, then disappeared into limitless space.

People did not seem ready for Christmas. It felt like meagre icing on an indifferent cake. Nobody wanted to spend. That evening the hotel restaurant was scattered with á la Carte locals and a few travelling salesmen. Garrick knew what to expect because Verity always checked everything out. In her professional eyes, quality meant cutlery laid to formulae accurate to 0.005mm centred on a single white orchid: it meant matching white damask tablecloths and origami napkins, with Wilton-weave carpets as deep as rain-forest moss and body-shaped chairs upholstered in pure textured velvets, beneath chandeliers like polished icicles. Shades of crimson textured the dining room walls. Behind a jungle of Kentia palms a pianist's fingers skittered over a keyboard.

Last night's waiters showed no recognition, directing him to last night's table. Then they'd been over-attentive to Vee, but now they fixed on Abigail. He sensed their curiosity and felt unjustly accused. People always jumped to conclusions. He ordered more wine and felt better, but as he replenished and emptied his glass he noticed Abby drank very little. The more their conversation flagged, Garrick resorted to his old stock anecdotes. Before long he was reduced to being himself, forgetting Anna, Varya, Gayev and Boris, while watching Abigail's lips.

"Abigail Had you thought . . . ?" With intense concentration he overcame any hint of slur. "If only we could live our lives knowing where Where our our actions would lead." A waiter dived in and topped up their glasses. "I mean . . . each trivial . . . or should we say each indiscretion? Any slightest risk . . . even the most passing pleasure. If we only had the advantage of hindsight beforehand? . . . If you see what I mean?"

As wines began to take hold they reminded of that series of flukes, which led him to Norston. After all, it began with a newspaper cutting. When they'd snipped out that advert, who could have predicted its outcome? Who knew where any action would lead? I fear thee, Ancient Mariner! I fear thy skinny hand! When alcohol was blurring his brain, his only defence was to laugh.

"Sorry?" Abigail was frowning. "I don't get it."

He leaned forward, helplessly grinning, elbows on table, chin in hands, at peace with the world, loving all mankind as his neighbours. "Don't get what?"

"You said Temple Storford?. You've been talking about Temple Storford." When he shook his head she protested. "Yes you have. On and on about her. And her kitchens."

"Are you sure?"

"And which room did you get in the end? . . . Room 112?"

He seemed to examine his wineglass, twisting its stem, noting the sheen, weighing it up in his hand, distorting the brilliant spectra, trying to refocus his thoughts. She couldn't resist.

"You're lying. You did!"

Out in Reception, laughing guests trekked from bar to bar clutching Champagne cocktails with mini-sushi on sticks while carols repeated on digital loops

"Affluent Christmas!" everything said, "Affluent Christmas to you! Affluent Christmas to you! We wish you affluent Christmas! Wealthy Christmas to you!" There was no escape from Goodwill. "God bless you merry gentlemen, let bargains come galore" rang through air-conditioning ducts, fire doors and sprinklers, repeated ad infinitum, "Ding dong merrily on high!" was followed by descants and counterpoint chants. Even the elevator sang its way up.

They emerged to a fanfare then processed to a joyous fugue, which broke into G major complete with antiphonal effects, climaxing as a triumphant chorus. Rooms 104,106, 108, 110, 112 . . . Garrick produced his entrycard with a snap. As if on cue the music cut out.

"You didn't believe me?" He held the card teasingly up to the lock.

Abigail knew that Stacey had broken every known rule. She'd spread her own petals convinced she'd always bloom and bloom. Inevitably she was going to seed. She had been deflowered and deflowered. There was a lesson there.

Garrick waited. "Okay? All bets still on?" He flicked his card through the receptor.

As the door swung open she felt no surprise. Memories clicked into place. It felt like dropping in on friends. Everything was as she remembered and just as she knew it would be, with the bed folded back and ready for occupation. Garrick's clothes lay neatly folded, his suitcases placed on a stand like the brochure. She mentally recorded the image knowing that Jilly Craske's trade-cards lay welcoming, secreted everywhere, despite Verity's 'Joie de Vivre' and 'Roman' whose fierce aromas were Verity's markers, her territorial statements. One single molecule, even a solitary atom said Madame Rochas! She knew instinctively what to do.

Having checked the leather-bound folder containing the "escritoire" pack, she hunted down every Jilly Craske card. This was her ultimate act of retrieval. Then with a mini-aerosol, she sprayed out the faintest of hints, one primal scent overwriting another, as Garrick looked on in surprise.

She nodded at striped pyjamas folded on the coverlet. "You wear those!" She patted a pillow and straightened a sheet, running a fingertip over soft linen. "Your wife? She didn't like fancy our room?"

His laugh sounded strained. "Something cropped up. She's always on call. There's satellite-tracking devices. Everyone's pinpointed down. They probably knew which side of the bed we . . ." He was visibly sobering up. "Never mind. Don't worry, I'll get you a cab."

He'd started to dial, then thought he could hear running water gurgling and drumming with echo-chamber effects.

"Abby? Where are . . . ?"

Her head appeared from the bathroom, hair dripping, shoulders bare. She gave an open-mouthed smile, pointed at the folder, then bobbed out of sight. Her after-image persisted. Her discarded clothes lay casually strewn on the carpet. Amongst House Rules and Price Lists he found dozens of trade cards for Jilly Craske's "Crowning Glory" alongside leaflets for "Club Arabica".

If Abigail were Olga, Chekhov would have written dialogue full of real meaning. No rhyming couplets. No pompous prose. Something witty maybe? Something cutting? Even romantic? Most of all, ambiguous. But Vee? Or Rosanna? Those Morozovas never once sang in a bath. Their passion went into their work. That's why their kids preferred Vee. She gave them a sense of direction. They sobbed when she stayed out at nights. She deserved their total devotion. He realized she'd not phoned him back, and he needed to know she'd got safely home. As he turned away, a hand slid round the edge of the door, felt for the light switch, and plunged the whole room into darkness.

"Oops!" Her breath seemed to come from nearby, "Now it's too late to go home. My mum'd go mad. I'm knackered. And it's freezing." Abigail's naked figure was rimmed with a sliver of light.

Common sense meant him telling her straight. It meant not pulling punches. The facts were straightforward. Married man. Two children. A mortgaged house in Lancaster Gate.

He felt a soft mouth at his cheeks and fingers unbutton his shirt. Next he was helping her tear off his clothes, ripping zips, shredding seams, spattering buttons like seeds.

Moments later they entwined in the sheets.

Garrick awoke with a start, his skull awash with liquidised brain. He extended his fingers and made contact with chilly white cambric. He was stretched out, naked alone half-in and half-out of the sheets on an extra-wide double bed. This wasn't Baker's Row and it certainly wasn't Lancaster Gate. He'd definitely drunk too much. Bright numerals came into focus. 07:20 they proclaimed, winking knowingly, so Vee must be out in the lobby packing her luggage and . . .

He jack-knifed to life! He tested the rest of the mattress. Yes. He was alone. By himself. He was swept with relief. It had all been a bizarre, grubby dream. Not that Coleridge was ever what you'd call 'sober', imagining ghost ships and conjuring nightmares at sea, nor were his mutinies, shipwrecks and murders real. Everyone's a fantasist. That was the human condition. The brain could generate wondrous effects. You could see them in Shakespeare. And even Chekhov. To be certain he made a quick search of the rooms. Tongue in cheek he checked wardrobes, lobby, and bathroom, but no sign. Nothing! No traces of lipstick. No screwed-up tissues. No sandy hairs in the basin. As if she had never existed. He was completely confident now. Those marks on his body must have come from the previous night. Even he couldn't manage two nights in a row!

It proved how vivid dreams could be! Not that they'd ever seemed real. Unless the desire had fathered the thought? As true and as corny as that? He sat on the edge of the bath and relaxed. In a flood of relief he almost felt sentimental. First he must contact Vee. She had driven for hours just to see him. Gratitude overwhelmed him. A full-blown hangover threatened, but their marriage had deserved celebration. He had nothing to feel guilty about.

He picked his way barefoot over the carpet as if crossing a minefield. Only then did he notice the video unit. Then everything fell into place. It was obvious now. He'd been dehydrated and drunk. A late-nite movie must have intercut with his dreams. The monitor screen was still fizzing away. What had occurred was a series of misunderstandings. His priority now was producing the show, and for the very first time Cinderella trumped Chekhov. Pippa and Trixie, James Carr, Lionel Parsons and the rest of the cast came to mind. Only one face was blank, pixilated and blotted-out.

The bed lay deserted Even the bathroom was tidy. As if no further proof were needed the mini-fridge contents were intact. Nothing else was amiss. He was well and truly alone. Why feel guilty for what hadn't happened? He popped a quick beer, gulping it straight from the can then decided to quickly phone Vee. She was always up early.

On impulse he checked the visitor's folder but all those Crowning Glory adverts had gone, as had the leaflet for Louise's nightclub. His scripts and textbooks reminded him rehearsals were due. Soon the whole cast would be hungover and waiting. Their party at the hotel had purposely excluded him, but what if they'd known he was staying upstairs? James Carr, Trixie, Pippa, and Lionel, with Reggie Buck and Orlando Marcel! Little did they know!

He popped one more lager before making his final inspection. After his shower he noticed he was missing a sock, and was pulling back bedclothes to check . . . then he saw. Crimson on fluoro-white cambric. Darkening stains on crushed linen. Raspberry blood on virginal white as forensic as a scene-of-crime.

As he stumbled back, he upended his suitcase skimming a postcard over the floor. He saw it was addressed to him. He held it up to the light. A naked couple lay entwined in an idealised landscape. Jupiter peered through a wadge of cumulo-nimbus fringed with an aura of sunbeams. It was archly baroque, yet implicit with threat. He turned it over. "Tragic Lovers in Classical Landscape" it said, "by Paul Delaroche (1797-1856)".

And beneath it in Verity's neat rounded handwriting:
"Gary honey, thanks!! See you soon. Much love from me, V, x x x,"
At that moment his phone started to ring.

CHAPTER TEN

FLASHBACKS

Heading back to Bakers Row, Garrick began to feel better. He even hummed to himself as he strolled. Light had started to seep through the darkness as if each turn of the Earth would wash any remaining shadows away. This was another immaculate dawn, a morning when nothing whatever would happen. But as the bus passed Castle Mount he almost expected Abigail's ghost. Now all things had significance. Everything hinted at meaning.

Back at his lodgings he plodded upstairs with his luggage, finding them unexpectedly steep. The narrow hallway still smelled of cats. An icy chill filled its stairwell. He did not bother to switch on a light. He could have managed blindfolded, knowing each distinctive creak of the stairs, recognising every individual step. He knew the topography of the handrail by heart because it bound all his rituals together. All this was familiar, predictable. He could switch off his brain and relax, and

Suddenly Out of nowhere Close-ups of body parts! Blurred noises Nipples, buttocks and bellies. He stopped in his tracks. Raw damp skin. Lolling tongue. Wide-open mouth. That freckled white skin. Tightly coiled pubic hair . . .

He tried shaking his head. Then more flashbacks. More revelations. Their implications appalled him. All his justifications were gone. He had secretly thought she was sleeping around because that's what young women did. He'd be on every CCTV. And what if porters or cleaning staff talked? Norston was a small gossipy town, but surely the management would be discreet. Compared with other incipient scandals, last night would hardly rate a mention. But even as he brushed this aside, some inner voice intervened, as calm and commanding as ever.

"Right. Main thing is Keep your head," Its clipped tones sounded almost quaint. "Do not panic. Keep totally calm. Your credit card's still valid even if it is overdrawn. More importantly, think, and don't feel. Steer clear morals or ethics. And finally Deny everything!"

The plot-line was clear. He had become his own dramatis persona. Now his subconscious was choreographing his moves, turning him into a puppet, scripting his dialogue too. It was the old eternal triangle plot. He was being produced and directed.

Somehow he managed to reach his little cramped landing, realising how closely he'd strayed into farce. More Bawd than Bard, he thought. Even as his door-lock clunked shut behind him his first thought was to contact Vee, make a clean breast of it and plead for forgiveness. But that inner voice cut in again, still sounding incredibly patient:

"Come on, don't be rash. How could Vee find out? Ask yourself that. So need anyone know? Consider the facts."

Not that he'd planned what happened. Nor actively set out to prevent it. This left one single outstanding question. Statistics. That is, what were the odds on pregnancy? After all, his was a marriage lasting ten years. He had a beautiful nine-year-old daughter and a wonderful six-year-old son. Whatever happened, his marriage was not under threat, but then again, his family photos looked tense in their frames. Apart from his mugging, Vee's visit had gone very well, thanks to Sanjay. She had been overwhelmed. Cut crystal was the perfect solution. It caught the anniversary mood.

He'd been flattered Vee asked him to manage her business. This was her act of commitment; her vote of total confidence. It proved she did depend on him, and he knew exactly why. Their Temple Storford visit had worked. More than that, their shared experience deepened their relationship and strengthened their love. His minor 'misjudgment' was no more than a blip in the great scheme of things. A mere biological glitch. Their motto was to forgive and forget.

He switched on the kettle, dabbing condensation from windows. Below in the street, a shaven-head with multiple rings in his lips was sticking trade-cards onto lampposts. A shivering hooker, hair dyed pink, sheltered in a bricked-up doorway. A Chinese waiter dumped bin-bags out on the kerb. Today any distraction was welcome. Everyone was their own work of art and everyone had their own act. In the pale morning light they looked insubstantial, but as sunlight skipped over the roofline, Baker's Row began to de-mist. How soon before all this was demolished to make way for one of Ruddock's grand urban vistas? Their Lebanese grocers? Their corner launderette? The Mediterranean sweetmeats? Soon only The Majestic would be left as the hub of a great urban wheel.

Because no rain was forecast, he decided to cycle. As he switched on his mobile it started to ring.

"Good morning Mr. Jones This is The Norston Castle Hotel. We've been trying to contact you, sir. Our cleaning service has contacted us We pride ourselves on attention to detail . . . first Floor tells us, a single sock was found in your room 112. It was clearly half of a pair. This has been laundered and can be collected by yourself at reception. We thank you for your custom. The Castle Hotel offers discounts for regular guests, and you can apply for Pegasus Points. Will that be all?"

He couldn't help laughing aloud. "You've really made my day! Tell you what. To show my goodwill, you can keep the sock as a memento!"

Firstly he needed a full change of clothes. Cycling was a serious business. He'd invest in nylon all-weather kit and aerodynamic helmet. First he'd empty his overnight bag. He tumbled it onto the bed. Socks, underpants, roll-necks, jeans and shirts, all crumpled out with the rest. As he picked out his wash bag, something heavy fell with a thud onto lino. Its dead weight lay wrapped in the Castle's gift paper. As he tried to grip it, a heavyweight object slid out. No sparkle, no rainbows, no glimmer. It seemed to deliberately shrink from the light. Despite its multiple facets it looked unacceptably cheap. An envelope was clinging with Sellotape. He unfolded the notelet enclosed.

'*THE NORSTON CASTLE HOTEL*', it read.

"*Dear Garrick,*" Vee had never addressed him as 'Garrick' before.

"*I guess you mean well,*" It said in her *large forceful writing*. "*As you well know, I never ever smoked. Or am I being dumb? More of your weird British humour? You made it pretty damn plain you hated our country house visit. While my momma said we'd damn all in common, it's taken me years to find out she was right.*

"*Remember it was you chose the Castle Hotel. It was you invited me down. I hope that's not a by-product of Chekhov. That'd be too damn ironic.*

"*You seem no way grateful for what I've done for you and the kids. Now I miss them so much more. Can't wait to get home. Hope I've not wasted those years. I guess we need major revaluation. Think about it.*

"*I gave it my best shot. Do not say I never tried! I'm waiting your apologies. By that I mean now!*

Vee."

He folded the note and stuffed it in his back pocket.

As he pedalled, the phrase kept repeating. "Serious revaluation." And this was before what happened next. What the hell did she mean? He'd have to find out. On Mondays most of the cast arrived semi-dazed after dashes down South, but he knew this time many stayed back. Their celebrations had been too close for comfort. He'd have to phone Vee before they turned up for rehearsal. Her notelet was still in his pocket. Urgent phone calls had to be made before they arrived.

Garrick was wheeling his bike with its rucksack of scripts towards the Church Hall when he first noticed Phyllis; hair freshly styled and trimmed, streaked and dyed as if she'd just left Crowning Glory. And wasn't she wearing new glasses? And a smart woollen coat? She looked sprightly, younger, even trendy. She gave a quick wave, but he decided he had not seen her. He'd have to phone Vee straightaway. He opened the porch door, slipped silently in, then ran straight into Trixie.

She kissed him enthusiastically. "Hi boss! You're late! Sorry pet, only jokin'!" She pulled her alpaca coat tighter. " It's near enough freezing in

216

there. Enough to freeze off Lionel's balls. If he's got any. They're too bastard mean to turn up the heating."

Lionel had appeared from behind her. "Oh how true, Trixie. How horribly true." He looked dapper in sheepskin corduroy. "I'd be better off playing Santa in Tesco's. There at least I'd be warm."

"Been there! Done it!" Reggie Buck was yelling to cheers. "One thing, Mister Director, in this town there's part-time comics what call themselves 'stand-ups'! Yeah? But they look like they're wilting to me! Got more fuckin' laughs before they was born! An' that was jus' by bein' born!" He stamped a foot and spread out his arms.

"Boom boom!" everyone chorused.

If Reggie Buck was a bigot he'd ended up playing himself, but pantomime needed mass confirmation. "Oh yes it does!" followed by "Oh no it doesn't!". It all came down to rites and responses like a congregation's chant. The mechanics came down to split-second timing, but James Carr was still holding forth about the 'Devaluation of Art' and their 'Noble Profession'.

". . . What's more, I spent the weekend re-reading Yuri Orlov's 'Stanislavsky'," James was now saying, "Such wonderful, wonderful stuff. The Moscow Art Theatre you see. And of course Anton Chekhov! Dear, wonderful, Chekhov. I love him." He turned to Garrick and beamed. "You should give it a go. He is all about intense dedication."

Still no sign of Abigail yet but no-one referred to her absence. Pippa was flashing her batwing eyelashes. Her lilac-pink lips smooched from her coffee cream mouth:

"The nightlife up here. It's a dream."

"'Scuse me Boss!" Reggie was raising a hand, "I've got another great idea. What if I do my Reggie Buck walk at the start of the scene?" He demonstrated his famous heel-toe, knock-kneed saunter like some double-jointed seal. "It'll make the whole show."

Truman and Goss suggested playing the two Ugly Sisters as ballerinas on points. Everyone wanted to talk.

Reggie was getting excited. "Another thought. Couldn't they play a long faaart on trombone when I enter?" He bent double, going bright red in the face. "See what I mean?" He blew a long raspberry through bloated lips. "The line before is 'Don't get the wind up!' And so, with my clever timing, it'd get a fantabulous laugh."

"Jesus Christ, Reggie!" Garrick gave a one-fingered gesture. "Just bloody play it for laughs!" And Reggie's large face compressed into a pout like a baby's.

Now the real nitty-gritty took over. James Carr began raising obscure metaphysical points about pronouns, syntax, and grammar, with intricate semantics followed by exquisite examinations of psychological inter-reactions, questioning entire motivations, and complaining about inappropriate rhymes. Consequently the more they rehearsed, the more laboured the scenes, like fighting inside a sack with both hands tied.

"Why'm I attempting pirouettes?" James was demanding, "One, I can't dance. And two, Baron Hardup is meant to be angry! It doesn't make sense."

Garrick raised both hands in despair. "It's not meant to make sense. It's meant to be funny. Humorous. Funny ha-ha. It's meant make people laugh."

By the time the choreographer came, there was still no sign of Abigail. When Fabian pointed this out, Garrick began to get nervous. Every time a door opened a yawning pit seemed to open before him. When it came to the steps of the Polka, Lionel and James felt their dignity threatened. They shuffled. They stumbled. They moaned. They complained.

"But you have to be dancing." Garrick pleaded. "That's what people do at balls!"

Reggie waved a suggestive finger. "Bit obsessed with the prince's balls, aren't we?" He thrust his hands on his hips. "It's enough to make rats turn into horses! And as for that fat, poncy pumpkin, if we don't take care it'll turn into some bloody great coach!"

They did not know how lucky they were. Garrick couldn't help thinking of poor bloody Chekhov, in and out of sanatoria, in and out of spas, exhaling aerosol blood, coughing up bronchial tissue with not an antibiotic in sight. To think he had died little older than Garrick was now.

He felt Verity's note burning its way through in his pocket. At least she had a sense of proportion. After talking it through with Roseanne she'd see it wasn't his fault he'd been mugged. Returning his gift was petty and crude. But misapprehensions occurred. It was he who would have to mend fences, just like his mother and father. Resquiat in Pace it said as they both shared the same granite block. What would Vee tell his kids about him? Truman and Wade were still arguing details when Garrick glanced round.

"Hi," Abigail mouthed, casually sorting out props.

Her sheer normality came as a shock. She was ambling offhandedly round as though nothing had happened although everyone knew she was late. It was she in her plasticised bubble: he in his metal-mesh cage. At the moment of death one's whole life is said to flash by. Now Garrick's life flickered like old-fashioned movies, all jump-cuts, jolts and defocused frames reduced to a single monochrome image. It was Abigail's inner strength against Garrick's reserve. Chekhov might have indulged the dilemma.

"Abby?" he whispered, "Abby? Later?"

Some sixth sense should have intervened but Garrick's mobile caught him out.

"Hiyah!" Verity's voice emerged from some outdoor acoustic. "I'm down here, live, in Wilton House. The Wilton House. Henry Herbert's. Yes? . We're doing roast venison haunch in their kitchens followed by fruits-of-the-forest gateaux and, yes, that Palladian Bridge in the grounds, it puts Temple Storford to shame." She noticeably changed down a gear. "Be straight with me Gary. You did get my note? We need a frank talk if we . . ." He heard a bell ring, urgent asides, then she rang off.

A split second later she phoned back.

He pressed the mouthpiece close to his lips. "Vee, I can't talk."

"Hi dad!" came a small voice, "It's me. Rachel says I've not to call."

"Mark. I can't speak."

He heard a deep intake of breath. "Mum didn't come home. She had to go down to location. Love you dad, bye." And the line had gone dead.

Occluded light was sieved through stained glass before draining away into shadows.

Elizabeth Scott parked in the single free space of what was left of Norston's old market. The once-thriving bazaar felt like a dinosaur park where bulldozers ravaged and raged. Mobile offices stood where stalls used to be, and earth-moving equipment rested under flapping tarpaulins. A massive American juggernaut was moored alongside like a battleship stencilled 'CRAIG DEMOLITION' next to containers labelled 'MANWESS GAS'. The message was clear; this was a major alliance. Her little hired Vauxhall looked pale and diminished.

She fixed a fake pass to its windscreen and sat for a moment checking her laptop, clicking on Garrick's full details. As she strolled up to the theatre past lines of trenches, she had a disturbing compulsion to gag. She took a deep breath, choked and looked round, feeling sick. That faint aroma? Like rotting eggs? She licked her finger, held it erect, before placing it on her tongue. The taste and smell quickly faded. Herds of dumper trucks were grubbing up debris as bulldozers churned geological cake. Their excavations ploughed through millennia as whole eras vanished and civilisations expired. All there seemed to be left was this hole. All Norston's past might there. She approached gingerly and stared into a vertical shaft.

At first she saw only blackness and then beneath a lattice of tubing and pipes she saw faint reflections, rising and falling as if with a tide. It seemed to have a life of its own. Like alien lungs. Her suspicions ran riot. Did underground tunnels connect with some arcane dystopian world? And wasn't that more than just a faint hint of odour?

'WARNING. GAS MAINTENANCE. DANGER' announced new fluorescent signs, 'NO TRESPASSING. BY ORDER . INTRUDERS WILL BE PROSECUTED'.

This wasn't her kind of story; she was the Human Interest Factor.

Phyllis examined Liz through gold bifocals. "Sorry love, they're at outside rehearsal."

Phyllis had enough to do. Recent announcements had come as a shock and details needed confirming. Checking up wasn't her job. She returned to her emails, glad to have brought her own paraffin stove, but Liz kept insisting she'd definitely made an appointment.

She waved her ID in Phyllis's face. "This is me. Elizabeth Scott! Look! And you know how often I've phoned?"

Sometimes bluffing could work but Phyllis was good at stonewalling, having honed her technique with the master himself. Rex Schulman himself had once praised her (Dear Rex. Lovely Rex. Sweet caring, adorable Rex) Lizzie took a seat and decided to wait. This was the journalist's burden. Reporters weren't welcome except with good news. Now it was evens, deadlock, and draw. This stalemate was broken by Manwess contractors dragging hydraulic equipment, reluctantly assisted by Josh. The young man's stare was forensic. It felt as if X-rays were scanning her body. Then as they moved on, Josh gave Liz a wave.

"What's it about?" Phyllis asked, "Your appointment?"

"Oh, nothing."

"Really?" Phyllis did not react. "Better wait till they've all broken for lunch, else they get tetchy. That's half an hour's time, but don't quote me." She returned to her keyboard, a finger poised over "delete".

As any journalist knows, waiting is fifty percent of the job, so Lizzie Scott decamped to the churchyard gates, stamping to keep herself warm. Once she would have walked into rehearsals, but artistes were too superstitious. Over the years they'd been ultra-thin-skinned about her reviews. Even Rex Schulman had taken offence. They all craved attention but only expected applause, and Garrick would be just the same. That's why he was still an enigma. When her researches led round in circles it struck her as odd. Too many things did not tally, leaving big blanks in his past. You could Google yourself to a standstill, but still his details didn't add up and the library clips didn't match. Other people were almost too easy: that young Roberts girl for instance. Shouldn't she still be at school? How come she was a work-study student whose mother behaved the 'Grande Dame'? Of course, Louise Roberts was well known for Club Arabica but over-enquiring might stimulate her defences. Her latest interview with Ruddock provided few clues, but she had the impression no Chekhov plays would actually go into production. When pressed he denied that (no follow-up questions permitted), while referring to Garrick's rendition of The Ancient Mariner's Tale. The man had too many distractions, he'd moaned. Without a truly profitable show the theatre would have to close down. Everything relied on their panto. The aftermath was undecided as yet, which implied those Chekhov Players were little more than a political scam.

Again she'd started to cough. This early morning fog contained enough micro-carbons to cause acute toxoplasmosis, so Den's Coffee Bar offered her a strategic view. As the Church Hall became veiled in mist she gulped down several black coffees and reached the squat Victorian porch just as Trixie and Pippa emerged, accompanied by Lionel who recognised her at once. She stood back to let Trixie and Pippa pass. Soon Garrick would enter her sights.

"Hello sweetheart, it's me. Now's your big chance!" Lionel's orthodontistry flashed. "You're the girl from the Mercury, right? Well I'm Lionel, and you nearly missed us." He tweaked two fingers to indicate 'quotes' and flipped his woven silk scarf. "That extra special interview'? Yes?"

Sitting alone in the dark of her office, mulling things over, Phyllis needed no electronic protection. The stairs were a faultless security system. She could recognise anyone's tread. On hearing Garrick's familiar footsteps she immediately switched on all her lights. Attack was first line of defence.

"Letter for you!" Her voice sang out as he reached the first landing. "Did she get hold of you?"

Garrick tried to not to hear. Rehearsals had been disappointing. The cast had been casually jokey, sharing newspapers, paperbacks and puzzles as usual while Orlando and Truman did crosswords, Wade Bluman played whist on his mobile, as others ran errands, knitted, or shared magazines. Everything seemed unnaturally normal . . . but Abigail's face kept intervening, spliced between his wife's and his children's, coming and going in mixes and fades.

220

Nobody mentioned the company party and Garrick said nothing. Like Trofimov he too was an exile. This was his Siberian outpost and history was repeating itself.

"I did try putting her off," Phyllis shouted down, "But you know how she is."

Garrick liked to believe he understood human nature. It came down to caring, but Abby had gone to such lengths to avoid him . . .

"Sorry?" He stopped in mid-tread. "Who?"

Phyllis was sorting files. "Well, if you don't know, it no longer matters."

He stared around her office, analyzing the details. Wadges of posters. Samples of programmes. Photographs, cuttings and Rex Schulman memorabilia. A framed photo of Arthur was hung with gold tinsel. Her china frogs wore bows of red ribbon. Plastic holly was everywhere, but what he noticed most was her hair. She had been restyled. She seemed younger, trendier, modern; confronting the world on its own terms. It made her look almost attractive, though her eyes appeared swollen and pink.

She held some documents out. "Top one's yours."

As she handed it over he noticed her growing assortment of bracelets and rings. A stack of identical envelopes lay at her elbow, hand-addressed in laborious writing. Glancing back as he left, he caught sight of her dabbing her eyes.

He was glad to escape. The turret was his sanctuary wedged between heaven and earth. Although it was barely mid-afternoon, streetlights glimmered through Kafkaesque mists and condensation dripped off the eaves. It was hellish to try not to think of his children. A wave of nostalgia gripped him. If he could not phone them direct at least he would write them a letter. He was about to bin Phyllis's packet, but a printed invitation slid out, deckle-edged, and headed with an embossed coat of arms.

"Lady Peggy de Vries invites Mr. Garrick to join her and
her friends at Temple Storford House for a Soirée to celebrate
The Majestic Theatre's 103rd pantomime season," Etceteras, etceteras

He propped it up on his desk. A Soirée? Even in Chekhov's day they'd seemed doomed. The Red Revolution had swept them away. But not here. Not in Britain. Not in Lancashire. At least, not yet. Soon the whole middle-class would implode. But first one must assert one's own aims, and Garrick meant to read all Chekhov's plays.

Outside in perpetual twilight the redevelopment site looked like the aftermath of a battle, strangely beautiful but inexplicably sad. Then out of this haze emerged pure déjà vu, evoking his very first day. There he was, Eddie Craig, distinctive in a company coat facing several acolytes. Garrick wiped the glass, pressing his face to the window. At that very moment Eddie Craig chose to turn round. When Eddie pointed all the helmets looked up. Defiantly Garrick switched on every light. This was his beacon. His lighthouse. His steeple. His wheelhouse. His masthead. He would not be cowed! But when he looked back they'd all disappeared as if they had never been there. Halfway down to the foyer he collided with Josh coming up.

Josh waved an order form. "Hi, the very man! I'm needing a new load of timber more canvas, some hardboard, chipboard, blockboard . . ." Counting them off on his fingers. "Here's the requisition. Sign here."

Garrick took the sheet without looking. "It'll get my full consideration."

"You don't get nowt for nowt, that's all."

"How very true!" Garrick mounted one step higher, forcing Josh to look up. "But you'll find in real life everything's ruled by a budget."

It came down to biological facts, basic psychosexual truths. Above all the alpha-male status. Garrick knew something that Josh did not, and felt quietly triumphant. With immense deliberation he folded the requisition away, calmly putting the kid in his place. Every symbolic victory counted, even if nobody noticed.

Josh gave a double thumbs-up. "Great. Soon as you can!" then hopped disconcertingly down, leaving Garrick marooned on one tread.

At the moment Lizzie was cornered by Lionel, Pippa and Trixie escaped. Priorities were clear. When photographers and paparazzi came snooping, they had to look at their best. Something had to be done. And done quickly. They almost broke into a run.

Cavanham Street was surprisingly busy. They moved against oncoming currents. Mothers with buggies, office-workers, teenagers, kids from school, all in a late-shopping race for Christmas bargains. Pippa's scalp began itching. When weather combines with pollution, hairstyles turn very lank. Restorative action was vital. Women of cosmopolitan tastes could not be caught minus lip-gloss, makeup, or vital sanitary ware.

Outside Crowning Glory, automated fairy lights were chasing each other around the new windows like mating fireflies. A Christmas tree lurked in the background. A line of fluffy overcoats occupied one wall surrounded by bagsful of shopping. No one looked up as the two actresses entered, nor was there any sign of Jilly. Pippa took a magazine from a pile. All these front covers featured one face. 'New Star of TV Kitchens' they said. The face was uncompromisingly bland. Soon all these very same publications would surely feature the Seraphim Twins? But Veronica didn't look up.

She continued working green mousse on a scalp. "Sorry like but Jilly i'n't in today. Just rings up and says as she's poorly!" Foam surged like a chemical weapon. "Now bloody look!" She nodded towards the waiting queue. "It's an invasion."

Trixie controlled rising panic, "Yes but this is urgent."

Veronica leaned confidentially over. "I know pet. Everything is. I mean, first Jilly's got migraines, cramps. Then hot flushes. The lot!" She shook her head resignedly. "I ask you. Walks into lampposts? Falls down stairs? Slams into doors? Trips over dog-leads? Slips on wet floors? Whatever. You name it." She returned to the still-foaming scalp, and turned the shower-head on. "Give us a call tomorrow, an' Jilly'll fit you straight in. Okay?"

"In that case, remember the Hair Lacquer Prayer." Trixie clasped both hands and closed her eyes . "Now let us spray!"

Pippa nodded. "That's hair today. An' gone tomorrow! . . . Okay!"

Garrick kept pressing keys. His fingertips must have doubled in size because numerals did as they pleased. "That's £2,432.50 x 21.5 x 17.5%!"

Mathematics weren't strictly neutral or even objective. From his own experience, no calculation was ever impartial, especially when working out budgets. Creative accounting was a contradiction in terms because the odds were pre-set. Digits took sides. This meant always siding with Ruddock and leaving his Chekhov Players as losers.

"£9,152.2812, VAT? . . . Oh bugger! That's got to be wrong."

People didn't come to see scenery, yet here was Josh was demanding more cash. Same with lighting and frocks. Josh was taking advantage, flaunting false charm. He took advantage of youth because that was his currency. Testosterone was a deceit. The fellow was a spendthrift with plans beyond his competence. Budgeting couldn't be backed up with blackmail. Expenditure had to be balanced. As for building sets? And hiring fancy furniture? Commissioning outlandish costumes? Garrick had to be wholly objective because Cinderella was only his first bridge to cross.

On its far side lay 'The Cherry Orchard' and 'The Three Sisters', like enticing mirages, receding and always receding, leaving Garrick trapped in accounts. Whichever buttons he pressed, outgoings became astronomical concepts . . . whereas income immediately dwindled. Likewise, credits always turned into debits stammering lines of additional zeroes.

If Cinderella were actively plotting against Chekhov, it could turn nasty. Like death and taxation, the panto could not be stopped. As a responsible boss he ought to update his assistant, which meant consulting Abigail. He considered, reconsidered, then slowly he lifted the phone balancing its weight in his hand, feeling its cool surfaces, dialling with a meticulous care then cutting it short and sitting back feeling shaken. He had gone to the rim and peered over as if into the Manwess's pit. He needed to dial home at once.

He heard the line connect, then ring. No one answered. No auto-phone kicked in. No message. No Vee. Not even Roseanne. Worst of all, no Rachel nor Mark. In his worst moments it seemed as if paternity could be revoked. He pictured them as newborn babies, tiny, red-faced and crumpled, minuscule fingers clutching at air. He'd felt each small head as it lay in the palm of his hand. Their latest hand-written postcards lay in his in-tray:

"Dear Dad, please buy me an inter-torsional link and a megabyte adapter for my virtual Netscape ZXO scanning device. Thanks . . . Mark"

"Dearest daddy I want gold-strapped high-heels and Lucy Doll panty briefs and mousy-styled furry headphones Pleeeease. Lots of love from Rachel, x x x"

For Abigail her meeting with Stacey was vital. Surely something must be wrong, because nothing appeared to have changed. She broke into a run. No deep-seated, gut-churning, physical turmoil? Why not? Sex to Stacey was just another routine like skateboards, skydiving, biking, dancing, whatever Already Abby was out of breath and shoe-backs were catching her heels. Maybe she couldn't find suitable words, but the moment was like over and gone. Why? When sometimes weeks passed in a blink, seconds could last a whole lifetime? Unless her drinks had been spiked? So where was the earth-shattering fun? It had happened, that's all. Just happened. As for love and romance? Everyone got crushes on boys. She felt cheated, frustrated, angry and tired. It was sod all to do with love, whatever that was. It could have been with anyone. Anyone! And not the husband whose wife's ring Abby had personally chosen! And whose hotel room she'd helped to select. She wanted to hammer her fists till they bled. She wanted to carve out her name on her wrists.

Outside Crowning Glory she stared at steamed-up windows. She wanted to yell, top of her voice, "Jilly! I done it! I done it! You've not!" Then Jilly Craske would go crazy and scratch out everyone's eyes.

At just such a moment everyone needed best friends. Stacey knew everything. She'd explain why other faces had flashed through her mind at the time, all of them mingling and changing.

Now she couldn't recall any details apart from, she hadn't enjoyed it. She needed to shower all the traces away then change every scrap of her clothes. If she couldn't put the clock back, at least she'd pretend it never took place. As for her mother's poetry stuff celebrating virginal bloom? Abby's brain shut off. She didn't have to face Garrick at all. She could turn on her heel and walk out. No problem. That's what Stacey would do. And what Abby most craved was Stacey's approval. From last night they were equals. With childhoods wiped out, they could meet on identical terms. They could challenge the strippers who ogled and juggled from websites. She anticipated Stacey's surprise. It was hard to control the excitement.

Stacey was shivering beneath the 3-sided clock above Walfords as bargain hunters jostled for presents. Abigail could not to be trusted. She'd give her another five minutes, that's all. No bugger kept to arrangements. She continued to pace the Brinkhouse Arcade in short skirt with high heels as a razorous wind goose-pimpled her legs. She was rubbing her hands when she heard Abigail's yell. Straightway she headed off. As Abigail followed, breathless and sweating, Stacey began to speed up.

Abigail broke into a canter. "Hey! Stacey wait! Bloody wait!"

When Stacey stopped dead in the central arcade, Abigail cannoned into her. Stacey smoothed down her coat with expensively manicured fingers then peered into a Visa-card-sized mirror, dabbing here, adjusting there as if Abigail did not exist. This was high performance art, a whole school of self-preening, indulging every nuance.

Stacey snapped her handbag shut. "An' don't dare say you're allergic to caffeine and cream 'Cause I need my next fix. An' quick! An' somewhere warm. Or my nipples'll turn into studs!" She took a mock-dominatrix stance, letting her shoulder bag swing. "This fucking arcade's a fast-freezer!" She strode off again, furiously rubbing her hands. "An' if it's all the same to you, I don't want no public discussion. Okay?" She grabbed Abigail's arm forcing her to keep up.

'Espresso Espresso' nestled alongside a florist where Christmas trees bulged in green mesh like giant bottle-brushes. Yes, Abigail thought, Stacey was wild. She was feisty and raunchy. She'd risk bodily organs and soul yet stay dead cool. You name it; she'd been there, done it, bought the personalised T-shirt and taken the requisite drugs. It was nothing ruled out. Nothing too freaky or skinky for her.

Abigail scooped chocolate foam from a large cappuccino and wondered how to break her good news. "Come on Stace? Are you mad because I was late?"

Stacey sighed. "Why is everything always you?"

"Yeah, but . . ." She sucked the foam in through her teeth.

"Yeah but what?" Stacey was breathing heavily now. "No. It's Sanjay!"

"But he seemed so-so . . ." Abby reached out and found Stacey's fingers unyielding. "Like Did he sexually abuse you?" Stacey looked so shocked Abigail floundered. "You don't mean he's like . . . gay?"

"Shit!" Stacey slammed the table. "It's not Night of the Vampires!"

Abigail floundered. Stacey always left you confused. One minute she's raging, next she's smiling and wiping tears from her eyes, then tugging from under her collar a golden rosette on a chain. She held it up to her lips, kissing it like some miraculous charm.

"Isn't it beautiful? No really. Don't say as I never warned you. Most guys only want full physical whatsit, not our inner minds! Not our true selves. Not our personalities, see." She sniffed and dabbed her eyes again. "Not our true, inner, deep spiritual selves. Not our purest virginal souls. We got to stay pure for that day."

Abigail felt the first icy cold twinges of doubt. "But, but . . . I don't"

"Don't worry. You'll find out. All they want's our bodies in bed. I couldn't believe as he'd do that. He couldn't take 'no'. Do you see? Yes, course you do."

"What Like not wanting to marry?"

Stacey slowly raised her right hand, holding it into Abigail's face. "You always want proof."

Stacey sat back and smiled through her tears. On her ring finger flashed a huge diamond ring, glittering with spectra of fire. Stacey leaned confidingly forward.

"Now do you get it?" she whispered. "We're staying virgin till then, I want to stand at that altar, knowing I'm chaste." She sat back, tearful and smug, uncontrollably smiling. "That's very important, you see."

Abigail waited. There must be a catch? She couldn't reset her body to zero. And her famous tattoos? And all the men she'd had? But Stacey's arms were noticeably bare. Gone were those dolphins and masks, vanished like washable transfers. Was it the same with her orgies? Her wild drunken scandals? Cutting-and-pasting? Everything fake like pulp fiction. The realisation was dawning. Everything was an act, but everyone trusts their best friends. Stacey was holding her ring to the light.

"'Course he's halfway through divorce. Lucky he's childless. Never sleep with married men, I say. Keep yourself pure till you've been blessed by the priest. That's what I always say."

"No you bloody don't!" Abby's anger was sudden and shrill. "Fuckin' liar!" People began to turn round. "So what was that stuff about fancying Garrick? He's married with kids."

"What's Garrick got to do with this?"

Abigail became icy calm. "Like you're always telling me, it's no big deal? An' dead right. It was easy!" As Stacey began to stand up, Abigail pushed her back down. "You said you'd screw Garrick if you got the chance. Well that's what I did."

Stacey held Abigail's stare. "No morning-afters to take?" She sat slowly shaking her head. "Can't help. I'm medically certified pure."

Stacey's scream rose above gurgling coffee machines as Abigail's toecap smashed into her shin. Stacey jumped up. Her chair toppled back. The whole café froze. With slow deliberation Stacey upended her purse, sending coins spinning, cascading over the table as a waitress approached. As the familiar metal-tipped heels clacked away then mingled with the roar of the traffic, Abby sat stirring the dregs of her coffee.

While Garrick shuffled manuscripts his mind was elsewhere. If all the world's a stage, the snag was human beings. They were too mortal to fit the Great Sagas. No heroes or heroines when everyone had obvious faults. Even blessed Phyllis. She guiltily put down the phone whenever he entered. And Fabian Wass was less and less sober, while Reggie was constantly farting, and Lionel behaved as if any humour was burning his tongue. There was too much human nature around. As Garrick's old man used to say, individuals are impossibly fragile, but pair them together, they're hell.

Louise and Abigail? Pippa and Trixie? Truman and Reggie? Even Eddie and Arthur? Opposites attract like life with death, night with day, theosophies with trivia, Chekhov with Cinderella Then add Fabian, Wade and Orlando, all treating life like rehearsals! And yet the show had started to gel. CINDERELLA WAS STARTING TO WORK! That was the shock. There were rare times when he could have kissed the whole cast. Sometimes he really enjoyed it, laughing aloud, laughing uncontrollably.

Everyone pushed for their ultimate laugh, aiming for stand-up ovations, experimenting with puns, absurdities or crude innuendo, anything for the twitch of a smirk. If laughter was the flipside of anguish, then a giggle was confirmation of life. It was there in the unlikeliest places. As in Buttons' scene when he introduces his pantomime cow to the two Ugly Sisters. Such moments of great human drama.

(Buttons enters, carrying a bucket and stool while leading in Daisy the cow)

Asphyxia: Hello Buttons, been milking again?

Buttons: You know me. I can never resist it.

Asphyxia: Ah yes" (holds up hands in mock delight). " And those big silly eyes. That bovine expression!

Euthanasia: And the cow don't look too brilliant neither!"

Those ancient music-hall gags! They'd festered so long they'd matured, and Garrick's repetitive honing of details was working. Those pauses, looks, and inflexions. Even the actors were starting to notice.

"You're awful!" Euphemia says to Dandini, "My mother warned me I'd meet men like you . . ." She pushes Dandini teasingly, who stands bolt

226

upright a moment, then topples rigidly over. "But I'd always thought they'd be younger!"

Yes, and the Baron's 'business' with closed-circuit surveillance, posing as if for a portrait got everyone laughing (shades of Arthur Ruddock were clear). Good old James Carr, the bastard. Even the ironing interlude (only developed to cover a scene-change behind) was another success.

(Phone rings . . . Buttons puts the iron to his ear!)

(And because poor Reggie Buck seemed unable to learn conventional words, let alone put syllables in order, everyone was prompting him)

Ethanasia. "I love cooking so much. Especially puddings. I'll have to join the Pudding Club!" (Wade Bluman's wide eyes challenge the audience to misunderstand as he stands heaving his well-padded bosoms.)

Asphyxia. "Yes, Euthanasia dear, I only have to look at you, sister dear .and I straightaway think . . .'tart'!"

Yes, he thought, 'tart' was right. Music hall screws Harlequinade. Their bastard child is Pantomime, where women's ambitions lead only to marriage, where wives are husbands' property and dowries have to be paid. He knew Verity's feminist hackles would rise at a culture where baby girls could be dumped on a hillside; where virgins fetched top prices; where daughters could be sold off in marriage like legalised prostitution, and menopausal women were witches. All of this in the name of 'True Love.' Such comic stereotypes dated back to the Greeks. The paradox was, a malcontent like James Carr seemed to keep getting laughs. Perhaps Chekhov might have provided an answer?

Now whenever he looked out across town, Garrick could see that where business and democracy met, the fault lines were constantly shifting. Religions, races and classes collided. Power and money have always talked. Manwess Gas could dig up whole networks of streets while bidding for Sudgas, Olveco and Estochem Heating, because Arthur Ruddock was pulling the strings while Eddie Craig put in bids to demolish year-old office blocks! Meanwhile Garrick's own options had shrunk, compressing his hopes, and extruding his life like cheap toothpaste. Sometimes he feared for his wife and his kids.

One day the clouds cleared. Sun shone. Birds sang. Everyone flogged away at rehearsals. Even the Church Hall got in on the act. Its tall gothic windows seemed to announce life was not merely rehearsal, but a provision for heaven. Or hell. Garrick noticed how Abigail's hair shimmered copper and gold in the sunlight. He wanted to scoop her up and bear her away but Lionel as usual was throwing a wobbly, shading his eyes and spreading his bony hands in despair. Reggie came padding behind him.

"How can I concentrate?" Lionel's deep tones turned into a wail. "First I get dazzled! Then Reginald never gives the right cue!" He shielded his eyes with both hands. "I never know where I am."

"True," agreed Reggie sadly, "That's me being creative". He warmed to his theme. "I'm an ad-libber, me! That's my trade. Spur of the moment an' that! Bit o'this. Bit o'that. Bit o'give'n'take! You give, an' I take! That's how it goes! But I don't get no say in the weather." He rolled his eyes, blinking frantically up at the windows and moaning.

"You see!" Lionel wailed, "Where's creative discipline gone? Why can't we go back and work on that stage?"

Garrick closed his eyes. Gags either worked or they didn't. The harder you tried, the less funny they got, but in his own humourless, ponderous way James was hilarious. That was the problem.

James only had to say, "Please, I'm trying to be serious," to guarantee titters, "It's about having background. Classical training's essential to understand iambic pentameters and internal rhymes," and he'd have everyone openly smirking. "That's Shakespeare and Marlowe, you see. And I've played them all. You cannot purchase experience. Because I interact with the greats. Together we created an unequalled period in post-modern drama." Then everyone fell about wetting themselves.

Undaunted, Reggie continued spontaneous business, disturbing Lionel's concentration because anarchy was the essence of humour, and clowns had licence to mock.

"You can't beat a nice Danish pastry". (Reggie batters cake mixture with large wooden spoon. Foam spatters everywhere). "No! .Else it makes one helluva mess!!" .(At this level, nothing much mattered but timing). "And tripe and onions go lovely with custard!" (Cue; the audience's groan of disgust! . . . Reggie is still pulling faces) "Yeah, an' mustard's great with ice cream!"

Asphyxia: "Honestly Buttons, that Cinders is so lazy. I've watched her. She's always snoozing and boozing, and slipping away for a pizza."

Buttons: (shocked). "Oh no she's not!" (Appeals to the audience) Is she, children?"

Euthanasia: "Oh yes she is!" (turns to audience for approval)

("Oh no she's not!!" the audience scream, conducted by Buttons).

Kids know what's expected: cheerleader and gang, priest and congregation, shaman and chorus. But rehearsals have to survive on thin air. No ricochet. No bounce. Just the unending curve of elliptical space, plus of course Reggie's puns on 'bottoms', 'stumps', 'choppers' and 'balls' ('Nudge nudge, wink wink! Know what I mean?'). Meanwhile the stand-up comedy show was running and running next door.

So why was his company working so hard for an audience of hundreds, when millions could be reached in one go? Mass media were waiting. Vee was successful. Everyone had their own website, but Abby had that Star Quality too. That inexplicable something.

As she followed the script with one finger, he watched her fingernail trailing the page, her moving lips mouthing words, glimpses of teeth, and the flickering tip of a tongue. Not even Reggie's inventions had thrown her. With Abigail present he could believe the past was wiped clean. Then Fabian yelled, "Coffee break! Everyone back in ten minutes."

After a morning spent in the church hall, they returned to the theatre to finalise progress on stage. Here Lionel was almost ecstatic. His dame postured and primped.

"Infamy!" Euthanasia was gesturing up to the back of the Circle. "Infamy Infamy! Everyone's got it in for me!"

The Ugly Stepsisters were meant to be making pastry which Buttons was supposed to be rolling out, all mimed to music and choreographed like a dance. With no music and no sense of rhythm, the disjointed scene was falling apart. From where Garrick sat in the auditorium Abigail looked almost too perfect as prompter, rimmed by a spillage of light. Neither had ever referred to that night but vivid reminders came back. Turning pages she crossed and uncrossed her long legs. He was too engrossed to see Phyllis heading directly for Pippa and Trixie who crouched at the back of the stalls. Perhaps he sensed a peripheral movement but other thoughts filled his mind.

Suddenly Pippa and Trixie approached. "It's Abby," Pippa whispered, "We've got bad news for her." They nudged each other and winked

'Norston General Hospital Trust. No Parking'. Its complex spreads like a town-within-town, its expansion dated by plaques above doors. 'The Westbury Wing', 'The Harris Extension', 'The de Vries Ward' soon to include 'The Craig Pathology Labs', 'Norrmark X-Rays' and 'The Ruddock Radiology Centre'. Add on Pharmacology, Chemotherapy, Osteology, moving onwards and onwards through varying shades of cream, grey and white.

A trio was following lines on the floor like some life-or-death mystery tour. They trudged through swing doors, up and down ramps, tracking some Yellow-Brick Road. To Abigail it felt like the maze to end mazes, surprised Garrick had acted as though they were off to comfort the dying! Left, right, left again, junctions, routes, like an interactive game. Following Pippa and Trixie they were overtaken by trolleys with patients wired up to jelly-bag drips, heads lolling, naked feet protruding.

They turned another corner, went through a lobby as double-glazed as an airlock, then entered the Edward Craig Wing, to be confronted by Disneyland murals. Maid Marion, Snow White and the Dwarves and of course Cinderella. Beneath a sign announcing "De Fries Maternity Block", Louise waited, clutching a massive bouquet. A sign announced 'Emergency Obstetrics Sponsored by Brinkside Plc. Post Natal and Incubators' then 'Paediatric Intensive Care'.

Trixie brandished her bouquet. "What's the betting? Boy or a Girl? It's gotta be one or the other!"

Louise turned to face them, eyes puffy and red. A chill seemed to blow down the passage, reducing the walls and dimming the lights. Louise plunged suddenly forward enveloping them in a surge of emotion, clutching Abigail to her. Here was the daughter conceived from her very own tissues. No Caesarean knives. No anaesthetics. Just terrible physical effort and pain. Bathed in concoctions of perfumes Abigail was once again reduced to a child.

Following a staff nurse down a long ward, Norston General passed like some giant Ferris wheel imperceptibly turning; an entire TV series compressed into one day. They became aware of the cries of the newborn mingled with whoopings of laughter Then more double doors, then more double doors. The nurse pointed to down the far end. Instinctively everyone lowered their voices. A messenger overtook them with bouquets of red roses.

"By the way, we don't allow flowers," said the nurse, pointedly, "But sometimes, we do make exceptions."

Ahead through frosted glass panels they saw moving shapes. A nurse burst in from a side door, propelling a trolley piled high with tubing and dials like debris from a recycling plant, then raced away. The Ward Sister returned looking uneasy, but everything seemed so clinically normal Abby began to have doubts.

"She must've known, surely?" Louise had a catch in her voice. "Women know. I mean, why keep it secret?"

Swaying pink curtains were patterned with animal shapes. In a coup de théatre the nurse swished them aside. "Abracadabra", thought Trixie. At the far side of a bed, sat a man, immobile, unshaven, unblinking, his face raw red, his collars frayed, and overcoat crumpled. Jilly appeared to be sleeping, a drip attached to her arm as if plugged directly into the mains. The man's eyes remained fixed on her face as Trixie leaned forward:

"Hi mate, how's she getting on?"

He muttered something under his breath. Jilly awoke and struggled to prop herself up, waving assistance away. Eyes dull as marbles peered from dark pits. Lank hair straggled a tightly stretched skull.

Louise tried to smile. "Hello Jilly. Veronica sends her love as do all your customers. But Veronica says, not to worry, okay? She'll keep the place ticking over." Louise drew Abigail forward. "Yes, and here's my little daughter. She's brought a couple of friends from the theatre."

The man was still craning forward; fists clenched into fury or prayer; white knuckles interlocked on the bedspread. His veins seemed to bulge. Arteries pulsed in his neck. A deep redness suffused his features. As he leaned forward Jilly Craske seemed to shrink back. Some private drama excluded the rest of the world.

Abigail was disturbed. Why had Jilly Craske kept everything secret? Stacey was right; biology rules! It's Alpha Male against all Womankind. It's got its own mathematics: ovaries plus spermatozoa, divided by one single sperm. One plus one equals two. Sex equals babies. Babies add up to sex multiplied a million times. Abigail pictured cross-sectioned embryos, placentas, and worse, the humanoid foetus itself, coiled like some ingrowing tadpole, growing and growing inside you and . . . obscure biological systems materialised from old textbooks, their implications flashing bright red. An internal slide-show added grotesques and monstrous freaks with everything upping the odds, and she panicked.

That night she had taken a terrible risk? Chlamydia, breast cancer, AIDS, whatever? Pregnancy was possible; probable even. Who knew the odds? She had been targeted, groomed, wined, and dined, possibly drugged into submission? Date rape, that's what it was. All that drink! It didn't bear thinking about. She made herself a solemn promise. Depending on how things panned out, she swore she would somehow get her revenge.

"Abby? Abby?" Jilly Craske found a faint voice. "Did they tell you?" She nodded towards the man who was visibly shaking. "It would've been a baby boy."

As Abby reached out, their fingertips touched. Static electricity crackled. At that moment time stood still, its tableau filled with the sound of her breathing as Jilly slumped back on the pillows. The man seemed to snap. He turned on Abigail as if she'd been found guilty and sentenced.

In that moment's distraction Jilly snatched at her tubing; ripped it away. Whirring pumps ceased. In the stillness came high-pitched bleeps. Dials flashed. Alarms buzzed. A red light zigzagged a monitor screen as Louise screamed for help.

A nurse pushed through ballooning drapes. She hustled everyone out. Halfway down the ward they heard bleeping stretch into a wail. Then a man's long drawn-out howl.

Garrick was pedalling home, inhaling hydrocarbons with snowflakes. Today without Pippa and Trixie, Reggie and Lionel had sparked off each other. This might yet be a groundbreaking production to raise the whole pantomime genre? The 'Archetype Cinderella' perhaps? Next the film of the musical, the book of the film and transfer to the West End then Broadway? And when Hollywood beckons, who knows?

The traffic was surprisingly light. At Jilly Craske's the lights were all off, like a gap in a row of white teeth. Nearby 'Blazer's Beautyland' dazzled with cranial massage, leg waxes, hairstyle and image consultants. Next door, 'Cut Price Goodwill' was burning kilowatts up. Not far away was 'Club Arabica'. The whole district would fit in a West London side street. The difference was more than just scale. He was seduced by that smoky red brick, blue-grey Welsh slate, cast-iron bridges, warehouse conversions, office blocks, and lines of shabby tenements. Here was tribal energy, a Lancashire spirit he'd never expected, and like any addict he'd soon be craving his fix. Vee would assume he'd gone native.

An icy wind distorted his vision. Transformation was the essence of drama. Sleet became frozen snow. Lights mutated to haloes. Neons turned into prisms. Apartment blocks became glacier cliffs. An iceberg was a stationery bus. Christmas lights were holograms seen through molten glass, like adverts for mass electrocution. By night they were starlight, bright, and exciting. Everything changed. The townscape blurred into the vast Russian Steppes.

He imagined two children as wide-eyed as Rachel and Mark. Early Siberian snows drifted round dachas where Chekhov and Pushkin huddled by earthenware stoves. Christmas in St Petersburg. Golden domes, huge glittering candles, heavy bronze bells and deep-throated chants of Orthodox mass; the rising soprano and resonant bass. Roads became frozen seas like the Baltic; all solid objects dissolved in a whiteout. Garrick raised both feet high off the pedals and freewheeled into the weather but once again some internal radar took the right fork heading for Club Arabica.

As snowflakes eddied and whirled he took shelter in a newsagent's forecourt. He was propping his bike by the doorway when a news-stand caught his attention. "TV Star's Local Husband Shock" it stated in 35pt And there she was. Verity! Happily grinning out of the paper, wholly unconcerned. If this were Norston Mercury, presumably he was that 'local husband'? . . . He skimmed the front page. They'd even got his bloody name wrong!

"Gareth Jones ex-showman directs local panto, Cinderella." it said,

"Good for a laugh, say panto stars Lionel Parsons and James Carr . . ."

In a sub-paragraph, headed "Garrick Brawl Fiasco", some interviewee had accused him of . . . "an alleged assault on an innocent Norston Castle Hotel porter, Anstey Fram, who was attacked and left semi conscious, needing hospital treatment. The victim now threatens to sue . . ." and so on, accompanied by close-ups of the porter, his face dark with bruising.

Another shot showed Garrick and Vee outside The Castle Hotel . No mention of his being robbed. No police statements. Instead there were shots of Garrick with Abigail from CCTV in the lobby, seemingly locked mouth-to-mouth. The by-line read "From our special correspondent, Elizabeth Scott", promising "More revelations to come".

He Instinctively he looked for his watch, overlooked 'DEATH OF REX SCHULMAN' and 'NEW COUNCIL BUDGET'. and panicked. How fast did bad news travel? Verity must not find out second-hand.

Some phone lines can be astonishingly clear. Each vowel, every consonant and syllable down to the slightest accent or pause, plus every intake of breath can be starkly reproduced.

"You fucking scumbag!" Vee was screaming, "You goddam son-of-a-bitch!"

Garrick had meant to break the news gently. He'd intended to draw on their common concerns and appeal to their long-lasting devotion. Instead he'd been scooped, bloody scooped, by that article faxed directly to Vee, together with transcripts of Norston FM. All thanks to Vee's new super-friend Lucy, the shit! Lucy was ultra-efficient.

Image, she'd claimed, was her agency's job. 'Damage limitation' meant changing any minus to plus then adding a few bonus points for good measure. Therefore more revelations were due. Every woman he'd ever known, and every dodgy deal of his youth; every drunk and disorderly, every possession of illegal substances, every violent misconduct! Whatever he thought he'd lived down. Once her puritan ethos took over, Vee could justify moral outrage: she'd make his old man seem benign. The implications were worse. He panicked at losing his kids and the nightmare of visiting rights, negotiating for minor concessions, and . . .

"What d'ye mean, you didn't knowingly screw her? Jesus God!" Verity's fury distorted the airwaves. "I don't give a shit! Not for that little scumbag! That sex-bunny asshole! You deserve each other. You're both full of shit!"

"But darling . . ."

"You'd screw any asshole. You promised you'd stopped! And I believed you! You and that . . . that little princess of demons! That little witch! You, you two-timing, blackmailing bastard! How do I know where your ass has been? I'm nailing a sign on our front door. 'Don't bring that fat poke anywhere near me. Not ever again' You're excommunicated, Gary. Eliminated. Debarred. I'm not risking clap or the plague, so don't you ever ever . . ." But Verity's sweet smiling face continued to gaze from his photos.

"Don't believe the media."

"Oh no? Why's that? When you keep giving me shit? Putting my whole new career on the line? I might be just a pastry cook, but it's made us all a pretty darn-good living, so far, and, and . . . anyway . . ." She continued

232

through her tears, "The same hotel and the very same bed! . . . That's, that's too cruel"

Yes, that was it. A classic, he thought. He'd have voted for her on a jury. Sadly forgiveness was not in the game. He'd have to fight back or lose both his kids.

"Okay Vee. I was wrong. I admit it. But let's discuss it reasonably. Think of our kids."

"Who the hell else am I thinking about?"

He sat on his bed and let her talk on. His own case was simple. His was the "Human Nature" plea, ie 'Man the Hunter' versus 'Woman the Home-Making Mom'. Sex was the primary masculine instinct. Furthermore, he'd been drunk, befuddled by medication and stress. If anything physical actually happened, it had been an uncontrolled 'corporeal act' with no emotional content. Either that, or he'd be forced to reveal how an experienced seductress played upon an exile missing his wife.

"Listen darling, I know how it must seem . . ." But the line had gone dead.

Garrick caught family pictures exchanging secretive looks as wallpaper patterns prowled round them. However, when Vee calmed down and reflected, she would have second thoughts. He was utterly certain of that.

Some years Norston never saw snow, so people took few precautions. Even when forecasters warned of 'sharp frosts' Norston Vale wasn't concerned because warm cocktails of gases promised galactic greenhouse effects, re-heating the planet, bringing palm trees and grapes to town, all in the Brinkside Development plan. Long warm summers and mild winters were guaranteed. 'Snow up North. Rain down South,' was already an old-fashioned cliché. And as Arthur Ruddock told The Mercury, The Chronicle, and The Gazette. "Who needs the Mediterranean? Think Norston Marina instead."

Although Arthur trusted his own predictions, he'd turned his central heating up a few notches, and Peggy de Vries ordered her gardener to cover susceptible plants. Even barelegged street-girls donned acrylic furs over thin cutaway blouses. Wise cynics like Garrick ignored idle warnings. Then overnight everything froze. Exactly as forecast.

He awoke to a chill that rolled from his ill-fitting windows across polar expanses of lino, right into the depths of his soul. He wondered why Vee hadn't rung. Leaping from bed he stumbled into a great wall of cold. As he stood, one bare foot on the other, he heard the phone ring, but the sound retreated back through the paper-thin walls, locating its source to next door.

Even as he was dressing, Verity filled his mind. Somehow theirs was a marriage that lasted. The pinnacle was their children: the only pain was Roseanne: their compromise had been Chekhov. When Garrick had promised to perform all his plays, peace was agreed. His single act of penitence would celebrate the Morozov line (and the whole American Morozoff clan), all because some distant Morozov niece had been vaguely related to Evgeniya Morozova, who'd had the good fortune to give birth to Anton Chekhov. So much for those ancestry websites. The truth was as oblique and as simple as that.

He smoothed The Ancient Mariner's binding, patted his Cherry Orchard script, and ran dry fingers over the spines of the rest. Books, books, books. 'The Seagull', 'Three Sisters', 'Uncle Vanya' and Ibsen's 'Doll's House', 'Ghosts', 'Rosmersholm', Dante Gabriel Borkman (most of which he genuinely intended to read). Either 'Cinderella' would be his downfall or rise. But standing there, shivering, he seemed to hear Edwin's voice. 'No man should make promises he cannot keep, nor aim to surpass his own father,' it said. So this was the price to be paid.

When the police asked him to deliver a witness statement, they'd been checking CCTV cameras. Now his insurers were getting steamed up. He scribbled down what details he could, shaved in near-zero water, before eating stale milk with muesli. All that really mattered was Vee. This was a storm in a teacup, and once she'd recalled their happy weekend she would be pleading for reconciliation. They'd shared so much together. This craze for celebrity cooks was as fleeting as hairstyles and gimmicks. She had a sentimental streak. She might even accept a share of the blame? He in turn would be generous and supportive.

In another redbrick terrace somewhere to the east of town, Josh had been stirred from deep sleep. Ringing tones split the dark. He scooped the instrument out of the blackness and felt the first wave of cold.

"Umm?"

"Ayup matey!" The voice wavered up to falsetto. "It's me Me!"

"An' who's that?"

The voice slipped back into Irish. "Don't give us that. It's me. Roddy."

Josh slapped a hand to his head. "I was asleep!"

His shoulders were aching. His back was stiff after two days constructing 'a turnspit and fireplace with miniature trapdoor' for the Palace Kitchen scene. This was not like assembling shop windows. Their Fairy Princess suffered acute claustrophobia. It needed invention. Work was a shit-easy routine for Roddy, poncing about in that van with his weird sense of humour. Showbiz was a disorganised world of recycled plywood and second-hand planks. It was cheap glues, polystyrene, canvas, sash cord, nails, staples, nuts'n'bolts, screws and . . .

"An how's you!" whined the voice, "An' your bitch?" Roddy's tone was all innuendo, ". . . Or haven't you heard?"

Josh suppressed a yawn. "Like I'm in bed, right? It's mid-Antarctic, an' my alarm doesn't smash our iceberg till seven! Okay?"

"Like, you really don't know?"

"No. And I'm cutting you off."

"Better not." Roddy began to sound almost gleeful. "You'd rather hear it from me."

"Such as what?"

"Okay, but I wasn't going to mention it, see, but Like, it's nothing you've done. Not personal like. We can't read other people's minds. I mean, that's why we need mates. An' why I've always backed you, no matter what whether you've backed me or not. But it's others what's got in the way. Blocked you from seeing the light."

Josh's eyes were adapting to darkness, surveying all the detritus of childhood, from posters of pop stars to composite toys spilling off shelves and from cupboards, exposing a lifetime of comfort. "Jus' cut the crap, Roddy!"

The silence seethed. "That's if you trust us? You promise?"

"Yeah, yeah, yeah."

"Now don't say I never warned you. But off you goes, as thick as short planks. You and your arty middle-class ways."

"Get on with it, Roddy."

"It's like it was down to someone to to tell you. I mean, right from us fitting them hairdresser's windows. Remember me warning? Remember? Because you an' me's mates. A team. That's what I was trying to warn you. Forget fuckin' headlines. Sod the press. That Garrick guy's crap. You'll get yourself hung out to dry. That bird's not worth it. She's just a tart what's . . ."

"You're slagging her off?"

Roddy's wit wasn't funny. His bitterness was tangible. Almost vindictive. Bitter consonants with sneering vowels. But to make people laugh you needed their tacit approval. They had to be accomplices. Someone should tell Roddy that.

But Roddy had only paused for a breath. "We made a great team, you an' me. Till social class and lack of respect . . ."

"You what?"

"No respect. All theatre's elitist! What's real is mass communications. I'm talking 'social awareness'. Irony. Satire. All that."

Roddy was sounding urgent, intense. "What's happened to morality?. Political morality? Ethics and that? I'll tell you what. It's like a stretched rubber sheet, where all of us roll to the heaviest point, then suffocate layer upon layer. That's like the secret of . . ."

Josh slammed down the phone. A worm in his brain had started to stir. He dragged the duvet back over himself.

As Garrick stepped out onto Baker's Row doorstep, the front door slammed shut behind him. Overnight frost with a sprinkling of snow had unified the whole street, but his brain refused to cool down. Vee still had not apologised, and as if this weren't bad enough, tonight was the dreaded 'Theatre Soirée', the classic cart before horse. With Lizzie Scott and set on exposés, a public soirée was the last thing he needed. Celebrations were too premature. He was not in the mood. The real danger was losing his children and with them the point of his life. But as always a tiny voice intervened. It insisted that notoriety paid, therefore all publicity was good. Be positive, it said, a major scandal would fill every seat in the theatre. Turn that to advantage.

Okay. Another part of his brain conceded, if it really were about bums on seats, then Lady de Vries and her alcopop parties might have some use. But if it meant crowds queuing for Hedda and Jörgen, because Garrick was being slammed in the papers and slaughtered on the Internet? Who'd care what led to HOUSE FULL signs? After Cinderella would come 'Cherry Orchard' and with it the chance to cast Liuba Ranevsky, Anya, Dunyasha and dotty old Epikhovdov. "Yes, Garrick Jones, you too shall go to the ball! Dare to be Gary!" it said, but too late, his prejudice had already triumphed. He would not be attending that supper. No matter what, his decision was conclusive. Definite. Final.

As he approached Craig Demolitions, the eastern sky was lightening and streetlights were switching off. Workers with padded gloves were dismembering girders, their arc-lances spattering fireworks. He tried to think as he walked and kept walking. Crossing lights changed with him half-across. All the traffic was hooting. He took the side alley towards the canal and its silence.

Here the water reflected his mood. Man could take comfort in nature. Along the broken coping stones, layers of mist drifted off water whose marbleised surfaces crackled with wafer-thin ice. It looked as bottomless as a loch. Verity hated all signs of decay. Desiccated willow herb and crystalline brambles clawed at his legs. Rust-tinted icicles dribbled down walls. Another new billboard had appeared on the towpath.

"BRINKSIDE MARINA. Soon to be Norston's Main Tourist Attraction" it announced, complete with computerised visuals. "Improvementation by Brinkside Developments PLC with Brinkhomes Property Co. Leases available now . . . Apply to Chairman, The Hon. George de Vries"

Just visible over the rubble, he could pick out the theatre like a dark iceberg alone in a squall. He'd need a smoke before he confronted the cast.

"Alone, alone, all alone," he thought, "Alone on a wide, wide sea."

Back at the church hall he dipped in through the tiny back porch, took a deep breath, then strolled calmly in.

". . . So will Garrick Fart-face be going?" Reggie was asking aloud, "I'll bet you ten quid to a Euro he don't, what with all that screwing around and . . . and . . . and . . ."

"Good morning."

As Garrick strolled forward everyone froze. "Good morning," they chorused back like a primary school, and Pippa and Trixie disappeared to wash mugs. Orlando Marcel hid the horse racing results. Fabian Wass slipped out for a smoke, leaving no sign of a headline nor hint of the papers. Everybody got down to work and professionalism was quickly restored. The only unspoken topic was that night's Soirée, but Garrick could read all the signs, then remembered he hadn't handed his statement in to the police. Events could so quickly run out of control. When someone suddenly burst into the hall Garrick instinctively bobbed out of view.

James Carr took centre-stage, oddly triumphant, waving and shushing for silence

"Everyone listen! The press is here! You can't move for cameras. Garrick's really stirred up the hornets!" He ignored Reggie's frantic signals. "There's film crews besieging the place. That's why he's not coming." He waved a grimacing Orlando away. "I've had so many microphones jammed up my nose. So I give them my usual ad-libs, plus a few brand-new ones for luck! This time Garrick's really buggered the . . . What? What?"

Garrick's head slowly emerged from the group. "Thank you James. You put it so well"

When herd instincts stir, all move in sync. Like the swarming of insects, flocking of birds, and the shoaling of fish, life is a biological process.

236

This was an act of survival. James found himself standing alone. Comedy gave way to farce as Pippa and Trixie raced up to Garrick, hugged and kissed him. The others clustered around shaking Garrick's hand, slapping his back, and pledging unwavering support, swearing this crisis had drawn them all closer together.

A tearful Lionel took Garrick's hands. "Remember, my dear the sum of the whole is greater than all its constituent parts. And we are mere constituent parts".

Pheromones filled the air. Everyone was talking, laughing and hugging. In the relentless entwining of lives this was pure Chekhovian force. In all the excitement nobody heard the back door.

Abigail found James Carr alone on a stool in the kitchen perched like a disconsolate gnome. He stared at the wall and ignored her, oblivious to the noise from next door. Abigail waited. Her fingernails cut into her palms with the ultimate comfort of pain. At last James shrugged an acknowledgement and pointed her towards the main hall. The scene was already set. Restraint might be the quintessence of Chekhov but as James knew, others too could be masters of timing. There was no greater pleasure than settling old scores. He repressed a smile as he ushered Abigail in.

It felt like floating on deserts of parquet. No one appeared to have seen her. Unless she were invisible? Perhaps as she'd slipped through that part-open door, her atoms dissolved before reassembling again?

With such paranormal protection she need not be cowed. She saw bright, eager faces bobbing round Garrick. By winning them over he thought he had got a free hand, but they didn't know what she knew. This would be her grand entrance. She was 'Heroine Righting Injustice'.

As everyone huddled and gabbled around, Garrick had an awareness as faint as the flick of an eyelid. But the surrounding surge of allegiance swelled to a climax. They cheered. And they cheered. He was being accepted; even respected at last. This was redemption on an almost cosmic scale. Such chances had to be seized. Seized or lost forever. But something was unsettling. Without knowing why, he found himself pushing supporters aside as if blindly following a script.

But Abigail must have been waiting. He ran across. He hugged and then kissed her.

A split-second's silence. Then the whole of Diwalhi exploded. *Pow! Zap! Zap! Flash!* Splatters of flashlights flared from high windows. Lens-shutters clattered and whirred. Photographers were balanced outside on ladders, cameramen on mobile cranes. Flash followed flash from above. Scoop on top of counter-scoop, each unique and exclusive, choreographed like a movie. It was atavistic and tribal with forces none could withstand. This was ambush and siege. Aluminium ladders. Cameramen tramping through bushes. Reporters like stunt men balanced on railings training their lenses through gaps.

In a moment's revelation Garrick foresaw the puns:

'King Leer!' 'Stage spite!' 'Chekhov Checked Out!'

He knew people believed what they read. Headlines sold. Exaggeration worked. Except why would anyone care? He was a nothing. No-one had been murdered. No-one had accused him of rape. All he had done was get drunk like any banker or statesman. Ordinary consenting sex in a bed. A hotel bed. Normal sex with a normal young woman. Nothing aberrant in that. In some societies girls were married at twelve but nobody talked about double-cross and betrayal and yet. And yet . . . worse, he had not heard from Vee. Despite leaving messages he'd not even received a single-word text.

As paparazzi crowded around, Garrick decided to transfer rehearsals back to the theatre, brushing off pleas from Elizabeth Scott and ignoring her promise of help. He made the fatal announcement. Everyone cheered, seized the chance and ran.

The main stage felt more secure than the church hall, although without radiators or heating it felt unremittingly cold. Gaping holes punctured walls. Twisted piping lay exposed. Trixie and Pippa shivered in thick knitted scarves. Lisetta Coll had brought hot-water-bottles from home. Lionel strutted in a glossy fur hat like something Chekhov mislaid. Unlikely outfits completed the sub-zero picture as rehearsals continued where they'd left off.

Pippa's blue fingers protruded from fluffy striped mittens. "Speaking as Union Rep, you're bleeding lucky I'm not calling a strike!" And received a round of applause.

Rehearsals continued on stage but Garrick could not concentrate. Vee was certain to phone any moment. The singing was off-key and every discord set his teeth on edge, but Garrick was becoming aware of a faint but insidious sound; an almost imperceptible bleeping. This was Verity's moment. He needed her to let him explain. He needed her absolution. Her complete understanding. Her simple compassion. He managed to crouch down, shielding the phone with both hands.

"Sorry darling." He made smoochy kisses. "Can't talk but I'll listen."

He could feel his heart beating as blood flooded into his cheeks. Compromise wouldn't be easy but he was prepared to concede that both of them were at fault.

"I am speaking to Gary Michael Jones?" a man's voice asked.

"What?"

"This," the sombre voice replied, "Is Harris of Messrs Harris & Nelson. Of Knightsbridge," Its tone sounded peevish. "Solicitors to Mrs Verity Anne Jones née Carr a descendant of the Morozoffs of Massachusetts, of the United States of America. Our client wishes to inform you that she . . . er . . ." Garrick heard rustlings of paper. "She intends to proceed with official separation proceedings in pursuance of her requested divorce. She proposes to serve notice on you . . . and asks if you have any comments."

"What?" Garrick cupped his hand round the mouthpiece.

"But at your wife's insistence we've contacted you in person." The caller sounded irritated. "Informally rather than writing. At the outset, so to speak. Note, this is at her personal insistence, not ours. It is not recommended practice. But as you know, Americans have a finely-tuned sense of fair play."

On stage Dandini played by Orlando Marcel, was performing garbled lyrics to the tune of 'Somewhere Over The Rainbow', suggesting they visit every household in the kingdom, bearing the infamous glass slipper for every

238

young virgin to try. And whomsoever it fitted would become Princess Charming, wife of the much-loved Heir to the Throne, complete with Grand Finale and walkdown through heart-shaped confetti.

"I suggest we make an appointment," the solicitor continued, "Some time within a few days."

"But that's impossible."

"Well, the decision is yours. Your wife has had the decency, the decency to ask us to enquire whether you intended to contest our action. Or whether you'd hoped for reconciliation services? Which shows great consideration indeed. If you should choose the reconciliation option then we shall organise a meeting at our chambers in Upper Montpelier Walk." Back on-stage, Dandini had lost track of his song.

"Okay," Garrick whispered, "Send me details. I'll come."

"In which case we'll need detailed arrangements, plus some specifics from you. First we'll have to . . ." But Garrick was called back to the stage.

Throughout the rest of a very long day not a soul mentioned Temple Storford nor the big party that night. Nor did anyone one ask if he'd go. No one mouthed the "Verity" word or treated Abby differently. Their studied politeness was almost uncanny. Neither had Arthur Ruddock contacted Garrick, nor had Lady de Vries, but even if nothing was outwardly different, everything had changed. An undercurrent flowed on. One thing for sure, he would not attend their bizarre celebrations. Provincial Soirées were absurd! Despite the press encamped outside, rehearsals continued on schedule. Some of the company waved as they left, as if to say "Sorry we shan't see you tonight, but that's how it is!"

Garrick by-passed the reporters and returned to his rooms. He found two new letters waiting in quirkily distinctive scripts. Small hands had struggled to master great tasks with pens that had wills of their own. Both had misspelled his address, spidery, childlike and very endearing. Their greeting cards were handmade and vivid. An angel with glued silver wings, a Santa Claus with cotton-wool trimmings, both bursting with life. To him such innocence seemed almost poignant because childhood would very soon pass. Before long they'd be hitting the 'screamager' phase, building up debts and studying for lengthy exams. Rachel would be a doctor perhaps? Markie more likely a chartered accountant? He tried to envisage their future. 'Blood of one's blood and flesh of one's flesh'. That was the parenting deal. But why wasn't he in their picture himself?

"Happy Xmas daddy I miss you, love Rachel XX. When are you coming home?"

"To my daddy, happy Christmas. Mummy is not here too much. Lots of love, Mark"

"Visiting Rights" came to mind. What had Vee told them? Did she tell them she had asked for divorce? And had they been told about Abigail yet? Questions only begged further questions because Vee would assume the pantomime was a ludicrous scam and Abigail was the excuse. She'd imagine he had betrayed both his family and Chekhov. She'd take it for granted he'd had a long affaire and that maybe his mugging was some kind of con?

He propped both their cards by his bedside. Those threats of divorce must have stemmed from Roseanne. It could never be Vee. Or was another man in the frame? Her producer? Director? Cameraman even? Anxiety turned into rage. Now he was the one who'd been cuckolded, wronged and publicly shamed, whereas everything he had done was for her. Only her. No-one could be trusted. Not even his closest of colleagues.

He checked the clock several times, synchronising and resetting alarms, wondering how he had coped without any watch and whether the police had retrieved it. He unearthed an uncrumpled shirt and still-packaged tie. He buffed up his frayed leather shoes and admired his new clean-shaven self in the mirror. According to 'Virilis', thirty-eight was the peak of man's life, so here he was on the cusp. Life like comedy was wholly dependant on timing. With just one single nudge he could easily end up middle-aged. Now was the time for action. He practised his grin and his image responded at once. He stooped prizefighter fashion, jabbing and hooking first Arthur then Josh. Opponents responded in sync. As both hit the canvas he counted them out then clasped his hands over his head.

Outside in Baker's Row strip-signs flickered as normal. Skimpy bar girls exposed trademarked buttocks and breasts. A few years ago, dazed Moldovans, Rumanians, and Filipinos had been tiny babies trafficked for rent, but death was in everyone's genes. Time was a Guillotine blade.

When his clock alarm buzzed Garrick was fully prepared. The moment had come. The decision was made. He downed a quick slug of vodka. Chekhov would have been subtle but Pushkin imposed codes of honour plus a pair of matched pistols in their silk-lined box. With referee and seconds appointed, a doctor in attendance, a clearing in birch woods and shafts of shimmering sunlight through mists, Garrick would soon be confronting his fate. This might be his finale.

He wound a scarf round his overcoat collar, paused on the little cramped landing, then headed out into the wintry Lancashire night.

CHAPTER ELEVEN

FINALE

Soirée guests would soon be arriving. Staff and caterers ran in ever-diminishing circles as Peggy de Vries and The Majestic's Board of Directors gathered for one final meeting.

At the far end of Storford Great Table, Lady Peggy sat in state as Arthur held forth from the other. The oak-panelled room smelled of beeswax and history. Its resonance rang like a courtroom. Family portraits stared straight ahead. Here Arthur felt very much at home, and considered with very good reason he was almost an honorary member. Let centuries come and go as they fancied, a telephone list could reverberate like The Book of Revelations and guarantee instant attention, but the death of Rex Schulman had come as the ultimate shock.

They'd received the announcement that morning. Everyone paid personal tributes. 'Genius, prodigy, luminary, great man of letters', adding that nothing would ever be quite the same. Each had their own recollection. Some were close to tears but Lady de Vries was outwardly stoic, which Arthur knew meant she was deeply moved. He allowed her distress to sink in but financial facts would have to be faced. At last he took a deep breath.

"Now finally, friends and colleagues . . . let me come to my main point!" The committee flinched in their Chippendale chairs. "Yes. The crunch!" One by one he locked onto each pair of eyes. "You all know what I mean This panto of ours. Our poor little Cinderella. She isn't just a pantomime, see." He rested both hands on the table before him. "Oh no, my friends. She is our bridging loan. Our sticking plaster, so to speak. Our annual profit, our public approval, our status, tiding us over towards an exciting new era. And we know what that means. Quite simply, the recreation of Norston.

241

Which brings us to our new Director of Productions." Several committee members looked sharply up. "He doesn't bear comparison with Rex. Our poor dear late Rex Not this whatsisname who's spattered all over the press Allegedly bringing our town into disrepute! But let's keep a sense of proportion". He caught their confusion. "Yes, that's what I'm saying. Don't they say all publicity's good? That's if you put it to use." He leaned confidingly forward. "And between you and me, we shall make use of it. We owe that to Rex. And in the end, it's all up to us And this is the perfect occasion. That's why we're here. To make our decision." He looked defiantly round. " We shall pass a unanimous verdict, knowing quite a few futures lie in our hands. Understood?"

Having learned to read between lines, the governors knew decisions had ways of backfiring.

Lady Peggy leaned forward. "It's not for us to cast the first stone. Rex would not have approved. Nor would my late husband." The committee all nodded. "So legal niceties must be observed for the good of our theatre and of course natural justice."

As usual Arthur chose the line of least resistance. "Madame is so right. Natural justice. Of course. Yes of course But let's face it, there's none of us immortals. Or not so far as I know. We can't accept headlines and hearsay. We must demand solid proof."

"Exactly!" Peggy smiled quickly at Arthur. "Garrick's signed a contract, and so have we. Which implies shared obligations. His Cinderella's only a taster. So when it comes to his main season I'm certain he'll make it awfully exciting. We look forward to wonderful Chekhovs. It is exactly one hundred years since he died. Then afterwards there'll be Strindbergs. And Ibsens. Maybe even a soupçon of Shakespeare? . . . With that we can apply for a grant."

Arthur half raised an eyebrow. "A shame he won't be attending tonight, our producer. Your Soirée ought to be everyone's highlight."

As Peggy leaned forward the panelled oak doors imperceptibly parted behind her. Only Arthur caught a glimpse of her son in the opening.

Peggy took a sip of Burgundy. "Thank you Arthur, so they say. But that won't stop Norston becoming the North's Centre of Culture tonight. We shall be Lancashire's primary city again." Everyone murmured approval. "And now, I've an announcement to make." Arthur sat up sharply. "As my special gesture of faith in our future, and in recognition of my family's lifelong involvement in Norston, I am making a unique proposal." The committee looked baffled, Arthur frantically scuffled through the agenda as Peggy watched in amusement. "Yes. After much consideration, I'm prepared allow 'The Majestic' to be re-consecrated as 'The Theatre de Vries!'

As usual in Norston the weather had turned. Cars churned up damp gravel; soggy lanterns skipped on long looping wires as fairy lights flickered round bay trees in tubs. At the far end of Temple Storford's main courtyard, under a concentration of lights, Lady Peggy de Vries posed beneath the massive portico, a silver fox coiled round her shoulders, putting aside her misgivings:

"Good evening everyone! Welcome to all my dear Friends of the Theatre. Greetings, greetings," repeated like a jammed disc.

Guests fell into line like a royal reception, shaking hands with each of the committee. Every visitor ran the same hand-wrenching gauntlet before being kissed on both cheeks by the hostess herself.

"Please go through to the banqueting hall Please go through to the banqueting hall . . . Please go through to the banqueting hall . . ." she chanted.

Attendance was noticeably higher this year. As candles glowed and chandeliers flickered, echoing spaces were filling with guests. Having gone to the bother of showering and shaving, Josh pushed through hordes of cameramen besieging the wrought-iron main gates. He doubted if Abby would dare to attend, knowing her unease among crowds. She was still avoiding him. To make it worse, gossip was adding new details with obscene allegations, none of which Josh believed. He'd heard recent talk of cancelling the pantomime which he didn't make sense. It brought back Roddy's anarchic views. Josh preferred measurements, materials, structures: that way you knew where you were. Heading for the free-flowing champagne, he edged past Arthur with Lady de Vries who greeted every guest as if snatching her very last chance while Arthur was kicking the parquet and grumbling:

"I told them 'No statement'. But will they take 'No' for an answer? No! So I doles out printed statements. But, oh no! They write their own bloody stories, carving slices out your soul."

Soon Peggy was reminiscing with Lionel about the philosophical nature of art, while outside the main gates, film crews in bobble hats gulped hot soup from vacuum flasks. Security officers prowled the grounds with dogs. The press corps was getting impatient. So far only James Carr had approached them, handing out his personal statement and volunteering to pose for shots.

In the long gallery, a string quartet was playing sanitised versions of popular songs. Wine was beginning to flow and Peggy was into her mingling phase, still shaking hands like a hustings. One of the actors knelt down and kissed her hand. Seeing her so entranced by James Carr was more than Arthur could take. He thought he knew people, but here she was, behaving in ways which stuck him as damned indiscreet. And where was the political nous? Democratisation was one thing, but a secure social structure needed certain barriers. That was the recognised Lancashire way. Socialism was dated and past. You didn't need a degree to see that. He'd once been a union convener himself. Even Lenin and Mao refurbished their images because society was always fragmenting. If he could see that, why the hell couldn't she? This was the twenty-first century and into its creditocracy phase, but Norston was proud of its backwater status. If all inherited status vanished, then where would society be? Only the presence of George beside him kept Arthur gritting his teeth. Not knowing what Peggy might do, he muttered excuses and mingled. Waiters repeatedly topped up his glass, obliterating his thoughts.

On one of these circumnavigations he caught sight of Phyllis. There she was standing alone. Her unexpected smartness caught his attention. New cocktail dress and diamante trimmings. Very trendy. Almost out of character. A pillar of our theatre, he thought, who understood systems and finance.

She'd keep her own counsel and know where she belonged. He placed a hot hand on her icy cool wrist, but she edged away looking startled, urgently shaking her head. Usually she'd have responded. This time everyone was putting on fronts because office staff were overcome, aping Manchester ways.

Amidst pyramids of hors d'oeuvres on tables looped with spruce and overloaded with silver salvers, he inhaled dangerous cocktails of spices, but made no attempt to suppress them. It was as if gilded platters were terraced with layers of fragrant hors d'oeuvres on beds of silk salad. Decorative leaves were adorned with ornately diced radish and carrot-like jewels sprinkled with Parmesan dust. Wild salmon and Atlantic prawns were latticed with dill and ringed with calamari and grapes. This was the annual feast of all feasts. It was the pinnacle of the year. Trays of vegetable quiches postured alluringly on tables as ornate as classic still-lives. Crystalline cake stands bore mounds of gateaux with Everest toppings of pastry and cream. Dishes of exotica glowed amidst candles like offerings on festive altars. Guests grubbed up handfuls as though they'd not eaten for weeks, revelling in conspicuous greed. People were eating themselves to a standstill. At the centre of all this consumption stood one single glittering ice-sculptured shoe on a cut glass pedestal, slowly melting away.

In this Josh saw a great truth. The Cinderella dilemma! Along with depression came misery, loneliness, failure, sexual frustration and anger. A shoe was only one half of a pair, like personalities split, unions broken, and lives set adrift. The classic bi-polar problem. He moved on from drinking to eating, hoping over-indulgence would deaden the pain. Seeing others wading in, his appetite sharpened and grew. Like speeded-up action, dips and crudités vanished, next hors d'oeuvres, then savouries, along with trays of pastries and crates of Chilean wine. After over-spiced tartlets he'd started on slices of quiche when Arthur approached with Phyllis at his heels.

It may have been this toxic excess which gave Phyllis that insight she preferred to ignore. She'd attended these soirées for years but Arthur had barely noticed, if ever. As conversation around them grew louder, alcohol loosened more tongues. It was 'Garrick and Abigail', 'Abby and Gary', punctuated by laughter. These absentees must not be allowed to take over.

Arthur took Phyllis's arm. "Time for formal introductions. Come on."

To her surprise she allowed him to lead her towards Lady Peggy de Vries. Sometimes one let others make pointless gestures even while plumbing the depths of one's soul. Ahead of them the hostess was perched on her personal dais surrounded by flowers and palms, necklaced with natural pearls, and distractedly sipping champagne. This was her imperial court, a throwback to some other era. But as Arthur and Phyllis approached, the babble slurred and fell silent. People were nudging and pointing. Peggy's face seemed to quiver then freeze. Arthur and Phyllis followed everyone's gaze

As the far doors closed a hooded figure slipped in. When Abigail theatrically flipped back her hood, there was an audible gasp. She wanted to whoop! She wanted to savour the moment! Who needed uppers or downers? This was the ultimate catwalk. So why was she feeling so empty inside? She'd slipped past the press pack unnoticed. Now all the faces were turned towards her as she slipped the coat from her shoulders and performed a self-conscious twirl. Within seconds that moment had passed. It was gone. People picked up where they'd left off with everyone speaking at once.

As Abigail glided forward, some edged away. Jilly Craske would have loved this. From somewhere at the back of her mind Abby glimpsed Jilly's corpse in its ice-drawer in that grey-tiled morgue. There too was Jilly's baby, premature and stillborn, as if birth and death had joined forces. Then came those echoes of Thomas's wails. Somehow she had to escape. Her inner self came to her rescue.

Somehow she'd stepped out of her body and found herself gazing down. Alone in her personal bubble, she glimpsed far below someone ambling towards her. At the moment Josh stretched out his arms, Abigail's disembodied spirit swooped down. It dived like a crane and zoomed into close-up. It felt cinematic and epic. Hollywood and The Bible combined.

At that same moment Josh saw Abby anew, her bare shoulders heightened with shimmering sequins, sandy locks shining with copper. Josh took the lead. Together they crossed invisible lines. Little gatherings parted before them. Like the Red Sea these waters would close and all be forgotten. The night's big sensation was over and finished before it began.

Suddenly Garrick appeared in the doorway framed like a movie. He paused for effect before strolling forward so recklessly calm that not even Chekhov could have heightened the moment. As he casually waved even he had not foreseen the effect. It was like an H.M. Bateman cartoon. The music creaked to a stop. Ice-sculpted swans plip-plopped into silence. Guests shuffled like biblical sands. In this sudden hiatus Elizabeth Scott edged towards Garrick. But Peggy moved faster.

"So, Mister Jones, you did make it!" Lady de Fries slowly shook Garrick's hand before standing back to observe him. "Or should we call you Garrick now?"

"You can call me whatever you want." He raised her fingers to his lips, tasting the diamonds and sapphires.

"How nice of you to attend," Peggy cooed, "If only at the very last moment. Let's hope your new-found 'fame' brushes off on our theatre In the nicest possible way." Garrick half bowed. "And your talented wife? One's heard so much about her." And knew she had hit home. "A cuisinière in her own right, so I hear? But I'm sure your 'Cinderella' will outclass any gourmet cuisine, Chekhov is so English you see. He understands us. He relishes the provincial. Such witty melancholia strikes chords with sensitive people. Don't you agree?"

"I'm not a literary critic."

"But you are our expert in drama. So why not produce us Nikolai Gogol's 'The Government Inspector' as well? That Russian classic? About this little nondescript man who arrives at some place off the map, and everyone thinks he's a man of importance? A Government Inspector, you see! All these small-town people from somewhere up in the Urals . . . !" She chuckles. "They fuss and fawn, and he lets them believe! It's a glorious satire."

From among the Roman philosopher busts Arthur Ruddock and young George de Fries in matching dinner jackets, watched events unfold. Arthur gripped George's shoulder, endorsing his own imitation with pride, admiring those features he recognised as his own. Experience had to be shared.

"Thing is, George, whatever gets said by others don't matter! You and me understand. Like osmosis. We carry on great legacies." He nodded at Socrates then towards Plato. "Solid best Italian marble! That's our tradition, Georgie. Solidity. The Norston tradition. No matter what else, you and me keep faith. It's what's in the blood. It comes down to trust. Team spirit. Right? It's our mutual interdependence and . . . not just that." Arthur sought adequate words. "You see, me and your mother. Believe me George, I've total faith . . . you and me, that's what I'm saying. A gentleman always honours his word. It's in our shared blood." He punched George playfully in the upper arm. "Am I right? Your Lordship?" and Plato imperceptibly rocked on his plinth.

When tradition becomes a bad habit it's hard to shake off. Madame's reception marked the apogee of her season. It is listed as 'Soirée of the Year' in Lancashire Times and reported in Manchester, Liverpool, Preston. The theatre board considered this annual bean-feast gave a boost to staff morale. The party was everyone's treat: from Bert and Phyllis to the stand-in pianist, to James Carr, Lionel, Pippa and Trixie and the rest of the cast. The Soirée was now both an end in itself and the consummation of everyone's hopes. For Peggy de Vries this was her great act of faith. With partying well under way and everyone talking at once, Arthur kept to the background, knowing that when Peggy's son took over the family trust, there'd be changes. Big changes. Real changes. That would be Arthur's own revolution as well. Progress was unstoppable.

Across the room James Carr cornered Garrick.

". . . So what is the nature of drama?" James Carr was asking. "Violence is integral and beauty is its antidote. Two sides of the Freudian coin. By which I don't mean sentimental insipid, innocuous or suppressing anything mildly offensive. We have to ask ourselves why?" James leaned forward. "So why over-sanitise? Take 'Cinderella'. Her real story starts where our show ends! With marital rape, multiple births, and probably death during labour!"

Garrick compulsively downed more Bordeaux. In the real world his wife was threatening divorce, his kids were distraught and Abigail was avoiding him. There was one other hell you could not escape. That hell was one's self. Merely by turning up, Garrick had made his big gesture, now others were blatantly cutting him out. As Garrick and Abigail circled each other from opposite ends of the room, Garrick slowly edged forwards, guest by guest, until he was almost in reach.

"Why hello, Mr Jones!" A suited man pounced. "From Manwess Gas? Chief Engineer, North Western Region? Big job, this! What with renewin' your flipperin' junctions an' mains." He wiped watery eyes. "Some over an 'undred years old, an' in a blitherin' state. Corrosion, see . . ." Garrick saw Abigail slipping away. "But speaking as a theatre buff, I loved your stand-up comics show. Dirty but witty!" He shook Garrick's hand and winked broadly. "Well done!"

A soft hand caught his arm. "Hello at last. Shouldn't we talk?" Elizabeth Scott disposed of her glass on a passing tray, "You mustn't blame your hotel if someone just happened to give me the nod that night. Like one of their staff? Who did kind of happen to take a few snapshots? For the record, that is. Plus the police always keep us informed. For public relations."

"Live by the press, die by the press? That it?"

She raised her eyebrows. "Really? A man of your talents? Don't you aspire?" She gazed around. "There's a big world out there, and I'm here to give you a chance before those red-label tabloids pounce and . . . and before agencies fill up their websites. With us you can still put your own point of view. You'll give us your story, exclusive? Okay?"

Anticlimax must have entered his blood. Garrick awoke several times in the night. Darkness clung like a physical presence, heavy, crystalline, thick. He propped himself upright. Time had speeded up, spitting him from a Black Hole into limbo. His whole body ached. His tongue was swollen and dry.

"Fucking soirée!"

Some bastard must have spiked his drinks. Those sensitive membranes between the emotions dissolved as events spiralled out of control. Except for the name of Rex Schulman, the rest was a merciful blank. Next he'd been sick in a cab then dumped on the doorstep .Oh yes, and the guy from over the landing had helped him unlock his front door. Somewhere at the back of his mind, among biblical texts and moral injunctions, another thought must have lain. A Trojan. A self-replicating virus.

He fumbled around in the darkness, found a switch, flicked Pow! He was padding along in a daze, nervously humming and ready to pee. There it was again. *Zap! Bang!* Everything hit him. Flashbacks followed flashbacks. Black and white in negative. Faces over-exposed. Press 'playback'! No one escapes their subconscious. With all synapses firing, their nightmares began to recur. Mix to himself on some landing-stage in sulphurous mists. Then Mark and Rachel on a ship's wooden deck in the darkness alongside him alone. Slowly but surely moving away Dark water lapping beneath them Two diminutive figures. Both stretching towards him, silently screaming.

"Daddy! Daddy!" They're mouthing, "Help us! Help!"

That widening gap is the Earth's crust. It is splitting, dividing, spewing out molten larva, leaving him spiked to the ice, receding, helpless and voiceless. New images come. Vee, blue in the face. Her head in a clear plastic bag, tight round the neck. It floats underwater, disconnected, mouth opening and closing, blue lips distorted. Like a ferocious painting by Bacon. Terror without any sound. Then Abigail's face drifts into close-up, eyes open-wide, lips like pink anemone pouting. She laughs aloud, exposing bloodstained teeth and forked flickering tongue . . .

Garrick leaned over the sofa and retched. There was no doubt any longer. If Vee had first seen that advert for Norston, it was Garrick who'd jumped without judging the odds. Now his children would set off for school with their futures in some other hands. But would they get decent breakfasts? Wash their hands? Do their homework? Trivia mattered, like brushing teeth and packing suitable lunches. Often he'd try to calculate where they were and what they'd be doing that moment. Would they so much as give him a thought?

Boxing Day would be 'Cinderella's' First Night! Lionel in that blue baroque wig, curtsying and camping around. Garrick still had presents to buy. Where was his bicarbonate? No, he needed caffeine. Images ran like a slide show. His wife, his children, their cats. Hot showers, warm central heating, comfortable restaurants, West End theatres, music and lights. In a flood of sentiment he dialled Verity's mobile, finding only a messaging service. He dialled every number he knew, scanning the memory bank, then thought of calling her solicitor direct.

As he hurried up Cavanham Street he noticed 'Crowing Glory' was shut, with a printed sign in its window. "Closed until further notice". Single blooms in silver foil were wedged round the door-frame. Scribbled post-its were stuck to the glass. Was it a birthday? People should celebrate more. A few doors away Craig Demolition was stripping another office block: like a virus they struck then moved on. By the time he'd reached the waterway footbridge, last night seemed remote.

The canal lay as still as buffed granite, as black and dead as chemical soup. Oil like corneal film stared reflectionless back, fringed with wafers of ice like the look of the terminally blind. How many people had jumped in and drowned? Mill workers worn to distraction? The newly bereaved? The depressed? Their carcasses rotting away in this mud? Within months this would ferment into lilies, with dragonflies zipping around. 'Venice of the post-industrial North'? 'Lancastrian Vegas'? 'Leisure Park for the Masses'? Once these arteries fed local industry. The railways changed that. Their bridges still spanned these canals, until like the very last cherry tree in the orchard; the final tall chimney was axed. Its shock waves shuddered the walls of the theatre.

Eventually winter would end, spring and summer return. Back gardens would bloom. Birds would build nests, window boxes burst into flower. Everything would germinate. But Brinkhouse Development and Brinkhouse Construction would continue drilling right up to the end, their pile-drivers shaking the earth. Garrick stared at the water. A beetle trapped in surface tension lay upside-down, drifting, legs flailing. He identified strongly. He willed it to swim or to fly. His instinct was to stretch out and save it. Leaning and straining, his fingers stretched out, when *whoomph*! A chunk of masonry plunged into water, barely missing his head. Flocks of pigeons took flight. By the time he'd spun round two mountain bikes had hurtled away down the gimmel.

The theatre was shrouded in mist with meltwater dripping from gutters. Garrick wasn't sure what to expect. Last night's soirée had been like an end in itself.

The union delegates gathered to greet him in hooded anoraks for the Arctic conditions. Ice crystals drifted round lights as if winter had invaded the building and resentment hung on the air. Garrick was prepared for the worst.

Pippa presented her list of complaints. According to 'Health & Safety Regulations' the 'workplace' should be shut down at once. Her thermometer proved it. 'The problem's these boilers?' The actors agreed, but what was he expected to do? Okay, yes yes, so the heating had failed? Sure, it was certainly freezing? And yes, it was definitely Arctic? Despite re-installation, temporary boilers were 'bronchially challenged', then failed completely 'due to prevailing conditions'. When the shouting match began, Garrick was conscious of Abigail's presence. By just existing she dominated proceedings, always avoiding his eyes. His arguments would not stack up. He knew he had lost.

When the actors returned, not only did they agree to keep working but offered to make contributions. Garrick was stunned. Acceptance made everything worse: winning felt like defeat. Phyllis had brought a spare mini-stove and Fabian hired in some Calor Gas heaters. Rehearsals proceeded in topcoats, mittens, and scarves, but somehow the show had gone off the boil. Its edge was dulled. Too many fluffed cues and mistimings. Through Garrick's eyes only Abigail sparkled. No matter how much he tried shutting her out, her tightly clenched fists always dragged something out of the void. It was time to take a short break.

Below stage the basement was clammy; the wardrobe was cramped. Sewing machines rattled away, surrounded by rails of grotesque concoctions. The Dame's and two Ugly Sisters' frocks were approaching completion. Ludicrous ball gowns were blooming like freshly picked flowers, lurid with aberrations. Valerie continued to sew as he entered, guiding ribbons and cloth through the ravenous needles. He plunged on through the digestive tracts of the building. The crunch was ahead and would have to be faced.

The scenery bay lay at the end of a passage. Grey light filtered through skylights like layers of fluorescent dust. Model stage sets were arranged on a workbench, florid sketches pinned to the walls. In a side bay Reg Diamond was finishing a staircase, stapling canvas to wood. Josh was painting a doorway, stripped to the waist, bulging with muscles, and oblivious to everything. Reg grinned through a mouthful of nails and Josh was more jaunty than ever.

Garrick looked round. Everything was too far advanced. He was being outwitted and Josh was too full of himself. They need not think they could lie back on their laurels. This wasn't the end of the story.

"I'm bringing forward our technical run-through." Garrick paused for effect. "Tomorrow sharp! Okay? Dress rehearsal's the day after tomorrow. First Night is Boxing Day matinée! Okay?"

Josh nodded casually up at a wall chart. "No problem."

Garrick's frustration ran riot. Vengeance? Vendetta? Revenge? After Temple Storford, flashbacks followed one after another. Abigail was everywhere. She recurred like a retinal imprint. Her laughter. His mugging. That rock from the footbridge? Black and anonymous cars. Everywhere shadowed and threatened. Everything fitting a pattern.

He found Phyllis painfully typing in mittens.

She looked up as he passed. "Garrick, it's urgent. Could you phone Mr Ruddock? About a press conference. Yes?"

Inside his office the air was so thin the walls had compacted, radiators fossilised, and water as solid as glass. His breath condensed into crystalline mist shrouding family snaps like the smiles of the bravely bereaved. Again and again he tried phoning. First Vee's mobile then home. From sheer desperation he tried her solicitor's office.

"Mr – Saxton – is – not – available," came the digitised twang, "But – please – leave – a – message – after – the – tone. Blee–ee–ee–ep!"

He sat with collar upturned and both hands in pockets. Once he had been so content. Perhaps his marriage had turned into clichés, but she could have turned the film company down. Producers are smart. They'd recognised Vee as a viable product. Her body language must have been clear. "You are what you eat" as she'd say, "What matters are fundamentals, not fashions."

Again his suspicions renewed. What if she'd known of their offer? Accepted before seeing that advert for Norston? The timing still jarred. Was Chekhov personally in on the plot? Her sudden obsession with Chekhov? Whisking him off to apply? Getting him out from under her feet?

As he sat there, daylight faded. He tried wiping a windowpane clear, but melt-ice froze into delicate fairy-tale forests. He scraped a crude hole with his nails. Through this small void, he glimpsed first flecks of snow . . . and made his crucial decision.

Up to the moment he'd slipped from the office, returned to his digs, then crammed a few things in a holdall, he'd been unsure what he intended. Having slipped a twenty-pound note under his neighbour opposite's door, that seemed to clinch it.

The southbound train clacked over points in a rhythmic rumble. Snowflakes settled and melted. The late service was packed. Travellers were jostling and coughing, compressing themselves into humanoid mounds. Whoever had bet on White Christmas must be calculating their winnings but Garrick was wishing he'd taken a flight. 'Christmas Special' meant pregnant luggage, hyperactive children, and weary adults. Soon he'd be home. He remembered that closing shot in the movie where the hero comes running as music swells to a climax. Tears brim in his eyes. His kids break forward and run, hands outstretched in slow motion, running towards him.

"Daddy, daddy! Poppa!" they scream.

He sweeps them up in his arms. The camera pulls out wider, and wider, and wider until they all shrink into dots on a distant horizon. Then the full credits run.

Real life was not like that. His children had quickly sensed he was the one who depended on them. Neither Chekhov nor Coleridge had their limitations reproduced in young genes. Maybe they'd misunderstood religion. One's progeny was one's sole resurrection. Each life was a link in that chain of command going back millennia, reprinted again and again. Its code was deceptively simple. No doubt his late father would be there at the opening night of 'The Seagull' then cheering on the 'Three Sisters', because Edwin wanted the best for his son. Perhaps his ghost was on this very same train?

Through dirty windows Garrick watched countryside pass. First comes that general awareness, then calculable pinpoints of light multiplying like stars reflected on low-flying clouds. He could feel every hour grind away and away and away . . .

They say you don't feel a pain till it stops: then comes the noise, the dampness and chill. Garrick tasted distinctive aromas. Without even opening his eyes he'd have recognised London. You have to escape to know a place clearly. By now he desperately needed his fix. Carbon monoxide and sulphur mingled with tikka marsala and grills. Norston was so different. It had such clear-cut boundaries. You could drive across in about half an hour, whereas London spreads like a fungal infection and follows the curve of the Earth.

The day felt surprisingly mild but it must have been recently raining. No sign of snow. Instead a pulp of discarded wrappers mulched underfoot. Newspaper headlines shouted of gangland and murders. Packaging blew on the wind. Outside Euston station the taxi queue shuffled and moaned, spitting gum as tourists and relatives yawned, then scrambled one place up the line as each vehicle rumbled away.

So Garrick waited. And waited. Beyond the station forecourt traffic crawled nose to tail. Wasn't a taxi meant to bypass delays? He'd stored up weeks of emotions for this. Anticipation was wearing him down.

His kids were happy knowing nothing of Norston, or Wales, or Edwin, or Chekhov, still less of Coleridge and his Ancient Mariner. This was year Zero to children. They took civilisation for granted, but if a single cog gets out of sync or a few kilobytes fail, the world could grind to a halt.

Again he tried ringing home. After several attempts he gave up. His arrival would be all the more spectacular. He pictured their astonishment and chuckled aloud, but as each cab arrived people surged forward, jostled, fought, then regrouped. Garrick was reduced to reading the billboards. A smiling young girl, all too much like Abigail, was advertising a new super-diet. He thought of Arthur Ruddock and Louise Roberts, and Phyllis, Pippa and Trixie, Jilly Craske, Josh White, Eddie Craig. Then Elizabeth Scott from that bloody paper and . . .

Vee of course would be upset. Of course. That's why it was vital to see her. Those weren't the headlines she'd wanted. And yet, with so many scandals and murders these days, why should his escapades count? Okay, the press distorted facts, so people jumped to conclusions. Here he was only a face in the crowd. As each cab's arrival led to pushing and shouting, Garrick heard someone out-yelling the rest. Syllables formed into recognisable words.

"Heyah Gary! Yeah, you! Gary Jones!" A large glossy Lexus was flashing every conceivable light, its driver frantically waving and pointing. "Hey man, it's me. Wanna ride?" Whoever it was, was pitching directly at Garrick. "Look man, don' fuck around! Jus' jump in!"

Garrick edged doubtfully over, suspecting some kind of scam. A semaphore of black hands and pale palms invited him over. The driver slid blue-mirrored shades up his ebony forehead.

"Why there Gary old fellow! Where the hell have you been?" came those high-pitched mock-gentrified accents, "Come on old chappie! I'll drop you wherever you want," and burst into irrepressible giggles.

Knotted bleached curls were threaded with woven extensions tied back over prominent ears. An open silk shirt gave glimpses of triple gold chains hung with menageries of charms.

"Gary old chap! Do climb aboard! It's the ol' team agin! It Gangey and Gary agin." Gangey opened the passenger door. "Don' jus' stan' dere! Tell us where you bin hiding." Cars behind started to hoot as Garrick scrambled aboard. "Believe me, old chappie, you're lookin' damn frightfully well!"

Gangey gave a two-fingered sign at the traffic, followed by a blast on the hooter. The car swung into the roadway. Garrick began to explain which way to head and how to navigate Lancaster Gate, but Gangey was nodding while heading the opposite way.

"No never min' dat. Meetin' you's got to mean some'ting importan'. You not bin down 'em studios, nor rehearsal room too, not for ages, man. I know you, Gary. You dip'n' you dive. What de latess scam? Not dat strip-dance musical, eh?" and he laughed at Garrick's expression. "No?" He waved aside Garrick's objections. "Me too. I'm off bitches as well. All dat nude dancing you ran! Yeah, mebbe big bucks,but fuck! You don' control no rights no more. An' dat digital editin' crap They paint in a fully raised todger what's bigger'n'better'n elephants got! Real kinky shit!" He shook his great mountain of curls. "Capitalism, man!"

"These days I'm more into Chekhov and Strindberg." Garrick said carefully.

"You mean dem Cuban cigars? . . . No, I know! I know! Dey writin' plays. I'm not fuckin illiterate, man! Don' forget I'm a poet. So what's wit you? All dat house-husban' shit! Well, it so 'appen I gone upmarket too. That's why I bin droppin' off frien's at the station."

"I'm surprised you recognised me."

"When I sees you stannin' dere, I forget you's like this. All tight-arse and tin-lipped. Same as dat Rocko, your agent fella. Show business, it changin', man. It skin flick an' dat stuff. Whole ting done in an editin' suite! Digits an' pixels! Gettin you doin' perversion, the lot. Nex' minute it on a website I mean, where de respeck? Don' categorise me. Know what I'm saying?"

Garrick suggested they ought to turn back towards Lancaster Gate. But Gangey seemed oblivious.

"Come on." Gangey was dwelling on something. "Look, I'm still waitin'! Come on! So it is your woman in dem magazine? Eh?" He turned towards Garrick and waited until Garrick reluctantly nodded, then Gangey gave a low whoop. "Great! An' on de box too! Verity Jones! Celebrity Cook! An' your own missus? Cookin'all dat bee-oo-tiful food!" His joshing sounded envious now. "To tell de troof, you make de right move. Yeah, management is where it at now. An' you done pretty good."

"It isn't quite like . . ." But Gangey kept looking at him not the road, and still they had not turned westwards.

"Jus 'ope she know she lucky, 'avin' you pushin 'er, Gary. Eatin' at nightspots. Wheelin'and dealin'! Know what I'm sayin? Well I'm plannin' on management too. Gettin' meesel' a new stable. Importin' intellectual women. Goin' upmarket Russian, Chinee, Abanians. Big dollars, right? Quality counts." He let out a long breath. "You mus' be rakin' in fortunes." As Gangey stayed heading east, that sweet smoky smell was not simple tobacco.

Garrick was becoming concerned. "My wife has a separate career. I'm just, only, merely a . . ." But the ghost of his father lurked on the back seat.

252

"You see I'm her professional advisor. Taxation awareness, you see. Without me she makes no decisions. Financial consultancy matters."

Ganj turned again to observe him, letting the roadway take care of itself. "Now you treatin' me like some Jamaican!"

He gave a long whistle dissolving into a sigh. People revert, Ganji was thinking, that was the shame; the brief link between them was severed. No more networking. No jobbing. No Clubland prospects. No conversation. No deals. If Garrick had signed up to Chekhov, Gangey was writing him off.

"Look, head towards Lancaster Gate," Garrick was saying. "Please. The far end? 9A, St Georges' Mews. That's back in the other direction Heading West, okay? Find somewhere to turn round."

"Like where?" Gangey stirred from a centuries-old coma. "Shit man! I aint no minicab. I don' carry no ninety-page map in me brain. I jus' a jobbing actor who built 'isself a swimmin' pool an' keep a race-horse or three."

Garrick found himself out on the pavement, waving at retreating lights. One single day had combined several epochs leaving Garrick out of phase. Decades must have passed within weeks; whole civilisations had come and gone. Now he was dumped at the kerb with Gangey driving away. A Time Machine switched itself on. A single still-frame flickered then whirred into action as if he'd just popped out the house and was picking up where he'd left off. He turned into Lancaster Gate with little clear sense of time, but when he got his missing watch back everything would fall into place.

He strolled along, noticing pea-lights strung up in trees and feeling at peace with the world. He was proud of his initiative. Because his visit was spur of the moment, he'd had no chance to buy Christmas presents. Ready cash would have instant appeal: he knew the kids would be thrilled. By the time he had turned at the junction for Sussex Gardens with just a few metres to go, he'd reached other major decisions.

"Vee darling", he'd say, "You're asking me to manage you? You want me to be your official advisor? Okay! Done! . . . I accept!"

Then he'd casually reveal the true facts of his panto, but guarantee Cherry Orchard next year. When Verity saw he'd no choice, everyone would be happy. Easy!

The familiar plaque announced 'St George's Mews' and Garrick strode through the archway into its 'oh-so-respectable' shades. Here Christmas lights glowed in sash windows. As in one of his recent dreams, he observed himself ringing the doorbell. But ringing at his own front door, surveyed by a yellow-eyed cat? He slid the Yale into its slot.

Nothing happened! He jiggled again. The lock was jammed! He checked all his keys then tried the deadlock. None worked. He tried ringing. Then banging. The weather had turned noticeably cooler. Sea breezes were blowing down from the Arctic where men froze to iced decks like a Gustave Doré illustration.

As he stepped back to check the house number a woman appeared, leading two poodles with holly sprigs tied to their collars.

"You're wasting your time," she remarked, and both dogs started barking, "They'll be closed till New Year. Best make an appointment." She pointed above him.

For Sale. No visitors without appointment.
Apply Branagh and Harvey, Kensington High Street

"Estate agents!" She snorted. "Leave 'em a message, that's my advice. Oh, and compliments of the season." Dragging her poodles away.

As usual every carriage was crowded. Travellers, tourists and weary commuters were texting away on their mobiles. The window seat was a welcome relief as latecomers trudged down the aisle dragging rucksacks and bags. This was the last train heading back and his life had gone into reverse.

They rattled through one godforsaken station after another. A group of students in bright paper hats gulped lager while munching crisps. Yes, he thought, these must be Norston-bound too; mass repatriation via Manchester Central. Perhaps his own brain would relocate too? These students laughing and joking were no more than Abigail's age. The dark girl with ringlets eventually came to the point of her gag.

"And so, and so he asks, 'But how can a false leg be that bloody painful?'" She waited for silence. "'Why?' he replies, 'Cause me wife smashes it over me head!'"

He felt a headache coming on. Abandoning rose-tinted lenses Garrick had peered into St George's Mews only to witness bare floorboards and walls! He'd straightaway taken a cab to the station then waited four hours for his train. At least, Garrick thought, he had followed his instincts. Vee was insistent on trust, but human nature infected us all.

Perhaps he should have posted a note through their front door or his kids would assume they'd been abandoned. How could his whole family just disappear, putting their house up for sale? Her solicitor had not forewarned him. A discreet Court Order was needed. He'd challenge any custody claims. He was certain that Roseanne who would be probing, cross-checking internet sites, and tracking his mediocrity down. They'd never forgive him for lacking distinction in Chekhov's centenary year. At least strip-joints and nite-clubs once had earned him a living. He was entirely respectable now, therefore;

a. No-one could prevent him from seeing his own children.

b. The law upheld justice.

c. A blood-parent had rights.

d. Every wee kiddie needed its dad.

He tugged a bedraggled script from his holdall. It fell open at page 10. Ten was the total years of his marriage. Ten, ten, ten! This was the decimalisation of wedlock. Exhaustion endowed it with meaning.

He needed a plan of campaign.

He'd contact her lawyers on Monday, politely requesting a meeting. Only then would he mention the house and enquire after his children. Alarming her would be counterproductive. Reasonableness was the style of the day. He would not come clean about his pantomime stunt until Chekhov was into rehearsal. Then Vee could come back to Norston bringing Rachel and Mark? Maybe they'd buy a new home and start afresh. Late at night on a train heading north, anything seemed possible.

He tried roughing a conciliatory message to Messrs. Sexton and Nalson. This would begin his new script:

Act One, Scene One. 'The Rest of his Life' . . .

Next morning he awoke feeling elated. When weather forecasters said "dry and cloudy with sun" it meant hollow-ground rays of sunlight slicing through occasional sleet in slow-moving shafts over moors. Almost a John Martin painting. Today it only meant sunlight and warmth.

As he set off, the demented old guy from over the landing grinned at him on the stairs. Ronnie Patel waved as Garrick passed down the street. Then Louis Murkadjee gave a thumbs-up. The Romanian hooker blew him a kiss, and Danny the bookmaker smiled as if Garrick had just won the jackpot. Everybody knew him. Everyone acknowledged him. That's what notoriety did. It laid a new skin on the landscape. Even Eddie Craig's sites appeared freshly cleared. Traffic flowed like fresh cream, and so far this morning Garrick had never given tobacco a thought. Soon his great saga would be fulfilled. The tragedy was poor Chekhov himself in days before antibiotics.

Garrick's London fiasco was like a parallel-universe and only half real. Its weight was off his mind. He knew it would all be resolved. He pedalled with inexplicable vigour. A heavy truck slowed to give way. A pedestrian smiled. The traffic lights were all in his favour. As he took a right-hand down Halifax Road, he was feeling euphoric. This is how his whole future would be. Anything was possible even if at Cavanham Street a passing bus blocked his path. He slowed and glanced idly up.

Across the whole bus and repeated over its back, was a single gigantic familiar face, ten times life-size. Beneath it the slogan:

'COOK AND LET COOK THE VERITY WAY!'

Her whole-wheat organic smile was crammed with health-giving comfort, gazing as if at a lover! Garrick swerved, wobbled, and lost concentration. Something violently struck his back wheel. He felt it buckle. As he crashed head-over-heels at the kerb, a black saloon accelerated away, its Manwess badge visible in the back window. Garrick sprawled on the tarmac, watching Verity's features retreating; literally the back of a bus.

As Garrick limped up to the theatre's glass doors still dragging the remains of his bike, he was approached by two girls bearing shoulder bags labelled "Brinkside Investments". They followed him closely, heads to one side, narrow-eyed and critical as he pushed at the doors with his bike.

"You an actor?" The paler girl sounded sympathetic. "Look. See. We got James Carr's signature." She held out an autograph book with a pen. "Best wishes," it says, "From a Royal Shakespearean star with lots of love, James Carr". Here you are. An' look at them kisses."

Garrick scrawled his own name over James Carr's, almost driving the point through the paper. Dumping his bike in the foyer, he hobbled upstairs. In knitted shawl and fingerless mittens Phyllis was one-handedly typing while answering phones. Her plaster frogs wore new tinsel bows. She gave a shy smile. It was oddly self-conscious and very un-Phyllis.

"Agreed!" she snapped at the phone, "Then make damn sure it is!" She rang off, evasively smiling. "Well, good morning Garrick," she cooed, "Are we glad to see you. And after that party.Oh dear! And the press! Someone said you'd gone running back home to London. He's no quitter, I told them But James Carr is so negative. Garrick'd not disappoint little kiddies, I told them, his very soul's in that panto. And I gave Manwess Gas a good roasting. I went straight to the senior management team. I told them we'd sue, just like you said."

"That's wonderful, Phyllis. Thank you."

What if he'd been seen? A B-List celebrity's husband, famous for being famous. Everyone would jump to conclusions. Wagging tongues would be spreading the word. Soon he'd fill the internet. Another phone started ringing. Within seconds all her phones followed suite. As he made to leave, Phyllis stretched out a restraining hand.

"That's not all. I had a word with Mister Ruddock." Her eyelids imperceptibly flickered. "On your behalf. I think he saw sense." She picked up each phone one by one, calmly plopping them back until there was silence. "You see, this town needs a publicity coup. We've got you and your lady-wife to thank. Yes, and your Mrs Roberts phoned. Said she had to talk to you. Very insistent, she was." She gave him an quizzical look. "About acting classes maybe? I'm all for anything that gets people in touch with their inner selves and And . . . anyway . . ." She looked almost embarrassed. ". . . But of course, that's if you do decide to stay on. James Carr said you had doubts, but . . . but seeing as your poetry readings went so well . . ."

"Er, Phyllis Just one small correction." Another phone started ringing. "This question of whether I'll stay ?" Another phone added more discords, then a third joined in.

Retreating upstairs to his office every muscle complained. As he entered the turret his cellphone theme played. He hoped it was Verity's call.

Mrs Roberts sounded distraught. "Garrick lovey! Thank goodness. It's me. Louise! "Sorry, but I've got to speak up. For nights I've been lying awake, thinking and thinking and . . ."

Abigail must have confessed! Embarrassment turned into shame. He felt like a rapist. Louise was after revenge. He'd be arrested and splashed all over the headlines. In moments of crisis he followed his instincts. He took a deep breath of cold air.

"Look, Mrs Roberts, you probably think I'm some sort of . . ."

"No no, it was me. It's preyed on my nerves ever since. I mean' .It didn't seem wrong at the time. I thought it was, like for everyone's good."

"I don't understand."

"Yes you do. We respect you, me and my daughter."

"As I respect you."

"No, listen. Remember those letters? When you first come? You know! You know! Those letters. You never ever took offence."

"Letters?"

"Yes yes! . . . You know. About my little Abigail? I shouldn't've written them, that's the truth. But when Jilly died, along with that poor, little, innocent babby and. It's been like God's judgement." She took his stunned silence as censure. "How can a man understand? I'd meant to protect her. All

256

them silly fairy tales! Cinderella shall go to the ball And all that stuff. Next comes disillusion, then worse." He heard her blowing her nose. "I wanted her to stay home with me, not work for you. I was wrong."

Was the call being recorded? He'd planned on restarting his life but events were conspiring against him. It could be a trick to make him confess.

"Look, I swear to you, Mrs Roberts . . ."

"You must've guessed it was me? Sending those anonymous letters? Oh come on!" Now she was sounding insulted. "It's preyed on my mind, but what else could I do? I only did it for her Sometimes we care too much and do daft things. Just to protect them."

"Never mind. It all worked out. In your place I'd have done just the same."

The incident seemed long ago and his family photos kept smiling.

"No, no," she continued, "there's more. Much more. What I'm trying to say is I'm trying to warn you! Jilly's boyfriend, partner, housemate, whatever It's egos. Men's egos . . . he's blaming you and he's well, he's obsessive. Threatening. Dangerous. Look what he did to poor Jilly". She gave a long heartfelt sigh. "There! Now I've told you. The man's a bloody psychopath! At least I've got that off my chest. Be careful, that's all I'm saying. If anything happens, then call the police. I'll not say anymore."

As she rang off, an echo chamber seemed to recycle her words. Unconnected incidents began to fall into place. Minor trivialities; apparent accidents, close shaves and near disasters. Their unresolved details filled out the blanks of a crossword. He thought of those memorial flowers outside the hairdresser's frontage. Was there a serial killer at large? All Garrick knew was, it was freezing and the canal had begun to ice over. The day those theatre boilers imploded, the North seized its chances and rolled down from the Arctic. Whole districts were turning to ice. Light was going fast and permafrost seemed to lie underfoot. Soon there'd be glaciers churning down Storford Moors. Global warming goodbye! In Norston he'd begun to feel safe, but now his perceptions were changing.

Below in the street, Manwess trucks manoeuvred alongside the big deepening shaft, clumsy and threatening. Traffic red in tooth and claw, jagged from bumper to bumper, rampaged over the site. A dumper truck raised its ominous shovel. There in the rubble, Garrick caught sight of movement. Probably Inuits building new igloos? He leaned forward and wiped at the glass, and saw someone below, motionless, watching.

On that freshly cleared tundra littered with debris where roads had no function and no destination, Eddie Craig leaned on his silver Mercedes, clapping his hands as if applauding himself.

He took stock of his expanding empire. He considered the Majestic's squat pediment. Its two stumpy octagonal towers topped with odd spires were clearly not 'great works of art'. No-one defended their architectural merit. That's why a quorum had been quietly assembled one lunchtime, documents quickly endorsed, then returned to the archives marked 'Confidential'. In an alliance of Left and Right, its 'preservation status' was discreetly but finally lifted, and urban renewal confirmed. The future was taking a visible shape, its territories daily expanding. Development grants were in the pipeline. Norston would rise on the crest of a wave. But first came the task of clearing that grimy historical site. Once he had finished, there'd be no sign anything ever existed.

From his post up at the window, Garrick kept watching. As a rising breeze blew, two other forms trudged out of nowhere, joining the first. Now all three clustered together. The first was emphatically pointing. Away to their left, strings of flashing orange lamps marked out Manwess's own deepening trenches like dysfunctional decor.

"Very Christmassy," Eddie was shouting, "Spot on for celebrations!"

Although Garrick could recognise Eddie, their body language was blurred. They looked like toy soldiers surveying defeat. Pigmies! Garrick took pleasure in that. He could have leaned out and stamped on them all. Despite all their meddling, The Majestic's future was assured. But as he pressed his face to the window, an icy chill rolled down the glass and spilled out into octagonal spaces. Soon it was knee-deep, rising like glacial waters from that canal. He needed a strong cigarette. There was a tap at the door. As it opened, he quickly switched on a light and reached for some scripts.

Abigail stood in the doorway, head bowed. "Her funeral's this afternoon," she whispered. "My friend. Family friend Jilly Craske. The hairdresser what . . . anyway she's . . ." She pictured Jilly's energy and fruitless attempts to succeed. "An' at Christmas as well." The banality sounded profane.

As Garrick reached out, the wide-open door sucked in more draughts. Caught in the cross-light Abby looked almost unreal, leaving his brain cells to fill in the blanks, letting another image emerge. A recognisable profile. A familiar silhouette. This wasn't just Abigail Jones. She was every woman he'd known. She was Maisie, Diana, Sandy, Susanne . . . and yes, she was Vee.

He'd meant to raise Louise's anonymous letters and Louise's open admissions, then his own doubts and regrets. He'd intended to ask how Abigail felt about him, and how she was coping? If indeed she were coping at all? Unspoken dialogues, undeclared thoughts! It only needed the playwright and script. Chekhov would have been perfect. Ibsen, Strindberg, Shakespeare, and even Oscar Wilde said more about life than he ever could. He wanted to speak through their words.

"So?" She looked him full in the eyes, "Is it alright if I go?"

Go? Did she expect him to nod and agree? Where was her commitment? Her dedication? You couldn't just dip in and dip out. This wasn't what he'd expected. Dress rehearsals were sacrosanct. Everyone knew the show must go on! If she aimed to be professional, then births, deaths and marriages took second place. One had to be cruel to be kind. This time he'd have to refuse.

Instead he heard someone saying. "Fine. Not at all. Buy some bouquets. Yes. Floral tributes, whatever. You know what I mean. A bunch or a wreath. Buy one from yourself and one from the theatre . . . and yes, one from me." He handed her a bundle of cash. "No no, keep the change. How's her poor husband coping?"

Then silence got in his way. He heard her footsteps descending the bare wooden stairs.

Without Abby's assistance, Garrick was left in a quandary, and Phyllis's prejudice confirmed that each new generation was more selfish than the last. Time was short enough before Christmas. The show would open on Boxing Day. But when Garrick explained Abby was attending the funeral of her nearest and dearest, Phyllis reluctantly agreed to assist:

"But only for Dress Rehearsal," she insisted, clicking her pearls like the snapping of bones, "And don't forget, it's Rex Schulman's memorial service next week. I hope no-one tries to get out of that."

Rex's had been a different, more beautiful era. Soured cream and smoked salmon bagels, gefilte fish and black tea, kosher scones and nostalgia jam. Now crude stand-up comics owned the stage, with one of them barely out of his teens. Grudgingly she joined Garrick down in the stalls, setting up office on her lap.

Despite bitter cold the theatre was milling with musicians, dancers, singers, and scene-boys, all chilled to the bone. Hopefully the warmth of their bodies might add another degree? 'The Technical' was their first run-through to iron out problems before the dress rehearsal itself. A stand-in musician played the new overture twice, including a medley from Tessa and the Skidoos. It sounded trendy, upbeat and jolly. The tabs shuddered up; new scenery creaked into place; the show juddered to life.

Lionel's 'Dame' in full-blooded masculine mould, mades his first entrance as if self-absorbed, then seems to spot the audience, with a "Hey! Who's this lot?" This is a primping, prancing stepmother dame. Six foot six tall and built like a boxer, she whirls Baron Hardup around, spinning his feet off the floor. James Carr is different: he gets laughs merely by being himself (pompous and very long-winded). These guys are pro's, Garrick thought. Jokes and business come thick and fast. Then Truman Fats Goss does his Caribbean tango showing them all about rhythm. Even the musician's impressed. James and Wade Bluman's feet are enormous when trying on miniature slippers (as black and white 'identical twins'). Just as amazingly, Reggie Buck's pastry scene works despite Garrick's fear he'll do gags about Verity's cooking. Even Phyllis is grinning. Despite stops and starts the show has begun to take shape. No-one has mentioned Abigail's absence, nor asked about Garrick's wife. For the first time the programme is knitting together.

"Oh titter you not!" Lionel warns, and Phyllis laughs.

Garrick pictured Rachel and Mark. Bugger Chekhov! Bugger the Morozoffs! Bugger their Centenaries! He was doing all this for his kids. They'd love these "It's behind you!" routines. This whole range of farting and pratfalls. By the time they'd reached the Fairy Glade scene, 'Giselle' was fused with 'Swan Lake'. Here was Linda, centre-stage, pointing her fairy wand at the backcloth surrounded by shivering fairies. Cinderella was meant to come trundling artlessly on, sitting at her open hearth, bathed in spotlights.

While Garrick cursed Josh, the fireside rolled in on its boat-truck complete with faint smoke as the curtain jerked uncertainly down. From the stalls came an outburst of clapping as Arthur Ruddock arose from the darkness with Peggy de Fries

"Brilliant!" Arthur was shouting, "Bloody superb!"

Peggy emerged in fur coat with pearls, dressed as for an Opera First Night. "Garrick my dear," she murmured with tears in her eyes. "It's so entertaining. No really!" She leant her cheek forward for kissing. "It's so very post-modern. It has a certain proletarian charm, with a kind of What do you say? Retro appeal?" She took Garrick's hand. "It's perfect for families. It's the ideal curtain raiser for Chekhov and Gogol. How about some Molière later? Or Giraudoux even? We could commission new apposite plays?"

"We need heating first."

"What?" Arthur looked apoplectic. "We need a technical chat, you and me," He jostled Garrick aside, "Don't talk to our patron that way. Blackmail's not acceptable here. Got that, shit-head?"

"There's bye-laws though. It's freezing."

"Bye-laws? You dare to quote byelaws at me? I'm paying you!" He waited to let it sink in. "Live theatre means dead, an' everyone knows it. Anachronism, that's what it is. We only subsidise theatre for Peggy and Phyllis. Because women still care."

"Don't forget the cultural . . ."

"Cultural shit! Jesus! Aren't you listening?" Arthur had gone puce with rage. "Fucking grow up!" As he was fumbling to put on a glove, his fingers lost touch with his brain. "We only hired you because . . ." sounding slurred, "To be totally, utterly frank, we, I'd, we'd . . ."

He waved wildly round, trying to control his fury, struggling to drag the right-handed glove over his straining left hand. Knuckles, wrists and joints seemed unconnected. As Garrick moved to assist, blundering fingers contracted; muscles and tendons refused to comply.

As Arthur struggled and staggered, Peggy came hurrying over. He waved her away. How could he help being left-handed? Couldn't she, of all people, see its significance? It wasn't some unique perversion. Not simply a flip of the statistics. It came from a very long line of left-handers. His father. His Granddad, his uncle. Now Peggy's son George. All shared the very same variation. Why be so deliberately dim?

As Arthur shuddered then lolled helplessly forward, Garrick managed to catch him.

When Abigail got to the bus stop Stacey was waiting alone. The drizzle started again, but as Stacey said, even if they were late for the funeral nothing would change. After some prayers, everything would be back like before, except Jilly Craske would be gone. That was all. The end. So they might as well pack up and go home. Would anyone know? And would anyone care?

But Abby's wrists were pulsating again. She'd always thought people didn't just die. Then it turns out she was wrong. Same as with Stacey's tattoos. Believing didn't make it true. So when Sanjay backed Stacey she might be part of some deal, chained like a dog to a door? Same as Jilly with Thomas. No cosmetics could cover that up. Or did Jilly not know she was pregnant? Or did she pretend she was not? Like, fooling herself? In a way that's what everyone did, and Abigail too felt a fraud; a Jilly Craske deal, who'd never lived up to anyone's hopes. Not taking exams. Failing diplomas.

Late for appointments. Women got caught in a trap. For all their excitement and glamour they too ended up in a coffin, thanks to the men in their lives.

The girls took cover from easterly winds. All Yorkshire and Lancashire froze. Christmas advanced like glacial gravel. Trees were stripped bare, with deciduous scaffolding shredded. Like oversized snowflakes, debris blew across lowlands and fells as one generation made room for another. Yet there was Stacey nodding along to her earphones, apparently deaf to the world. Soon they'd be up to their necks in a snowdrift; two little heads on a sea of white snow, their bouquets chilled to a crisp. Abigail ruffled those curiously odourless petals. What did "unscented" mean in the language of flowers? Births, marriages, deaths? Or just an absence of feelings?

Stacey leaned over. "I was like thinking, Abbs She thought you was great, Jilly did. Really. Went on about how you'd, like be a big star!" She avoided Abigail's eyes. "She'd got her work room out back papered wi' her certificates Finalist in this'n'that. Short-listed for everything else. Semi-finalist Hairstylist of the Year. Finalist for the Pompadour Cup .Not like some other tarts I could mention!"

She pointed up at the billboards. Red and gold slogans blazed across billboards:

COOK AND LET COOK!
GREETINGS FROM VERITY JONES

By the time they'd reached the cemetery chapel, mourners had progressed to the grave. The two inched up a well-trampled path to where the grieving were huddled. A priest was intoning an arrhythmic dirge. Undertakers blew on their hands. A surprisingly large congregation murmured responses, many in tears. Scarves fluttered. Frail hands clamped once-a-year hats to bowed heads. Louise Roberts and Jilly's assistant stood bareheaded in seemingly limitless pain. Down at the graveside pallbearers strained on the tapes. Only as the coffin was lowered did Abigail notice. A miniaturised casket was lying on top, matching in every small detail.

Both sank below layers of green plastic matting. And were gone.

"Hair today and gone tomorrow," as Jilly herself used to say, but her epitaph ought to read: "Jilly Craske, who changed people's lives simply by rearranging their hair." No film-clips, old movies, nor signs of Hollywood here as mourners scattered handfuls of soil, raw eyelids blinking back tears.

That's when Abigail heard it again. A man's stifled wail. Part despairing, part fury.

Outside the chapel a display of red roses spelled out "FROM THOMAS" as if crucified on an easel surrounded by transparent bundles, arranged like floral specimen packs. This was mass murder of flowers, she thought, their body-bags dripping with chilled condensation. As the skies darkened, these sacrifices mimicked events. Their cellophane shimmered and crackled beneath the first flecks of wet snow. Monochrome bleached out any colour.

At this very same moment, back at the theatre, Cinderella was being granted Three Magic Wishes. All her dreams would come true.

So far in the course of his life, Garrick had learnt one thing; that nothing exists in isolation. So, when paramedics whisked Arthur Ruddock away, the man was forgotten as if he had never existed: as if a switch had been tripped. Only one thing mattered. Whatever happened, the show must go on, and Garrick was fully committed. By now those magic wishes were due to be granted, even if half the costumes weren't ready. The final few scenes were devoted to tying up ends.

Garrick felt free to sit back, hands clasped behind his head. Everyone loves transformations . Whizz bang! Drums roll! Cymbals clash! Sparks fly! Everything happens at once! Linda casts off her shabby disguise, twinkling her fibre-optic wand, revealing her Good Fairy self in an explosion of sequins. There was something wondrously corny about it. Forget digital tricks. Real magic takes place in the mind. It says 'all things are possible' in ways Chekhov and Ibsen would have never have thought. It talks to the kid in us all. Whatever Verity thought, Pantoland led to fulfilment. It battled evil spirits and villains. It guaranteed love, changed poverty to riches, illness to health, loneliness into glamour, and dreams into reality. No arthritis, retirement homes, prolonged sickness, nor lingering agonised deaths But as always his thoughts slipped back to his children: to Rachel and Mark.

Linda is raising a polished glass rod. "Cinders! Your wish shall be granted!" She spins on points in a series of slow pirouettes as the drumbeat starts to roll And keeps rolling "But one word of warning!" (Yes, always that unavoidable catch). "You must be home before the clock has struck midnight. Remember that, Cinders! Before yonder clock has struck Twelve!"

On the day, hundreds of kids would be catching their breaths. No magic trick was complete till that roll on the drums. Then a crash on the cymbals, rumblings, curses. A massive explosion complete with burst of green smoke. Then there it is! A glitter-faced coach drawn by a panicking pony led by a bad-tempered groom.

Even scene-crew and builders were cheering. Garrick joined the applause. You had to believe. You wanted to, even if anticlimax was waiting. But where were his children? Why was Vee punishing him? Putting their family home on the market! Could the Morozoff Mafia sneak them off to the States? He'd get a court order! He'd invoke the Court of Appeal. He'd go to the House of Lords!

He found himself frantically patting his pockets, groping around for a smoke. He had to get out. Having already gulped several litres he'd have to empty his bladder. Any pretext was welcome. Any excuse to escape Lionel and Josh! The Management Toilets were banned to all but himself.

As he pushed at the door, a gust of ammonia mingled with Eau de Verbena. He stopped in his tracks. There was Josh stepping up to a stall, unzipping himself without glancing round, then facing the urinal, offhandedly starting to whistle. An immature youngster, his balls barely dropped. Garrick clenched his teeth. At the most primitive level this was a challenge, an inter-generational clash. Survival of the fittest, it said, but as the classic Alpha Male, Garrick had the advantage. Here was some skinny frame confronted by potential paunch. Garrick's was the dominant status. Maturity would always prevail.

He edged up to a niche and rigidly stood to attention, fixing his eyes on the copper-stained tiles. Then he tried to relax. Meanwhile Josh peed with unrestrained vigour as forceful as a high-pressure hose. He even glanced round and continued to whistle. Garrick felt himself tensing up. This was an outright intrusion! A trespasser! An illegal! It was crude psychological warfare. But the more self-conscious Garrick became, the more his internal plumbing contracted.

Josh turned and glanced casually down. "Hi Gary. Impressed by my new crystal coach? New seating, bigger wheels, brand new axles, much bigger shafts. Everything bigger! An' better! Okay."

Josh shook himself, spat into the drain, and strolled over to the washbasins. When Josh turned the hand-dryer on, Garrick slumped forward, his spinal column contracting, his forehead adhering to tiles. He clearly pictured Abigail, she and Josh grappling and groaning. Bastard! Bastard! *Bastard*! Josh strutted out to the dryer's electrical roar, as if to a burst of applause.

Garrick was repeatedly washing his hands when he felt muffled vibrations. The water in his washbasin shimmered. From somewhere he heard a low crump, and automatically ducked. Though he couldn't quite pinpoint a source, it seemed nearby, yet at a great distance . . . It must rate on the Richter Scale? An earthquake? A terrorist bomb? Muslim extremists? IRA bombers?

Out in the auditorium he heard shouts and felt subsonic vibrations. As he made his way stagewards through gloom, short-sightedly grasping at seat-backs, the house tabs seemed to sway.

Suddenly Lionel burst through them followed by Trixie and some of the cast. "Honestly! Garrick!!" Lionel stood, hands on hips. "I mean, it's bad enough being frozen to death. Now all this, this terrible banging! We can't even feel ourselves think!"

Trixie was into her union role, demanding evacuation procedures according to Health and Safety rules, HSV416, sub-section 233a. Fabian as official Safety Rep was investigating, she said. Then on cue Fabian appeared, helplessly shaking his head.

"Not our bloody stage carpenter kid?" shouted Garrick

"Nope. Some guys from Manwess wearing earmuffs like bloody great turtles! They're blasting out old excavations." Fabian folded his short stubby arms. "So I told them 'Fuck off' And they went!"

Abigail and Stacey were sat on the rear seat of the afternoon bus as it sniffed its way back from the Chapel of Rest. Soon schools would be out with juniors packing the aisles. On the day she'd reached sixteen Abigail had said, "Sod off" to them all. That day she'd changed sides, because boundaries were meant to be crossed and turning points had to be turned. Now her old school books were lining the Norston canal.

Stretched across the rear of their bus, Verity's wrap-around smile said it all, emblazoned across every bus-stop and many prime sites in town. 'Cook And Let Cook!', 'Cook And Let Cook. Yes, that's Cook And Let Cook! The Big New Hit Series'. Through networks of pinholes, passengers watched pedestrians stare. As heavy clouds fooled street-lamps into premature life, the darkness was almost alluring. Their journey seemed never-ending. Just as she'd done many times lately, Abigail thought again of that ghost ship in Garrick's poem, and gave an involuntary shudder. Jilly's death had felt like The End, but surely each ending was only another beginning? Soon even those scars on Abigail's arms would be less than a lacework of lines.

"What I mean is . . ." she began, "If Jilly hadn't tarted me up . . . and if . . .You know what I mean." Stacey shot her a look. "No no, what I mean is . . . What then?"

"Who cares? I'm getting a headache!" Stacey continued to peer out through the mesh

Dress rehearsal rumbled on despite minor hitches. The news was that Arthur was being kept overnight for specialist observation, so Lady P with young George had both rushed over to see him. "A suspected minor heart attack", they'd reported, with Arthur prescribed a strict diet plus rest. After treatment he'd soon be out and about, but a course at a gym was advised.

Amazingly no-one noticed Abigail's absence. At one point, the Ugly Sisters are fighting to try on that tiny glass slipper (Left at the ball by Cinders, who'd overrun her time-coded spell, and who'd changed back to a dogsbody skivvy while secretly the daughter of a disowned princess who'd shamefully married beneath her, but technically of royal blood .and therefore not morganatic, thereby confusing the plot).

As James Carr moaned, "Grand Finale follows Grand Bloody Farce". Or as Reggie put it, 'One smack on bare buttocks is worth more than hundreds of poems'. Slapstick would always win out, the more vulgar the better. Nothing had to make sense. Reluctantly Garrick agreed. Pantomime did give satisfaction. It wasn't exactly 'The Seagull' or 'The Three Sisters', yet its formula worked; it upended logic. Mix in familiar gags like two grown men in enormous bustles and bra's trying to force bunioned feet into a minuscule Perspex slipper. Result, wicked stepsisters frustrated! Stir in Reggie Buttons leading Prince Pippa towards Cinderella. Whereupon Trixie knowingly tries on the slipper. And hey! Surprise, surprise!

"It fits!" everyone's screaming, "It fits!. It fits! *It fits!*"

By the time the cast had gathered for notes, the elemental cold had returned. It seemed to freeze on their faces and weigh down their clothes. Soon everyone shivered, and Garrick's thoughts turned back to Vee and his kids. He was slipping away discreetly to phone when James Carr caught his arm.

"Excuse me! Ladies and gentlemen!" James shouted. "I have a little surprise for you all. As you've been so wonderful, and we've a phenomenal season ahead . . . including some of the world's greatest classics . . . I've purchased a small gift for you all. We've recently got used to its flavour!" He whipped a sheet off the side table, revealing six magnums of Harrison's Sparkling Pomagne.

James Carr raised his glass to Garrick. "So let's drink to this absolute rascal! To Garrick! Cheers! We owe our forthcoming season to him!"

Garrick plucked thoughts from the air. "Er . . . Ladies and gentlemen, thank you so much. Thank you. But let us not forget. We've got the world's greatest master, Anton Chekhov, still to come. This is his centenary year. One hundred years since he died. He's all the inspiration we need And I myself

264

feel so inspired by By my family my son and my daughter even my mother-in-law, and . . ."

But their attention had already moved on.

Brinkhouse Development Corporation's directors assembled for formal pre-Christmas drinks. This was the season of company parties, annual functions, and unrepeatable offers. Shopping was at fever pitch, holidays were approaching.

The company's latest headquarters bulged with all that was modern and warm. Finest multi-national taste was subsidised by Euro-funds betting on Norston's potential. In Eddie Craig's view, Brinkhouse had scored every scorable point. It proved that to create you had to destroy, because space could be easily recycled. This triumph of glass on twenty-two floors combined hemispheres, rectangles, curves, with a crisp assembly of cubes, all costing some sixty-five millions. Volume wasn't down to dimensions, but to foresight and style. No-one remembered the Victorian courtroom which recently stood on this spot.

Take white rugs and white marble floors; add fibre-optic pinpoints to cutting-edge electronics, titanium edgings, and polished chrome. White-upon-white eliminated unfashionable shadows fulfilling new mathematical truths. Everything was modern and new. The Board watched themselves in a dozen reflections. Their very presence fulfilled the Heisenberg rule. The new oval table was carved and inlaid by Aho of Chelsea. At one end sat young George de Vries. At the other sprawled their newest and biggest investor who'd flown in direct via Heathrow. In such surroundings everyone felt superhuman, even big City names like Williams-Thorneycroft and Lightfoot & Preece.

First George de Vries read out a prologue, grateful for all Arthur's coaching, then their new chairman responded.

"Thank you, amici," Lambrusco said, "Bene! Molte grazie!" before slipping back to Canadian vowels. "Hi. I'm proud to be joining you guys. We'll be hearing from Arthur Ruddock tonight, but afterwards he'll be takin' life more more easy Okay? We upgrade to a Euro-dimensional scale, accelerating leverage to expedite propositions. That's us, Mythras Internationale SL, with on-site advice from Craig Demolition UK."

He faded down lights as images flicked on-screen, flipping from picture to picture. Plans, elevations, projections, faster and faster, talking jargon and concepts, with images merging into each other. This was another New World. Lambrusco's words washed over them as each celebrated themselves. Now every bank would want to invest. Eddie craned forward and waited.

Lambrusco gave a big smile. "Okay, to sum up. All our projects remotivate schedulisation. But what's even better . . . !" (Click to long shot of a glass and chromium city, full of parks, marinas and trees) . . . "Norston UK will become a 21st Century city. A second millennium centre, pushing top global standards." (Image follows image on-screen) "New roads, new shopping centres, new industries, new parking centres, waterway centres and multi-berth marina, new railway and transport centre. Yeah, and the really good news, my friends. The entire site has been secured!" A murmur of surprise. "Yep. Sure has! And you better believe me. We've'a come to a closure and transfer agreement with The Majestic Theatre Trustees!" He looked over the rim of his glasses. "That's what I said! It shuts itself down on February 10th. That's finito! Then we at Brinkside merge with Temple Storford Estates!"

Some loud intakes of breath. Others exchanged furtive glances.

Lambrusco laughed aloud. "Sure. We reintegrate as 'Fecundo Estates'. New Venice of the UK. Marinas, apartments, romantic canals and investments .Novella Venetia . . . That's our Christmas gift to investors. We need your formal confirmation, that's all. Your normal signatures on dotted lines!" With a flourish he waved all his papers and waited.

Silence was broken with murmured "Hear hears" which gradually built to applause, and then everyone started talking at once. Eddie Craig seized his moment. He stood up and rapped on the table.

"Forgive me Mister Chairman, but there is summat else." He lowered his voice. "Brothers. I ask you, witness my promise." He placed his right hand on his heart. "The day as we bash out the very first bricks of that so-called theatre," He winked at Lambrusco. "I'll donate to every one of you here, a magnum of the finest Champagne. Aye, and best vintage at that."

As laughter masked a sense of unease, soft hands were tactically thumping the table. Eddie Craig smiled to himself, and easing his bulk to one side, softly, silently belched.

Back at the theatre toasts had been drunk. James Carr's generosity was so unexpected his recklessness swept their inhibitions away. This must be a dawning new age. Everyone was inspired. When alcohol gets into the bloodstream one thing can lead to another, and no-one seemed concerned with the cold.

Their party pieces were dusted off and old solo acts were reprised. This was the moment to let your hair down. After Truman Fats Goss had extemporised reggae to Reggie's discordant guitar, James Carr recited two Shakespeare sonnets. Then Pippa and Trixie sang "Love me baby" from Solenoid Cuckoos Greatest Hits'. Emboldened by this, Ted Frink the pianist and Tracey the wardrobe assistant, rendered that Jim Bratby classic "Let's live and let's live!" in an orgy of self expression.

Carried along on their fervour, Garrick found himself overwhelmed. Suddenly all that was impossibly complex became absurdly simple, and all that was distant was well within reach. He was accepted at last with no further need for deception. He was legit. One of their clique. He wandered around in a daze. He was happy: happier than he'd been for some time. He drank to Arthur, to Phyllis, to Abigail, to his wife and to each of his children as people kept topping his drinks.

He awoke with a grunt, slumped on a hamper with clothes rails drooping around him. With each breath he inhaled the smell of stale sweat mixed with greasepaint and spiked with fumes of spilled wine. The wardrobe store was under the stage. He was dizzy and freezing. His mouth was dry and his tongue was like polystyrene. The whole cast had partied then gone. His brain would not co-operate. When he tried to sit up he felt sick and ashamed.

266

Waves of sentiment burst through defences. It was time to be home with his kids, replaying their first spoken words; those "ma-maas" and "shoo-shoos" through threads of saliva. Each phase of their lives was one initiation after another. Okay, he hadn't been too sure of his role, but at last he could admit some mistakes. It was no-go the diapers! No-go the kids' buggy! The albatross had got its revenge. He was as much at sea as that Ancient Mariner. If this were his personal exile, it might well be Siberia, the Crimea, or even the slopes of the Urals.

Then, as his eyes adjusted, he noticed a paper cup within reach. He stretched out and sipped at dregs, letting them fizz on his tongue. Time to change direction again? Maybe enrol on a culinary course because marriage was all about sharing? Chekhov would understand that. His Prozorov family knew all there was to know about exile; Olga, Masha, Natasha. With his own insights, Garrick ought to produce The Three Sisters? Not that he knew what he was doing. Everyone turned a blind eye, but surely Phyllis and Abigail had noticed? Everywhere he'd left clues.

When he tried standing up, his brain rolled around. His co-ordination was failing. He felt so light-headed he could have floated up through the ceiling. All it had taken was cheap fizzy wine. He knew exactly how Coleridge felt, drugged to the eyeballs, opiumed up to the gills. No wonder the poet saw ghost ships, seabirds, and boatloads of the dead. Around in semi-darkness, hanging costumes retained the shapes of their wearers like discarded husks: every fold, every crinkle and crease. Did they live secret lives? Living out dualities? Copying identities? Mimicking souls? In just such a way, his own children imprinted themselves upon him as each generation was forced to break free from the last. He regretted not spending Thanksgiving at home. He'd sleep throughout Christmas dreaming of being with them.

Then a streak of malice curdled his thoughts. Why was Vee starring? Why she? Not himself? Why soufflés and entrecôte steak? The more he tried to rationalise the more everything blurred. Cooking was a measurable craft. Dough either bloodywell rises or doesn't. A roux either thickens or not. It was a cross between craft and a science and not what he'd rate High Art. Not Shakespeare, nor Miller, nor Chekhov. At once he regretted his thoughts. He should be commissioning plays, planning great innovations, giving seminars, setting up the Majestic's own website.

Cramp snatched at his legs, leaving him nauseous and stiff. He drifted like the Coleridge poem. He noticed he had started to shiver. Whenever he tried to stand up, he felt giddy. Next moment he slumped as if all his strings had been cut, sprawled against a costume rail, imagining Abigail's body. Only then did he remember. She had gone to that funeral. And never returned. Why had he not noticed till now? When someone dies, you know you'll not see them again . . . But the living as well?

Something had to be done. The whole heating system would have to be checked. Garrick was responsible. Personally accountable. He would inspect the engineers' progress. Now. It was his duty. He managed to drag himself to his feet and stagger around to their site. Signs exclaimed, "Maintenance by Manwess Gas" and "No Naked Lights by Order". Around a dismantled boiler lay convolutions of pipes, twisted panels, crushed baffles, adapters, and junctions. Holes had been drilled through walls and floors. Strips of bent piping writhed like a snake pit beneath them.

> "I fear thee Ancient Mariner!
> I fear thy skinny hand!"

Those extractor tubes presumably vented high on the roofs? He tried tapping piping. Unearthly rumbles led nowhere. The main valve looked loose. He idly tried a few turns. No effect. No hiss of gas. No obvious smell. Nothing . . . How could they possibly finish in time?

> "I fear thee and thy glittering eye
> And thy skinny hand so brown . . ."

By now his fingers were numb and his lungs were like fibreglass wadding. With intense concentration he somehow got out of the basement. Once at ground level, he took a short cut across stage, planning to ring Manwess from his office, but as he made his way from the wings an irresistible force seemed to take over again.

Its unseen hand guided him to centre-stage where louvres cast equivocal shadows. Yes, he thought, this was the clown playing Hamlet. This was the Idiot playing King Lear. He was feeling light-headed again. Facing the steel safety curtain backed by iron bars and asbestos, some x-ray vision cut in. He could scan a full house and silence its roar of applause. This was the Superman trick. By inhaling intense adulation, its molecules passed through the lungs, infiltrating his blood.

Was this what he tasted? That aroma? Like condiments maybe? Bittersweet. Mustardy. Choking. He swivelled his tongue, tasting its tang in the air. An aftertaste at the back of the throat. But as Verity said, flavour is all in the mind.

Ghosts fled like lost souls, then flooded back when he'd passed. Dry-fingered corn merchants jostled with music-hall stars, cinema projectionists, dance bands, and whole generations of local de Vries. Garrick saw no sign of live builders. No watchmen. No security guards. Manwess Contractors were failing. Their engineers wanted to work overnight. They'd asked for twenty-four hours to complete. Their deadline was clear. If things weren't concluded on time, then he'd sue. Bloody sue!

With immense effort he mounted steepening stairs like climbing Mont Blanc with lead weights. On reaching Phyllis's office he had to sit down surrounded by spriglets of holly, assorted frog baubles, and shrivelled sprigs of mistletoe. A Norston Marina Calendar was autographed "From Arthur Ruddock with much love".

Garrick struggled breathlessly up his last stairs, leaving all the doors ajar, painstakingly propping each open. Even hungover he still applied practical logic. Everybody knew heat rose. And Garrick's room was the highest point in the building. Therefore, he'd let that warmth circulate upwards? Why not make use of physics for once? It made irrefutable sense.

Reaching the top of the stairs he scrambled over the threshold. His octagonal turret seemed an especially appropriate space. This was his own private eyrie. Without the conditions for life nothing could either grow or decay. He wedged the door open an optimum 45 degrees to let the warm air in. On the edge of his desk stood a crimson candle unlit in its dish of wax holly; its tag wished him Merry Xmas. He gazed out into the night, facing exactly southeast towards London. The skies briefly clouded. Temperatures had started to rise. Wherever they happened to be at this moment, Mark and Rachel would hopefully be fast asleep. He mouthed them both kisses hoping these could be psychically mailed. By now Arctic winds should have blown themselves out after trekking over the great Northern Steppes. Still no sign of frost. And no forecast of snow over Christmas: only a debilitating chill, which drifted from Ancient Mariner regions and settled near Garrick's heart.

He filled a styrene cup with neat vodka and decided on one last attempt to phone home. He switched on his desk lamp. Its halogen brightness seared into his retina. Bright became dark, red into green. Yellow turned blue, with everything going vice-versa. Hazy images floated across his cornea. Distortions imprinted his vision. As his eyelids started to flicker, he fought to stay awake. Then, there it was!

Emerging from nowhere it was suddenly, unbelievably, summer! An idyll of bird song and trees. Two oxen pulling a hay cart. Fields of shimmering corn. Tinkling cowbells. The rustle of birches and flicker of aspen. Apples and cherries beginning to ripen. Chattering beech-thrushes. Faint singing of peasants rhythmically timing the sweep of their scythes. And there, visible above the trees, the gleam of an onion-dome church. And look, there's Yasha arranging the luggage, Abigail mooning about on the drive, and Madame Ranevsky fluttering round. There's Rachel, Mark and Verity riding off in horse and trap, its wheel rims grinding the gravel. He's waving frantically now, but they seem unaware of his presence . . .

His head hit the desk with a thud. He sat up sharply. Some images remained. Little Markie, young Rachel. It was proof he wasn't alone. Existence wouldn't just end with himself. His immortality lived on in their genes. He'd keep their pictures sewn into his wallet . . . after all, who'd cooked their meals and changed their diapers? Who'd wiped their bums and nursed dying washing machines?

He took a quick gulp of the vodka. Phyllis's gift would give him a boost; her celebratory candle in its holly wreath. A glow would cheer everything up. He opened his briefcase to look for a cigarette lighter, but something was distracting him.

Peering down from his window he seemed to see swarms of flitting figures around a huge beetle, glinting under a streetlight. Distorted forms were elongated by shadows. They scuttled like armies of ants. It was Brothers Grimm's version of dwarves, hobgoblins, and elves. It was like Gustave Doré with something of Albrecht Dürer. It was Hansel and Gretel, and Little Tom Thumb, Rumplestiltskin, wolves, forests, huge mountains, gothic towers, and creatures from deep in the mind.

This had to be seen to be believed.

"Verity?" he called, but she still didn't come, "Vee darling, bring Chekhov to see this."

Out of the blackness came pinpoints of light like St Petersburg lanterns, or candles in the Ranevsky household, or birch fires in the Karelian forests. He felt the urgent need for a smoke. A nicotine fix was all that was needed. His system cried out for care, but the scented red candle demanded instant attention. It said, 'I am the spirit of Christmas, so don't be such a goddam Scrooge!' speaking in Verity's voice.

He retrieved from the briefcase his forbidden gas lighter banned along with tobacco, ignoring an innermost urge to be sick. He needed a boost. He picked up his cigarette lighter, flipped it open and shook the transparent tube.

After his meeting with Ricky Lambrusco, Eddie Craig was triumphant. Consultation, activation and then consummation; that was how everything worked. He loved the night air as it came rolling down from the fells; he relished crushed earth at his heels, knowing History lay underneath. Great change never relied on consensus: it needed massive investment. Wise men heeded Eddie's advice because history was the Lives of the Great.

He posed with a cigar in his mouth, one hand in the flap of his coat. Solitude was his friend. One final battle would complete his campaign. He took a celebratory breath in the darkness, legs apart, chin jutting out, taking stock of his sites in the wind. Thin clouds broke for a moment, illuminating how much he had conquered, trench by trench, minefield by minefield, charge by charge against superior forces never heeding the wound nor counting the cost. Around him spread dereliction. Eddie could savour a factory chimney gone here; a tower block dismantled there; cotton mills, weaving sheds, dye factories, workshops, all flattened. Only one structure intruded. Its twin subsidised towers rose like a cathedral pastiche. 'Majestic' was a complete contradiction!

A modern entertainment complex was needed, complete with motorway access. Lancashire would be the hub of the world with Norston connected to similar centres like Paris, Rome, Madrid, Berlin, Vienna, New York, Los Angeles, Moscow, St Petersburg, Bombay, Beijing, Sydney, London. Eddie would visit the hospital next morning and give Arthur Ruddock the news. Victory would soon be complete. He'd explain his revised schedules, and catalogue latest plans for . . .

He could make out a gleam in the theatre's left tower when the building was meant to be vacant! He felt an irrational anger. Who did that Garrick think he was? Rex Schulman? He'd become a thorn in the flesh, sniping at Norston's core values. Surely he would not be working through Christmas?

Hearing another vehicle approach, Eddie flung his cigar. It fizzed in the mud as he ducked into darkness. A dark Ford saloon freewheeled till it ran out of momentum, pulling up under a street lamp, its engine still softly running. A 'Manwess Gas Staff 'sticker was visibly glued to its windscreen. Eddie groaned. No doubt some little hooker was performing her rites on their overstaffed management team. This is what the South had exported: underage sex and hard drugs. It was living proof the whole district needed razing. Randy young bastards in glossy Mondeos, sniffing cocaine or cheap glue, proved he and Arthur were wholly, morally righteous.

Against low-scudding sodium-lit clouds The Majestic Theatre looked like a disfigured church. It was marked green and purple on Eddie's new revised plan. Everything about it was wrong. Its misshapen towers jerry-built for Victorian merchants, its unstable foundations, terminal damp, rotting timber, and crumbling brick exposed on three sides to Eddie's freshly cleared deserts, was signatures away from becoming a World Class Marina.

Eddie turned up his collar and edged behind a parked tipper to take a more sheltered view. Here he was free to indulge an uninterrupted stillness. Elderly men were allowed to dream dreams. He slid his last Havana from its aluminium tube, bit off its end, and edged the roll of fragrant leaves between his moist lips And felt good Bloody good! He bent his head away from the breeze, folded his hand as a windbreak and pressed the gas lighter . . .

ZAAAAP!! A great flash lit the sky! A blinding Hiroshima! Followed by a blast of hot air! .Eddie ducked, spat out his cigar, and felt the very Earth shudder. For Godsake! All he'd done was flip a small flame! Then *BOOOOM!* Bricks and debris hailed down around him. An earthquake? A landslide? Another Twin Towers? Some unknown volcano must have breached the Earth's crust. Next, molten larva would come spewing up, and ashes cascade from the skies to make Eddie's own efforts seem puny. He could already read the Mercury's headlines, "Volcanoes erupt in Town Centre! Local Pompeii! Norston buried in ash!"

He curled up, instinctively covering his head as debris rained down. Beside him dropped a Manwess sign warning 'Danger Beware!' Then sudden stillness and silence All he had done was light a cigar? Or was God reading his mind?

He heard a car engine revving. He twisted to get a good look. A Ford Mondeo was slowly reversing. Its shiny black carcass speckled with granules was backing away from the inferno. It put on a spurt, spun on the handbrake, then skidded away as if leaving the scene of the crime before Eddie could register details. He wished he had noted the number-plate.

The theatre was ablaze. Huge flames rim-lit its silhouette casting an orange-red glow. The shell was outlined against clouds whose vapours surged then condensed into dark droplets of rain. As their first spots fell, fat and heavy, Eddie brushed splats from his face.

"Well done, Lord," he whispered, "That's what we'd call in the business, 'God's Work'."

Up on top of Castle Mount, entwined in the old public shelter, Josh and Abigail stopped for a moment, unintentionally prolonging their climax.

"It's thunder!" Josh gasped, as involuntary muscles contracted.

"Mmm," Abigail murmured, caught in mid-spasm, deliciously holding her breath, "Uuuhh Yeah! Yeah! . . . Same for me!" She shuddered and groaned. "It's thunder! But Stacey'd not understand!" Then she thought of that night in the Castle Hotel and laughed aloud as she came.

Odd spots of rain grew to a patter; first syncopated, then drumming down hard on the roof as Abigail's fingers trailed Josh's stubble and ran round the rims of his ears. Suddenly everything seemed to make sense. When the theatre season was over they'd both be free. No doubts or regrets.

She felt a flood of relief. "Just listen to that." She lay back and stared at the ceiling, "That weather's got no sense of timing!"

Josh felt her body relaxing beneath him then suddenly tauten again.

"Oh Jesus Christ!" she murmured, "I can't wait to get out this whole shitty town! I can't wait! I can't wait!"

But lying there in the darkness, Josh shuddered without knowing why.

The End

Bibliography

CHEKHOV, The Hidden Ground, by Philip Callow,
published by Constable.